BELAIR COVE

A NOVEL OF LIFE, LOVE, AND LOSS IN A PRAIRIE CAJUN VILLAGE

BELAIR COVE

A NOVEL OF LIFE, LOVE, AND LOSS IN A PRAIRIE CAJUN VILLAGE

By Dianne Dempsey-Legnon

Hardcover ISBN: 978-1-105-05857-8
Paperback ISBN: 978-1-105-05858-5

For Prairie Cajuns

Coup de Main

Coup de main in Cajun French means a helping hand. The Prairie Cajuns survived by helping each other within small communities of families and neighbors. They shared work, food, and friendship. My mother often leaves the following message on my phone, "Di, This is Mother. We're having a *coup de main* at [so and so's] house on Sunday. See you there. Love you. Call me back so I'll be sure to put your name in the pot."

Family and friends supported me in the writing of this book. I am grateful to the French and Cajun storytellers in my family, especially my parents who shared their stories with me. I am proud of my heritage from whence this story came and to my parents for the retelling.

I belong to a writing group. My writing group has met faithfully twice a month for over five years. They willingly gave of themselves, providing editing suggestions that were both nurturing and unflinchingly honest. They showed continued enthusiasm for the project for more than a year. To these dear friends, I am truly thankful: Kay Couvillon, Nettie McDaniel, Marion Rosser and Margaret Simon. Special thanks to Kathleen O'Shaughnessy for sharing her love of editing with me. On occasion, others drifted in and out of our writing group and provided solid advice. I appreciate their input as well. Ann Dobie has always been there to inspire me.

My dear friends Loraine Allain, Lana Downing, and Mary Jane Doise were instrumental in helping me bring this novel to fruition. Others listened, read excerpts, and encouraged me along the way. My family had unwavering faith in my ability to tell our story. I love you for that Sherry and Richard, Laura and Ellis, and my brothers, Wayne and Kim. My younger sister, Peggy, spent years researching the family genealogy; I am thankful for her willingness to share that information with me. My daughter, Amy Dempsey, who read and commented on one of many drafts and my stepsons, Chris and Steve Legnon, and their wives, Michelle and Mandi, provided encouragement.

My dear husband, Michael Legnon, has stood fast by me these last few years as I kept to myself and did the work. He is a constant in my life and never failed to listen as my characters slowly materialized. His understanding and cooperation made it easier for me to fulfill a promise to my parents. Finally, in memory of my late husband, James Wiley Dempsey, I am grateful for the years we shared. In acknowledgement to his family, especially Billie Anne Richard, for encouraging me to live and love again, I am thankful.

I could not have done this without the help and support of all the aforementioned, a true *coup de main*. To all of you, I extend my deepest gratitude for your generosity. Time, talent, and friendship are valuable gifts, and you shared yours with me in the making of this story.

Merci beaucoup!

Hospital Vigil 1965
Lafayette, Louisiana

Marc Willis's footsteps echoed as his black cowboy boots pounded the gray and white checkered hospital floor. In a nearby double room, a metal bedpan clanged and the sound rang out across the long and lonely corridor. Leaching antiseptic hope, the smell of bleach permeated the hallway. Last night, he had slept on a pallet made from chair cushions and blankets. His early morning theatrics of twisting and stretching had not yet worked out the stiffness. Placing one shoulder on the surface of the door, he nudged it open. Marc Willis had refused to leave his grandmother's side, and she had refused to leave her "old man."

His grandmother was sitting there beside her husband of more than forty years.

"*Mémère*, here. I've brought you a cup of hot coffee and a biscuit. Take it. You need to eat something."

His grandmother was dressed in one of her shirtwaist cotton shifts whose tiny flowers gathered loosely around her small bosom. A tattered sweater draped over her shoulders. *Mémère* looked up from her vigil and smiled at her grandson, lean as a young sapling and twice as tall.

"*Cher*, I'm not hungry. I'll take the coffee, though." She reached for the Styrofoam cup, blew a few times, and sipped.

Marc Willis pulled up a chair next to her. They sat in silence sipping *café au lait*. The only other sound in the stark room was the constant whir from the oxygen tent. A fine mist settled around them.

Unexpectedly, *Mémère* cleared her throat and patted Marc Willis on the leg. "Son, you need to get on to school. That's the most important thing, school." Their eyes met. "*Pépère* would not want you sittin' around here mopin' like this, so go on. I'll be fine, just fine. That cute little nurse, the one from Church Point, is on duty this mornin'. She'll do right by us. She'll explain anything the doctor says if I don't get it right away. Her French is pretty good. Don't you worry!"

Marc Willis squeezed his grandmother's hand and whispered softly in her ear, "I'm not the least bit worried about you two. Why, y'all got a lot of livin' left in you. But, ooh-ooh-wee, you are right, *Mémère*, that little nurse sure is fine. Why do you think I'm still hanging around here?"

Marc Willis's grandmother spoke to her husband, "Hear that, old man?" She looked at Marc Willis and sighed. "That'd sure make your grandpa happy. Why, tha's what he's been sayin' all along. That boy, Marc Willis, he needs a good Cajun girl to keep him straight."

A tender smile spread across her wide, wrinkled face. "Y'all been watchin' over us like a mother hen. Why, every day somebody's sittin' here beside me. Don't you get it? I need some private time with your grandpa. And you, you go on and get to school." She motioned as if to shoo chickens from the yard.

Marc Willis had spent enough summer vacations on the farm with his grandmother to recognize that tone. She had always been a strong-willed woman. It was born from years of living by sheer grit. There were missing pieces to her life story, things that she kept secret. Those who knew rarely hinted at or whispered about it. She always said, "It's best we let sleeping dogs lie."

Marc Willis winked and proposed a compromise. "What if I was to go and settle in that little room next to the chapel and do some studying while we both wait for that cute little nurse to come on by? You wouldn't deny your favorite grandson a chance to impress the woman he might one day marry, would you, *Mémère*?"

Satisfied with their bargain, she shook her finger at him. "You are such a flirt. Don't you give that pretty little nurse false hope, though? You got lots of school left to go."

Marc Willis reached for his knapsack, and then he winked. "I wouldn't do any such thing. Cross my heart."

An eerie stillness settled around the room as the door slowly shut behind him. It was as if all of the enthusiasm that comes with joyful living vanished with his going. *Mémère* shivered and pulled her sweater tighter around her shoulders. The metal chair scraped the floor as she pulled it closer to the bed. She picked up her husband's leathery hand and held it gently. "I sure do love that boy. That one reminds me of you more than any of our other grandsons."

No response.

Pépère's persistent paleness sent fear up her spine faster than heat lightning before a summer storm. She glanced around the sterile room, an expanse of white—white walls, white sheets, and white mist coming from the oxygen tent. Her husband's white hair rested on a white pillow. The whiteness took her back to their childhood. A jumble of bygone days swelled and filled her head and heart. She pressed the top of her husband's hand to her cheek. "It was all so long ago."

Thus, she began to talk to him. She began by recounting their beginnings, as if it were a tale about others, in hopes of bringing her husband back to the present through the back door. As the precious hours slipped away, and family members came and went, *Mémère* shared her story with her children. They in turn translated her words into English and repeated it for the younger generation. It was a tale of a simple Prairie Cajun girl, Angelique. The year was 1906 and the place was Belair Cove.

Table of Contents

xiv

Part I

Première Partie

Roly Poly
Belair Cove, Louisiana

The Cove sensed the arrival of a long growing season. The rush of March winds lifted winter's gray curtain from the prairie. The temperatures had been unusually mild, the early spring moist. Belair Cove was in perfect balance, and the soil was ripe for planting. The farmers looked forward to wagons filled with the reward of their upcoming labors.

Villagers had gathered at Sacred Heart Chapel for a special Mass of thanksgiving. Afterwards, families hurried home in anticipation of a hearty meal outdoors and a chance to enjoy the beautiful weather. Not wanting to offend any of the families, Father Lalonde followed the dirt path that wound its way from one farm to the next. He found good company and crocks of delicious food at each stop along the way. Father Lalonde rubbed his too-full belly as he approached his final destination, Vidrine's place.

Father quickly scanned the scene before him. He could hear the loud voices of young children in noisy conversations. He turned toward the path leading him to the shade trees beyond the pasture. The muffled laughter of younger children drifted and swirled across the fallow fields as he made his way. Father noticed a jumble of shoes and socks heaped carelessly against the whitewashed fence. The children were playing Roly Poly and he waved at them as he walked by.

"You boys better watch out, that Angelique can throw as good as any of you."

One of the boys pretended to pitch an imaginary ball over the tin roof. Several others waved at Father in disagreement. One remarked, "Aw Father, you ain't seen Jean Marc throw. He's got the best arm around here." They pointed to the tin can that marked Jean Marc's last throw.

Angelique ignored their antics as she held the ball lightly and tossed it back and forth between her hands. It was a white sock stuffed with cotton and shaped similar to a firm hardball the size of a man's fist. One of the boys had tied a string securely around the opening. She smiled and breathed deeply: the first hint of spring blossoms, an explosion of pink azaleas.

"Thanks, Father. Good to have you on my side."

Angelique's best friend, Marie Rose, flushed with excitement; the feather-dusted freckles on her plump cheeks glowed. She bounced repeatedly as she edged nearer to Angelique and tugged on her arm.

"Angelique, you think you can make it? Jean Marc's last throw went a far piece."

Angelique stood in sharp contrast to Marie Rose. Angelique was tall, sun-drenched, and slender. She wore a simple green dress made from a flour sack; tiny yellow flowers dotted the fabric. She had rolled up the long sleeves and tucked the full skirt toward the midline of her waistband to resemble pantaloons. A streak of dirt striped her forehead.

Marie Rose whispered into Angelique's ear, "My mama says you should always let the boy win even if you can beat him. Pride and all."

Angelique shook free of Marie Rose's hold and spat on the ground. "You heard Father Lalonde. You know I can do anything as good as any old boy."

Angelique stepped back, her brow deeply furrowed. Overhead, two sparrows held a tenuous grip on a narrow twig. She studied the tops of the trees as the branches stiffened, swayed, and fell limp after each gust of wind. She calculated the distance and took three steps further back. Then with all her might, she flung the sock over the roof.

"Roly Poly!" she shouted. "I gotcha this time, Jean Marc! Take that, you big braggart."

The two girls darted toward the opposite side of the house. Angelique's long braids flapped as she ran, and each twist of her hair shimmered as if it were a coffee bean nugget tinged with gold. Marie Rose bumped Angelique as they sped around the corner and came to a stop.

The words "Roly Poly" bounced from one child to the next and echoed back to them. All eyes were staring up at the high-pitched roof. The cotton-stuffed ball was still soaring. It had already tipped the arch of the tin roof and started rolling in a lopsided spiral.

Damon waved his long, skinny arms at Jean Marc. "Whoopee, I think she's gonna beat you this time."

At first, the white ball tumbled slowly, and then it picked up speed, spun swiftly down, down, down until—an unexpected gust of swirling wind blew across the tin roof. Everyone gasped. The hard ball was shifting off course. It was wobbling a little to the left toward a rusty piece of tin sticking straight up from the surface of the worn roof.

Angelique stomped her feet. "Hell and damnation, that ain't right. If it snags on that, I get another toss. You hear me, Jean Marc Fontenot?"

Jean Marc hooked his fingers around the straps of his overalls and a slow, sheepish smile spread across his boyish face. "Uh uh, not on your life." His deep-set brown eyes shone with golden specks as he pointed his finger at her and asserted, "This your last try. And you better not let your papa or Eula Mae hear you talkin' that way!"

Angelique squinted at the sun using both hands to shade her eyes as she watched the ball wobble.

"Hey look," Damon yelled, "the wind done took it. Bounced right over that crooked piece of tin."

Dozens of toes quickly lined up on either end of the finish line drawn in the dirt. The ball came to rest with a dull thud. Damon took a stick and marked the distance amidst a collective gasp of *oohs* and *aahs*. The white sock rested on one side of the line and the tin can on the other. Angelique's throw had landed barely an inch past Jean Marc's.

Angelique clapped her hands and squealed with delight. She grabbed Marie Rose to dance the Cajun jig. They twirled around and around until they were both dizzy and finally stopped.

Marie Rose stuck her tongue out at the boys. "I told y'all she could beat him."

Jean Marc's shoulders slumped, his face sullen.

Angelique planted her feet firmly to steady herself, widened her eyes, rested both hands on her hips, and twisted from side to side. "Well, looks like you ain't gonna get a kiss after all, Mister High and Mighty. Ain't you been told? Shouldn't count your chickens before they hatch. Didn't your mama ever tell *you* that?" Angelique tapped her foot and opened the palm of her hand. "Hand over my shiny nickel."

Damon huddled up with a few of the older boys and whispered something not meant for girls to hear. They shoved each other repeatedly, whooped, and hollered. They quieted as Jean Marc inched toward Angelique. He reached deep inside his worn pocket and pulled out a nickel, one of several he had worked hard to earn. He stepped forward to drop the nickel into Angelique's waiting hand.

Before releasing the coin, his fingers feathered the length of her open palm ever so slightly.

Angelique quickly closed her hand around the nickel; Jean Marc's fingers had sent an unfamiliar quiver through her. Even though her face flushed a rosy color, she looked directly into his eyes. In the hushed moments that followed, the wind whistled between the oaks, a dog barked, and a baby cried. Somewhere in the distance, they could hear that Angelique's Papa had taken up his fiddle.

Damon's throat tightened as he watched. The pupils of his blue eyes dilated in anger. He smashed through the circle and shoved Angelique and Jean Marc apart. Pulling Angelique toward him, Damon surprised her with a loud kiss – *pwahp* – right on her lips.

Damon turned to Jean Marc and scoffed, "Got to take what you want, Jean Marc. Don't you know that?"

Angelique slammed her closed fists against Damon's chest, knocking him off balance. He stumbled backwards and toppled to the ground. She tried to kick him, but Damon quickly rolled out of harm's way and burst into laughter. Wiping her face clean with the back of her hand, Angelique spat at him.

"I hate you, Damon Vidrine."

Damon righted himself and teased, "You know you loved it, Angelique."

Jean Marc erupted, "Why you lousy…I'm gonna take somethin' all right, the hair right off your hide."

Damon and Jean Marc lunged for each other, arms and legs thrashing, fists flying. Jean Marc fell to the ground. The children hastily encircled the two boys.

"Come on, Jean Marc, get up. Whip his ass. He ain't nuthin' but a big bully. Watch out for his left, that's it."

Marie Rose shouted, "Give him a black eye, Jean Marc. That'll fix him."

Angelique tightened her grip around the nickel and backed away from the scuffle. With her free hand, she took hold of Marie Rose's arm and tugged. "Come on. Let's get out of here before Eula Mae hears them."

Too late. The shutters flew open and slammed against the house; Eula Mae craned her long, skinny neck through the open window. The sun struck her dark face, setting it aglow like a polished midnight river stone. Her thick, wiry hair stuck out in every direction in spite of the red scarf wrapped around her small head and tied at the nape of her neck. Eula Mae, her dark eyes threatening, banged a wooden spoon against the side of the house when she saw Damon and Jean Marc fighting again. Startled, the rest of the children pushed and shoved against each other awkwardly. They tried to move away from the combatants and Eula Mae's accusing eyes.

"I declare, you two boys are gonna be the death of me. Stop that this instant! Damon, your mama says for you to git in this house and wash up. Supper be ready shortly."

Eula Mae shook her bony finger at the rest of the brood. "Y'all go on home now. Git. Tha's the last words I'm gonna say." Whenever Eula Mae barked the "last words," all of the Cove's children scurried to obey. Her people had sharecropped in the Cove as long as any of the white families had. She had cared for most of their children at one time or another, treated every one of them as if they were her own, and earned their respect in the process. They scattered like the little sparrows, "*ti-pops,*" at the tops of the trees.

"Angelique, what you doin' here child? I done told you to stay away from them boys. Go on home, girl. I be at your place next to bring you some supper."

The sun had begun to set heavily on the edge of the waning daylight. The only children who remained were Damon and Jean Marc as they wrestled on the ground. Damon had finally pinned Jean Marc down and was about to throw a lethal punch when he heard Eula Mae give her final warning.

"Don't make me come out there. Damon, I'll git your papa and he'll take a switch to the both of you."

Damon froze, fist in mid-air. Jean Marc took the advantage and shoved Damon sideways while scrambling out from underneath. Both boys popped up and began to circle each other cautiously with raised fists. Damon chanced a look over Jean Marc's head at Eula Mae. She had made her way onto the front porch by then and was standing there waving her broom in the air. Damon gave up under the pressure of Eula Mae's watchful stance.

Damon slowly lowered his fists. "Aw, it ain't worth it. Just so's you know, Eula Mae, he started it all."

Jean Marc waited warily. He was not sure if Damon truly intended to back down. Finally, Jean Marc relaxed his shoulders and dropped his arms at his side.

Eula Mae waited for a few more seconds and then returned to her chores. She had long since vowed to keep her opinions to herself;

it would never do for Damon's mother, Mrs. Hippolyte Vidrine, to know her thoughts. That woman seemed oblivious to the past and the recklessness of youth that repeats itself with each succeeding generation. However, Eula Mae could not overcome her frustration. For too long, she had watched as Damon bullied Jean Marc. Her tiny body stiffened and her regal chin jutted out in defiance.

She mumbled under her breath, "Mark my words, that Damon's a bad seed." One day, she knew, Jean Marc was going to give Damon his due. When that day came, she would turn her eyes the other way.

On the other hand, if anyone asked her about Jean Marc, her response was very different. She would tell people: "Wish that boy could see that he be just like the stars shinin' in the night sky. I'd bet that child never made no fuss from the day he was born." Eula Mae poked her head out of the window once more. "I'm checkin' on y'all to see if you boys a listenin' to me. Damon, git on in here."

"Yes, ma'am."

Eula Mae turned to leave. Jean Marc backed up and began to circle away from Damon with the intent of heading toward home. Damon scurried to stick his foot out, deliberately tripping Jean Marc. He then darted up the steps onto the porch and plunged his hands in a basin of water waiting at the back door. Splashing water over his straight black hair, he looked over his shoulder at Jean Marc and smirked. Damon stepped inside the house and shouted a bogus apology to Eula Mae.

Jean Marc laid there with the wind knocked out of him. After several seconds, he rose and stumbled off while throwing solid punches in the air. "I'll get you for this, Damon," he vowed. Jean Marc saw Capsay, his Catahoula Hound, running to catch up with him, "*Mais*, there you are."

Jean Marc bent on one knee and Capsay pounced on him and began to lick his face. Jean Marc stroked Capsay's fur, but steadied his gaze further down the road. Angelique had long since disappeared around a bend. He did not begrudge Angelique the shiny new nickel even though he had spent days in the sweltering heat to earn it. However, Damon stealing a kiss from her was another matter entirely.

"Capsay, it ain't right. Just because he lives in a big fine house smack in the middle of the Cove, it just ain't right."

Jean Marc knew he could earn more nickels when his mama made more fig pies. He would just have to get up early to beat the old black crows. They could pick a fig tree clean in a short time.

"Folks sure do gobble up mama's pies, a nickel a piece. I might consider bringin' some lemonade to the fields next Saturday. I reckon fig pies make a fella real thirsty."

Jean Marc picked up a stick and threw it for Capsay. The Catahoula Hound returned with the stick between his teeth and his tail wagging. He dropped it at Jean Marc's bare feet.

Jean Marc reached for the stick. "Capsay, I sure wish Eula Mae hadn't heard the fight and come out to break us up. I woulda whupped the life outta Damon this time. I coulda done it, too." Jean Marc looked at his pup to see if he agreed. Capsay barked and barked. Jean Marc threw a few more punches into the air for emphasis, and Capsay put some distance between himself and Jean Marc's anger.

"Aw, shucks, come here, boy. I ain't gonna hurt you." Jean Marc tapped his thigh and waited. "Come here, boy." He knelt in the dirt as Capsay licked his face clean. Jean Marc ran his fingers across his smooth chin: nothing. Damon had already begun to shave. "Capsay, one day, I'm gonna be a man and build me a nice house off the ground. Gonna have wood floors, a wood burning stove, and a cistern, too." Jean Marc pushed his unruly brown hair back from his forehead, straightened his drab overalls, and stood tall. "Mais, tha's what I'm gonna do. Ain't gonna sharecrop for Damon's folks, for sure."

Revenge

The *carencro*, a single black carrion crow, tugged on the carcass of a dead opossum, ripped off a small portion, and gulped it down. He cawed out to the others that he had found food. Two crows swooped down to feast on the remains. From Sacred Heart Chapel, on the opposite side of the road, one saw only their dark heads as they bobbed up and down in the drainage ditch.

Sacred Heart Chapel was, like its name, the core of Belair Cove. The white wooden façade rested against a backdrop of ancient oaks dripping with gray moss. To the left of the chapel was the cemetery, where families had buried their dead since the village began. On the tombstones were the familiar names of many Acadian and French families: Fontenot, Boudreaux, Vidrine and so many more.

It was the First Friday of the month, and only a few of the faithful were at the Benediction service. While kneeling in front of the altar, Jean Marc and Damon threatened to topple each other over as they squirmed impatiently. They leaned first on one knee and then the other. They kept looking over their shoulders at the elderly congregation, mostly women, who droned on and on.

When Father Lalonde spoke his final "Amen", the two boys popped up like jack-in-the-boxes. They pulled off their robes and tossed them into a heap at the back of the church. They burst out of the double doors at the entrance. The frightened crows protested loudly, flapped their wings, and flew away. Father Lalonde rolled his eyes to the heavens when he saw the pile of robes tossed aside so absentmindedly. He beckoned the two altar boys to return, but they had evaporated like morning mist.

Jean Marc picked up his pace as he ran, but he was no match for Damon's long strides. Damon was two lengths ahead as they raced around the next bend. Damon reached the fence line first. He turned, faced Jean Marc, and while running in place boasted, "Ha! I win again." Damon veered to the right to avoid the pecan grove and the men hard at work. He headed for a group of younger boys playing stickball with a tin can in the side pasture. Damon thrived on competition.

Jean Marc came to a stumbling halt; he leaned forward and rested his hands on the top of his knees until his breathing slowed. When he lifted his head, Damon was no longer in sight. Jean Marc heard his dog Capsay barking incessantly. He spotted him tied to a tree; the rope around his neck extended its full length. Jean Marc walked over to nuzzle the young pup.

"Hey, boy. Ya missed me, huh? Good dog."

From under the shade of a pecan tree, Uncle Gus beckoned to Jean Marc, "About time you get here. Been waiting for y'all."

Jean Marc responded, "Can't wait to get started."

Today was the start of the first fall *boucherie*. Last Sunday's lottery at Gus Fontenot's had settled the schedule. Each family name had been placed in a bowl for the drawing that determined who provided the calf for butchering. They shared the meat equally and repeated the practice based on the schedule. Jean Marc had waited anxiously as his Uncle Gus drew a slip of paper from the lottery bowl.

Gus looked at Jean Marc, shook his head sadly, and moaned, "It gonna be a while, son."

Crestfallen, Jean Marc seized the slip of paper Uncle Gus had pretended to toss aside carelessly. He had to see it with his own eyes. He smoothed the slip of paper out and read the date aloud. He was confused, and then Uncle Gus winked.

Jean Marc whooped and hollered, "I shoulda known you was pulling my leg."

They had drawn the first date and Gus had promised Jean Marc that he could help carve the hindquarter this time. Jean Marc was hungry to learn. He studied the flurry of preparations going on around him before rushing to his uncle's side. Jean Marc listened, intent on every word Uncle Gus spoke. Nodding his head, Jean Marc watched as Gus positioned the hindquarter on the table and used the edge of his hand to show the exact angle of the cut. Gus patted the slab of meat a few times and then handed Jean Marc the knife. "Careful now. It's mighty sharp."

Jean Marc gripped the handle firmly and placed the blade exactly where his uncle had shown him. He paused to search his uncle's face for reassurance before sinking the knife into the muscle.

With his uncle's approval, he made a deep slice in the hindquarter of the calf.

Jean Marc promised, "Uncle Gus, I'm gonna make you proud."

"You doin' fine boy, keep goin'," Uncle Gus said as he handed the slab of meat to Uncle Emile, who put it on an old scale.

Knife in hand, Jean Marc made a second careful cut.

"I think the boy's caught on to this. Yep, mighty fine butchering," Uncle Emile exclaimed.

"I think I got the hang of it, for sure." Jean Marc wiped his sweaty face on the sleeve of his shirt and turned around to see if Angelique had heard the compliment.

Angelique was helping Eula Mae scrape the cowhide. She had her nose pinched up tight and was making peculiar faces. She looked up and saw Jean Marc staring back at her while Eula Mae continued to jabber on about her technique for drying the skins. "Pay attention, Angelique. This gonna make a fine new seat for them old kitchen chairs. They be as good as new when we done."

Jean Marc winked at Angelique. She stuck her tongue out at him. He burst out laughing and then went back to business. Jean Marc slipped the knife blade into the meat, carved out the last roast, and carried it over to the table where it was to be salted. One of the women took it from him and rubbed the meat with special seasonings, turned it over, and rubbed the other side.

Jean Marc admired the choice cuts laid out on the table. He yelled across the yard, "All done. Uncle Gus, which cut of meat we gonna get this week?"

Gus walked over, selected a rump roast, and sliced it into smaller pieces. "We get first choice, boy."

Jean Marc watched as Uncle Gus slipped their portion of salted meat into the glass jar. He sealed the lid and handed it to Jean Marc. "You gonna git this home?"

Damon called out, "Hey, Jean Marc, leave that, we need you on the team."

"Ain't got time."

Jean Marc set the jar down only long enough to untie Capsay and tap his thigh twice. Capsay ignored the command and headed in the direction of the game. Capsay snapped his head from side to side, ready to pounce on the tin can that the boys were kicking around.

Jean Marc called out firmly, "Capsay, here, boy."

Capsay balked and backed away. Once again, Jean Marc gave the command. Capsay hung his head, but complied. He nipped at Jean Marc's ankles as they headed home together.

Jean Marc studied the land as he walked each bend of the winding road. Past the barren fields, he could see the rolling hills and the tall prairie grass fading from verdant shades of green to golden hues. A few remaining wildflowers dusted the landscape. Giant oak and pine trees forested the backlands bordering the coulees and bayous. This place was his future; he straightened his shoulders. He dreamed of the day that he would have a farm of his own. He passed by Uncle Hanray's place, then his Uncle Emile's farm, and Uncle Farreaux's. Jean Marc crossed the road and stopped to admire the corn planted on the Vidrine property. The Vidrines owned more than most on both sides of the road.

"Capsay, one day I will own a big piece of farm land, me."

Jean Marc cradled the jar with one hand and stroked the dog with the other. "*Mais*, Capsay, guess who I will take for my wife?"

Capsay barked loudly and cocked his ears.

Jean Marc chuckled. "You like her too, eh boy? Good dog." Jean Marc bent down and Capsay licked his face. Jean Marc whistled as he continued on his path home. He felt lucky to call any place home. He shuddered to think what might have become of him had Uncle Gus not taken him in when he was orphaned at a young age.

Even so, home was a simple structure made from sawed lumber located on the highest point of the land. The house had a steep gabled roof and a porch that wrapped around the front. A fence separated the family garden from the crops surrounding the property on every side. When he reached home, he buried the jar under the steps of the porch.

"We're done here. Capsay, *Tante* Odette promised me a good supper tonight, a slab of hot cornbread, *bouillie* made from the entrails of the butchered calf, and corn *maquechou*. Ooh-wee, that's gonna taste good." Jean Marc's mouth watered. "Except supper's gonna wait for a while 'cus I got me an idea how I can earn a few more coins." Jean Marc raced back to Uncle Gus's place. He kept alert for neighbors who wanted help carrying their portion of meat home.

Mr. Vidrine was shouting, "Damon, Damon. Where the hell is that boy?" Damon had spent most of his day skirting the edges of the busy workers, playing with the boys, and flirting with the girls. Mr.

Vidrine was embarrassed as heads turned to witness his frustration with his son.

Emile used his chin as if it were a pointer and muttered to Gus, "Lookee there. Things never change. Damon's just like his papa at that age, think the world owes him, he does. That boy ought to leave dem girls alone."

Gus glanced toward Domitile Vidrine. Their eyes met. Domitile stood up, ready to counter Emile's harsh words.

"Been a long day, Emile," Gus said. "Leave it alone. We all done here. Go get yourself a beer."

Jean Marc saw a chance for easy money, to lower a jar down, deep into Mr. Vidrine's well. Jean Marc pushed forward between the three men and said, "For a nickel, I'll carry that, Mr. Vidrine. What you say, eh?"

Domitile's steel grey eyes settled on the eager boy. He smiled warmly down at Jean Marc and handed him a jar of salted meat. "You best be gettin' along then. You gotta crawl under the house and put this here jar next to the chimney. It's real cool there. Bury it deep. You hear? I'll meet you back at my place in a bit."

"No problem, Mr. Vidrine."

Jean Marc's broad smile faded as soon as he set off for the Vidrine place. This delivery would be more difficult than he had anticipated. But, he was up to the task.

Neither he nor Capsay noticed that someone was following them. Skirting ditches and hedges and staying several yards back, Damon trailed behind them. He carried a knapsack over his shoulder.

When Jean Marc arrived at the Vidrine house, he sucked in his breath, knelt, and ducked under the front steps. Capsay followed on his haunches. Jean Marc paused for a few minutes to allow his eyes to adjust to the darkness. His knees raked across the unleveled dampness as he crawled beneath the porch and headed in the direction of the chimney. It was cooler and drier there.

Jean Marc heard Mr. Vidrine's voice approaching as he called for his old bulldog, "Peanut, Peanut, come here, boy."

The wooden planks on the porch creaked under the footsteps of the older man's weight. He settled in and the rocker began to squeak to the rhythm of the up and down motion. The smoke from his pipe scented the air.

Jean Marc returned to his task under the house. He prayed that he would not come across an ornery snake. He made a wide sweep ahead with a stick and then patted the damp ground searching for the hollowed out spot.

"It gonna be worth it," he said to himself.

"There, right there." Jean Marc's hands found the slight indention where the meat jar had rested in the past. Using his fingers, he dug deeper, then settled the jar firmly in place. He swiveled around to exit when he saw Damon crawling straight toward him.

"What the heck?"

Damon whispered, "Shh, watch this. I'm gonna get my pa."

Damon had a small sack slung over his back. Peanut was coming up the rear sniffing at Damon's pocket. Damon loosened the string on the sack, pulled out a corncob, and a bottle of turpentine. He soaked the corncob in turpentine; the stench brought tears to their eyes.

"What the hell you up to, Damon?"

The dogs inhaled the stench of the turpentine and started to move away from it. Damon was faster; he grabbed Peanut by the snout and tucked that old dog under his arm. He looked up at Jean Marc and said, "Pa loves this damn dog more than anything."

"I want no part of this." Jean Marc scooted on his elbows in an attempt to grab the turpentine-soaked corncob from Damon.

Damon quickly reached around with his free hand and rubbed the corncob on Peanut's behind. Peanut growled, squirmed and twisted, until he finally broke loose. Damon reached into his pocket, pulled out a scrap of raw meat, and waved it under Peanut's nose. Crawling to the edge of the house, Damon tossed it far out into the yard. Both dogs raced from underneath the house to chase the meat, and the boys scrambled to hide behind the barn.

Capsay reached the scrap before the old bulldog. Peanut let out a deep throaty growl and lunged for the young pup's neck. Capsay yelped, but he was quick to get away. Shaking himself loose and ready for a fight, Capsay turned to face Peanut, snarled, and bared his teeth.

Suddenly, Peanut stopped short and shuddered. He started shaking his backside akin to a jar of churning butter. Rubbing his behind to ease the burning fire, poor Peanut scooted across the grass. Capsay made off with the raw meat and ran toward Jean Marc.

Meanwhile, Mr. Vidrine had dropped his pipe and leapt from his rocker. He called out Peanut's name repetitively. The old dog continued to drag his rear end over the cool grass. On occasion, he would jump, turn, and twist, but nothing seemed to help.

"Peanut, what's wrong with you? What's wrong wit my dog? Peanut, you goin' crazy?"

Peanut just kept on spinning like a top.

Damon ran up beside Jean Marc and whispered, "I got him good. Didn't I? He punished me yesterday for nuthin'."

Jean Marc frowned. "I'm gonna get you for this. Peanut bit my dog. I ought to tell on you."

Damon shoved Jean Marc against the side of the barn and held his arm against Jean Marc's throat. "You ain't gonna do nuthin' of the sort, now, are you? Besides, that stupid dog of yours ain't hurt none." Damon released his chokehold and ran around the far corner of the house. He called out to his father: "Pa, what's ailin' Peanut?"

Jean Marc rubbed his throat and bent down to examine Capsay's shoulder. The cut was not deep. With some care and healing herbs, it would mend quickly. Hearing the chatter of birds, he shielded his eyes and looked up at the clear blue sky. A flock of black crows soared high above his head. They flew toward Uncle Gus's backyard. Jean Marc shouted in frustration at the only thing that he could, the scavengers. "Y'all a bunch of mangy critters. Gus ain't got scraps for the likes of you."

Jean Marc brushed the grime off his overalls and followed Damon to the front of the house to claim the nickel he had earned. "One of these days you gonna get it, Damon Vidrine."

The Hospital Vigil

Mémère patted her husband's hand while he slept. "Why, when I look back over it now, I guess y'all was always fightin' with each other. As far back as I can remember."

Mémère knew that she still had that nickel she had won from Jean Marc. She had kept it all these years, a reminder of how simple life might have been. It was tucked away somewhere in a bureau drawer, nestled inside the first white handkerchief she had ever sewn. She remembered finishing the edges of that handkerchief with a fine stitch. She had embroidered small flowers on all four corners and the letter "A" above one floret.

"We were so young. *Pépère*, those were happy times."

Across the hall, Marc Willis rubbed his tired eyes and closed his books. It was more important than ever that he score well on this botany test. Good grades might be the only thing that stood between him and Vietnam. He checked his watch and then made his way back to his grandfather's room. He tiptoed in and heard his grandmother's sweet voice. "Mémère, who you talkin' to?"

She chuckled. "Some might say I'm a bit crazy. I thought it might help if he could hear stories from the old days. Get him to thinkin'. You know, bring him back."

Marc Willis placed his hand on top of hers.

"Well, who knows, you might be right. Why don't you tell me a story?"

"What do you want to hear about?"

Marc Willis considered the question for a few seconds and shook his head. "When did you first realize that *Grand-père* was the one?"

She smiled. "You know, I used to be a real tomboy."

Catching the *Blossom*

The boys lay low amongst the tall grasses. A cow mooed. Damon tilted his head. "Jean Marc, when I say go you run like a skunk's chasin' you."

"I ain't too sure about this, Damon. You done got me more than one whippin' lately."

"Aw, we ain't gonna get caught. I'm tellin' you, just run alongside 'til you see an open boxcar and hop on in. Now, don't get spooked if there's others sittin' inside there. Just find you a spot, set yourself down and let your eyes adjust to the dark. Then, we'll be in Ville Platte lickety split. You tired a walkin', ain't you?"

"Yeah, takes more than an hour. What about Angelique? We told her we'd take her with us."

"We ain't takin' her with us. Angelique's papa'll skin us alive. I told her we were goin' Wednesday after next. Besides, we get the lay of the land first and maybe take her with us next time. Wait here."

Damon crawled up to the tracks and put his ear next to the hot metal. He scrambled back to Jean Marc. "She's a comin'. Get ready."

The wind rustled in the trees. Damon slapped at the annoying mosquito sucking blood from his arm. Jean Marc lay flattened against the hard ground, his nose buried deep in the earth. He loved the smell of the sweet grass and the rich loam.

The *Cotton Blossom* was speeding down a section of track hidden deep in the woods. The two boys remained pressed to the earth and tuned their ears to its familiar sound. Having raced against the train often, they knew that she was very fast. Still, even the *Cotton Blossom* had to slow down coming around this next bend. That would be their chance to hop aboard. Suddenly, the train appeared through a section of saplings splitting the backlands in two, the same way she separated Belair Cove Road. She was all grit, spit, and engine, not like a white cotton blossom at all.

Damon shouted over the sound of the train's engine, "Get ready. This is it." He darted from the shelter of the prairie grass and never looked back.

Jean Marc popped his head up and sprang into action. His heart was pounding as he ran beside the boxcars that flew by. He was gaining on one when he caught sight of Angelique's blue dress out of the corner of his eye. He waved his arms and yelled at her above the deafening roar, "Angelique, get out of my way!"

Angelique sprinted even faster to catch up with him. "Not a chance. I'm gettin' on!"

Breathing hard, Jean Marc gritted his teeth and slowed his pace until he came to a gradual halt. The *Cotton Blossom* chugged around the next bend without him. "Darn, girl, you ain't nuthin' but trouble."

"Ain't right, leavin' me behind like that," Angelique shot back.

The two looked up the tracks to see Damon swinging into a boxcar. Jean Marc reached for Angelique's hand. "Come on. We'll find something else to do around here."

Angelique waved as the last car disappeared. "I'm gonna ride that train one day, head right out of Belair Cove. See things I've never seen before."

"And leave Belair Cove?" Jean Marc said, "You go right ahead, you. I ain't ever leavin' here, me. This is home."

The fading train sounded as if Belair Cove sighed in relief upon hearing this. A rabbit scurried across their path. A small fox ambled to the edge of the trees, lifted its head, and then darted deeper into the woods. The morning dew evaporated as the bright sun shone down and warmed the earth. Jean Marc and Angelique walked away hand in hand.

Blackberry Cobbler

Angelique had grown up on the edge of Belair Cove; people used to say she was a little heathen. Despite being poor, she had a reasonably happy childhood. Her mama, Azalie Belair, had been from the Cove. She lived only long enough to twirl Angelique's curly dark hair around her own finger, look into her tiny hazel eyes, and admire her angelic face. Azalie kissed the sweet, silky skin of her forehead and named her daughter Angelique, after the angels in heaven. Azalie died three days later. Papa, Alduce Belair, had done his best to look after his daughter with the help of Eula Mae. As she grew, Papa always struggled to "do the right thing by my girl."

However, Angelique was a tomboy through and through. When she turned thirteen, Papa wanted her to start wearing dresses and act more like a girl. Angelique much preferred her worn dungarees. This morning was no exception. She stuck her head out the back door of their old shack. No sign of Papa. She sprinted as fast as she could across the length of the pasture toward the backlands. As she ran, the swish of her dungarees against her legs promised, *"free, free, free."* Angelique did not look back until the trees hid her from view.

Angelique crossed the piney woods to the root-tangled edge of the bayou, and headed toward the old, deserted boat dock. She followed the markings that she left behind last fall, an "x" scraped into the bark of several trees. She grinned when she spotted the bramble of bushes laden with blackberries, her secret supply yet undiscovered by others. Angelique popped a ripe berry into her mouth and tasted its sweetness. Satisfied, she began to plop blackberries into her bucket: a cobbler would be a wonderful surprise for Papa.

Angelique heard him whistling before she actually saw Jean Marc drop his fishing line into the water almost directly above her head.

"Hey, what you think you doin' up there?"

"What the hell, Angelique, you scared me to death. What *you* doin' down there?" Jean Marc pulled in his line.

"What's it look like I'm doin'? Pickin' berries. A cobbler for Papa."

"Now, look what you've gone and done, scared all the fish, you did."

Jean Marc propped his fishing pole against a sad little sycamore angled over the bayou. "Aw, here, let me help you. Then maybe a fella can have some peace. Besides, your papa and I got something in common. A blackberry cobbler would taste real good."

They gathered berries until Angelique's bucket was full. After that, Angelique sat with Jean Marc while he fished the murky bottom of the river. She wiggled her toes in the water, fidgeted with the leaves that were within her grasp, and looked all about, not a bird in sight above her head. Upstream, several small fish jumped in and out of the water. She squirmed impatiently.

In a soft whisper, Jean Marc began to share his knowledge of the backlands. He talked about the drag of the current. He explained that the twisted roots under the water were a haven for all types of small creatures that depended upon each other. He bragged about the catfish that frequented his favorite fishing hole. Sunlight poured into the surrounding trees and birds warbled while they waited. A turtle, its big round eyes dark and serious, plopped into the bayou.

That was the first time. He reached over to run his finger across a berry stained cheek and leaned in to catch her scent. It was the most natural thing to do; he kissed her gently on the lips. Neither said anything afterwards.

It was close to dark when they headed home—he carrying a fish in a basket and she with a bucket full of berries. Angelique glowed like a firefly at dusk and Jean Marc stood tall, his chest was puffed out like a rooster.

They parted at the first bend in the road. Angelique walked home alone and skulked from one tallow tree to the next. When there was no sign of her papa, she made a dash for the back door of the shack.

"Papa? Papa, you in here?"

When no answer came, Angelique plopped the bucket of blackberries onto the kitchen table absentmindedly. She shed her dungarees and stuffed them into the bureau. Snapping her dress off the bed, she hastily slipped it back over her head. She raised the lid of the old trunk at the foot of her bed; the hinges squeaked. Angelique fumbled around looking for the nickel, the same nickel that she had won off Jean Marc some time back.

"Aha, there you are."

Angelique turned the cotton sock upside down and shook it until she heard the nickel ding as it rolled away on the floor. She chased after it and slapped her palm down before it found its way under the bed. Searching for a handkerchief, she rummaged through her sewing basket. She placed the nickel into the center of her handkerchief and folded it carefully upon itself. She kissed the white center lightly and tucked it under her pillow for safekeeping.

The next evening, Angelique arrived at Jean Marc's house carrying a warm, fresh blackberry cobbler. She glowed as she handed it to his Aunt Odette. "I made it myself."

Jean Marc rushed to take his aunt's place at the door, looked back over his shoulder, and whispered to Angelique. "If you like, we could meet back at the old dock again."

"*Mais oui*, yes," she said.

Angelique started for home. It was a blue-black, starry night—a heavenly canvas over Belair Cove—the kind of night where dreams come true. Jean Marc stood outside and watched her walk away. His pulse quickened and his breath became shallow. He remembered Angelique's ripe lips stained with berries, a memorable image of pleasures yet to come.

They found their way to the bayou as often as they could. They met at the spot where the dappled sunlight cast a shimmery glow over the fallen willow tree. There, they learned to trust each other. Although neither spoke of it openly, Jean Marc and Angelique dared to envision a future together.

Until now, Jean Marc seldom mentioned his childhood, the time before he came to live with Uncle Gus. Angelique was curious about his knowledge of the backlands and questioned him repeatedly about where he had learned this or that. He slowly revealed the truth about his early years, at least as far back as he could remember.

"There are some things that don't add up. But, I learned long ago to leave well enough alone. Can you keep a secret?"

Angelique swore on her mother's grave.

"I know folks around here talk bad about them, but my mama was part Indian. She died from the fever when I was little. Mama, she taught me a lot."

Jean Marc taught her much about the ways of his mother's people. Angelique's curiosity made her an eager student. She came to love the backlands as much as he did. As often as she could, she followed him when he went hunting. He taught her to stay downwind of animals, to listen for the tiniest snap of a twig or the swish of the grass, and to examine the bark of a tree. They studied feeding habits of various animals. She learned that a chewed-up pinecone could identify a certain animal. They tracked deer, squirrels, rabbits, and tiny birds.

"Angelique, over here. See, a squirrel ate this. That squirrel got him some mighty big teeth. See how it's all ragged and frayed. Yep, I'm sure tha's a squirrel."

Sometimes, Jean Marc would fish and Angelique would wander away to collect flowers and interesting plants. She placed them carefully into her pouch—her guise for being in the backlands in the first place. Later, Angelique would bring them to Eula Mae's and take note as she explained the medicinal benefits of each.

Angelique's knowledge of the backlands expanded swiftly. She looked at the trees, the birds, the deer and the turtles with new eyes, Jean Marc's eyes.

Jean Marc always walked ahead when they were together. He would help pull Angelique up from the lower bank of the bayou. He cleared the branches from her path and put his arm out in front of her at the slightest threatening sound. In the woods, they came to depend on each other with only the slightest look or touch. At the end of a day's adventure, they sometimes kissed goodbye. They dared not stay until dark, when the stars shimmered across the night sky.

Bal de Maison

Young girls in Belair Cove married at a tender age, far younger than those who lived in larger towns. When their daughters turned fourteen, Cajun mothers started scouting suitable husbands. The true guardians of the Cove, the elderly women who kept careful watch for such things began to take notice of the attraction between Angelique and Jean Marc. They gazed at each other dreamily, always seemed to be in the same place at the same time, and danced the last dance together on Saturday nights. There was talk that they might make a good match.

Angelique and Marie Rose were coming of age and it was time for their parents to find acceptable suitors for marriage. They were excited about the upcoming *fais do-do* at Marie Rose's house. The two teens chitchatted like hens as they prepared for the evening.

"I sure hope Antoine asks me to dance," Marie Rose said. "He's a good man. Papa thinks he would be a fine catch. Don't you think so? A good man is all you need. That's what Mama says."

They each gripped an end of the dining table and pushed it against the wall. Marie Rose unfolded the tablecloth, covered the table with it, and smoothed out the wrinkles. They arranged the chairs around the outer perimeter of the living room.

Angelique picked up Eula Mae's pecan cake from the sideboard and placed it on the center of the table. She deliberated on Marie Rose's question for only a second. Antoine was puny and pale; on the other hand, he had kind eyes. "It's the way he watches you when you're not lookin'," Angelique replied. "Yes, I think he really likes you."

Marie Rose blushed and raised her eyebrows. "I felt his eyes on me a time or two. It gives me shivers up my spine, in a good way." The two young women laughed and hugged. Arm in arm, they turned to give the room one final inspection.

Angelique spoke first, "Everything's ready. I say it's time for us to get gussied up for this dance. I have a feeling it's gonna be a special night for both of us."

Marie Rose frowned. "Sorry, I can't. I gotta finish gettin' Jacque and Pierre's things ready to wear."

"I ain't believin' this. Can't your brothers take care of themselves? They ought to shine their own shoes."

"Mama says I can't go if they're not satisfied with what I've done." Marie Rose slumped over a pair of black boots, picked up one of them, and busied herself swirling polish over it.

"I'll never understand why your mama favors those big-lazy-good for nuthin' boys. They ain't no better than us. Here, let me help you with that."

Angelique took the boot from Marie Rose's grasp, sucked deep into the back of her throat, and then spat on it. Marie Rose chuckled, snatched it back, and began buffing it to a deep shine.

"Don't you worry about me. I take care of myself. Why, I done got that pretty green dress all ironed and ready to wear since the middle of the week."

"Well, then, I guess I should leave you to finish up here. I still got a few things to do."

She left Marie Rose ironing her brothers' shirts.

Angelique walked slowly home; her mind filled with warm thoughts of her own future. Her dreams that were once fragile things had strengthened through the telling of them and taken on a life of their own. Angelique had shared her dreams with Jean Marc on many a lazy afternoon as they wandered through the backlands. He had never once made fun of her when she talked about needing more schooling, traveling outside of Belair Cove, or even her desire to raise a large family of her own. Like the air that she breathed and the gravity that kept her tethered to the earth, Angelique believed in life's possibilities. Maybe Jean Marc would find the courage to speak to her papa; it might even be tonight.

Angelique pressed her hands to her stomach cramps and quickened her pace toward home. "Nothing is going to ruin this evening." Papa would not allow her to go to the dance if he found out she did not feel well. She chastised Eve for disobeying God and bringing this curse upon woman. She would have to stop in at Eula Mae's and get some fresh rags.

Angelique found Eula Mae in her back yard calling the chickens, "*P'awk, p'awk, p'awk, pwawk.*"

"Eula Mae, you hoo!"

Her hand filled with grain, Eula Mae waved Angelique over. She motioned her toward a beat up old chair. "I'm hankerin' for a Rhode Island Red. What you think about that? I done seen one in the catalog at Sylvester's Mercantile."

When she was close enough to observe Angelique's pallor, she said, "Uh oh, what's troublin' you child? You sit a spell and tell old Eula Mae everythin'." She threw out the rest of the feed and wiped her hands on her apron.

In the kitchen, Eula Mae put a pot of water on the stove to boil. She set out her only nice teacup and saucer. From the pocket of her apron, Eula Mae took out a small sack of herbs and untied the string. She selected a few dried leaves of evening primrose, crumbled them into the cup, added the boiling water, and swirled the tea with a spoon.

"I got just the medicine you need to fix that belly ache," she said as she handed Angelique the hot brew. They went outside and sat together under the shade of the old poplar by the gate. Angelique frowned at the dark mixture settling at the bottom of the teacup.

"Drink up. Tha's evenin' promise in there. Gonna ease your monthly. It's hard to find around here."

Angelique stirred it with her finger and watched as the little particles settled once more. She closed her eyes and sniffed at the ingredients before taking her first sip. She shuddered at the unusual taste.

"I be thinkin' it's best for you to stay away from that dance tonight, child." Eula Mae pointed to the cup of tea. "It's likely, tha's the best evenin' promise you gonna get. Yessiree." She chuckled at her cleverness and shook her arthritic finger at Angelique. "You heed my warnin' good, you hear. No dance tonight."

"Eula Mae, you worry too much. Like you said, this gonna fix me right up. Besides, I feel better just bein' around you." Angelique swallowed the rest of the herbal tea and stood up to leave.

"Not without takin' a few good eggs to your papa, you ain't," Eula Mae chided.

Angelique knew that it would do no good to argue. She held out her own apron and shaped it into a bowl.

Eula Mae filled it with fresh eggs. "That'll do, Eula Mae. Six eggs. I got to get home."

Balancing the eggs afforded Angelique the chance to proceed slowly past Jean Marc's place on her way home. It was early yet and she wanted assurance that he was going to be at the dance. Her heart skipped when she spotted the metal tub in the back yard, hot water rising to meet the already sweltering heat of late afternoon. Angelique lifted her shoulders to meet her ears, rolled her eyes up to heaven, and beamed. *"Merci, Bon Dieu."* Tonight, Jean Marc would smell of soap scented with sassafras, all fresh and clean.

Angelique swayed slightly to an imaginary dance tune as she strolled home, blue sky above and solid earth beneath her feet. The sudden sound of thundering hooves from behind startled her. Brandishing flags to announce the upcoming dance, Marie Rose's rascal brothers and Damon shot past her on horseback. They fired their pistols in the air several times to alert the neighbors.

The eggs nestled in Angelique's apron crashed to the ground. She shook her fist and cursed the riders. Damon burst out laughing at her as he sailed past. With swift muscular movements, he turned his horse around, leapt off, and dropped down in front of her.

"Here, let me help you with that."

Marie Rose's brothers circled the two of them a few times; the horses kicked up a swirl of dust.

"Oh, sweet Angelique, let me help you," one of them said as he mocked Damon.

"Mon amour let me save you," teased the other.

Damon warned them both to back off with a simple, single glance. The two set off down the road, leaving Damon and Angelique behind. They stood on either side of the broken eggs splattered on the road.

"Well, it's a little late to help me. Don't you think, Damon?"

Damon winked. "Angelique, you sure are a feisty one."

"Never you mind what I am, Damon Vidrine. You owe me six good eggs."

Damon jumped over the mess and made a grab for her waist.

Angelique sidestepped his grasp and skirted away, out of reach. She looked over her shoulder at him and she marched away. "I've got no interest in the likes of you."

Damon yelled, "How about I just buy you the whole goddamn henhouse?" He watched her walk away, leaving him alone on the dusty road. He mounted his horse and rode after her.

"What the hell I done now? Want a ride to your place?"

Angelique motioned him away.

"Please yourself then. Walk home alone, but I'll see you tonight. Save me a dance, you pretty little thing." Damon jerked on the reins and trotted off to catch up with his friends.

The Promise Fades

Angelique tucked in her calico blouse and smoothed out her dark green skirt. A crowd had already gathered outside Marie Rose's place when she and Papa arrived. Angelique bounced in the seat as she heard the sound of Cajun music drifting her way.

"Hurry, Papa."

"Hold your horses, girl."

Papa tugged on the reins and the wagon came to a stop. He moved so slowly. It seemed to take him forever to step down from the wagon, hitch the horse to the fence post, and collect his fiddle.

Angelique kicked her leg out from under her skirt and climbed down without any assistance. She straightened her clothes once more and stepped briskly toward the music that vibrated in her very bones. She dodged several children playing a game of tag in the yard.

Angelique rushed inside searching for Marie Rose. Noticing the chaperones sitting in a row against the wall, she slowed her pace. Remembering her manners, she nodded at each of the women as she made her way around the crowded room. Lena Breaux's mother rushed past Angelique and headed for the dance floor. She swooped over to the young man who was dancing with her daughter and tapped him on the shoulder. The two no longer touched.

Eula Mae sat some distance from the rest of the local women. Her foot tapped the floor to the beat of the music. She shook her head in disapproval when she saw Angelique.

Angelique hugged her affectionately. "Don't you be mad at me."

"Child, I'm here because I knowed that you'd be comin' here anyways. You as stubborn as my ol' mule, Baptiste. How you feelin'? Like I done told you, there ain't enough evenin' promise in that tea to last you the night."

❖ ❖ ❖

Papa shuffled across the room to the far corner where the other musicians made a space for him. Felix Soileau was keeping time for the band with his *ti-fer*. Papa lifted his fiddle to his shoulder, picked up the beat, and joined them in the lively tune. A few couples stepped lightly to the music as they circled the room. Nearby, Marie Rose feigned shyness behind downcast eyelashes each time Antoine attempted to hold her gaze. They steadily moved toward each other as if it were a casual occurrence and started a conversation.

In the back bedroom, mothers were rocking their babies to sleep while their husbands gambled in the barn. Out back, shouts and curses told the tale of wins and losses as cards tumbled onto bales of hay. Old Mr. Chastine stood near his wagon. Several men waited in line to buy his special homemade brew. Damon and Marie Rose's brothers decided to start their evening by drinking a few beers.

It had been a long day of anticipation for Angelique. She pressed her hands to her belly. By the time the dance floor filled, Eula Mae's remedy was beginning to wear off. She was upset that Jean Marc had not yet made an appearance. He was loitering outside and drinking beer with Damon. When they finally strolled through the doorway, Jean Marc was unusually loud and his speech was slurred. He stumbled his way over to where she sat and asked her to dance. She refused.

Jean Marc flushed. He looked around to see if anyone had observed the slight. "Angelique, what's the matter? This ain't like you."

"I ain't feelin' like dancin' right this minute. Tha's all."

Drunk with false bravado, Jean Marc immediately turned to the girl standing next to them. "Solange, you want to dance with me?" Solange did not hesitate to put her hand in his. Jean Marc danced with her twice more while Angelique watched. Though her heart broke, she pretended indifference.

Damon seized his opportunity. Angelique accepted his offer of a dance. She did two more rounds with him to spite Jean Marc. However, she refused Damon the last dance of the evening. She scanned the room quickly searching for Jean Marc, but he had simply vanished. Angelique stood there holding back tears as she watched Marie Rose and Antoine pass her by. A few old biddies puckered their lips and rolled their eyes at Angelique's predicament. The last dance signified far more than a two-step around the room.

On the way home, Papa questioned her incessantly about Damon Vidrine. He went on to provide his opinion about Damon and his redeeming qualities, though there were few. Angelique did not want to hear anymore. "Papa, please, I don't want to talk about Damon Vidrine. He ain't right for me."

They rode home in sullen silence.

Domitile Vidrine, Damon's father, showed up early the next morning brandishing a small sack of tobacco for Papa. He and Papa walked the fields with their heads bent in deep conversation. Angelique knew that Domitile was expounding about the merits of his fine son. Angelique stood barefoot behind the open door and prayed for a miracle. None came. Domitile Vidrine invited Papa and Angelique to Sunday dinner, week after next.

Papa decided to wait a few days before he mentioned it to Angelique. He needed time to consider certain things, turn it over in his head and think about their future. "What's a poor man to do?" he confided to Eula Mae. Eula Mae reserved judgment. She understood Alduce's heart.

Unfortunately, Alduce and Eula Mae were not getting younger. He did not want poverty to follow his only child all the days of her life. He was nothing but a poor sharecropper like his father before him, farming *cote-a-cote*, side by side, with freed blacks like Eula Mae's family. "Poor is poor in these parts," Angelique's *grand-père* used to say. Not much had changed.

Papa had a keen eye for the beauty hidden in a piece of unfinished wood. Under his caring capable hands, the soft grains surfaced and he constructed beautiful furniture in the hours he was not working the fields. It took time and tenderness to nurture perfection, but few in the Cove could afford that quality of artisanship. Therefore, Papa focused on simple, serviceable pieces. Papa saved his carpentry earnings in a sock tucked underneath Angelique's moss bedding. However, they often emptied the money sock. Even if the crops were good, they still had to pay the landowner. There was no money left to buy basic supplies such as flour, sugar, or salt. One year Papa replaced the roof on the house they rented because the landowner refused to take care of the problem, and he bought medicine when Angelique had fever the summer she was nine.

Papa often shared his vision with her, the dream of a better life for the two of them. It was her favorite fairy tale when she was little. Angelique would fold herself into Papa's arms and he would begin, "Papa has some big plans for his little girl."

"Tell me again. I want to hear the secret plans, Papa."

"One day not too far away, I buy us our very own tools. Then, we able to work the ground like this." Papa would hold Angelique's hands in his and together they would scrunch up their faces and pretend to work very hard.

"Our crop is good, ain't it Papa? What happened next?" Angelique's eyes would light up.

"Yep, crop's good. So now, we get half the yield instead of farming thirds." Papa would hold up two fingers for Angelique.

"This is the part where you're supposed to tickle me, Papa?"

"*Mais oui*, that's right." Papa always pretended to forget. He would poke Angelique's sides, and she would squeal and wriggle with delight. The story would continue.

"The next year we buy fertilizer, seed, and maybe a mule."

Angelique pretended to plant a seed in the palm of her hand. "And then." Impatient, she would rush to the finish. "And then with a few good crops, God willing, we buy our very own farm." Angelique would clap enthusiastically: "The end!"

Papa would add, "Even if it's small, just a few acres would do. No more sharecroppin', then no more rentin', and best of all no more beggin' for loans from the Jewish banker in Ville Platte. Nosiree. He's a kind man, a good man for sure, but...."

They chimed in together, "a man's gotta feel his own land under his feet."

Papa would touch his index finger to the tip of Angelique's nose, tuck her into bed, and whisper, "Goodnight, my angel."

"I love you, Papa."

Unfortunately, Papa's dream remained a bedtime story that he told year after year. He could not seem to get ahead of the rain, drought, or the boll weevil. Domitile Vidrine, on the other hand, found better fortunes.

Although it was not much to brag about at first, Domitile had been lucky. He owned land, and over time, the land turned a profit. He was able to borrow against it during the hard times and managed to pay off both the loan and the note, eventually. It was peculiar how one lazy curve on Belair Cove Road could distinguish itself from another and define a man's destiny. Domitile Vidrine was the envy of Belair Cove. There would be no sharecropping for Domitile's grandchildren.

By the time Angelique turned fifteen, a few of the other young women in Belair Cove had already accepted promises of marriage. Papa observed these young girls with their aching backs, hands stuck in the dirt, and babies on their hips. They had little to show for their effort. Papa wanted something different for Angelique.

"*Ma petite* Angelique, she could have a future with that Damon Vidrine," Papa confided in Eula Mae, "a better future than most around here."

Sunday Dinner at the Vidrines

"I ain't goin', Papa. I don't want nuthin' to do with the likes of Damon Vidrine. It's like I told you, he ain't right for me. My heart is set on Jean Marc. Please, Papa."

"You just hold your horses. This ain't nuthin' more than a Sunday dinner. I'm only goin' to eat a whole hell of a lot of Hippolyte's delicious fried chicken. We'll be home long before suppertime. Besides, I'll know what's best for you when the time comes."

Papa opened their front door to the morning. As the sunlight splayed across the sparse room, Angelique turned. Her beauty filled him with pride and admiration.

"Angelique, you sure are a pretty little thing. Look just like your mama. Come on now, girl, we best get over there."

Domitile Vidrine and his wife, Hippolyte, came to the door to greet Angelique and Papa when they arrived. Domitile ran his hand over his balding head and scratched his big ears as he greeted them, his grey eyes looked everywhere except at Papa. Damon, it seemed, was gone.

"Damon had good reason for what he done. That Pierre Boudreaux wouldn't let up for a second. He provoked my boy is all I'm sayin'. All the same, I sent him off for a spell to visit his *grand-mère*. She wanted to live by the bayou and moved to Washington sometime back. That one sure straightened me out when I was a wild young thing. Why, *Grand-mère*, she come all the way out to the piney woods to fetch me back to Belair Cove. It all turned out pretty good. She gonna do the same with Damon, for sure."

Domitile raised his bushy eyebrows and motioned toward his own wife. "Whew, *Grand-mère*, she a mean old thing. And this one here, she startin' to act just like her mama." Hippolyte slapped his arm. Domitile laughed at his own joke, his leathery face sagged while his jowls shook.

"Besides, he ain't gonna get in trouble over there. Washington, Louisiana done dried up. Been years now since the last steamboat passed through."

Angelique heard a completely different account of the incident involving Pierre Boudreaux. Marie Rose told the truth of it as they left church that morning. Damon got into an argument with her brother over a horse race the night before. Damon pulled out a pistol and shot him.

"He was actin' all wild and crazy like. Pierre probably gonna be blind in that eye for the rest of his life. Domitile better do somethin' with that one. He's just plain mean. We all tired of his mischief and this time, it's serious. My pa's goin' to talk to the sheriff about him."

Papa had heard the same version of the story that Marie Rose shared with Angelique. Because Papa had always been as thin as a walking stick, the bulging blue vein in his long neck pulsed. Yet, he was a man of few words and tried to hide his frustration as he joined the Vidrine men at the table.

Angelique followed Papa to the table. Damon's young cousin, Flavia, reached for her arm. "No, not yet, it ain't your turn. The men go first."

Angelique observed the Vidrine women, Hippolyte and her daughters, Marie and Celeste. They were busy tending to children, stirring the pots, and serving the men. Angelique could not believe it when Damon's uncle shook his empty glass at his wife and she rushed forward to fill it with fresh milk. Several of the men ate second helpings. They remained at the table and discussed recent news, the price of cotton and corn, and made predictions about the weather. The women cleared the table and washed their dirty dishes.

Finally, Domitile Vidrine pushed his chair back, stood up, and led the men to the porch for a smoke. Angelique sat down with the women to eat. The children continued to play outside while they waited for their turn to eat. Later, Angelique railed at the inequality of it all to Marie Rose. On the other hand, she was relieved that Damon was gone. In Damon's absence, Angelique would have a chance to impress upon Papa her love for Jean Marc.

As time passed, Jean Marc did not appear at any social occasions in the small community, nor did he meet Angelique down by the river any more. Jean Marc had taken a chance of his own. He hoped to prove to Angelique's papa that he was a worthy suitor for his daughter.

Jean Marc chose what he could afford, a small plot of land on the outskirts of the Cove. He went to visit the Jewish banker in Ville

Platte. The older man listened to Jean Marc's plans for a better future.

"How old are you son?"

Jean Marc lied. "I'm older than I look, sir, turned eighteen last December. More important, I got me a powerful need to succeed. If you take a chance on me, I'll turn that pitiful place around. I know I can do it. Just need enough to get started."

Jean Marc walked across the street to the lawyer with cash in his hand and purchased the property. His hand was steady and sure when he signed the papers. From that day on, Jean Marc had little time for boyish things. He was a slave to the land.

Angelique was frustrated. Jean Marc had not attended a *bal de maison* in so long that she began to play the fiddle with Papa and the band instead of avoiding other dance partners. Only twice did Jean Marc make an appearance. The first time was to tell her of his purchase.

"Angelique, I got me a little place. It's not much, but one day…"

Angelique squeezed Jean Marc's hand in approval.

A few months later, Jean Marc returned. He plodded inside before the last dance and found his way to Angelique. He was unwashed and far from sober.

Angelique placed her fiddle on a chair and accepted his offer to dance in spite of his appearance. He whispered words of defeat, "Angelique, I been tryin' so hard to get ahead but the land done beat me down. What I bought ain't good for nuthin' and I'm deep in debt."

Angelique responded, "Well, that make you just like the rest of us. Don't it? If we worked at it together, you might have a better chance."

Jean Marc shook his head from side to side. "I could never let you start a life with me like dat. I got to turn this thing around first." He left her standing on the dance floor, alone.

Angelique ran from the room with tears streaming down her face.

Damon reappeared in Belair Cove after his *grand-mère* died. When he returned, the first thing he did was call on Angelique. He intended to convince her to marry him. Damon found her trying to catch stray chickens near the henhouse. He watched her while a cacophony of squawking chickens scattered in all directions.

"Looks like y'all got trouble here."

Angelique hid her surprise at finding him standing there and put her hands on her hips. "Well, Damon Vidrine. Don't just stand there. Aren't you goin' to help me out?"

Damon jumped over the fence and joined in the fray. He snagged a chicken by its legs and tossed it back into the henhouse. Feathers floated through the air as they scrambled to complete the task. Breathing hard from their effort, they succumbed to fits of laughter.

"I probably could have rounded up those chickens on my own. Anyways, thanks. Can I offer you something to drink?"

Damon took off his hat and sat on the porch steps. "That's a mighty fine idea."

Angelique went inside and returned carrying a cup of lemonade and a slice of sweet dough pie. She handed it to Damon. Not wanting to sit beside him, she stood facing him while he ate.

"Um, um, there ain't nuthin' like Eula Mae's pies. I been missin' them."

Angelique hissed, "What you sayin'? That I can't bake a pie?"

Damon wiped his mouth on his forearm. "Well, could be you learned a thing or two since I been gone. All I'm sayin' is it's might tasty. A fella could be charmed by a girl when she's as beautiful as you and can make pies like this."

"I ain't lookin' to charm nobody."

Damon changed the subject. "You musta left the latch undone for them chickens to get loose."

"Why, I did no such thing!" Angelique grabbed the tin cup from his hands and tossed the lemonade out into the yard. "I best be getting back to my chores. Lots to tend to around here. Good day to ya."

Damon's eyes turned to steel; he reddened and squared his jaw. He quickly recovered and sauntered over to the latch to examine it. He fiddled with the catch. "Well, sure enough, I can see that this latch is loose. I'll come by this evening and tighten that for you." He turned and walked away before she could answer.

Hard Times

The sweltering heat smothered the Cove. It had not rained for over a month. The ground blistered and cracked. Deep crevices spread across the landscape. The yields became scarce and insects plagued anything that remained. The trees and bushes in the backlands were dry as kindling. It would only take one spark to start a forest fire. The starving woods animals scattered in search of food, and the people of the Cove suffered.

The long drought continued to threaten the Cove until the day the rain began to fall. Relief spread across the land. However, once the rain started, it would not stop. The deep crevices and hard ground could not absorb the rushing waters. The gullies and bayous spilled over, and the Cove lay flooded. The remaining top soil washed away.

Papa took off his hat, wiped his brow, and set it back on his head as he stood in line. He stepped up to the makeshift desk set up under the big oak tree. Damon counted out the coins while Domitile Vidrine sat behind the rusty, wooden barrel and recorded his profits. In Papa's pocket was less than his share of the crop money. It had been another tough year and he had little to show for it. There had been even fewer commissions for new furniture, Papa's usual *lagniappe*.

Papa crept to the front of the line. He pulled on the string of his pouch and spilled his few coins out onto the barrel. Domitile winced. Papa counted the coins one by one, and then pushed them toward Domitile. Damon picked up Papa's meager earnings and Domitile scratched a record of the payment in his gray ledger.

Domitile placed his thick index finger over his lips. His long fingertip thumped the end of his Roman nose. Without looking up, he mumbled, "You're a might short, Alduce, and I done already had to carry over the loss from last year." Looking up, he continued, "You gettin' way behind."

Papa looked steadily at Domitile, who stared back at him in silence. Domitile swatted at a few flies buzzing around his face. Papa lowered his head and tucked his hands into empty pockets. His overalls hiked up past his ankles as he balled his pocketed hands into fists and jiggled them.

"Ain't got no more money, Domitile. Any chance I could clear out the back pasture for you and get it ready for planting next spring? That might pay down the debt, come close to makin' us even." Papa twisted his straw hat. The edge frayed, and bits and pieces floated to the ground. "If not that," he continued, "maybe, Hippolyte needin' some new furniture for the house. I could build something real nice for her."

Domitile tapped his pencil on the ledger, shifted his eyes away from Papa, and frowned. Domitile crooked his finger and signaled for Papa to come closer. Papa bent his head low enough to hear. "Alduce, they ain't got enough hours in the day for even you to do all that. Why don't you stop by this evenin'? We could talk about this predicament. Have a sip of whiskey."

Domitile Vidrine glanced at his son, Damon, and then back over to Papa. Damon whispered into his father's ear. Domitile favored his son with a nod and continued his conversation with Papa.

"You and me could, possibly, agree to somethin' that would settle this debt once and for all."

Papa secured his hat on his head. "I'd take kindly to considerin' what you got to say."

Alduce looked at himself in the cracked mirror, licked the palm of his hand, and slicked his hair back. He had thought long and hard about what task Domitile might demand of him and figured on answering any request with the same response: "I got me a good strong back and I can do the job." He squeezed his toes into too-tight Sunday shoes, laced them up, and headed out the door.

It was a short distance to Domitile's house. Papa simply had to jump the ditch, cross the dirt road, and jump the ditch on the other side. Domitile was sitting on the porch. He had a fifth of moonshine and two shot glasses on the small table between the two cypress rockers. Pipe smoke curled around Domitile, clouding his face as Papa stepped on the porch. Papa took out his pipe and began to stuff tobacco into the chamber. He lit the tobacco while Domitile poured a round of drinks.

The two men reminisced about the good old days. They discussed the weather at great length as well as the boll weevil. Papa waited for Domitile to weave the conversation toward the real matter at hand. The rockers squeaked as dusk began to lower its curtain around them. Finally, Domitile stopped his rocker, cleared his throat a few times, and turned to Papa.

"Alduce, you and me been friends for a long time. Our children have grown up playin' together, right here in this Cove. My boy has had his eye on your Angelique as far back as I can recall. Damon's turned out to be a fine strappin' boy. I believe that time he spent over in Washington with his *grand-mère* helped him to settle down."

Domitile slapped the porch floor with his feet to set his rocker in motion. "Good match for your girl, I'm thinking." He continued, "What would you say if we set our minds, you and me, to gettin' them two together?"

Alduce pursed his lips and remained quiet for a moment. The mockingbird sang an unfamiliar call, a final tune for the evening. All was quiet.

"Domitile, you done surprised me. I come here to talk about payin' down my debt. This ain't got nuthin' to do with what I owe you. Instead, you talkin' about my baby girl marryin' your boy. I got to think hard on this."

Alduce Belair scratched his forehead. He pushed aside the conversations he recently had with his daughter. Her heart seemed to be set on Jean Marc.

He asked himself, "What's the best thing for my baby girl? What's the best thing for my Angelique?"

Domitile studied Alduce's face, and spoke again. "And to my way of thinkin', it wouldn't seem right for Angelique's pa to be in debt to Vidrines if they were married. Nosiree, we'd be family then. Anyway, you ain't got to come up with a proper dowry. Y'all ain't got to do nuthin'," Domitile added.

Domitile's pipe died out. He banged it on the rocker's edge, refilled it, and struck a match. He puffed several times, and smoke curled its way into the air.

"My boy would be a good husband to your Angelique. Give her nice things. Oh, and by the way, that back pasture you mentioned this morning, it needs clearin' out. That old place of mine been settin' empty for some time. It could be fixed up real good. You good at that sort of thing."

Domitile stopped his rocker in forward motion, planted his feet firmly, and steadied his gaze on Papa. "In time, that house could be yours. The land it sits on, too."

Alduce flew out of the rocker, stepped off the porch, and paced in front of Domitile. He chewed on his lower lip until it bled. "My Angelique, she deserves the best," he mumbled to himself.

The evening air was heavy and still. Domitile inched to the edge of his motionless rocker. "And the money you owe me: erased." Domitile's hands made wide sweeps in the air. "Of course, I'd be countin' on a brood of grandsons from that girl a yours. That Angelique got good bones. I'm needin' strong boys to work my land."

"Tha's a mighty fine offer, Domitile."

Alduce knew it to be true unless Domitile Vidrine had suddenly become a *feu-follet*, a devilish trickster. The past had shown Domitile to be a fair and just man. Alduce was not a gambling man; however, the odds were in his favor. He quickly weighed all the possibilities. Domitile had proven that he could keep Damon in line. Certainly, the boy must love Angelique, or Domitile would not have made such a fine offer. Without a doubt, a son would probably be born into the Vidrine family.

Alduce thought it over. He needed to convince himself that he was doing the right thing for Angelique. *Jean Marc could never give Angelique the things she deserved. What future was there for a half-breed? Gus's brother had married that Indian and raised her son as his own. No one in the Cove really understood how that happened. Yet, Gus did a good thing taking that boy in when his brother and the woman died from the fever. He had always treated Jean Marc fair. Now, Jean Marc was a grown man and Gus had sons who would inherit his land. Yes, in time, Angelique would forget about her foolish crush on Jean Marc.*

Alduce concluded that the Vidrines could give them everything they wanted. Angelique would be set for the rest of her life. He would be set for life. He could live out his time in a nice house, debt free, and watch over his many grandchildren in peace and contentment. He could spend his time building the kind of furniture that families keep for generations, starting with a house full for his own daughter. It was true that Angelique came from good stock. There could be several heirs born into the Vidrine family. That was all that was required to clear his debt.

"Yep, this is the best thing for her. Bein' poor make her worse off in ways she don't even realize," Alduce Belair spoke his thoughts aloud.

Domitile stood up and put out his hand forcefully before Papa could change his mind. "Then it's done?"

Alduce nodded in agreement. The two men shook hands. Domitile slapped Papa on the back repeatedly.

Reeling from what had just happened, Alduce hurried home. He had gone to Domitile's house that evening looking for work and willing to tackle any project that he could accomplish with his back. This, this was more than he had ever hoped for. Angelique and Damon were to be married. Alduce was quick to push aside any notion that he had just traded his precious daughter so that he could be debt-free and own a little piece of land.

Eula Mae was looking forward to spending the morning picking berries with Angelique. She was swinging her basket and humming a gospel hymn as she ambled toward the Belair shack. The sudden interest the girl had in learning to bake was no surprise to her. *That Jean Marc sure has a sweet tooth.*

Eula Mae stopped short when she heard loud voices shatter the quiet morning; a thunderous argument came from inside the shack. She hastened to the door and pushed it open to find Alduce and Angelique nose-to-nose. They were shouting at each other.

Papa was waving his hands definitively and his whole body shook. "It's done. I done told you. This be the best thing for you girl. Tha's true."

Angelique paced. "I ain't gonna marry no Vidrine. They're awful mean, the whole lot of 'em."

Eula Mae dropped her basket and gasped. "Alduce, what you gone and done?"

They both turned to face Eula Mae.

"It's about the land, Eula Mae. You ain't nuthin' if you ain't got land. You know that. Jean Marc can't give my girl nuthin' except what she already got. And that's nuthin'. I don't want her livin' like this no more." He pounded his fist on the rough-hewn table.

Angelique grimaced. "What's wrong with what we got? I got everything I want right here."

"Think about it, girl. You want your children doin' without, like you've had to do? You got to have money to make money. Damon gonna have all that land one day. Tha's it. I ain't gonna talk about it no more." Papa folded his arms across his chest.

Angelique paced around the table. "You can't do this to me. I want Jean Marc. Eula Mae, try to talk some sense into Papa, please."

Eula Mae stared defiantly at Alduce. "Child, that ain't my place. If your papa wants to act the fool, there ain't nuthin' I can do."

Turning his back to the two women, Papa walked over to the stove and poured himself a cup of hot coffee. He blew into the steamy cup. "All I'm askin' is for you to give Damon a chance. Angelique, you can love any man if you set your mind to it."

Angelique stepped back as if struck. She put her hands over her face. "Oh, Papa, you can't mean that."

"Now you listen here, Damon Vidrine gonna be callin' on ya real soon and tha's all there is to it. Set your mind on it 'cus it's done." Papa slammed his tin cup on the table and the hot coffee burned his hands. Leaving the door wedged half-open in the dirt floor, he flew out of the shack.

Angelique rushed into Eula Mae's open arms.

"Ain't nuthin' I can do 'bout this, child. You gotta make the best of it. Life ain't fair, and though I hate to agree with your papa on this one, it's a good chance for you. Tha's all ya pa's wantin'."

"What about what I want?" Angelique cried out.

Eula Mae looked out of the open door as she held Angelique in her arms. She watched Alduce's straight back as he stomped away, his obstinancy stretching across the silent space, drifting out into the morning light, and disappearing around a bend of Belair Cove Road.

Courting Angelique

Damon began courting Angelique a few days after their fathers struck the agreement. He came by almost every day with some small token of his esteem: a hair ribbon, a sweet tart, or a bouquet of wildflowers. He was oblivious to her indifference and unrelenting in his desire to gain her favor.

"Angelique, we gonna have a real good life together. I'm gonna make sure you have the best of everythin'. Fine smellin' soaps, Sunday dresses with pretty lace and more ribbons for your hair." Damon scooted closer to her on the swing and reached for her hand. Although Angelique did not pull away, she remained limp and unresponsive.

Angelique was waiting—waiting for Jean Marc to brave this challenge and fight for her hand in marriage. Instead, it seemed that he had given up. She had not heard from Jean Marc in several weeks. Marie Rose confided that her brothers said that Jean Marc had decided not to oppose Damon's right to court her. He felt unworthy. Nevertheless, Angelique knew that he had not left the Cove. She did not need Marie Rose to tell her that. Angelique could feel his presence.

Angelique could not free her mind of thoughts of Jean Marc. She would be standing beside Damon in the middle of the road, at a dance, or at Sylvester's Mercantile and her eyes would wander. Angelique would escape the drudgery of daily chores to roam the backlands in search of him. She avoided his farm and the prying eyes of neighbors. Instead, she would follow their old trails and wait for hours at their fishing spot. She prayed that he would come to her. She searched for the right words—the ones that would convince him that they belonged together.

He must not think himself unworthy. It makes no difference that he is part Indian. It matters not that he never knew his real father or even that he's poor. Most folks in the Cove are poor. And as far as his secret past, who cares? There are probably others with hidden secrets. Either way, it does not matter. All that matters is that he captured my heart.

Jean Marc never made his way to the backlands. He was determined to stay away from Angelique. However, he confided to

Uncle Gus, "This ain't what I want. I got to put my feelings aside and think what's best for her. Unfortunately, that might be Damon, 'cus I can't seem to turn this farm around. If tha's the case, there ain't nuthin' left here for me anymore."

Gripping the beer bottle firmly, Jean Marc wiped his nose with the back of his hand. He gulped the last of its contents down and threw the bottle across his parched field. The land had not been kind to him.

Meanwhile, Damon persevered.

"Angelique, think about your old papa. What a good life he gonna have! I can take care of him. He'll be able to set his weary bones down each evening on a place he can call his own."

Damon edged closer and Angelique tensed. When he leaned in and kissed Angelique, she drew back as if stung by a hornet. Anger overtook him and Damon turned away, his eyes dark and dangerous. He rubbed the side of his face, his index finger stroking the mole on his left cheek. When his anger soothed, Damon spoke, "Angelique, we gonna be married and I've a right to set my lips on yours."

Angelique shot back, "Our gettin' married was not my idea to begin with, Damon Vidrine. It's somethin' you and Papa cooked up. Don't worry, I'll do my duty as a wife when the time comes, but I won't be likin' it one bit."

Damon did not respond since she had at least acknowledged that they were indeed to be married one day. Still, he pleaded his case, "Woman, you gotta give me a break."

He never really proposed to her. She never really accepted. It just was.

The first Sunday that Damon showed up at church, it stunned Angelique. He slid into the seat next to her and Papa. He participated in the Mass with practiced reverence and responded boisterously in all the right places. Damon was not like himself: he allowed her to walk ahead of him, put out his hand to steady her on the steps, and led her to the shade of the oaks. Following Mass, he greeted and complimented the local matriarchs and made inquiries about the well-being of their children.

After a few Sundays, friends and neighbors began to regard them as a couple. Angelique received jealous glances from several young women in the Cove. One in particular, Lena Breaux, teased, "She's the lucky one, I'd trade places with her anytime she wanted. Damon's so handsome. And rich, besides."

The little church solicited donations to help the poorest of their village, and the Vidrines were often generous in that regard. Thus, it was no surprise to Angelique to hear Father Lalonde speaking highly of Damon after Mass one Sunday. "Angelique, tha's a fine young man you got there. And it's clear he's smitten with you. Best we announce the Banns of Holy Matrimony before his eyes begin to wander elsewhere."

Angelique turned pale and her knees almost buckled.

Damon stepped up beside her. "Oh, Father, there ain't no chance of that." He placed his hand on Angelique's elbow, squeezed, and whisked her aside.

Angelique was not upset with Father's words. It was what she saw over his shoulder. She stared past Father, past Damon, past the old oak at the side of the church. She was unprepared, after all this time, for Jean Marc to show up anywhere, much less at the church after Mass and on this particular morning. Yet, there he was. He was sitting on a blanket under the shade of an oak tree with a shapely young woman.

Angelique did not recognize her. She stared at the two of them as they set up their picnic lunch. They teased and pushed each other playfully. A huge stone settled heavily on Angelique's chest and threatened to smother her.

Damon demanded Angelique's attention. "Angelique, what do you think? Father is right. I'm gonna tell him to begin announcin' the Banns startin' next Sunday. We get married soon after that."

Damon took her silence as an affirmation.

Hope Lost

Jean Marc hastily scanned the weathered barn door for a knothole, and from there, he could watch and wait. He laid his eyes against the rough wood and looked across the pasture into the black night beyond the boundary of the imposing oaks. He spotted her running swiftly toward the old barn, toward him. A pale blue shawl covered her thick brown hair. His breath surfaced in short quick gasps as if he were drowning. Angelique's simple white smocked gown wisped softly around her lithe body. The moonlit shadows revealed all to him. He should never have agreed to meet her.

The rusty hinge of the old door squeaked as he pried it open to allow her to enter. She slammed against his broad chest. Shifting his weight, he countered the sudden impact. His strong arms surrounded her as he quickly shut the door against the dark night.

"Jean Marc, what are we gonna do? Let's run away together. We don't have to live here," she moaned.

Jean Marc pulled away, removed her shawl, and cradled her face in the palms of his calloused hands. "Angelique, my precious Angelique."

Angelique looked up and sought solace in the depths of his coffee-colored eyes.

"No, no," she said. "I've seen that look before. Don't tell me you agree with Papa. I will not accept Damon. Do you hear me? I cannot. You of all people should know that. I have always loved you. I want you Jean Marc! That girl you were with on Sunday, I'm sure she means nothing to you. You have to go to Papa. He'll listen to you. You have to reason with him! Tell him. Tell him that you can provide for us. It will happen soon enough. You just need another year."

"It's too late, Angelique. It is what must be done. Don't you see? I have nuthin' to offer you. Take a good look at me." Jean Marc stepped back. His overalls were threadbare and patched in places. His faded cotton shirt had frayed from years of wear.

"I have nuthin'. I am nuthin'. Your papa is an old man, *mon amour*. He is doin' what any man in his shoes should do. I'd do the same except I ain't even got no shoes to stand in right now. Your pa needs to rest easy knowing that you taken care of. Damon can do that. I cannot."

Jean Marc sighed. "Anyways, I'll be leavin' y'all soon enough."

"What do you mean? Where are you goin'? Jean Marc, tell me, what crazy thing have you gone and done?"

Long tendrils of brown, curly hair covered Jean Marc's face. He pushed his hair back and grabbed it tightly at the bronzed nape. He squared his shoulders and faced the woman he so dearly loved.

"Signed up. Signed up as soon as I heard you and Damon was gonna marry. There's goin' to be a war on soon. That damn fella they call the Kaiser, why, he's tryin' to take over the whole damn world. They need strong men to fight. They need men like me."

"What! Why'd you go and do a fool thing like that? I've heard Damon and his father talkin' about this. It ain't nuthin' that concerns us."

Angelique crumbled into the dank, musty hay and rocked absentmindedly. Her wavy chestnut hair fell loosely over her face, and her olive skin paled to white. Angelique set her face in a stony expression, but her eyes glistened with tears. "Then it must be as Papa wills it."

Jean Marc saw resignation slip through Angelique as swiftly as water through a sieve. He tried to reach for her once more. Angelique jerked away. "You're *capon*, you coward," she spewed. "Leave me be. A better man would fight for what he wants."

Angelique spun past Jean Marc. Her absence created a momentary stillness like the eye of a violent storm. Emptiness settled all around him. He put his eye to the knothole and watched her fade like bayou mist along with all of his hopes and dreams. He slammed his fist into the barn door. "Last summer's drought ain't only dried up the damn fields."

Jean Marc felt deep regret for the day he had stood before those two lawyers in Ville Platte. Barefoot, straw hat in hand, he handed over the sum of five hundred dollars for the fifteen acres. Who knew that it would flood that first year, and the next summer would be the driest ever? The weather had not been in his favor and Jean Marc's optimism had withered under the weight of his waning dreams.

Jean Marc hung his head and closed his eyes. "This be the best thing for you, my sweet Angelique."

Angelique stumbled back the way she had come, her feet crunching on the dry grass. She sped past the oak grove that secluded the Vidrine house from the surrounding farmland and outbuildings. She ran toward the shack across the road, the place she and Papa called home. Afraid of what she might say or do if Papa were still awake, she decided it would be best to first talk to Eula Mae. Angelique turned toward the woods and the familiar footpath along the bayou.

Angelique could not wait for Eula Mae to respond to her quick knock on the door. She rushed inside. "Eula Mae, what am I to do? Jean Marc's gone and enlisted." Angelique fell to the floor and dropped her head into the familiar lap of comfort.

Eula Mae was sitting by the shadowy light of the kerosene lamp. Angelique startled her, and she pricked her finger on a needle. Eula Mae tossed her mending on the floor; she had no string of comfort to thread together, but spoke softly. "I done told ya, there ain't nuthin' I can do about this. There ain't no talkin' your *père* out of this one."

She stroked Angelique's wavy hair, and lifted Angelique's hand. She traced the lines on Angelique's open palm as she had done so often when she was a child. The reading was the same—difficult times were ahead.

"You gonna stay the night with me. Ya hear? I'll send Josef over to tell your papa that you stayin' right here."

Eula Mae picked up the shirt she had been mending off the floor and set it on her sewing pile. She woke her grandson, Josef. Bypassing the scary, dark woods, he cut across the field to Papa's house. The old wooden bed creaked as Eula Mae pulled the covers over Angelique. She waited until Josef returned and the house grew quiet, and then she pulled her rosary from her pocket and made the sign of the cross.

The meeting between Angelique and Jean Marc was no secret to Damon Vidrine. He had stepped out for a smoke and witnessed Jean Marc sneaking toward the old, abandoned barn. He wondered what Jean Marc was up to and watched closely, until he saw Angelique. He was certain that either the published Banns or the news of Jean Marc's enlistment must have sparked this reunion.

Damon's mother, Hippolyte, returned from a church meeting last Wednesday to report the latest gossip to Domitile. When he heard the news that Jean Marc had enlisted, Domitile stood up so quickly that his chair fell backwards. "Why in the hell did that boy go and do a fool thing like that?"

Hippolyte was quick to respond, "Don't make no difference to us, does it? All I know is that he is out of our lives once and for all."

Damon laughed. "Why the hell y'all so upset? Jean Marc means nothing to us. It's like you said. Jean Marc Fontenot is *couillon*, a fool. Good riddance."

Domitile opened his mouth to say something but thought better of it and stormed out of the room. Hippolyte folded in on herself. She had her own suspicions about Jean Marc, but nothing that she could confirm.

Damon had watched anxiously as Angelique rushed from the barn. The meeting had been brief. He considered how hastily Angelique had departed and concluded, at last, he had won. This severed the unavoidable end of childhood friendships. He had pushed for a swift end to Angelique's infatuation with Jean Marc. Damon alone loved her best. He would forgive her this final encounter. She would soon realize that he alone was her destiny.

Damon had observed Jean Marc when he left the barn. He slouched miserably, his head was down, and he dragged his bare feet. Jean Marc was defeated. "Now, Angelique truly belongs to me. Wild things need tamin' and I am man enough. Jean Marc has no backbone. He is no match for her." Damon spat into the dark night. He took one more puff on his cigarette, smashed it under his feet, and looked up at the full moon.

"Angelique, you will forget him."

Part II

Deuxième Partie

The Wedding

Eula Mae and Angelique were sitting on the old swing under the oak when they saw Damon's mother waddling across the road with a bundle in her arms. Hippolyte placed her sack carefully on the porch step. She took a few short breaths, wiped the sweat off the shadow on her upper lip, and tucked a stray hair into her bonnet. "Couldn't you see me comin' and tell that I needed some help? This is mighty heavy."

Hippolyte removed the covering on the silver punch bowl. "This has been in my family for generations. It needs a might touchin' up. I think Eula Mae here is just the person for that job. She would want to do somethin' special for your weddin' day."

Hippolyte continued to unpack tarnished punch cups and place them around the bowl. "Uh, uh, uh. If only it could tell the stories, so many wonderful celebrations back home in Poitiers. That's where my people are from. Poitiers, that's in France."

Shutting her eyes against the sunlight, Hippolyte laid her hands over the bowl as if to feel its stories. "Don't even recall who had it first and how it got carried here."

Without lifting her head, Eula Mae commented, "Huh, me, I done seen one just like that a few years back at that Fontenot baby's baptism. That was before they lost their crop in the flood of 1900 and then got cleaned out by folks who was sittin' pretty on high ground."

Hippolyte pretended she had not heard Eula Mae. "Ain't it a beauty. Just needs a bit of touchin' up."

Angelique laid her porcelain tub of peas down and picked up the punch bowl. "Hippolyte, I do thank you kindly for the offer, but the weddin's gonna be a simple thing. Just family. My cousin, Henri, offered his place for refreshments."

Hippolyte continued as if Angelique had not spoken. "We'll set out this punch bowl with some nice fresh lemonade right under the tree next to the church. Then everyone in Belair Cove can be included in the celebration. Make it a real event."

Hippolyte twirled and her hips jiggled. "It's goin' to be a beautiful fall day for sure. I can feel the air a changin'." Hippolyte grabbed onto the porch post to steady herself after all that spinning.

Being careful not to spill a single pea from the bowl resting in her lap, Eula Mae leaned to the side and lifted the bucket of empty shells. "Ain't that something, you bein' able to predict the weather and all." Barely missing Hippolyte, she tossed the shells out into the yard for the chickens.

Hippolyte stuck out her chin and stepped aside. "Let's wait and see what Damon thinks about this." She left the tarnished silver pieces scattered on the porch.

Eula Mae shook her head. "I ain't cleanin' that thing." Eula Mae returned to shelling peas, and Angelique was gathering the stray punch cups on the porch when Damon rode up on his horse. Eula Mae shook her head and rolled her eyes. "Ain't took Hippolyte long to get to Damon. This porch be busier than a beehive."

Damon jumped up on the porch, walked over to Angelique, and kissed her on the lips. "Mornin'. Look at you sittin' here all pretty. Angelique, I do think I'm a lucky man. I heard my mama done already dropped by for a visit. Now, about this weddin', you'd make a man proud if you could go along with her just this once. That'd be a fine thing if y'all got along real good and all."

From his shirt pocket, he pulled out an envelope and tucked it in Angelique's hand. "Here, you gonna need a few things for the weddin'. Get yourself somethin' real nice."

Angelique closed her hand around the envelope and squeezed with her fingers. The thickness hinted at a sizable sum of bills. "Damon, I don't need your money. I have my own ideas about the weddin' dress and was plannin' on makin' it myself. This gonna be a simple weddin', remember? We talked about dis."

Damon looked down at the drab punch bowl sitting on the floorboards. "Aw, come on girl, make that old woman happy. Let her have her day."

Eula Mae picked up her bowl of peas and walked off in a huff. "Well, I ain't never heard anything like it."

"What's wrong with her?"

Angelique paled. "Maybe she thinks I should have some say in my own weddin'."

"Well, maybe she ought to mind her own business."

Angelique exploded. "She's the closest thing I got to a mama."

"Oh come on, baby, I didn't mean nuthin'. You got to see it from my way of thinkin'. I'm caught between the two women I love."

Angelique waited until Damon left before counting out the crisp bills. "Eula Mae, come look at this. Can you believe this? We could do a lot with this money. Don't need no fancy things."

"Yoo hoo!" The two women looked up when Marie Rose called out to them.

Eula Mae remarked, "Like I said, busier than a beehive. Child, you go on now. Take Marie Rose with you. You two go and do what the man said; spend that money on a weddin' dress, one that'll make you look beautiful. Spend it all. I'll finish up here."

Angelique held the small cloth purse tightly in her hands. She kept feeling for the envelope hidden there as she and Marie Rose traipsed down to Sylvester's Mercantile in Ville Platte. Marie Rose was excited and questioned Angelique all the way there: Did she want lace? Did she prefer linen? What length would she like the dress to be? What kind of undergarments should she wear? She burst through the doors of the mercantile with the reluctant bride-to-be following close behind. They made their way up to the long wooden counter.

"Mornin', Mrs. Sylvester. Can we please have a look at the catalog? Angelique is gonna choose a dress for her weddin', and I'm here to lend a hand."

Marie Rose was surprised to find young Antoine standing on the ladder, stocking shelves at the back of the store. She paused for a second. "And a good mornin' to you, Antoine Sylvester." Marie Rose extended every syllable of his name as she spoke and gave him her most enthusiastic smile. Then, she turned her attention back to the wonderful task of shopping with somebody else's cash.

Marie Rose thumbed through the pages of the catalog. She squealed loudly with each turn of the page. She folded over the corners to mark her favorites. But, Angelique showed little interest in the dainty dresses trimmed with satin and lace and clutched her purse close to her chest.

"Marie Rose, I don't need to spend all of this money. I want to set some aside for safekeeping. A simple dress will do. Besides, I'd feel silly in something fancy like that."

Marie Rose smoothed out the corners she had marked and licked her index finger to begin flipping the pages searching for a simpler dress. "It's your weddin'."

Angelique responded with sarcasm, "That's what I'm told, anyway."

Angelique glanced out of the store window at passersby. What little enthusiasm she had fell flat as a deflated balloon when she saw Jean Marc walking down the sidewalk, arm in arm with the same young woman from the picnic. Marie Rose followed Angelique's gaze to Jean Marc and his lovely companion. The couple sauntered past the front window of the store. Marie Rose put her hand softly on Angelique's arm.

"Did you git to meet Jean Marc's cousin, Bena? Sweet girl. Came all the way from Opelousas for a visit. Poor thing said she couldn't let her dear cousin go off to war without spending a little time with him. Wasn't that nice?"

"What? Cousins?"

Angelique walked up to the front window and stared at their backs. Marie Rose followed. "You didn't recognize her? She was here once before. That was years ago. I thought sure you had met her at the picnic. That was the same day Father announced your intent to marry Damon out in front of the church."

Angelique's hands flew to her mouth. "They're cousins? Oh, *Bon Dieu*, what have I done?"

Marie Rose pulled Angelique from the window. "What's the matter, honey?"

"I didn't know. I thought he was sweet on her and now, I'm gettin' married to Damon."

"Oh! Honey. You sure you want to do this?"

The door to the mercantile opened. The bell rang sharply as three children flooded the entrance. With greedy eyes focused on the candy jar at the counter, they pushed past Angelique and Marie Rose. Their mother followed them inside. She apologized for their improper behavior.

Angelique was lost in thought and ignored the woman. After a few seconds, she remembered why she was there. In a dismissive tone, she said to Marie Rose, "Never mind. It's nuthin'. Nuthin' at all. Let's get back to them dresses." They walked back to the counter.

Marie Rose spoke with less enthusiasm, "Well, let's have another look at some of these pretty dresses. We can find something you'll like."

Angelique turned back to the catalog. She pointed to the first thing she saw, which was a long-sleeved pale crème dress cut on a bias so that it was fuller at the bottom. The skirt would swish around Angelique's ankles when she walked. She pointed to the matching gloves and hat as well. The hat had a short veil that would cover her eyes and the bridge of her nose. The gloves had tiny pearl buttons at the wrists.

"That's perfect, Angelique. Now, what about shoes? What about these little heels? They'd be perfect."

"Papa bought me a fine pair of shoes last winter, simple brown lace ups. That'll do." Angelique slammed the catalog shut with a loud thud and wandered over to the tobacco bin. She would bring some home to Papa.

Marie Rose turned to Mrs. Sylvester for help. "Don't you agree that Angelique should get the matching shoes?"

"Well, that would certainly complete the outfit." Mrs. Sylvester looked from her son to Marie Rose while hoping for an additional sale.

Marie Rose tapped her foot on the floor. "She'll take the shoes. They're perfect." Once more, Marie Rose reached for the catalog and flipped through the sections looking for a nightgown. She found one, picked up the catalog, and carried it over to where Angelique stood. She looked over her shoulder to make sure Antoine was not watching and pointed to the gown.

"Angelique, I think there are a few more things that you might need to consider." Angelique continued to study the brands of tobacco. Marie Rose shook the catalog in front of Angelique's face and widened her eyes pleading, "Angelique."

Angelique pushed the catalog aside and walked out of the store.

Marie Rose marched back over to Mrs. Sylvester and handed her the catalog. "She gonna get that one." Marie Rose batted her pale lashes at Antoine and giggled, her freckled cheeks the color of a red hot pepper. Antoine lowered his eyes to the order form and began scribbling for his mother. Marie Rose raced out to catch up with Angelique.

"I don't get it. Why ain't you excited? If it'd be me, why, you'd have to scrape me off the ceiling about now. Is it Jean Marc? You still got feelings for him, ain't you?"

Marie Rose looked back over her shoulder to find Antoine sweeping the sidewalk and watching her. Marie Rose grabbed Angelique by the arm. "I think you right. Antoine likes me."

Angelique was grateful that Marie Rose turned her thoughts to Antoine. She could not have answered the question about Jean Marc.

Her true feelings did not matter anymore. Angelique offered no further resistance as her wedding day drew near.

Papa was relieved. "You're a smart girl, Angelique. I knew you'd realize it's for the best. Damon will be a good provider. Look at all them fancy boxes you got here."

Angelique's new garments arrived. She opened the parcel slowly. The crisp paper rustled as she lifted the dress out of the box. She held it up in front of her for Eula Mae and Papa to see.

Eula Mae pressed her palms to her heart. "You gonna look so beautiful, child."

Angelique looked forlorn, and a worried Papa left the room.

Eula Mae advised, "You make the best of it. It's like my old *grand-mère* used to say, 'Girl, you got to marry a boy that loves you a lil bit more than you love him…Tha's the only pull a woman got in this world'."

Angelique hoped that both Papa and Eula Mae's *grand-mères* were right and that she could indeed choose to love Damon. She wanted to be like the candle that burns and gives off a bright light. In the face of light, all darkness vanishes. Angelique mustered all of the courage that she could.

"Lord knows, I'm gonna try."

Eula Mae scrunched up her shoulders.

"Tha's my girl."

Fall came early and the sun-drenched prairie glistened. The Cove smelled fresh and clean. Lifting up the silvery side of each shiny leaf, a balmy breeze danced through the trees. The inhabitants of the Cove paused from their labors to revel in the cool air. The young and old were frisky like newborn pups. Angelique's wedding day was quickly upon her.

Jean Marc sulked behind the shady water oak beyond the watchful eyes of the gossiping old women. He peeked at the inhabitants of Belair Cove as they rolled up in their buggies and filed into the church, one after the other. No one could blame them for not wanting to miss this big event. It was all he had heard everyone jabber about ever since the publication of the Banns. They had gossiped amongst themselves.

"I'd kinda thought she fancied Jean Marc Fontenot instead of that Damon Vidrine. Sure is a shame. My way of thinkin', they'd a been a better match."

Jean Marc tugged on his simple cotton shirt, a farewell gift from his cousin Bena, stitched by her own hand. Bena had always been good to him. "I can't have you goin' off to save the world lookin' worn out. It wouldn't be right."

Jean Marc stepped out from behind the tree trunk after the last wagon emptied and old Mister Broussard shouted at his wife, "Hurry up, woman. We already late."

Jean Marc watched his own footfall on the first step at the front of the church and laid down a sack of his belongings. *Was this really happening?* The wooden board squeaked unmercifully and a frightened squirrel scurried up the nearest tree. His leaden feet trudged up the next three steps. He placed the palm of his hand on the front door, counted to ten, and inched it open. His shadow stretched the length of the center aisle and fell short of the altar. His throat constricted and threatened to cut off his breath when he saw Angelique framed in candle light at the front of the church. She was more beautiful than he ever remembered. Shutting his eyes, Jean Marc tried to capture her as a photograph in his mind.

Jean Marc stood rigid and waited. He waited until he heard Angelique speak her vows. Heads had to lean closer, benches creaked, and the candles on the altar flickered. She spoke the binding words in a rushed whisper; the flower petals in her bouquet shook.

Damon faced the congregation rather than his bride. He scanned the crowd until his eyes came to rest on Jean Marc at the back door of the church. Damon's lips curled up and he repeated after Father, his voice ricocheted off the walls. Afterwards, he pulled his bride roughly to his side and saluted Jean Marc.

Angelique's eyes followed Damon's gaze to the back of the church. She swooned at the sight of Jean Marc standing there. Her bouquet slipped from her hands and fell to the floor.

Jean Marc's body jerked as the finality of their words sank in. Their vows, once spoken, forced him out of the door. He picked up the sack, threw it over his shoulder, and stumbled away from the church. Like the *Cotton Blossom*, he steadily picked up speed until he was nothing more than a fading figure, every running step distancing him from the memory of his beloved Angelique and Belair Cove.

The newly married couple stepped out of the church, stood under the canopy of oaks, and received friends who came to wish them well. An old wooden table covered with a white tablecloth stood opposite the cemetery. Hippolyte hastily began setting out shiny, silver punch cups and pouring sweet lemonade into them as she beckoned guests over.

"Isn't this a gorgeous day? From the very start, I predicted it would be a perfect day for my boy."

Marie Rose admired the decorative punch bowl as she made her way in the refreshment line.

"It's lovely, isn't it? Why, it's been in my family for generations. Eula Mae shined it up all pretty for today. Oh, there she is. Eula Mae, get over here, I need your help," Hippolyte said.

Eula Mae stepped behind the table and picked up the cake knife, ready to serve Marie Rose a slice of wedding cake. Hippolyte quickly reached for the cake knife in Eula Mae's hand. "That's not what I meant, dear. Gather up the dirty cups and wash them out? I got some hot soapy water waiting for you out back."

Eula Mae shot her a menacing look, jerked her hand free, and persisted. "I dun churned the butter, gathered the eggs, and baked this here cake especially for Angelique. Be damned if I ain't gonna cut some for these nice folks. Besides, I ain't the hired help today."

Hippolyte bristled. "Well, I never."

Eula Mae sliced a generous wedge of cake for Marie Rose and placed it on her plate. Marie Rose smirked at Hippolyte and walked past Eula Mae. "Don't let that old witch get the best of you. Your cake is absolutely delicious and you deserve to slice it."

"Thank you, child, for saying dat." Eula Mae smiled and chatted amiably as she served the next few people in line. In her own good time, she relinquished the cake knife, picked up a tray, and began collecting dirty cups. She regretted letting her temper get the best of her.

Gathering the cups, Eula Mae slipped in and out among the guests. Mrs. Broussard was chatting with Mrs. Sylvester. "Why that Jean Marc Fontenot, he ain't even stopped to eat cake or drink lemonade."

Eula Mae floated past Papa, Domitile, and Gus. They were huddled together in deep conversation. Jean Marc's presence at the back of the church had not escaped Domitile.

"I'm concerned for that boy."

Gus responded, "Jean Marc'll come back safe. I know it."

Papa chimed in, "I reckon this the best thing for both of them."

Papa left the two men, picked up his fiddle, and went to find his married daughter. He hugged Angelique, kissed her cheek, and offered to play a tune. He played several slow melodies. Guests swayed to the romantic rhythms and chose to linger until late afternoon.

At the day's end, Angelique walked beside Damon and his parents back to the family home. There had been no time for Damon to build them a house of their own. They ate a quick supper with his parents while Damon ravaged her with his eyes. He took her hand and led her to his bedroom as night set in around them. There was no time to change into her new nightgown that Marie Rose had chosen so carefully. Her wedding night was clumsy, awkward, and ended in a heated rush. Damon rolled over and was instantly asleep. Angelique was grateful that it had been short-lived.

Hippolyte moved around the kitchen noisily. She stored the top of the wedding cake in a metal tin and sealed it shut. She explained to Domitile, "This'll be for their first anniversary." She hung the tin by its handle from a nail sticking out from a beam in the ceiling. It swung loosely from side to side and finally came to rest as she busied herself with washing out the punch bowl. She placed the dried punch cups in the silver bowl and wrapped it up for safekeeping. She opened the cedar chest in her bedroom, lowered the bowl inside, placed her wool blankets over the top, and shut the lid.

In The Beginning

Angelique heeded Eula Mae's advice on the day of her wedding. Eula Mae had made her wiry body as tall as possible standing on her tiptoes. She had cupped Angelique's two hands in hers and with big brown eyes filled with pure love, said:

"Now child, listen good, 'cus I gonna give you my best advice 'bout marryin' like my mama done me when I jumped the broom. I say it so's you understand. Here it is. Even though the man thinks he's the boss, it's the woman who tunes the marriage to make a good sound. Tha's all I got."

Eula Mae squeezed Angelique's hands hard, handed her a small bouquet of flowers, and motioned for her to walk down the aisle. "You go on now." She had made the sign of the cross and prayed for the best as Angelique walked away from her.

In the beginning, Angelique tried to alter the music of her heart to a new beat, that of a married woman. She blamed no one for the fact that she was married to Damon. She did not blame Papa for wanting a better life for both of them. She wanted an easier life for him also. Jean Marc was gone, possibly never to return. She put away childish dreams and focused on the present, her life with Damon.

The fact that Damon was attentive made it easier to commit. She watched as he rose at dawn, handed her a warm cup of *café au lait*, and with a swat to her behind, headed for the fields to work the family farm. On occasion, she surprised him at noon with a hearty picnic of bread, fig jam, and boiled eggs. Sitting under the sycamore at the edge of the property, she bubbled over about plans for their new house. He returned in the evening content to sit by her side. Angelique fed Damon a nightly feast about her vision of their life together.

Yet, weeks went by and there were no signs that Damon intended to build a house. He seemed content to toil on the farm beside his father by day and nuzzle her under the roof of his parents by night. Angelique gradually became disenchanted. She was the one stuck in the house with his mother every day.

Hippolyte often whined, "Out of my kitchen, I don't need your help around here."

Angelique was out of sorts with no space to call her own. She put on her overalls and headed for the field, but joining the men was "out of the question," according to Damon. Angelique pleaded with her husband. "Damon, there is nothing for me to do here. We need our own place."

To appease her, Damon took Angelique to the mercantile under the assumption that she needed some "pretty little things." He insisted she select several bolts of colorful fabric and beautiful threads. Angelique carried the material to Eula Mae's house, and they stitched a fine wardrobe for Sunday church. Angelique was pleased with her new garments.

Damon whistled as Angelique made her way toward the buggy. "Turn around girl and let me have a look at you. Whew, you lookin' good. Makes a man proud!"

Still, Angelique was bored. Against Damon's wishes, she began visiting Papa quite frequently. Her visits often extended late into the afternoon. Papa was proud to show her the progress he was making on the old place. He would press his hands on the refurbished walls. "Lookee here, baby girl, as good as new. Your papa gonna spend his days chatting with the birds, feeding the deer out back, and waitin' for grandchildren tha's bound to come along real soon."

"Oh Papa, It does me good to see you happy."

"By the way, when Damon gonna start up on your place? I'm most done here and ready to help."

"I'm not sure. He works awful hard on the farm. And weekends, he needs to rest."

Angelique woke to Damon nibbling on her ear. She ignored him, rose, and paused to enjoy the view of the Cove from her bedroom window. Her laundry hung from the clothesline and blew softly in the breeze. All thanks to Hippolyte.

"Damon, we need a place of our own."

"Aw girl, let my ma spoil us for a little while longer. Soon, I'll begin to work on our house," Damon promised as he pulled Angelique back into the bed.

Angelique pushed him away. "I ain't got time for that. Got church this morning and gonna see Papa later. I mean it, Damon Vidrine. I want my own place."

"Ain't right you spendin' all your time over there. You married to me now."

Angelique had intended to spend the day with Papa, but thought better of it. Maybe, if she eased the tension that was brewing between her and Damon, he would start on the house. She made her way home from Papa's place by cutting across the green meadow long before the sun dipped low on the horizon. Angelique pushed on the back door to her mother-in-law's house. It was stuck half-open and Angelique shoved hard. The door banged against the back wall.

Hippolyte was startled. "Oh child, what you doin' always scarin' the life out of me like that?" Her large frame cast out most of the light as she rushed out of the kitchen. A circular shadow swayed on the wall with her passing.

Angelique looked up to see the tin can swinging from its hanging place on the beam above the kitchen table, the wooden milking stool positioned perfectly underneath. She climbed up on the round stool and stretched to reach the tin containing the top of her wedding cake. She looked around for something to use to open the can. She snatched a knife resting on the tabletop. Knife in hand, Angelique tiptoed to the doorway to confirm Hippolyte's whereabouts. She was sitting in her porch rocker. Angelique stepped back inside and pried the lid until it popped off. She peered inside. A large portion of the cake was gone.

Angelique burst onto the porch and stood in front of Hippolyte. She waved the tin in Hippolyte's face. "Go on, look inside this tin. See what I done seen. You ain't foolin' me no more, old woman."

Hippolyte flushed. "What are you talkin' about? I was checkin' your weddin' cake to be sure it was still good. And just as I suspected, it was startin' to spoil. I cut the bad part off, tha's all. What's wrong with you?"

Angelique turned the container over and dumped the rest of the cake out into the yard. The chickens came running to peck at the cake on the ground. "Hippolyte, you should be ashamed."

Domitile and Damon walked in from the fields.

"What's goin' on here?"

"Damon, I can't take this. Why don't you ask her, just ask your mother what happened to our wedding cake." Angelique threw her hands in the air and ran back inside.

Hippolyte was as red as a rooster. "She come out here actin' all crazy. Accusing me of eatin' y'all wedding cake. Threw it out right there in the yard. I ain't ever seen anything like it."

Domitile interrupted. "Let's all calm down. Hippolyte, supper ready? Get it on the table and let the dust settle a bit."

After the men ate their dinner, the two women sat at the table alone. There was an icy chill in the air. The only sound in the room was the screech of their forks as they scraped across the plates. When they finished, Hippolyte plated each a slice of sweet dough pie for dessert. She placed a particularly large portion in front of her chair and handed Angelique the last portion, mostly crumbs. Angelique simply stared at Hippolyte, stared her down until the old woman cast her eyes to the floor. Angelique left the table.

"I'll get the dishes started."

After the incident, neither of them ever spoke about the tin of supposedly spoiled cake. They both knew the truth. However, Angelique continued to beg Damon for a place that she could call home. "When you gonna start our house?"

"Damn it woman, we ain't been married three months and you already turnin' into a nag. Can't you think of nuthin' else?"

Angelique and Damon's whispered arguments tumbled with them into the night. Although intimacy between them was rare, Angelique was thrilled when she realized that she was expecting a baby. Domitile and Hippolyte were exuberant. Finally, under pressure from his father, Damon broke ground on the new house.

The sound of Damon's lone hammer echoed through the drab February days. Belair Cove was unusually still. It moaned and groaned in response to America's call to war. Many of its young men had either signed up or been called away for military service. The sound of young men cavorting was no more. Saturday night revelry that used to stir the dust and shake the barn rafters faded. The Cove folded in on itself in apprehension.

Angelique was in a hurry for their new house to be completed. She tried to supervise all matters of the construction. She peered over Damon's shoulders in an attempt to advise him. "Damon, Papa says that you have to shave that board this way."

"Damn it, Angelique, get back to the kitchen. Your papa don't know everything. Leave it to me. I don't need him or anybody else tellin' me what to do."

Damon crammed two ill-fitting boards together.

Progress on the house was slow. Damon found much to do in Ville Platte that had little to do with construction. He confided with the bartender, *Ti Blanc*, "You a lucky man. Ain't got no wife to nag you. Tell me that there's more to life than this."

Ti Blanc wiped down the counter. "You're a fool if you don't realize how lucky you are, Damon. Go home."

Damon swiped his hand in the air in disagreement and staggered out of the bar that night as he did on many other nights. One evening, Domitile was waiting up for Damon when he returned. A letter was sitting on the kitchen table. He handed it to Damon.

"This is not good, son."

He had been married six months, his wife was pregnant, and the frame on the new house was not finished when the army drafted Damon into military service. The morning that Damon left was unusually warm for late spring. His parents by her side, Angelique watched as Damon walked away with his back straight and his gait proud. He turned back only once to shout, "I'm gonna get those devils, make you proud of me."

Angelique stared out across the road and continued to watch until heat waves distorted Damon's image, and he faded into the distance. She vowed not to allow her fears to magnify her troubles; she would make the best of things as they were. Angelique walked away from a whimpering Hippolyte with renewed conviction.

"I predict this heat ain't gonna get better. I got me lots to do before this baby comes. I best get crackin'." The weight of her responsibilities did not dampen her sense of freedom.

Since most of the young men were across the ocean fighting in the trenches, each family in the Cove needed every able body in the fields. Even so, after supper they would gather at Angelique's unfinished house, light fires outside, and work on closing in the frame and roofing the structure. They labored late into the night. Papa worked steadily beside Domitile. Eula Mae carried tray after tray of fried chicken out to feed the weary workers.

Domitile insisted Angelique sit in a chair and rest. She reluctantly agreed. She had tripped over some loose boards and nearly fallen the night before. "Can't have nuthin' bad happenin' to my grandson," Domitile warned.

Domitile's kindness toward Angelique grated on Hippolyte. "Our son is off fightin' a war and you got her sittin' here like the queen bee. What she done to deserve that?" Domitile soothed his wife's ruffled feathers with a swat to her behind. "Don't you want that boy to find his wife and baby waitin' for him at home when he come back? Tha's what I'm thinkin'."

Angelique did the only thing she could to lighten the burdens of her neighbors as they labored on this, her first home. She played the fiddle for them: lively jigs and reels. Hammers pounded to the beat of the music. Voices rang out over the Cove and filled the heavens with song as they worked.

In a short time, her home was habitable. Angelique folded her four Sunday dresses and placed them in a pile on the floor of her old room at the Vidrines. Domitile would carry these over later. Angelique doubted if she would ever fit into them again. She made a neat stack of the things that she had sewn for the baby and tucked them into her basket.

Angelique reached for her Bible resting on the side table near the bed. She caught sight of the edge of the forgotten handkerchief tucked near the center of the book. Angelique had not been able to bring herself to throw away her first embroidered handkerchief and the nickel hidden there, Jean Marc's nickel. She sat on the bed holding the white handkerchief until the baby stirred and kicked. Angelique sighed, rubbed the mound that was Damon's child, and placed the handkerchief on top of the baby's things.

Twice Angelique wobbled across the yard from the Vidrines carrying her few personal possessions. Papa showed up with a few surprises: cypress furniture that he had constructed—nothing fancy. She ran her palm across the smooth surface of her new table and smelled the fresh wood.

"Oh Papa, it's perfect, real sturdy."

On her first night alone, Angelique ate a cold supper and sat in one of the cane-backed chairs in front of the unlit fireplace. She could not shut her eyes, and stayed up late into the night thinking about the future. Angelique dispelled any concerns she had about what might await her when Damon returned; that time would come soon enough. Instead, she imagined warm evenings by the fire surrounded by her growing family. Papa had surprised her with one very special gift, a cradle. She tipped the waiting cradle with her toe and watched it rock. She finally dozed off after planning a special Sunday dinner for all those who had made this day possible.

Sunday dinner never happened because Adelaide chose that day to come into this world. It was a difficult birth. Angelique's baby girl arrived on her own terms, early and breech. Only Eula Mae's knowledge of birthing saved the infant.

"What have we here, a spunky little thing just like her mama? Uh uh, this one is sure to be trouble," Eula Mae chuckled as she finally slipped Adelaide from Angelique's womb. Eula Mae washed the child in water blended with sweet aromatics blessed by Father Avi.

Angelique fell in love instantly with her daughter. Adelaide had a funny little squished face and a head full of straight black hair that stuck out in all directions. Angelique set aside any concerns about the Vidrine obsession with her bearing sons.

Domitile hid his disappointment. "Don't you worry none, the next one gonna be a boy."

Being a grandmother suited Hippolyte. "She looks just like my people. Look Domitile, she got my dimple when she smiles."

Though life on the farm was difficult, Angelique was, for the moment, content. She had a house, had won the favor of her in-laws, and had a beautiful daughter to hold. She was free to do as she pleased.

The Hospital Vigil

The sweet little nurse from Church Point looked at *Mémère*. She reached for a tissue and questioned, "You mean that your father forced you to marry that awful man?"

"Oh, it wasn't really like that, child. He did what he thought best at the time."

Marc Willis interrupted, "*Mémère*, I've got to go. Aunt Adelaide said she'll be coming by later this afternoon to keep you company."

"Oh, y'all worry too much. I'll be fine. You go on."

Marc Willis and the nurse walked out of the room together.

"Your grandmother is a remarkable woman."

"That she is."

Marc Willis was getting in the elevator when the nurse stopped a co-worker in the hall to retell the touching story she had just heard. It was not long before other nurses started visiting the old couple in Room 227 as the story continued. They repeated the most interesting details from one shift to the next.

Wounded

Domitile checked his pocket watch one more time and tried to reassure Angelique. "Train should be here any minute."

Holding Adelaide in her arms, Angelique paced in front of the depot. The baby had her whole fist in her mouth as she rubbed her gums. Angelique wiped the saliva on Adelaide's chin with a handkerchief and straightened the baby's bonnet. Angelique scanned the distance under the midday sun. She saw great big puffs of smoke billowing up to the sky and folding into the clouds. The shrill whistle of the train disturbed the still morning and startled them. Adelaide started to cry. The *Cotton Blossom* rumbled, hissed, spit, and slowly came to a halt.

There was no heroic welcome for Damon Vidrine, a man whose military career ended under unusual circumstances. Damon kept secret the details of his injury, the result of a fall from a moving truck following a night of carousing. The form letter sent to Angelique simply stated that her husband suffered an injury in the course of service to his country.

With crutches under his arms and the weight of his regulation army bag slung over his shoulder, Damon lurched off the train precariously.

Hippolyte sprang forward to grab him. "Oh, son, what they done to you? Everything gonna be fine now that you're home."

Domitile took the olive green bag from his son's shoulder and pointed at the buggy. "You look a might pale."

Angelique was the last to step forward. She inched closer, being careful of the crutches, and kissed Damon lightly. "How you doin'?" She was fighting to keep a strong hold on Adelaide, who was trying to wriggle away from the nearness of this stranger.

Damon laughed. "I take it this wiry little thing is my daughter? I like her. She's got fire in her eyes."

From the start, Damon was difficult. His leg throbbed, he was wobbly on the crutches, and he hated being housebound. Angelique tended to his injury each morning and tried to be attentive by night.

By day, she still had crops to take care of, cows to milk, chickens to feed, dinner to put on the table, and a child who needed a mother. Angelique did her best to be patient, but Damon demanded more of her time than Adelaide.

Damon's wound healed eventually, but his leg remained stiff, which caused his gait to be awkward. He made no effort to step off the porch and back into life. He became masterful at telling Angelique what to do, while doing nothing himself. His disposition became bitter, and his demands tiring:

"Angelique, where are my clean shirts? Get me my supper. Can't you do nuthin' right around here?" Then, claiming that it eased his pain, he would reach for the jug of whiskey.

Angelique quickly grew to resent his presence and constant interference in her work routine; her patience had worn as thin as corn silk. She would snap back, "Damon, it don't make sense, you sittin' around mopin' all day. You ain't usin' the crutches any more. To my way of thinkin', it's time you get out of that chair and into the fields. I can take care of Adelaide."

Damon would fume at her temerity and stomp his crutch on the floorboards, rattling the rafters and frightening Adelaide. Angelique put distance between them. She would throw the supper plates into the sink, scoop up her baby, and march over to her in-laws' house across the field.

Domitile and Hippolyte were distraught by Damon's jagged edge. They kept insisting that Damon get out of the house, help with the farming, and take an interest in his wife and daughter. In the end, they ran out of excuses to explain Damon's poor behavior. Neither of them seemed capable of influencing him. Everyone was in a state of agitation, until Angelique announced that she was pregnant again.

Damon was excited when she told him the news. "This one gonna be a boy, for sure."

Angelique did indeed pray that this child would be a boy. Everything about this pregnancy did feel different. Nothing would ease her morning sickness, and she felt exhausted even at the start of the day. She had shared her hope with Eula Mae. "If this baby is a boy, maybe that will give him reason for livin' again. Might take his mind off his gimp leg."

Eula Mae rolled her eyes. "Humph, it ain't his leg tha's the problem. I think he left what little sense he had somewhere out there at that Texas army camp."

Damon seemed to have renewed interest in life after the news of the baby, but he still had limited enthusiasm for life on the farm and did as little work as necessary. Instead, he often made his way into the saddle and headed for the gaming tables in town.

Angelique was frustrated. There was so much more that they could accomplish on the farm if only she could convince him and they worked together. She began to hound him about his responsibilities and her concerns about their dwindling assets over these last few months. Night after night, she scanned the ledger and tried to juggle their shrinking cash. On the other hand, he walked out of the bedroom dressed in his Sunday clothes with coins jingling in his pocket. One night, Angelique shook the ledger in his face.

"Damon, you promised. We got to talk about this."

Damon ripped the ledger from her hands and threw it on the floor. "Like I told you. That's man's work. You don't worry your simple little head about that."

Angelique blocked the doorway. "Where you goin'?"

Damon balled his hands into fists and stepped so close to Angelique that their noses almost touched. "You'd better get out my way, woman."

Angelique stepped aside. She listened to the fading sound of the horse's hooves. She reached for the ledger and set it back on the tabletop, buried her head in the pages and wept. Then she sat for another hour with pencil in hand, but finally gave up. She turned the kerosene light down low and went to look in on Adelaide. One glimpse of her precious child could restore Angelique's faith in God. She tucked the covers snug around her sleeping baby and stepped outside to look at the stars. She listened for the familiar sounds of the Cove as it settled into night. Like feathers shaken loose and drifting back to earth, Angelique allowed herself to do the same. Blessed night always comforted her.

Damon walked into the bar. "*Ti Blanc*, pour me some whiskey. Might ease my sufferin'. I hate being stuck in this shithole."

Heads pivoted to see who had made such a brash statement. Recognizing Damon, the locals paid no attention to him. Town pride was at stake.

Damon sat sulking, nursing his drink. His thoughts wandered back in time... before the war, before he got married, before Belair Cove changed. He remembered a time when people showed him some respect. He would gloat as he threw his father's money on the gaming table during a round of cards and watch the envious faces. After winning a bet on a horse race at the local bush track, he would lift his arms high above his head and revel in the thunderous applause of the crowd. Friends would rush to him at parties and laugh at his jokes, and all the pretty girls used to flirt hinting for the last dance at the *bal de maison*.

Damon eyed his empty glass. "It's all gone."

"Want another shot?" The bar tender stood ready to pour more whiskey. Damon tapped his glass in answer, and watched as *Ti Blanc* poured the dark, liquid fire.

At the opposite side of the bar, Gus Fontenot was among the men who were ignoring Damon. Uncle Gus was sharing the contents of Jean Marc's most recent letter with them. He repeated that Jean Marc thought he was faring better than most of the men in his company because he had grown up barefoot, working behind a plow, and hunting with a rifle in the backlands. Damon placed his elbow on the bar and twisted his body around to listen.

When Damon had heard enough, he spewed, "Why in the hell is it that all this town can talk about is Jean Marc Fontenot?" He slammed his glass down and whiskey splashed everywhere. Damon stormed out of the saloon.

Uncle Gus shook his head and folded Jean Marc's letter in the breast pocket of his overalls. Several others had sons fighting across the ocean, and since few in the Cove could read and write, Jean Marc's letters were anxiously received. Any snippet of news was welcome. Jean Marc's letters came regularly; Gus waited for the mail at Sylvester's every Saturday. When a letter came, it brought the war home to Belair Cove.

News of Jean Marc's Bronze Star fueled Damon's next outburst one Saturday morning. He was in the store with Domitile buying shotgun shells when Gus received an official government letter. With shaky hands, Gus turned the letter over repeatedly. He carefully peeled opened the top of the envelope, pursed his lips, and touched the folded piece of paper inside. He steadied his gaze on Domitile at the back of the store.

"I hope nuthin has happened to our boy."

The paper rustled as he pulled it out of the envelope. He looked up at the waiting assembly in the store. Customers inched closer. Mrs. Sylvester set her pencil and pad down on the counter. Upon entering the store and seeing all the somber faces, Felix Soileau quieted as Gus unfolded the letter.

Gus looked at Domitile. Domitile nodded slightly and Gus began to read silently. The hushed crowd waited. Gus finally let the air escape from his chest in a great rush of relief. He smiled.

"He's fine. That fool boy done gone and took the lead, run up some damn hill and took it for our side, almost single-handed, he did."

Men patted each other on the back and the women lifted their hands to their hearts in a collective gasp. Everyone, except Damon, seemed relieved. From the back of the store he spewed, "Lies. All lies. Jean Marc probably ain't seen no action. Probably sittin' pretty behind some desk kissin' the general's ass."

Domitile seized his son by the collar and pushed him hard against the wall. His face was beet red. "Tha's enough, son. Show some respect for our boys still fightin' over there." Domitile pulled Damon through the crowd and out of the store. Domitile and Damon crossed the street and headed for the Buckhorn Saloon.

Gus followed and found the two of them sitting across the room from each other in the saloon. Damon was at a round table in the far corner playing cards while Domitile sat alone at the bar with a draft beer in front of him. He appeared to be deep in thought and an eerie sadness surrounded him. Gus pulled up a stool and sat next to Domitile.

"You and me, we know that war takes a lot out of a man. Ain't no shame in the way your boy come home like he done."

Domitile stared sadly at his old friend. "I done made some mighty big mistakes in my life. Can't change the past. I'm ashamed of them and of the way Damon acted back there. And, you know I'm proud of Jean Marc."

Hiding behind his cards, Damon secretly observed his father and Gus. This was a familiar scene, their shoulders slumped and heads bent in hushed conversations. They had done this many times. When he was twelve, Damon had eavesdropped on his father and Gus, only to discover something he wished he had never heard. Damon threw his cards down on the table, which ended the round and caused grumbling from the other players. He walked over to join his father and Gus. "What y'all talkin' about over here?"

Domitile set his beer down and ignored the question. "Son, we best be gettin' home."

"Humph, ain't like y'all got anything important to talk about anyway. You go on home without me, old man. Leave me the hell alone."

Gus and Domitile walked out of the saloon together, while the story of Damon's outburst at the mercantile spread faster than the boll weevil. The Broussards told the Boudreauxs, who told the Chaissons, who told the Breauxs. After that, some began to avoid Damon.

Angelique heard the story from Marie Rose, but she had no more patience or pity for her husband. She had enough troubles of her own. Hippolyte and Domitile had come to rely on her for many things. Domitile began to count on her to help him balance the family's books. This was no easy task in these trying times. They were all struggling to keep the farm going, and Damon's absence most evenings weighed heavily on her.

Hippolyte's offer to stay with her one Saturday night was an unexpected surprise. Angelique welcomed her company. Hippolyte took charge of Adelaide, readied her for bed, and rocked her to sleep. The two women stayed up late mending and talking. The next morning, Damon was surprised to wake up and find his mother in their kitchen cooking breakfast.

"What you doin' here this early?"

"What you think I'm doin'? Tryin' to give that poor girl a break. She's pregnant and you ain't anywhere to be found. She's got Adelaide besides. Tha's a handful, son."

Damon ran his fingers through his black hair and flushed. He marched off looking for Angelique. He found her outside balancing a bucket of milk in one hand and trying to open the pasture gate with the other.

"What you think you're doin', Angelique? It's too early to set the cows out for grazin'."

"I've been doin' this by myself for quite a while now, Damon. You ain't got nuthin' to say about what's done around here. Let me alone."

Damon stepped in front of Angelique. "Woman, gimme that bucket."

"Get out of my way, Damon Vidrine."

Damon struggled to wrench the bucket from her hands and milk sloshed around their feet. Angelique slipped in the muddy mess and Damon steadied her before she fell. The near mishap stifled any desire for further argument between them.

Hippolyte had been watching them from the window and came rushing outside. "Damon, what's the matter with you? The baby could have been hurt." He raised his hands high in the air and backed away. Hippolyte took the milk bucket from Angelique and handed it to him. "I don't know what's got into you, son. Take that into the house." Hippolyte walked Angelique back to the house with her arm around her.

Whether or not we are willing participants, life goes on. Angelique's life disappeared in tiny bits and pieces from repeated drudgery. Her loveless marriage was a trap. Empty of joy except for Adelaide, her life had a surreal quality.

After her initial morning sickness subsided, Angelique went to the cotton field long before the sun came up, before Damon stirred. Life was easier that way. Eula Mae and her grandson, Josef, joined Angelique in the fields most mornings. Today was no exception. Josef adored Angelique and would do anything to be by her side. Josef wanted to help Angelique gather cotton, but the itchy burlap sack was bigger than he was tall. He tripped on his own feet to the amusement of everyone and tumbled head first into the rows of cotton. Josef's heartfelt enthusiasm was greater than the job at hand.

Eula Mae wiped his eyes and decided to find a more appropriate task for him. "I think I got just the job for a bright young man like you. A very, very important job. You think you up to it?" Josef nodded his head, his eyes bright and eager to please. He was proud to bring drinking water to the field hands. In addition, Josef kept a close eye on Adelaide under the shade of the tall pine trees.

Angelique had given him strict instructions. "Josef, if she gives you any trouble, you just call out like I told you and I'll come runnin'. Hear?" Angelique felt reassured when Josef called out to her as she neared the end of each row. "Green pepper. She be fine."

And everything was fine for a while until Josef began waving his arms, jumping, and shouting from the back of the wagon. "Red pepper, hot pepper!" Angelique dropped her sack and ran. Adelaide was sobbing by the time she reached the bassinet. Adelaide's ragdoll was missing. There would be neither peace nor work until she had her doll. Angelique jostled her baby in her arms while Josef hurried home to get it.

Josef held the doll high in the air as he hastened back. "I found it. Everything gonna be fine. Here you go, Little Girl." He tickled Adelaide on the nose with the ragdoll, and she laughed as she reached for her cuddly. Angelique set her daughter down in the basket. Josef continued to play with Adelaide until Angelique disappeared between the rows of white cotton.

At the end of the day, the sunset's amber glow illuminated the field. Angelique dragged bare feet across the dusty earth. She had been there from sun up to sun down. Angelique sidestepped a narrow row of bare cotton plants. She heaved her full sack to the wagon and lifted the strap off her neck. Damon watched her, but made no offer to help.

"Damon, would you take care of the weigh-in today? I've got to go and get Adelaide from Josef. And there's still supper to prepare."

Domitile lifted Angelique's sack onto the wagon. "Don't you worry about this, Hon. We got it."

Angelique hastened toward the grove of old pine trees. She peeled off her dirty gloves with the clipped fingertips, and slapped her hands across her dusty overalls. She pushed her bonnet off her sweat-drenched head and let her hair fall loosely.

Josef puffed up with pride. "Me and Little Girl here had a real good day, Miss Angelique. Yep, we did. She didn't make no fuss. She like a sweet green pepper all day long. Well, 'cept for this mornin'. Me and you, we fixed that though."

Angelique reached into the bassinet and lifted her baby out of it. "Oh, there's my sweet little pepper. Josef, I knew I could count on you." Angelique shifted Adelaide to her hip, and then looked to make sure that Damon was not watching her. She placed a nickel in Josef's hand.

"Thank you, Ma'am. I like keepin' Adelaide." Josef ran off to join his grandmother.

Hippolyte walked up to Angelique and matched her step for step as they headed home. Hippolyte clapped her hands together. "Give that baby to me and go on home. Adelaide, come to *Grand-mère*."

Adelaide squealed in delight, bounced merrily, and spread her arms wide for her grandmother. Angelique handed the child over. "You're a good woman, Hippolyte."

Hippolyte blushed. "Well, somebody got to see that she's cared for proper. You ain't got nuthin' left to give at the day's end."

"And you do."

"I might be her *grand-mère,* but women of my age can work circles around you youngin's. Now, you go on and put them feet up. They swellin' right before my eyes."

Angelique could only smile at Hippolyte's gruffness and she thought, *she got a heart after all.* She watched as Adelaide bounced happily in Hippolyte's arms. She relaxed her shoulders and the tensions of the day fell away. Damon had chosen to labor with her in the fields all day, she had filled her sack with cotton, and not one of those nasty caterpillars had stung her. Angelique hummed a happy tune. Although she missed playing her fiddle, Angelique measured time in thanksgiving for her small victories.

The Vidrines Mourn

Angelique headed home from Eula Mae's with fresh greens for Domitile's birthday dinner. She had been counting her blessings as if they were a mantra: *plenty to eat, clothes on my back, a roof over my head. And of course, there's Adelaide, my beautiful daughter. Another baby on the way.* The train whistle blew and interrupted her thoughts. The *Cotton Blossom* blared again as it sped down the tracks and across the dirt road, a gust of wind lifted and twisted the hem of Angelique's skirt. She watched the caboose fly past and the train faded out of sight. The familiar sense of hopelessness returned. "I got to shake this feeling."

Angelique and Hippolyte had planned a surprise for Domitile. Supper tonight would include all his favorites: pot roast, new potatoes, and smothered greens. Damon had promised he would join them for the birthday celebration. Angelique sighed in relief when she saw him enter the kitchen behind Domitile and walk over to the sink to wash his hands. Next, he sauntered over to the table and sat heavily in a chair waiting for Angelique to serve him.

Domitile walked over to the black stove and lifted the lid to the pot. "Everything smells so good." He grabbed his plate off the table and served himself.

Angelique did the same. She carried her plate to the table and sat down next to Damon. He bristled and held up his empty plate. "Angelique, what you think you're doin', woman? Serve my plate, won't ya?" Angelique froze.

Domitile reacted. "Son, where you been? Lots changed around here. We all eat together, now. Both your mama and Angelique have been workin' as hard as any man in the field. Without them, I couldn't keep this place goin', and I need you with us. Almost plantin' time again."

Damon jumped up; his chair toppled to the floor. "What you talkin' about. I pull my weight around here. And, maybe I don't like the changes."

With his fork still in his hand, Domitile pounded his fist on the table. "What's wrong with you, Damon? You're a husband and a father. Angelique needs you. We need you here on this farm. All this gonna be yours one day."

Damon ripped his napkin from his shirt, threw it on his empty plate, and stormed out of the house cursing. The hot roast bubbled in the pot. Angelique lifted her fork to her mouth. Domitile righted the chair Damon had turned over and sat back down.

Hippolyte spooned a heap of potatoes onto her plate and joined them. She patted Domitile's hand. "He's just all spit and vinegar, like when you was a boy. Remember how it was?"

"Why you bringin' that up? I did good by you, didn't I? You ain't got nuthin' to complain about, Hippolyte. But that boy of yours, don't seem like he gonna ever settle down."

"He's gonna come around. You'll see."

On Monday, Damon joined his father in the field before dawn. Domitile pulled the mules to a stop and handed the reins to his son with a nod of his head. Hippolyte lifted her head and smiled. Damon turned the soil over row after row while Domitile and the women made tiny burrows and dropped seeds into the freshly turned earth. They toiled together until sundown.

Domitile winked at his son in approval. "We sure put in a good day, today. Ought to be a real fine crop this year. What you think, son? We get a lot done working together like that. Well, I got to clean out them stalls before dark."

Angelique pressed her hand to her aching back. "And I got to fetch Adelaide from Eula Mae out at the Breauxs place. I was afraid she might catch Josef's cold if he kept her today."

Hippolyte shook her head. "You done enough for one day. I'll walk over to Eula Mae's for you, see if she can keep Adelaide for a while longer. Damon, you can handle the rest, can't you?" Damon's eyes darkened and he glared at Angelique. Without a word, he unhitched the reins, slapped the old mule with it, and led her away.

Angelique walked home quietly. She stumbled into the kitchen, pulled off the cloth covering on the crock, and dipped her spoon inside foraging through the grease for a piece of pork. Unfortunately, the crock was empty. Discouraged, she shut her eyes and started to wonder what she could throw together for supper. Nothing came to mind. She stepped out onto the porch to breathe fresh air and watch the fiery shades of twilight fade away. She sat in the rocker, tipped her head back, and listened to the sounds of evening. Her breathing deepened and she dozed off.

It had been some time since Damon spent all day behind a plow. The heat had worn him down. He was tired and hungry. Unfortunately, he came home to find Angelique asleep on the porch. There was no fire and no supper waiting for him. Damon stood there fuming, and then he kicked Angelique's rocker hard.

"Damn it, Angelique. You got my pa bamboozled. You ain't worth nuthin'. Where's my supper? I'm beat."

Angelique was startled awake. "Why you got to be such an ass, Damon? Get your own damn supper. I'm puttin' in as much time as you and I been doin' it for longer. And I'm big and pregnant, besides."

Damon spun, sneered, and grabbed Angelique's face; his fingers pressed into her jawbone.

Angelique gripped his wrists with both hands as he yanked her from the rocker. "That's enough Damon, stop it."

Damon started to walk her toward the door. "I said I want my supper and I'll be damned if you ain't gonna fix it." In the distance, they heard the muffled echo of laughter, young boys fishing by the bayou.

"You're hurting me. Let go."

He pulled her closer and then thought better of it. He abruptly dropped his hold on her. Angelique teetered as the weight of her midriff threw her off balance. She began to tumble backwards off the porch. Angelique's scream froze in her throat, and Damon lunged to catch her, but missed. She landed on the grass with a heavy thud. Damon leapt down to her side.

"Shit, don't move."

He felt for broken bones. None. He put his ear to her swollen belly. All seemed quiet. He rested a hand on her stomach.

"Are you hurt? Damn it, talk to me."

Angelique fought his touch. "Get away. Get away from me. I hate you."

"You crazy bitch."

Damon left Angelique lying there. He walked back into the house and picked up his jug of moonshine. He slammed the door to their bedroom behind him.

Angelique waited until her tears dried and her breathing slowed. A rabbit scurried under the house. A crescent moon hovered up above. She felt her womb and asked God for forgiveness. Angelique had wanted another child, however, she had not wanted to bear

Damon's child. Rolling over on her side, she pushed herself up. She felt between her legs for blood: nothing. She sat on the bottom step until her fear subsided, and then she went inside.

Angelique pulled herself to the basin, worked the pump, and dipped a cloth into the cool water. She sank into a chair and washed her face, arms, and legs. With shaky hands, she squeezed the cloth dry and set it down. Angelique lowered herself to the cold floor near the hearth, curled into a ball, and rested her hands gently on the mound of her hard, round belly.

"Please, God, take care of this little one."

Angelique dozed, but awakened when she felt a sudden, sharp jab in her abdomen. The labor pains were coming fast. Fear gripped her and she screamed, "Damon! Damon, get the doctor! It's too soon. Oh, God, it's too soon."

Only half-awake, Damon stumbled into the kitchen. He froze when he saw Angelique doubled over in a pool of blood. He found a blanket to cover Angelique and placed a pillow under her head. "Don't move. I'm gonna go next door for help."

"I need a doctor. *Depeche toi*, hurry."

In sheer panic, Damon shouted as he burst into his parents' home. Breathless, they rushed back to Angelique's side, but it was too late. She was squatting on the floor leaning over her lifeless baby, a boy. Angelique stared at them, her face scrunched in grief. She began to rock and weep. "He's gone. My baby boy is gone. If only Damon hadn't grabbed me."

Hippolyte could not contain her grief. Her shoulders shook as she heaved deep sobs. Damon lifted Angelique and carried her to their bedroom, which smelled of stale whiskey. The only sound came from Hippolyte's whimpers as she wrapped the baby in her shawl.

As Damon eased Angelique onto the bed, he forced his lips to her ear and begged for forgiveness. "*Cher*, this one just wasn't meant to be. I'm sorry. We'll have another baby. You'll see."

Angelique demanded, "I want Adelaide. Bring Adelaide to me."

Hippolyte hurried to get Adelaide. The tension in the room was thick, and Adelaide began to cry when Hippolyte tried to place her in her mother's arms. She wiggled free, toddled to Damon, and lifted her arms signaling him to pick her up.

Hippolyte intervened. "Come on child. I'm gonna get you some sweet milk."

Domitile had gone to get Angelique's papa, and he brought Eula Mae along. Papa glared at the dirty glass and the whiskey jug at the foot of the bed and then at Domitile. Domitile could still hear Angelique's accusation ringing in his ears. Anger threatened to consume him. He turned his back to his son and with leaden feet left the room.

Eula Mae cleaned the lifeless infant and wrapped him in a soft patchwork quilt. She handed the baby to Damon. "Here's your son. Go and bury the boy."

Damon left the house. Angelique turned her face to the wall, pulled her legs tightly to her breast, and used her arm to bury her face. Papa bent over his daughter. He pushed her wet hair back and kissed her forehead.

"Please, Papa, leave me alone."

Alduce was numb. He needed to be alone, too. Weak and weary, he walked out of the house and stopped to rest under the gnarled fig tree. He looked up: the sun was rising over Belair Cove. He leaned his head against the tree trunk and shut his eyes from the morning light.

Alduce later shared his worries with Eula Mae. "If Angelique paid more attention to Damon? Then he might give up his drinkin' ways and stay home. I should have never left that child to run wild. I should've gotten married after her mama died. A good woman could've taught her what she needed to know about being a wife. She needed that as much as readin' and writin'."

Eula Mae's heartbeat stopped for an instant. She glared at Alduce for a second before she reached into the bucket of soapy water, pulled up one of his shirts, and slammed it against the washboard. She scrubbed forcefully, water sloshed everywhere, and the buttons scraped against the metal board until they popped right off the shirt.

"You talk to her, Mae. Damon's a good provider."

Eula Mae shook the wet shirt at him. "Ain't no fool like an old fool. Tha's what I say. Alduce Belair, open your eyes. It ain't your girl tha's the root of this. She can't do nuthin' with the likes of that devil. Trouble follows that one." Eula Mae tossed the shirt back into the water and searched the floor for lost buttons.

"Every young man's gonna sew a few oats before he settles down. It just takin' him a bit longer, tha's all. Me, I think, Angelique needs to pay him more attention."

"And when she got time for that? She's already workin' her fingers to the bone for the whole lot of 'em. When's the last time she paid you a visit? Nosiree, got no time for nuthin'. I done lived in these parts longer than you. Enough to say you don't understand all tha's goin' on here. Now, I mean you no disrespect, but you's wrong about this."

Alduce picked up a button and handed it to Eula Mae. "What we gonna do, Mae?"

"We gonna keep a sharp eye on her. Tha's what we gonna do. Somethin' ain't right. If she don't come here, we goin' over there whenever we can. And it might be good to let Marie Rose in on this, too. They used to be so close."

After his conversation with Eula Mae, Alduce started dropping in on Angelique for brief visits. He often found Domitile and Hippolyte there as well. Papa would play with Adelaide, chat with Domitile or Hippolyte, and join in whatever task seemed most pressing. Hippolyte was the first to invite him to stay for supper one night after they had all worked together late into the evening.

"You can't have nuthin' over at your place to eat. It's late. There's a hot gumbo settin' on this here stove, enough for all of us."

Papa became a regular visitor. Not long after that, Alduce and Domitile began to schedule a friendly game of checkers on lazy Sunday afternoons. Angelique was happy to have her family around her. It was not long before she picked up her fiddle and music became a part of the afternoon ritual.

Marie Rose was distraught when she heard about the death of Angelique's baby boy. She had observed the subtle changes in her best friend over the last few years. After Marie Rose's marriage to Antoine Sylvester, she and Angelique had deepened the wagon tracks between Ville Plate and Belair Cove. However, it soon became evident to Marie Rose that Damon was a challenge and she started keeping her distance. Besides, she did not have much free time.

Marriage had been good for Marie Rose. Her Antoine never ceased to dote on her and their growing family. However, after old Mrs. Sylvester died, the store in Ville Platte demanded her constant attention. It became increasingly more difficult for Marie Rose to travel the five miles to Belair Cove. Most families made it into town once or twice a month for supplies and the latest news. She loved those occasions when Angelique or old neighbors from the Cove dropped in. It was unfortunate that, lately, Hippolyte seemed to be the only Vidrine dispatched for gathering supplies. Marie Rose missed Angelique.

Marie Rose traveled to the Cove for weddings and funerals, and during times of crisis. Following the death of Angelique's baby boy, Marie Rose made haste to her door. With Adelaide clinging to her side, Angelique was quiet and withdrawn. In the awkward silence, both women watched Marie Rose's two mischievous boys as they darted in and out of the house, jumped off the porch, and threw rocks at the chickens.

"Stop that right now. You boys are askin' for a whippin'. Come over here and sit down. Be still now. We gonna pass out some of these cookies I brought." Marie Rose handed each of the boys a few cookies.

Angelique delighted in their little faces. They looked so much like their mother. Both boys had freckles dusted across the tips of their noses. "I envy you, Marie Rose. The way Antoine looks at you. You seem to work so well together, day by day in the store, knowing each other so well that a glance between you says it all. Antoine puts you and the children first above all things. It's how we both hoped it would be." Angelique brushed aside the tears that slid down her cheeks.

Marie Rose squirmed in her chair and did not know what to say. The boys were fighting over the few remaining cookies. She focused on their behavior and divided the cookies equally between them. Marie Rose was embarrassed at her own thoughtlessness. She should have left the children at home with Antoine. Her sons were a reminder to Angelique of what she had recently lost. "I am so sorry, sweetie. There'll be more babies for you, and one of them's bound to be a boy."

Angelique smiled. "Well, now, enough of that. Let's talk about other things. After all, there is a war on. That is probably not the best subject either. But, I must have some news about all of our boys fighting overseas. Belair Cove has so few good men left."

"I fear our boys from the Cove are in the thick of it. I'm almost glad Antoine has such poor eyesight. They say Jean Marc's been assigned to some important job, translating French to English. Jean Marc writes about once a week and sends news back about any of our own boys when he can. Otherwise, we wouldn't know anything at all."

"Well, that's good to hear for sure. All our boys are gonna get through this and come home safe. I feel it in my bones. They know how to deal with hardship."

Marie Rose continued chatting about the young soldiers from Belair Cove. Then she changed topics. "Oh by the way, have you heard the rumors? They say a teacher gonna be assigned to Ville Platte soon. Our children gonna get a proper education then."

"That old *grand-mère* of yours sure did scare me to death when she taught us. Do you remember the time Damon and Jean Marc stopped up the chimney and she got so mad? We had no school all morning until she sorted it out, all that smoke?"

They reminisced and laughed about their home schooling days, until Marie Rose's boys became too restless and she decided it was time to leave. Angelique watched as Marie Rose pulled out onto the road and shouted, "I hope you realize how lucky you are."

For Angelique's sake, Marie Rose was dismissive. "Antoine eats cookies every night in bed with a full glass of milk, crumbs everywhere. I hate it."

Angelique laughed and waved until Marie Rose faded in the distance. She did not believe that God had truly blessed her own marriage. It did not matter, because there was no escape. Therefore, she would have to make the best of it. What else was there to do?

Angelique Gives Up

After the loss of their son, Angelique was not surprised to find Damon trying to make amends. From the first day that she felt well enough to dress for chores, he coddled her. "What you think you doin', woman? I expect you to rest for a long spell, yet. And don't be liftin' nuthin' heavy 'til I get back."

At first, Angelique was only slightly impressed that Damon stayed close to home and worked the fields every day. Overtime, Damon's changed attitude swayed her. He worked hard from sunrise until dark without complaint, and returned home limping, filthy, and exhausted. He threw water over himself in a basin that she left at the back door and dried off with a towel. Damon would often amuse Adelaide while Angelique put supper on the table. He would stomp through the house and pretend to be a bear. He'd growl, "Where's my baby girl?"

Adelaide would shriek before realizing it was her papa, and then rush into his arms; her chubby legs jiggled as she ran. Angelique so loved her child. It warmed her heart to watch them together.

Angelique's melancholy began to lift as Damon found subtle ways to reach out to her. "I think what you need is some time away from here. You ought to get out of this house and go visitin'. Do you good to see Marie Rose." He would lean his cane-back chair on two legs after a meal and rave, "Mighty fine supper you fixed for us tonight. Make a man proud to be your husband."

Angelique began to postpone evening chores; she would pull Adelaide onto her lap and rock her to sleep. She would listen to Damon while he shared events of the day or revealed his plans for the next. Angelique began to accept his teasing tug on her hair and later the kiss he would brush against her cheek.

"It might be nice to get your papa over here some evenin' for a little music. Do us all good, I'm thinkin'."

Although Angelique's grief eventually subsided, no matter how hard Damon tried, she could not warm to him when he turned to her in the heat of night. She lay there stiffly, waiting for the end. She did not want more children so soon after the loss of their son. When she felt the first days of a new morning sickness, it hit her like a slap in the face. She felt ill from the very beginning of the pregnancy. She was not ready to tell Damon. Angelique needed time to be sure. Everything about this pregnancy seemed different.

It made Angelique angry when Damon found her vomiting off the back porch and he rubbed his hands over her soft belly. "This one's gonna be a strong boy."

Angelique whispered, "So was the last one, Damon, so was the last one." Damon did not hear her comment because he had already raced across to his father's house to share the exciting news.

Weeks passed and Angelique continued to feel nauseated. Her strength slowly waned and she became withdrawn. She would pull away at Damon's slightest touch. "What's gotten into you, Angelique? You should be happy. I'm here doin' everthin' you want and we've got another baby on the way."

Papa studied his daughter closely, gauging how she felt. "Angelique, you happy about this?"

"Let's just hope it's a boy," she said.

Papa found her apathy disconcerting, and he hovered nearby to keep an eye on things. He became part of the patchwork of their daily lives, caring for the animals, helping with Adelaide, and on most evenings, not leaving until long after supper. Practicing the fiddle with her papa became the one nightly ritual that Angelique enjoyed. After Papa left, she would not go to bed until she heard Damon snore. Damon would wake in the mornings to find a cold breakfast on the table, and Angelique would already be outside tending to chores. Damon grew restless and succumbed to old habits.

"Angelique, you ain't doin' right by me. A man expects to fall asleep next to his wife at night. And I ought to have a hot breakfast waitin' for me in the mornin'. I can't remember the last time…" He paused when he saw her face constrict and changed the subject… "I need a clean shirt to put on."

"I ain't cleanin' your shirts as long as you wearin' them to gad about struttin' around Lord knows where."

Damon grew tired of tripping over Alduce on his doorstep, his presence a constant hint of Papa's mistrust. He resented the lack of privacy with Angelique. One evening, after Papa departed, Damon reached for Angelique as she went to set the fiddle on a chair. She pulled away from him in disgust. He ripped the fiddle from her hands.

"You're my wife. You belong to me. I don't take kindly to you puttin' that old man before your husband. I don't want to come home and find your lazy ass sittin' on the porch playin' that thing with him again."

"What are you sayin', Damon? You ain't makin' any sense to me. Lower your voice. You'll wake Adelaide."

Damon threw the fiddle at her. It slid across the table and landed on the floor, barely missing Adelaide as she lay sleeping. She woke and started to cry. Angelique ran to her.

"Watch what you're doin'. That fiddle almost hit her."

"You ain't listenin' to me, woman."

Damon sucked in his breath, clenched his jaw, and lifted the table off the floor. He slammed it down again, shoved it against the wall, and trapped Angelique behind it. Then, Damon stormed out of the house. Angelique pushed the table away from her and clasped her hands together to stop them from shaking. She crumbled to the floor beside her daughter, who was crying loudly.

"Quiet, Adelaide, It's all over. He's gone. Come here."

The next night, as Papa prepared to leave, Angelique smiled faintly at him and placed her fiddle in his hands. "Papa, Adelaide's gettin' into more and more mischief these days. I got to keep a better eye on her. I'm feelin' awful sick with this new baby. Chores ain't getting done while I'm sittin' here playin' my fiddle. I'm thinkin' it's best if I leave it at your place for a while. Save it for special times. I'll let you know when it's a good time."

Papa noticed the scrapes on the underside of the fiddle. Angelique's hand shook as she handed it over to him. He gripped the fiddle between his fingers and looked from her to Damon.

"There ain't no trouble between you two, is there?"

Angelique pressed her hands to her slightly pregnant belly. "*Mais non*, Papa, everything's fine. This baby ain't like the last. Tha's all. I'm just tired."

"I understand. Tha's fine with me. I'll keep this for you. You can come 'round anytime, you and Adelaide."

"I'll try, Papa."

Damon stood quietly by her side until Papa was gone. He put his arm around Angelique and nibbled at her neck. Papa disappeared in the darkness.

Angelique's *joie de vivre* had stifled, like the cold embers of the fireplace at daybreak, nothing left to rekindle. She no longer cared what Damon did or did not do; however, she did not want Adelaide in the midst of their battles. Damon's need to control Angelique became elemental. It happened in subtle ways, a look or a tug on her arm. He would whisper soft, polite threats that only she understood.

"Don't do that or you'll be sorry."

Angelique recognized that she would have to find a way to keep the peace. Damon had distanced himself from her, often not returning until midnight. He sought solace from drinking and gambling of one kind or another. Angelique did not care; it was easier this way for both of them. It was as if she were the mockingbird, altering her song to survive.

Angelique learned that if she remained docile, Damon left her alone. He could not bully her if she stood fast in agreement with all he said, if she walked obediently behind him, if she offered no opinions, nor shared any secret desires. It was easier to pretend, to put on her Sunday dress and place her arm in his on those rare occasions when they ventured into town together. It helped that Damon was predictable. Angelique had only to figure out what she wanted most, and then "by going through the back door," as Eula Mae might say, suggest the opposite.

After the morning sickness subsided, Angelique often wandered to the far edge of the backlands near the east boundary of their property. She would sit where she could enjoy the ducks on the neighbor's pond. While Adelaide chased mosquito hawks and butterflies, Angelique would pick the wildflowers at her feet and return home to arrange them in a pitcher.

One day, she looked up to find Damon staring at her as she approached with a bundle of flowers in her arms. He was leaning against a fence post with both hands in his pockets. He gazed out in the direction she had come. "Think I'm gonna plow up the ground, plant me some grapes back there. Make some wine. Good money in it, they say. Sell it at festivals, things like that."

Angelique shrugged with feigned indifference. She waited until later, when Damon was within earshot, and pretended to speak her mind to Hippolyte. "Have you heard? Damon wants to plant grapes out back across from that pond. He thinks the soil might be good there. What you think about that? I'm just glad he ain't paid any mind to the rich soil right under his nose. The sun shines bright most days right off this porch. I sure don't want some old twisted grape vines stretched across the side yard. I'm considerin' that spot for plantin' me some flowers."

A few days later, Damon was plowing up the side yard. Angelique looked forward to watching the grapes ripen. She would be able to pick fresh grapes right off the vine from the back porch. It would be a tasty treat for Adelaide. Fresh fruit would be good for the child growing inside of her, too. She would have plenty of grapes for making jelly. It was a safe bet that Damon would probably never make any wine. Some things had a way of working themselves out.

Like Alduce, Eula Mae had taken care to observe Damon's comings and goings. She would wait until he was out of sight and rush over to Angelique's place. Angelique was always pleased to see Eula Mae walking briskly up the road, her straw hat wider than her tiny shoulders. Josef was never far behind. He reminded Angelique of a young sapling that would one day grow into a solid oak. The three of them would make quick haste of morning chores while Adelaide napped. Afterwards, the women would sit and visit while Josef entertained Adelaide, his reward a piece of sweet dough pie.

It was a wet, winter day when Angelique sent Josef to clean out the stalls in the barn. He sloshed across the yard whistling, in spite of the drizzling rain. Eula Mae leaned on her broom and laughed. "That boy was born happy. He growin' like a weed though. Be ten on his next birthday."

Angelique set Adelaide down on an old patchwork quilt under the covered porch and handed her a rag doll. "He's gonna grow up to be a fine man. Big one for sure, but a kind man all the same."

At first, Angelique could not figure out where the screams were coming from until she heard Damon cursing and the *thwaping* sound of a belt. "Josef! Damon! Damon, leave Josef alone."

Eula Mae threw her broom down and dashed toward the barn."I'm going after him. You stay here." Angelique chased after Eula Mae.

Damon had Josef by the collar when Eula Mae entered the barn. "Y'all kind ain't gonna steal from the likes of me. What you doin' in here, boy?" Damon raised a leather strap to strike Josef.

Eula Mae screamed, "You better not touch my boy."

Angelique came up from behind Eula Mae and took hold of Damon's raised arm. "Don't you dare hit Josef. I sent him in here to muck the stalls. It ain't been done by the likes of you."

"You gettin' in my business, woman? Maybe I need to beat the both of you."

Angelique wedged her pregnant self between Damon and Josef. "What you gonna do Damon, push me down again? There'll be witnesses this time." Angelique hit her mark.

Damon released his hold on Josef and smashed his fist into the nearest stall railing. "Aw. It ain't worth it." Damon spat on the ground. "You ain't no better than them."

Josef scrambled to Eula Mae's side. Angelique wrapped her arms around both of them. "I'd rather them than you."

Damon picked up a shovel and threw it at Angelique. She caught it before it could do any harm. Damon brushed by her, knocking her off balance, and stormed out of the barn. "You better do a good job mucking them stalls, you hear me boy."

Eula Mae bristled. "Leave us alone."

Angelique turned to look at Josef. "I am so sorry. Did he hurt you?"

"No ma'am, I jumped around too much for him to get a good lick of my hide."

Eula Mae asked, "That man ain't nuthin' but a wily old snake. And let me tell you, if he ever does either of you harm, he'll have to reckon with me, and then the Lord. Why you puttin' up with that, Angelique?"

The three of them walked slowly back towards the house. In the heat of the moment, they had abandoned Adelaide. They found her sitting on the porch steps. She was frightened, confused, and crying. Eula Mae picked her up, kissed the tip of her nose, and hugged her tightly. "Oh my sweet child, we didn't mean to leave you like that."

Angelique went inside and started a pot of coffee. She handed a hot cup to Eula Mae and took Adelaide from her. "It was easy to stand up to Damon to protect Josef."

Eula Mae stared at Angelique in the silence where love rests. She knew that Angelique might ignore any attempt to instruct her in ways of standing up to Damon; nonetheless, she spoke. "Child, you ain't got to give up yourself to be married to no man. You can't do that no more than the sun can stop from shinin'. Ain't natural."

Drying their wet clothes, they stood with their backs to the fireplace. Eula Mae took note of Angelique's rigid backbone and the firmness of her jaw. Eula Mae reckoned she would have to go to confession again on Saturday next. For some reason, she could not hold her tongue. She vowed for the umpteenth time to speak no more of this. Only Angelique could answer the questions of her own life.

Angelique slept fitfully that night in spite of Damon's absence being a blessing. She dreamt about a black and white checkered floor and a little girl in a pink ruffled dress with a bright bow in her long brown hair. She saw God holding out his arms. The little girl ran and jumped into the halo of warmth and comfort. All the hurt and longing washed away, the empty places filled with the love of God. She awoke when the child of her dreams wept with joy. Angelique dried her eyes and prayed to the saints to help her remember the details of her dream. She mulled over the possibility of sharing it with Eula Mae, but thought better of it.

The *Traiteuse*

Madame Pitre had lived in the farthest depths of the backlands for so long that the locals often joked that she resembled petrified wood. She possessed the power of healing, like her mama before her. Using an assortment of medicinal herbs, she could cure anything from sunstroke to consumption. Her incantations and unusual rituals were legendary among the people of Belair Cove and known to spark romance and thwart evil.

Angelique had heard the story of how *Madame* Pitre had cured her of a terrible earache when she was ten months old. Eula Mae's home remedies had not worked and she had insisted that Alduce take Angelique to the *traiteuse*. Angelique was lethargic and a high fever scorched her body scarlet red. Fear mounted with every step as Papa carried Angelique deeper into the woods late one evening. The path was barely visible. Suddenly, like an apparition, *Madame* Pitre stepped out from behind a river oak, crept right up to Angelique, and put both of her hands over her ears. She spoke in strange gibberish, what Alduce assumed were special prayers.

Papa recalled that two egrets squawked, flapped their wings, and took flight. The dark leaves in the trees had rustled, and the gray, stringy moss shuddered. Papa's dog had jumped and howled as if he were sounding an alarm. Alduce had opened his mouth to speak; the *traiteuse* motioned for him to hush.

Angelique had fought *Madame* Pitre's hold on her. The louder Angelique had wailed, the louder *Madame* Pitre recited her prayers, and the tighter she pushed on the child's ears. Then, all was tranquil. Angelique looked up at Alduce with a final whimper, her tiny shoulders jerked, and she quieted. It seemed that *Madame* Pitre had healed Angelique. No fever, no earache. She had fallen asleep in her papa's arms on the way home, an angelic expression on her tiny face.

Other stories about *Madame* Pitre were equally compelling. The *traiteuse* had predicted that the Thibodeaux child would be born with hands like a frog. The child indeed had one webbed hand. However, after the recent incident at the mercantile, even Eula Mae cautioned Angelique to stay away from her.

Almost everyone shied away from the *traiteuse* ever since she had predicted the Great War long before it began. *Madame* Pitre had been out gathering plants when she came across the spider. No one could read the signs of the "writin' spider" better. She rushed into the mercantile stammering, grabbed anyone who would listen, and shook them repeatedly. Her shabby sack dress hung limp over her scrawny shoulders. Sprigs of herbs, twigs, and roots were spilling out of her apron pockets.

"I done seen it," she screamed. "The writin' spider, right there between them trees yonder by the side of that shed. The writin' spider done spelled it out. There's bad things a comin', bad things."

From the back of the store, Antoine remarked, "*Madame*, we done seen bad times. They can't get much worse."

"I'm tellin' ya. The writin' spider done wrote a "W", dat mean a great big war." *Madame* Pitre's eyes bulged and her hands shook. She spun around in a circle pleading for believers.

Antoine pulled up a chair for her to rest. "*Mais*, calm down. Set a spell. If you say it's so, then it's true."

Madame Pitre fell into the chair and tugged at Antoine's shirt sleeve. "I'm telling you, the writin' spider done wrote it."

The Great War did come four years later. It stole the strongest of Belair Cove's young men and scattered them far from their Cajun homes. Many remembered *Madame* Pitre's warning and concluded that she must possess unusual powers.

It was for this reason that Angelique plunged farther into the dark woods, farther than she had ever been before, searching for the old woman's home place. Her compass was Bayou Debaillon's soggy bank. Along the way, she came across a writin' spider's indecipherable web spun between the limbs of a sycamore. She studied the pattern, but nothing revealed itself to her. Angelique pressed on. She ignored the cuts and scratches on her legs from the underlying brush as she parted the last tree limbs in front of the ramshackle house. She lifted the rope on the gate and scanned the yard. Two hound dogs resting in the shade of the shack lifted their droopy heads and set them down again.

Still, Angelique was reluctant to step inside their boundaries. She cleared her throat. "*Madame* Pitre, *Madame* Pitre, I'm needin' your help."

"Who's there?"

"It's me, Angelique, Ezore Belair's girl."

The *traiteuse* peeked out from behind the corner of the shack and shook her head. "Ezore be dead a long time. I was mighty fond of that sweet girl. Lord, keep her."

Madame Pitre navigated the obstacle course in her yard and reached the wobbly gate. The hound dogs were lolling at her side. Her eyes studied Angelique from head to toe.

"You look just like her. All right, what you want wit me?"

"I'm pregnant."

"Uh, uh, I can't help you child. I'm about healin' folks and tha's all they is to it. What you thinkin' about?"

"No ma'am, I'm wantin' this baby. I just wondered if you could tell me if it's a boy or girl. I got a little girl already. I need a boy."

Madame Pitre shook her head. "Wait right here."

She went inside her shack and returned, carrying a rickety wooden chair, and offered it to Angelique. "Sit here. I got just the thing. This here will tell what you want to know." From her pocket, she produced a shiny metal ring with a string attached.

"What you gonna do to me?"

"Just hold still."

Reciting incantations, she swirled the ring over Angelique's swollen belly. Slowly it started to turn, and then faster and faster in the same direction. *Madame* Pitre faced Angelique.

"Child, it's another girl."

"Are you sure? Could you just try it again?" Angelique's shoulders sagged and her face fell.

"I'm sure as I can be." Madame Pitre scratched her scraggly grey wisps of hair.

Madame Pitre patted Angelique's shoulder and sighed. "I be right back." A few minutes later, she appeared carrying a cup of steaming black tea. The *traiteuse* pulled up an old crate and sat directly in front of Angelique.

Teardrops rolled off Angelique's face. "I'm sorry I bothered you. I ain't cryin' for lack of love for this child, but for what it means for all of us. Damon won't give me any peace if this baby ain't a boy."

"You married to Damon Vidrine. He one of Domitile's boys. This a real fix you in. That Damon's the bad seed, to my way of thinkin'."

"Damon's got no brothers," Angelique answered.

Madame Pitre was puzzled. She coughed several times as if she were choking, steadied her gaze on Angelique, and scooted her crate in even closer. "Never mind that. Now, you listen to me." She looked down into the swirling tea leaves in the cup and back up at Angelique. "You stop that snivelin'. This baby gonna be a girl. Tha's done. What I can do is tell you somethin' else. You gonna be all right, child. I'm sure of that. In the meantime, you got to get God's strength back inside ya."

Madame Pitre's toothless grin lit up her wrinkled face. She used her crooked finger to poke at Angelique's heart. "All the courage you need is right in there. You go on home. Everythin' gonna be all right. You gonna see. And remember it's like the Bible says, 'Pride goeth before destruction and a haughty spirit before the fall'."

Madame Pitre says it's all gonna be all right. Angelique headed home. She stopped to sit for a while at the edge of the bayou. The sound of the water lapping against the cypress knees and fallen trees soothed her. She took off her shoes, set them aside, and dropped her naked feet noisily into the warm muddy water; it is always best to scare the snakes. She fell in sync to the rhythm of Bayou Debaillon. Angelique and Jean Marc had spent a good part of their childhood here. Her breathing slowed as she let the memories take her to a better time.

Angelique swatted the black ant crawling up her arm. She watched a small catfish swim between her dangling feet. The bayou was a constant in her life, as much as the rising sun, the prairie grasses, and the train tracks stretching across Belair Cove. Her life remained timed to the music of the Cove and its bayou. Angelique figured that searching for answers would not be the key to her survival. She needed to surrender to the way it was, at least for the time being. There was some peace in that.

After all, she had Adelaide, Papa, and Eula Mae to think of. Soon, there would be a new little girl to love. "This child will carry me forward. Carry. I like the name, Carrie."

Resonating across the Cove, the muffled church bells of Sacred Heart rang out. The crickets joined in and reminded Angelique that it was getting late. She plucked her shoes from the watery edge and stood up. "Courage, I can do this Lord. *Madame* Pitre says it's gonna be all right. Oh and Lord, about Jean Marc, please, bring him back safe and sound. I didn't mean all those awful things I said to him before he left."

The Hospital Vigil

Adelaide's heels clicked as she strode up to the nurse's desk, asking for directions.

"Are you a relative?"

"Yes, I'm Adelaide Vidrine."

The nurse questioned loudly. "Did you say Adelaide Vidrine?"

Another nurse pushing a cart down the hall stopped to stare. At the desk, the nurse in charge raised her eyes from a mountain of paperwork.

"Room 227, down the hall and to your left, ma'am."

The nurses gathered back at the nursing station and whispered. They had all heard about Adelaide.

"Oh, Adelaide, I'm so glad you're here. Come. Come and sit with me."

Adelaide choked back her tears.

"How's he doin'?"

Mémère struggled with her answer.

"Only God knows."

"Mama, I made so many bad choices in my life. It took me three marriages to tell the difference between a good man and a bad one."

Adelaide stepped further into the room and winced at the sight of *Pépère* motionless on the bed.

"I blamed him for everything that went wrong."

"That was a natural thing for you to do."

"But, I wasted so much time."

"You come around in the end."

"I should have told him."

"Don't fret. He knows your heart. Now, come sit beside me."

Jean Marc Meets Lady Luck

Although the news would not reach Belair Cover for weeks, Jean Marc reveled in the fact that the war was over. Like so many other young soldiers, he could not wait to get home. However, there was one major concern. Jean Marc was bringing home an unexpected surprise, his new wife. It was even a surprise to him when he had proposed and she had accepted. Before he could say Roly Poly, a Justice of the Peace in a small village outside of Paris had married them. Tomorrow they would be on their way to America.

Jean Marc had come to love his young bride in the short time since they had met. She was intelligent, beautiful, and had a caring nature. Elizabeth had left London and come to Paris in search of one of her brothers who was missing in action. It was a reckless thing to do, and with little result. She had roamed from hospital to hospital in hopes of finding him. She finally gave up her search, but found plenty others who needed help. She took a job in an American hospital and spent tireless hours at the bedside of the maimed, scarred, and frightened soldiers.

Jean Marc had gone to the hospital to visit the crazy kid who saved his life only hours before the war ended. He stopped by every morning longing to find Jim Felterman sitting up or opening his eyes, any simple movement would do. Each day, his condition worsened. The last day of the young man's life, Elizabeth came and sat beside Jean Marc to wait his passing.

She pulled up a chair, sat next to him, and whispered, "I'm going to stay with the two of you for a little while." She reached over, took the patient's bandaged hand in hers, and then turned to Jean Marc offering the same. They sat that way until the last, and then some.

Jean Marc had witnessed death all around him for longer than he cared to remember, but sitting there holding this girl's delicate hand shattered his reserve. He wrestled with the silent tears streaming down his face. Elizabeth sat quietly by his side and waited until he composed himself. She stood up, squeezed his shoulder gently, and walked away without saying one word.

Jean Marc waited outside the hospital ward for her that day. She walked out carrying a worn satchel. He leapt forward.

"Going somewhere? Here, let me help you with that."

"No thanks, I've got it."

"What's your name? I just wanted to thank you for what you did back there."

Elizabeth hesitated, dropped her satchel, and then walked right up to him. She kissed him full on the mouth. Jean Marc was quick to respond. When Elizabeth pulled away, she looked horrified.

"I can't believe I just did that. I apologize. I don't know what got into me. I, I wanted to thank YOU… for what you did over here."

"I just did what I was supposed to do. No thanks necessary, but kissin' you is the best thing that happened to me in a mighty long time. You taste better than sweet wine. I'd like to offer you a cup of coffee."

"I've got somewhere to go."

"Can I see you tomorrow?"

"No. I'm going home today. To London."

"Oh, you got somebody special waiting for you? There's a little coffee shop on the way and I'll walk you to the train after that."

Elizabeth shook her head and reached for her satchel. Jean Marc did the same. A brief tug of war ensued. She looked up at him. The sheepish grin on his face rendered her defenseless, and she dropped her grip on the handle.

They walked to a small cafe together. They noticed neither the two cups of cold espresso sitting in front of them nor the lateness of the hour as they talked on and on, the connection between them immediate.

Elizabeth glanced at her watch. "Oh dear, I think I might have missed the last train out."

Jean Marc reached across the table and grasped her hands in his. "Please, don't leave me."

Elizabeth stayed with Jean Marc that night and every night after that. From the beginning, she knew the date he was scheduled to ship home. As the time approached, the two were despondent at the thought of parting. The weeks passed quickly and they had clung to each other seeking comfort. She had lost so much: two brothers to the Great War. She had never known her father, and grief had stripped her mother of any sense. The woman had run off with some stranger. In the end, it had been easy to convince Elizabeth to come to Belair Cove. Still, the night before their departure, Elizabeth wept.

Jean Marc cradled her in his arms and rocked her like a baby, "Everything's comin' our way. You gonna see. You gonna love Belair Cove."

"Jean Marc, I trust you completely. It's not that. Home is wherever you are and I know we are going to have a good life. It does make me sad to know that I will probably never see England again."

Jean Marc remained awake long after Elizabeth fell asleep. He dropped his pillow lengthwise, pressed it against her side, tucked the covers all around her, and left the room. He needed to walk, to think.

What would he do if she was unhappy in Belair Cove? He had not exactly told her the truth about what life might be like there. He had painted a pretty picture: a peaceful place that follows the twists and turns of the bayou, rich farmland as far as the eye could see, and hundred-year-old oaks and pines like sentinels protecting the people. To him, Belair Cove was a living breathing thing.

"Lizzie, in springtime, the azaleas bust open in a hundred shades of pink, and in the fall, when most places are stripped to the bare bones, everything is green. Well, except for the tallow trees. Ah, the tallow trees. They set the Cove ablaze with tongues of fire."

Yet, Jean Marc knew very well that Belair Cove could be a harsh place. There were things that he had failed to mention, such as the lack of real money. Jean Marc had not told Elizabeth that most people were sharecroppers and scraped by with what little they had.

He had not shared the hardships of trying to work that pitiful piece of land that the banker, mercifully, had bought back from him. The banker had felt that it was his duty to help him since he was a young soldier going off to war. Hoping to start over when he returned to Belair Cove, Jean Marc had put aside every penny he could spare from his army paycheck. Yet, he worried. *Would the money he saved be enough?*

For many Prairie Cajun men, gambling represented hope and ran thick in their blood. Some would wager on anything. They gambled on cockfights, horse races, card games and hunting. Jean Marc knew what misfortune could befall a gambling man. He had seen it happen more than once. He concluded early on that he worked too hard to push his luck. Jean Marc gambled only on occasion and then only with small change. In France, however, Lady Luck followed Jean Marc when he gambled, especially at *bourré*.

At first, Jean Marc had passed up the sidewalk card game near the docks, not far from the room he and Elizabeth shared. Walking home one night, he watched a soldier with fiery, red hair scatter his cards and walk off in a huff.

"What they playin'?" Jean Marc asked the carrot top as he passed by.

"Poker. And if I'd had any sense, I would've stayed out of that game." The freckle-faced soldier pushed his eyeglasses back up on his nose, and widened his lips in a straight line. He turned his pockets inside out for Jean Marc. "Those guys are pros."

Jean Marc stood back for a little while and watched the players, all army infantry. These men had nothing left to lose. They had survived death and destruction at every turn, their innocence stolen.

A dark haired soldier turned to Jean Marc, "We lost a player. You want in?"

"Could be. Gimme the low down," Jean Marc answered. He listened as the soldier explained the basic rules of the game. "Sounds simple enough."

Making room for Jean Marc, the players shifted positions. The soldier with the dark hair introduced himself. "You'll forget our names, easier to remember where we headed, I'm New York."

It did not take long for Jean Marc to recognize that poker had as much to do with the man as the cards. Unfortunately, Jean Marc was losing. He paced himself, betting less on losing hands and faking it at other times. He tried to keep his opponents guessing. It paid off because ever so slowly the cards turned in his favor. He counted his winnings in his head. Jean Marc checked his watch. He had not left a note and worried that Elizabeth might wake up and find him gone.

"This next one's it for me boys. I got to get goin'." Keeping his cards close to his chest, Jean Marc fanned them out in front of him, five cards of the same suit. *It might be foolish but just this once, maybe…*

New York licked his lips while everyone waited in suspended silence. "What you say, fellas, let's make this one interesting?" New York looked around the circle before placing his bet.

Jean Marc observed how he ran his tongue over his lips, a sure sign that he was bluffing. Several of the other players dropped out. All eyes turned to look at Jean Marc.

"You in or out? Let's see you match this."

Jean Marc hesitated for only a second. "Like I said, win or lose this is the last hand for me." Jean Marc pushed his previous winnings into the center of the pot. Then he laid down his last army paycheck, signed it, and set it down as well.

The New Yorker slicked his hair back. "This is the real deal boys. Let's see what you got, Louisiana."

Jean Marc walked away from that game with one thousand and seven hundred dollars and a grin that could carry him across the ocean back to Belair Cove with pride. Back at the hotel, he blew on Elizabeth's face and watched as she blinked and opened her eyes.

"Wake up sleepy head. I've got a big surprise."

She woke to find Jean Marc lying beside her. He was waving the money in front of her face. Elizabeth rubbed her eyes, reached for the bills, and sat bolt upright.

"Jean Marc, where did you get that? What have you done? I don't understand."

"Robbed the bank down the block. It was easy," he teased until he saw her panic-stricken face. Jean Marc rolled over, spilling the truth as they both tumbled onto the floor tangled in bed linens and laughter.

Just One Glimpse

Angelique was buying groceries at the mercantile when she learned that Jean Marc was coming home. Jean Marc's guardian, Uncle Gus, had been pacing in front of the store. "Mornin' Angelique. I'm waitin' for the postman. He ought to be here any minute." Gus had stretched his thick neck for an anxious look down the street. He smiled as wide as the quarter moon when he saw a ball of dust whirling toward him.

The mail carrier slowed his horse, hitched the reins to a post, and reached for his saddlebag. "Gus, you like a faithful old dog. I thought I might find you here." He threw the bag over his shoulder and Gus followed him inside the store.

Gus asked, "Got a letter for me?"

"Hold on, Gus." Antoine took the mail from the carrier and rifled in the saddlebag to search for a letter. He found a postcard and handed it to Gus.

Gus waved it a few times as if fanning a flame, and then gave it to Marie Rose. "Jean Marc usually writes letters. This ain't good. Would you read it?"

Marie Rose placed her glasses on the tip of her nose. She stared at the photo then turned the card over. Other customers—including Angelique—moved forward to listen. Marie Rose raised her eyes to Uncle Gus. "This one comes all the way from Germany."

Marie Rose began to read Jean Marc's words, *"Uncle Gus, keep this photo. This is where I was when the war ended. I'll be home real soon. I got a surprise for y'all."* Marie Rose finished and handed Gus the postcard.

"Is that Jean Marc, the one in the middle, ain't it? He looks different."

Gus looked at the photo, nodded, and passed the postcard around for everyone to see. Jean Marc was standing in front of a building with two other soldiers. He had a rifle slung across his back and a gun in a holster. He had a crop of short hair and a full mustache on his face. The soldiers in the photo were linked arm in arm and smiling.

When it finally sunk in, Gus started shouting, "He's comin' home. That boy's comin' home!"

Angelique wanted to feel that postcard in her hand; then again, she knew better. Word might get back to Damon if she showed any interest. She left hastily and forgot to collect her purchases.

Marie Rose ran out after her with the bundle. "Angelique, He's coming home. What are you to do?"

Angelique was abrupt. "There's nuthin' to do. I'm a married woman with a child and another one on the way. It's as I said before. Jean Marc is nuthin' to me."

Later, Angelique had to ask the Lord for forgiveness because she had told a boldfaced lie. Wondering what it would be like to see him again, she was plagued with thoughts of Jean Marc. The postcard had not mentioned the date when he would be returning home. Not knowing was tearing her apart. Luckily, she could count on Marie Rose.

Marie Rose dropped by for *café au lait* one morning to report the news about the new telephone they had installed at the mercantile. "And guess what, it was Gus who got our very first message. I jumped out of my skin when that thing rang. Why, I had to get out here and tell Gus the news right away."

Jean Marc would be arriving by train Tuesday, the day after Papa's birthday. Angelique marked the days in her mind according to the tasks already on her calendar while Marie Rose continued to chatter. She had promised to clean the church for Father on Saturday. They were going to celebrate Papa's birthday a day early, on Sunday. Monday, she had committed to helping Hippolyte weed the garden. That is when she concocted her plan for Tuesday.

It was a brazen decision, and no good could come of it. Yet, here she was walking alone on the road in the mid-day heat, big and pregnant. She was hoping for just one quick glimpse of Jean Marc's rugged face, to feel his nearness, and to let it fill up the empty place inside of her, even if only for a moment.

Angelique slipped out under the pretense of taking the broken hoe to the blacksmith, Felix Soileau, for repair. She would risk all for just one glimpse of Jean Marc. She had to reach the station before the train pulled in.

The unsightly tracks cut right through the middle of Belair Cove splitting it in two. Here, it did not really matter what side of the tracks you lived on. The tracks were only an obstacle to step across on your way to nowhere. Angelique treaded carefully; her eyes focused on each unlevel crack. Since the accident, she had a fear of falling. She would not risk losing another baby. The train whistle blew in the distance and Angelique quickened her pace.

She hated to think about the last night that she had seen Jean Marc. She had said such cruel things to him. She remembered the way he looked at her on her wedding day. It saddened her to know he had witnessed her vows to Damon. However, wedding guests said he looked strong and brave, ready for war.

Angelique hurried toward the sound of the coming train. She had always loved that sound. Today, the train was bringing Jean Marc home. Sweat dripped down her face; Angelique held her enlarged belly as she pressed forward. She skirted the main street, turned the corner, and trudged through the alley near Doc Simeon's office. From there, she could see the crowd at the depot. No one would notice her. The shrill whistle blew and the train screeched to a halt. Angelique perched on the wooden handle of the hoe to steady herself, her breathing labored.

The conductor lowered the step. One after the other, several strangers stepped onto the platform, their faces obscured by billowing puffs of steam, but no Jean Marc. Angelique watched as a lovely woman carrying a suitcase stepped down. Slowly, she turned her head to the left and then the right before moving forward. Angelique grew anxious and felt weak-kneed. Where was Jean Marc? Her eyes remained glued to the exit door. *Maybe she had misunderstood. Maybe something happened and his schedule changed. Please, God, let it be today.* Then, there he was.

Jean Marc tossed his army duffel bag out first, stepped off the platform, and bent to pick it up. When he stood up, Angelique studied every feature of his fine chiseled face and proud posture. He had indeed changed. He looked older, rugged, and powerful. Jean Marc caught up to the young woman, placed his palm across the small of her back, and drew her close to him. She turned and smiled. The familiarity pierced Angelique. A welcoming throng of family and friends quickly surrounded them. Angelique pressed her body against the building, covered her mouth with one hand, and hidden from view, she sobbed. The sounds of celebration drifted in and out. Angelique knew she did not belong here.

Shucking Corn

It was a good year for corn, mid-July and sweltering hot. It was the second day that the women sat canning corn under the old chinaberry tree. Their wooden chairs formed a tight circle, and they moved them as needed to follow the shade. They were soaked in sweat, covered in flecks of corn, tired, and cranky. Pregnancy made Angelique's discomfort even worse. She paused to fan herself with her straw hat, lifted her eyes above the canopy of shade to study the clouds, and announced, "I wouldn't mind a late afternoon shower today."

Hippolyte tossed tomatoes, bell peppers, and onions into a large cast iron pot resting on the fire pit. She raised her wooden spoon in response. "In due time, God will provide." The peppers and onions snapped and sizzled in the hot oil. Hippolyte moved around the circle dipping a large ladle into each porcelain bowl and scooped out the freshly cut corn. She carried it to her large cast iron pot and tossed it into the mixture. She stirred the corn *maquechou* constantly to keep it from sticking to the bottom and burning. After it was cooked, she would seal the corn in glass jars.

Marie Rose inhaled the aroma. "Hope we break for lunch soon. I'm hungry." Marie Rose had decided to join the circle today. It was a rare opportunity for her to spend time with Angelique.

Angelique pushed unruly ringlets of dark brown hair from her damp face with stiff fingers and hugged Marie Rose. "It's been too long." She motioned for Marie Rose to pull up a chair and sit by her.

Lena Breaux had been sitting next to Angelique. Marie Rose squeezed her chair in between the two. Lena picked up her chair and moved across from them in a huff. They ignored her. "Well, I told Antoine that I just had to spend the day here with you. But, I do feel a little guilty that he's stuck inside the store all by himself today."

Marie Rose barely escaped a soaking as one of her boys tossed a cob of shucked corn into the large galvanized metal bucket at the center of the circle. "You boys better watch what y'all doin'. Spillin' water every which way. Get on out of here!" The knife waved around in her hand as she spoke, and it seemed to strike fear in their hearts. They headed for the fields to see what havoc they could cause there.

The splashing water had cooled Angelique's bare legs and swollen feet. A bowl sat precariously in her lap as she went back to slicing through layers of corn. Using a short, thin blade, she shaved the cob just a quarter inch then turned it over and shaved again. In order to cream the corn, she continued to circle the cob. Finally, the knife sunk deep into the core and swept across it firmly in one direction releasing the yellow milk. Angelique's fingers cramped while the repetition allowed her mind to drift aimlessly. She paid little attention to the motion of the knife blade as it moved up and down.

"It's gonna be a while before we break for a bite. Ouch!" Angelique stopped to suck blood from her finger. She looked up to see Lena Breaux staring at her. Lena immediately lowered her eyes. Angelique looked at Lena, a shapely young woman with dark hair curled around her strong face. There were rumors about Damon and Lena Breaux. Marie Rose had seen them together in Ville Platte, as they jostled playfully and leaned against each other. When Lena's family found out about this, it would surely end. A memory surfaced for Angelique. *I was the same age as Lena when Papa decided it best I marry Damon.*

"Lena, what's your plans for the future?"

Lena crossed her legs in the opposite direction and stuttered, "Ain't got none 'til the boys come home. Marie Rose, you know everythin' that goes on around here. When are the rest of our boys comin' home? I might be able to talk about a future, then. Meanwhile, I want to hear all about Jean Marc's homecoming celebration." Lena Breaux had hit her mark.

Angelique shuddered. She knew too much about that all ready. She had seen some of it with her own eyes and had heard even more from Damon. They had been sitting at the supper table when Damon said, "Well, the Cove is safe tonight. Our almighty hero, Jean Marc, has returned, came in on the train, he did. Folks was clappin' and huggin'. And guess what? He had a woman with him. She was a pretty little thing, a blonde, blue-eyed little fox, English woman, they say. Guess Jean Marc knew there was nuthin' here for him."

Damon studied Angelique closely. He waited for her reaction to the news. Angelique had learned long ago to hide behind a blank mask.

The women in the circle bombarded Marie Rose with questions about Jean Marc's bride. Yes, Jean Marc was back. Yes, she had met his wife. Yes, she was pretty like everyone said. With each answer, Marie Rose noticed that Angelique grew more restless. Angelique bent to pick up her tin cup off the ground and took another sip of the remaining coffee, cold and bitter. She tried to ignore Marie Rose's youngest scraping a tin plate with a fork, the sound grated on her last nerve. She was numb from sitting for so long and her feet were stinging as they fell asleep. She stood up to stretch and looked out toward the fields. Marie Rose's older boys raced in and out between the rows of tall corn stalks.

Angelique watched the wagon roll forward and stop. Damon heaved a burlap sack into the wagon and motioned to the boys to stay out of his way. Damon had replaced his father to drive the team. He left the older men the task of breaking ears of corn, tossing them into sacks, and dragging them to the end of the row. Once the wagon was full, Damon headed for the circle and the shade of the trees. He hopped down from the seat in one easy fluid motion and landed on his good leg. He rolled up his sleeves and lifted a large sack onto his shoulder.

He dropped it in front of Lena Breaux, "Ooh-ooh-wee, y'all lookin' mighty fine today. And Lena got that yellow ribbon tied up in her hair like dat."

Lena Breaux touched the ribbon and blushed.

Adelaide ran to meet her father and started jumping up and down clamoring for his attention. "Papa, I want to ride in the wagon. Can I, Papa?"

Angelique interrupted, "Adelaide, you come back over here. I need you. Keep twistin' like I showed you. You big enough to get every bit of silk off that corn."

Damon picked up Adelaide. "Oh, I don't think a little ride in the wagon could hurt none. Now could it?" They drove off together with Adelaide squealing and hopping around like a rabbit.

Lena Breaux gazed fleetingly at his back. "Tha's a fine man you got there, Angelique." Lena's mother tilted her head and opened her eyes wide silently scolding her daughter for such a brazen comment.

Angelique seethed as she swallowed her unspoken response and stared at Lena Breaux. That is when she first saw them in the distance; Jean Marc and his wife were standing on the other side of the gate. *Oh Lord, Why today?* She tried to smooth her hair back, brush the corn off her face, and loosen her dress that clung to her widening girth. It was impossible to hide her swollen belly, even though the child was not due for five more months. Angelique used her hands to lift herself up and slid further back in her seat; the bowl in her lap wobbled. She wrapped her feet around the inside of the legs of the chair and braced herself.

Jean Marc opened the gate to let Elizabeth pass through. She barely reached Jean Marc's shoulders. The descriptions Angelique had heard about her were true. Elizabeth was indeed a fine porcelain doll, ivory skin, flushed cheeks and silky blue eyes veiled behind thick brown lashes. She had braided and coiled her long blonde hair in a tight circle at the back of her head. She wore a tan straight skirt; the white blouse tucked inside revealed a tiny waist.

Jean Marc stopped to pick a few blackberries growing against the fence and handed them to her. Elizabeth ate the berries and licked her fingers clean. Jean Marc secured the gate and reached for her hand. The couple strolled toward her, hand in hand. As they made their way across the pasture, they disturbed a flock of house wrens. The birds scattered and lighted once again in a pecan tree nearby. Their sudden appearance had surprised and flustered Elizabeth. She waved her hands wildly over her head. Jean Marc's laughter rang out over the prairie.

Angelique felt hot tears forming on her dark lashes and her nose began to run. *He's happy. Look up, look up.* She practiced Eula Mae's wise instructions, lift your eyes toward heaven and there will be no room for tears.

Lena Breaux noticed Angelique's tentative expression and looked over her shoulder to discover the cause of her discomfort. "Well, speak of the devil. There's Jean Marc and his bride comin' this way."

All heads turned.

Jean Marc tipped his hat and waved. "Ladies, how y'all doin' today? This here's my wife, Elizabeth."

Elizabeth removed her new bonnet and smiled. "Good day." Her eyes sparkled as they rested on each person in turn.

She laughed lightly and spoke softly, asking questions about canning corn while Jean Marc translated her words to Cajun French. Elizabeth turned to Marie Rose and thanked her for the scented soap. Marie Rose put her head down and did not look at Angelique. Jean Marc tapped his hat against his leg as Elizabeth made her way around the circle; his shirt was drenched with perspiration. He kept glancing at Angelique.

Finally, Jean Marc faced her and spoke, "Lizzie, this is Angelique Vidrine."

"Hello, Jean Marc has spoken highly of you," Lizzie said with a lilting accent and a cheery smile.

Angelique looked at Jean Marc, but she directed her response to Elizabeth with a shrug, "Tha's because I taught him how to fish."

Jean Marc slapped his hat on his thigh. "Tha's not true. You know I taught you everything you know about the backlands includin' fishing."

He walked right up to her, leaned in under the straw hat, and planted a friendly kiss on her cheek. "It's been a long time, Angelique. I see your family's growin'?"

Damon caught sight of Jean Marc and his bride as they made their way toward the circle of women. A cloud of dust trailed behind him as he raced back with a half-empty wagon. He leapt from the seat and hugged Jean Marc as if nothing was amiss between them.

Over Jean Marc's shoulder, his eyes took in all of Elizabeth. "Well, what have we here? I come home from the war with nuthin' but this bum leg. And look at you; you bring back this fine young filly."

Jean Marc moved to Elizabeth's side. "Elizabeth, this is Damon."

"I'm right proud to meet you, pretty lady." Damon went to stand behind Angelique, put his hand on the back of her neck, and squeezed possessively. "I got me another little one on the way. Angelique looks best when she's expectin'. Don't you think?"

Jean Marc answered, "I do believe that you and I are two lucky fellas."

Damon lifted his eyebrows as if in disagreement and winked at Lena Breaux. He walked over to Jean Marc and slapped him hard on the back. "What you say? Let's leave the women folk to the canning. They have enough sacks here to keep them busy for quite a while. How 'bout a drink for old times?"

"Sorry, maybe after Elizabeth and I get settled in."

Damon gritted his teeth at this perceived slight. "Well, another day then, *mon ami.*"

"To be sure," Jean Marc nodded.

Adelaide called out from the wagon, "Come on, Papa, let's go."

Damon swung himself up into the wagon and headed back the way he had come. He snapped at Adelaide, "Will you stop movin' around for Christ sake."

Jean Marc put his hat back on. "Well, ladies, we best be gettin' back to town. Elizabeth and I got a lot to do today." Elizabeth placed her hand through the crook of his arm.

After they left, Angelique unwound her tense body from the chair and excused herself. She hastened in the direction of the outhouse in order to hide from prying eyes. She escaped behind a tree, leaned against the rough bark, and covered her face with shaky hands. Angelique listened as the women in the circle chimed in, "It sure is good to have Jean Marc back home."

Jean Marc Cashes in His Winnings

Jean Marc was a patient man. When he returned to Belair Cove, he chose to hide his winnings and wait for the right opportunity to buy land. He kept repeating to Elizabeth, "Everythin' gotta be right."

Jean Marc hid his money in an old sock and pushed it deep under their mattress. He thought it would be a long time before he could realize his dream. However, within days of his arrival, certain events fell into place like a well-played hand of cards, some his doing and others the hand of fate.

Jean Marc's Uncle Emile died. Emile, a committed bachelor, had no wife or children of his own. Jean Marc was overwhelmed when he learned that his uncle had left him his small farm. "Gus, I can't take Uncle Emile's land. It ain't right. That belongs to you and your brothers."

"We done all talked about this long before you even come home, boy. You made us all real proud over there. Besides, we got enough for our own. Your cousins know about this and they all agreed. Emile went fast and this is what he wanted to do. Give you a real start on things."

Uncle Emile had been a kind and unassuming man. He had lived in a tiny shack at the back of his property. Jean Marc and Elizabeth welcomed this blessing and moved into the shack. As luck would have it, Uncle Emile's property bordered thirty acres of prime land that came up for auction. The Prejeans had abandoned the place when they could not meet the lender's note. Jean Marc seized the opportunity. Buying that property the next week emptied his sock of its contents. He was now the proud owner of a sizable farm.

Elizabeth never complained about their humble quarters, but Jean Marc was in a hurry to build her a proper house. He knew he had to find inexpensive materials. Uncle Gus suggested that he offer to tear down the old Vidrine barn. It was abandoned and rotting out back near Angelique's Papa's place.

Jean Marc approached Domitile. "I could clear out that old barn and haul off all of the wood and such. I'd keep what's good for my trouble. Agreed?"

Domitile had often asked Damon to strip the dilapidated old barn, but he had done nothing. Domitile sighed, recognizing the offer as a good deal. The two men shook hands on it.

Jean Marc disassembled the old barn board by board and hauled off anything useful to build a house. Uncle Gus and Uncle Hanray showed up the first day with hammers in hand. Aunt Maudrey and Aunt Odette pulled out every nail from the boards. Jean Marc and his cousins worked late into the night organizing the materials. Rotting boards were trimmed and planed, nails straightened. They salvaged everything that was usable including the tin from the roof. The rest was firewood.

It was not long before Jean Marc and Elizabeth had a house that mirrored his dream, simple and practical. Jean Marc was pleased that Elizabeth had adapted well to her new surroundings. She felt secure with all of Jean Marc's family around her, and before long announced that she was pregnant. Jean Marc sped up the pace and planted a vegetable garden at the side of the house. They built a sturdy barn and chicken coop. He fenced in their property as well as the house.

They had mature fig and pecan trees on the perimeter of their land. Elizabeth loved to bake, and it was not long before her fig cakes and sugar cookies received praise from the neighbors. Elizabeth planted azalea bushes in the front yard while Jean Marc made plans to grow cotton.

There was one aspect that they could not alter: Damon and Angelique had the farm next to theirs. Their houses were set far enough apart, yet the distance not so great that, with a good rifle, one could have picked the other off his front porch.

Hippolyte was beside herself about the new neighbors. It was not idle curiosity; it was akin to an old wound that would not heal. She marched across the yard several times a day spying on Angelique's new neighbors. She would swoop through Angelique's house unannounced and sashay straight to the bedroom window, her great bosoms undulating. Hippolyte would peek through a crack in the shutters and remain there until she had something to report, "Oh did you see that? They puttin' up a fence between us like we might traipse across their fine property or somethin'... EEEE, did you see what they got over there, a house full of fine folks like they visitin' the queen of England." Afterwards, Hippolyte always tried to find something to satisfy her sweet tooth in Angelique's pie keeper. The hinges would rattle when she slammed the door shut.

Her snooping and obvious envy agitated everyone. Domitile received the brunt of Hippolyte's meddling. "This is all your fault. You should a never let him set foot on my property and tear down that barn. And I told you to buy that other piece from the Prejeans a while back, but no, you ain't listenin' to me."

Domitile tried to hold his tongue and did not respond, but Hippolyte crossed the threshold of his reserve. Her constant gossiping and nagging reminded him of the failures he saw in their son compared to Jean Marc's industrious ways. Domitile had no more patience. "You ain't nuthin' but a nosey busy-body. Stay out of their way, tha's all we got to do."

Hippolyte struck back, "Why they got to live so close is all I want to know. Why I got to look at that every day?"

"I ain't gonna listen to this. You agreed to leave this one be a long time ago, woman. Don't start up now. That boy deserves his chance to have somethin', to be somethin' more. It ain't ours to question."

Damon saw Jean Marc's presence as an intrusion on his family, one that posed a serious threat. Jealousy began to consume his waking thoughts. Angelique bore the brunt of his hostilities that became more difficult with each passing day. She could do nothing right in his eyes, and the strain took a toll on her. Having Jean Marc and his wife living so close might be more than she could endure.

All of the Vidrines watched as Jean Marc and Elizabeth breathed life into the land. It was clear their home was simple abundance. It was the gathering place for friends and relatives. Their days seemed to bear none of the struggles that plagued their neighbors.

Angelique worried about the new neighbors as well. Crossing paths would surely become a daily occurrence, and if the first evening it happened were an indicator of things to come, life would be difficult. Damon was sitting on his front porch cleaning his shotgun when Jean Marc walked by.

"Evenin' Damon. Now that we settled in, how about you and me go huntin' together sometime? Be like old times."

Damon did not answer. He removed the cleaning cloth from the barrel of his shotgun and loaded it with a round of shells. Then he jumped up, aimed his shotgun at Jean Marc, and yelled, "Bam!"

Jean Marc dove for the nearest cover. He hit the ground and rolled into a nearby ditch. "Hell, Damon. Ain't you got no sense? You ain't ever gonna change, are you?"

Damon burst out laughing. "Scared ya, didn't I? Ah come on, can't you take a joke? It's like you said, we used to have fun in the old days."

"I spent too many damn years in the trenches duckin' enemy fire to ever think that was funny."

"War's over, or ain't you heard?"

Jean Marc picked himself up off the ground. "You're a goddamn idiot. You know that?" Years of hidden anger at his childhood enemy surfaced. "Why don't you put that thing down and step off your porch?"

Hearing their raised voices, Angelique rushed to the door. "What's going on out here? Stop this nonsense. Y'all ain't kids no more. Jean Marc, get out of here."

Jean Marc apologized, "Sorry about this, Angelique."

Damon lowered his gun and pulled Angelique to his side. Wriggling free from her husband, Angelique nodded in response. She was not sure with whom she was angrier. She longed for a diversion, a place to escape, but there was none.

The Festival

Angelique opened the door to the mercantile. The bell was barely audible above the sound of loud voices. Marie Rose and the town sheriff were in the midst of a heated disagreement. Using her hands to add meaning to her words, Marie Rose stood behind the counter pleading her case. "Main Street has to be roped off."

"Why can't you just tie a piece of string to their wrist when they pay?" he said. "Then, they can do whatever they want. Tha's all we need." The sheriff threw a quarter on the counter for his chewing tobacco and left abruptly.

"That's crazy. I ain't got time to tie string to everybody that's gonna come to this festival." Marie Rose's hands flew up in frustration. She was in charge of the town's first festival and things had run amok.

It had been fifty years since the incorporation of Ville Platte and the last census showed they numbered six hundred strong, a good enough reason "to pass a good time." Actually, any reason would have sufficed. Marie Rose had talked of nothing else for weeks. She had organized a parade, a few sporting events, a baking contest, and a street dance.

"Angelique, you have to help me out here. Antoine checked the Farmer's Almanac this mornin'. He says it's supposed to rain on festival day, the sheriff here is givin' me a hard time, and the band has gone and canceled on me."

Marie Rose's voice rose two decibels. "I'm ropin' the street off. I'm tellin' you. Angelique, I need a big favor. Think Damon would let you play on Saturday night?"

Angelique lifted her shoulders to her ears, spread her arms wide displaying her pregnant belly, and looked up at Marie Rose shaking her head "no."

"*Mais*, that don't make no difference, none at all. Please. Please. You and your papa, y'all the best around here anyway."

"Marie Rose, it probably ain't gonna rain, but if you want me to, I could get over to the church and light a candle or, better yet, convince *Madame* Pitre to conjure up some sunshine. She might do it if she thought it'd drum up some business. She could cure folks if they get sunstroke. That'd be easier than convincin' Damon to let me play on Saturday night. Besides, I'd be embarrassed to stand up on stage like dis, fatter than a stuffed turkey at Thanksgivin'."

Marie Rose pleaded, "If I can find a way to convince Damon to let you play, will you do it?"

"Well, for you... anything, of course. But, that'll never happen."

Marie Rose had an idea. Although she had never found him appealing, Felix Soileau, the blacksmith, had always been sweet on her. He was kind, but had a small barrel chest and a large bulbous nose. Nonetheless, she enjoyed Felix's occasional flirtation while Antoine looked away. Felix had never married. Some said he was waiting for Antoine to die of one of his imaginary ailments so that he could step into his place.

Recently, Marie Rose overheard Felix tell Antoine that Damon owed him money, a gambling debt. That is when she concocted her plan. If she could get Antoine to pay off Damon's debt to Felix, then have Felix convince Damon that he would forego the debt if he allowed Angelique to play—that might just work. They could reimburse themselves from the profits after the festival.

Festival day arrived and Angelique had dressed carefully in a light blue smock. Around her shoulders, she draped a lightweight, cream-colored shawl that she had made. The shawl had an intricate pattern of white flowers along the edge. Her dark hair encircled the back of her slender neck in a tight bun, but several wispy curls escaped and framed her face.

Angelique was grateful to feel the fiddle in her hand. She stored it behind the counter at the mercantile when they arrived. Angelique questioned Marie Rose as to how she was able to get Damon to agree.

"Oh, I am sworn to secrecy. All that matters is that it's done."

Angelique gave up on learning the truth and decided to concentrate on Adelaide. Playing some of the games at the festival would be fun. But, where was Adelaide? No Adelaide.

Angelique dashed out onto Main Street. She scanned the children's booths and food tables in front of the church. Peering up and down the street, she was frantic. There were several men gathered at the farthest end near the blacksmith shop. The wind carried the loud bursts of triumph from the shooting events. Damon headed in the direction of the noise. He had not noticed Adelaide trailing after him.

"Damon! Adelaide's right behind you!"

Damon picked her up. "How'd you get away from your mama like that?" He met Angelique halfway and tried to hand Adelaide over to her.

Adelaide squirmed. "Papa, I want to go with Papa."

"Your mama's right for once, little girl. I got more important things to do right now. You go on."

Angelique bribed, "Adelaide, how about I get you some fresh lemonade?"

While waiting for the parade to advance down Main Street, Angelique and Adelaide sat on a bale of hay in front of the mercantile. The stage where Angelique would play loomed in the distance. There were so many people, some of whom she did not recognize. Angelique was fidgety.

Marie Rose stopped by, hugged Angelique, and kissed Adelaide on the forehead. "Look, blue skies. Thank the Lord. We'll put Adelaide to bed inside if she gets tired. Don't you worry none. I'll keep my eye on her."

"Eula Mae gonna see about Adelaide, but what about me?" Angelique pressed her hands to her bulging waist.

"You'll be fine the minute you start playin'," Marie Rose ventured.

"Hippolyte was fussin' about this all mornin'. I'm not sure it's right."

"Ain't nobody gonna say nuthin'. Oh look, Jean Marc."

Angelique and Marie Rose watched as Elizabeth completed the entry form at the baking tent while Jean Marc held her plate of cookies. Jean Marc waved. Marie Rose motioned for them to come over.

"Elizabeth, so glad that y'all came. I see you entered the bakin' contest."

Elizabeth blushed. "Jean Marc and his family insisted I bake a batch of cookies for today."

Jean Marc bragged, "Just wait 'til you taste one of 'em. They are my favorite." He looked around. "Where's Damon?"

A cheer went up from the shooting range. Felix Soileau came huffing up the street. "That Damon, he's the best shot around. Done won me a whole heap of money bettin' on him."

A mob of boys started yelling, "The parade's comin'. The parade's comin'." Excited faces turned toward the train depot at the end of the street.

Marie Rose lit up. "*Mais*, I better get busy, me." She disappeared into the crowd.

Damon sidled up behind Angelique and wrapped his arms around her. "Wanna bet on who's the best shot in these here parts? Mornin' Jean Marc, Miss Elizabeth."

Jean Marc tipped his hat and complimented, "I hear congratulations are in order."

Ignoring Jean Marc, Damon picked up Adelaide and lifted her onto his shoulders. He eyed Felix. "You enterin' the *boudin* eatin' contest? I'd bet on you. Might win me a whole heap of money then."

A caravan of wagons went grinding and creaking down Main Street. The sheriff led the way on his black horse. He sat tall in the saddle and waved his hand from side to side. He was wearing a black banner draped over his chest with the word *Capitain* written across it in gold lettering.

Angelique chuckled. "Why, that Marie Rose, she's a little devil. I see how she convinced the sheriff to rope off the street for the parade."

Adelaide applauded as each passing wagon sent ripples of laughter and a cacophony of heckling out into the street. They rolled by with colorful advertising signs displayed on the sides. Next, the entourage of prominent landowners of Ville Platte rode by, the entire family waved from the backs of their wagons. Some sat on the floorboards banging on pots with spoons, ringing cowbells, and shouting at friends.

A cowboy stole the show dressed as an Indian chief, his face painted for war. The onlookers, except for Jean Marc, burst into laughter. Elizabeth brushed Jean Marc's arm tenderly.

Jean Marc reflected, "Sometimes, it's hard to forgive folks for poking fun."

Angelique overheard him and interrupted, "It's ignorance that grips the heart of some folks. They just don't know any better."

Damon added, "It's Indians tha's ignorant."

Ready with a sharp response, Elizabeth fumed and turned to face Damon.

Jean Marc shook his head. "He ain't worth it Lizzie."

Angelique scolded, "What's wrong with you Damon?"

Damon looked from one to the other. "What, I ain't said nuthin' but the truth."

Elizabeth looked from Jean Marc to Angelique and understood that she, too, knew of his ancestry. An uncomfortable quiet hung over them. All eyes turned and focused on the street.

The parade seemed more like a *charivari*, a noisy celebration usually reserved for second marriages. Marie Rose and Antoine's wagon was last. The boys were throwing hard candy to the throng of children chasing their wagon. Jehan Boudreaux rode his donkey with a sign advertising "a nickel a ride," and that was the end of the parade. The donkey spooked when three rowdy cowboys blew their cow horns. The donkey bucked and threw Boudreaux off. He jumped up and chased after her. The crowd cheered, the parade was over, and revelers stepped into the street.

Papa wandered over to Angelique. "Reckon we ought to grab a bite? The Buckhorn's serving up a tasty pork jambalaya for a quarter. Now, the Fist to Cuffs got the chicken gumbo. Which one you want?"

Even before the gumbo cooled in the bowl, dancers started getting itchy feet. "*Mais* Angelique, when the dancin' goin' to start?"

Papa lowered his spoon. "You hold your horses. We comin'. Y'all grab some chairs and set 'em up outside for the women."

Several men quickly obliged and snatched chairs right up from under the customers. They lined them up along the plank sidewalk. Papa handed Angelique her fiddle, Domitile picked up his guitar, and Felix clasped his *ti-fer*. They were ready. Damon plucked a chair from the wall and carried it to the stage for Angelique. He took to the stage as if it were his.

Someone from the crowd yelled, "What you gonna play for us, Damon?"

"Shut up, Gaston. Wouldn't do to have my lady tirin' out on y'all."

Angelique felt the tension ease from her muscles. She adjusted the chair and sat down. "Thanks, Damon. Tha's kind of you."

Chaperones settled themselves in for the evening. Angelique glanced at the older women. Hippolyte sat at the center of the row, frowning up at her daughter-in-law. Several others were shaking their heads and whispering; a few stared. It was unseemly for a pregnant woman near the end of her term to be out in public, much less sitting on a stage with a fiddle in her hand.

Damon followed Angelique's glance. He bent down over Angelique and whispered in her ear, "Even those old biddies see how ridiculous you look sittin' here." He kissed her on the cheek.

Angelique dropped her bow. Damon picked it up, handed it to her with fanfare, and winked. He raised his hands to the waiting crowd. "Y'all have fun, now."

Papa and Domitile broke out in a lively Cajun jig. Angelique sat motionless. Papa slowly inched toward his daughter encouragingly. Angelique searched the crowd for reassurance. Jean Marc's soulful eyes met hers. He smiled and pretended to play an imaginary fiddle. Angelique stood up, raised her fiddle, shut her eyes and picked up the tune. Papa stomped his foot hard in response. The floorboards drummed the beat. Everyone cheered, young men grabbed a dancing partner, and the party began. Even the older women tapped their feet.

Angelique played for nearly an hour before she sat down.

Papa called out, "*Ayeee*, any a you fiddlin' boys out there want to come on up here and help us out?"

A newcomer to Ville Platte jumped up on stage and the band played on while Angelique sat on the sideline holding a sleepy Adelaide. Angelique searched the crowd for Damon and spotted him talking to Lena Breaux. She feigned indifference and watched the dancers. She saw Jean Marc as he led Elizabeth around the circle. Jean Marc was no longer the boy she remembered. His hair was short, army style, his stance confident, and his muscular physique made him appear more mature.

"ONE, two, three, ONE, two, three," Jean Marc counted aloud for Elizabeth as they circled the room to a Cajun waltz. He pressed his palm into her back as he guided her past the other dancers. Elizabeth was a quick study and soon they moved to a rhythm all their own.

Angelique closed her eyes for a moment and inhaled deeply as she imagined herself twirling in Jean Marc's arms. Suddenly, she felt a tight contraction rip through her entire body. She pointed to Damon and told Adelaide, "Adelaide, go get your papa, hurry."

When Damon arrived, Angelique struggled to stand and pressed her hand against her aching back as another contraction began. "Damon, we got to leave right now." As they departed, she looked over her shoulder at the happy couple one last time. Jean Marc had his head thrown back and his deep-throated laughter echoed across the prairie. Angelique whispered, her voice barely audible over the sound of the music, "At least one of us is happy."

Marie Rose stopped by a few days later to see Angelique's newborn baby girl, Carrie. "*Cher, ti bébé.* Angelique, she's beautiful. Marie Rose set a parcel down on the table. "A few things for our little Carrie."

Carrie slept peacefully in her mother's arms. Angelique glowed when she looked at her second child. "This one gonna be easy."

Hippolyte broke up the pleasantries, "Gimme that child. I best give the puny little thing a bath this mornin'." Angelique handed Carrie over to her mother-in-law. Carrie started to whimper as Hippolyte sashayed out of the room, a cold draft left in her wake.

"What's wrong with her today? She is more ornery than usual."

Angelique whispered, "She ain't as bad as she pretends. I hurt her feelin's, tha's all. She wanted me to name the baby after her. I just flat refused. Went on and on about the name Hippolyte being the name of some ancient goddess. Can you imagine that?"

The two women chuckled.

"What'd Damon have to say about all that?"

"Oh, Damon, he could have cared less, he wanted a boy."

Marie Rose rolled her eyes. "Huh, men. *Mais,* I think the name Carrie is perfect, me. And that goddess business, Hippolyte must have been some awful wicked goddess if she was one. *Et bien,* oh well. I'm more interested in talkin' about the festival." Marie Rose scooted her chair closer to Angelique and flushed with the memory.

Adelaide snuck into the room. Wanting attention, she wriggled between the two women. "I liked your parade. I wanna do it agin."

Marie Rose lifted Adelaide onto her lap. She took Adelaide's hands and clapped them together. "Oh, we will surely do that just for you. We sure will, *cher*. We gonna have lots of festivals. And your mama's gonna play for all of 'em. The crowds love her. Why me, I got big ideas for Ville Platte. More and more travelers are makin' this a regular stop on their way west and then decidin' to stayin' on."

Angelique complimented Marie Rose, "You makin' a big difference for all of us. You make me proud to know you. I recognize the good tha's comin' and what that might offer my babies. Soon Adelaide'll be ready for school."

Hippolyte returned carrying a tray with coffee. "Carrie sleeping like an angel since I been lookin' after her. Thought you two might like a taste of my coffee. Adelaide, come on out here and help me collect the eggs this mornin'. Let these ladies talk grown-up talk."

Angelique sat quietly while Marie Rose added milk and sugar to her coffee. "Marie Rose, remember when we used to lay in the grass waitin' for the train, when we were kids?"

Marie Rose nodded. "Yeah, you'd crouch like a fox waitin' and then you'd dash after that train calling out, 'Hey, *Cotton Blossom*, gimme a ride. Take me with you.'"

Angelique shut her eyes and listened for the familiar sound of the wheels on the tracks as they got louder and louder – *thwap thwap, thwap thwap*. "I can still feel the thrill inside of me, the moment when she whooshed by like a black dragon. And when the caboose became a tiny distant speck on the track, I always felt a letdown. Always wanted to get on that train and see where she took me, all those faraway places. Never been outside this Cove. It never dawned on me that Jean Marc would be the first to leave this place. Not once."

Marie Rose inserted, "That was like yesterday. Some folks been askin' Jean Marc about the places he saw, but he ain't sayin' much. Guess it bein' war and all. He really never was much of a talker."

Marie Rose hesitated. It seemed that Angelique was not vaporizing into thin air at the sound of Jean Marc's name, so she continued. "Oh, did I mention that Elizabeth took first place with her cookies? I tasted them myself and they were pretty good. You ought to give her a chance, Angelique. She could be your friend."

"What are you talkin' about Marie Rose? I don't think tha's a good idea at all. Please, let's not talk about them."

"Well, just consider what I said about Elizabeth, won't you. Y'all livin' so close to each other."

Angelique put up her hands, "No more about them. All I want to talk about is the festival. I loved it all, especially, seeing friends and family, and the sounds of the children laughin' and playin'. Oh, and playing the fiddle. Folks did seem to like the music."

Angelique shut her eyes to give weight to her words. She was back there again—her fiddle resting on her shoulder, tucked under her chin against the warm wood, her bones responding to the vibrations.

The Difficult Birth

Angelique had promised Marie Rose that she would consider her suggestion carefully. She vacillated between being happy for Jean Marc and feeling great hostility. Jean Marc certainly deserved a life of his own. He had done what he thought was in her best interest at the time. The truth was that he had betrayed her, given her up so she could marry Damon.

Early one morning, Angelique confided in Bessie while she squeezed her udder, "I ought not be thinkin' about Jean Marc so much. What you think old girl? How come such a coward come back from the war a hero? And I'm stuck with Damon. *C'est la vie.* Whatever happened to the catechism of *Grand-mère*? Do good, stay right with God, and only good things will happen to you. Well, *Grand-mère* was dead wrong."

Unfortunately, Angelique encountered Jean Marc or Elizabeth almost daily. It was difficult to see them together, always holding hands, whispering, and laughing. Elizabeth reminded Angelique of a skittish young doe. Angelique made every effort to avoid them as much as possible until the day John Watkins, "the Watkins Man," rolled into Belair Cove.

His covered wagon was overflowing with kitchenwares, and a red sign on the top promised a money back guarantee. The wagon rattled and clanged with black cast iron pots that scraped against the sides. Watkins sold tonics, poultices, and magic salves in addition to hardware. Potential customers came running from their houses or fields to follow the Watkins Man. His wagon came to a halt in front of Sacred Heart Chapel. Children pushed and shoved to get a closer look. Elizabeth and Angelique pressed forward with the crowd while the vendor shouted.

"The Watkins Man has plenty of room! Step right up, folks! As I was saying, this here elixir will cure your aching belly. All you need is one dose of this. Yessiree. The secret ingredient told to me by my old friend, a real Attakapa medicine man." He patted the dark bottle with syrupy contents.

The Watkins Man was sporting a fine suit and bow tie. He used a yellow handkerchief to wipe his sweaty brow. His long mustache twirled at the edges of his sallow cheeks. A strip of leather held his hair back in a ponytail. He picked up his guitar on the seat and started playing a Cajun tune, *"Jolie Jeune Fille"*. He would stop occasionally to tell a joke, and then he would start the song again.

The children loved it when the Watkins Man came to Belair Cove. They knew from years past that he would hand out tiny sugar squares to the little ones at the end of his sales pitch. Begging their parents to buy something, they danced around the wagon.

Angelique glanced at Elizabeth. It did not look like she was pregnant. Angelique had overheard Jean Marc's aunt, Odette, sharing the news outside of church a few weeks back. Odette had gone on and on about how elated Jean Marc was at the news.

Elizabeth smiled and approached Angelique. "Angelique. How are you on this fine day?"

Angelique turned and whispered, "Do you think the Watkins Man can cure whatever ails Hippolyte?" Angelique laughed at her own joke.

"I'm afraid not even the Watkins Man can cure crankiness," Elizabeth blurted.

Angelique burst out laughing. "I like the way you think." Angelique bought a bottle of liniment for Damon's lame leg. Elizabeth purchased a bar of scented soap for herself and some salve for Jean Marc. They left together.

The next day, Elizabeth appeared at Angelique's door with a plate of cookies. Angelique offered her a place at the table and set the cookies down. Elizabeth cleared her throat. "Angelique, you may have already heard, I'm expecting a baby. I nursed soldiers during the war, but I know very little about having a baby. I'm too embarrassed to ask Jean Marc's aunts. And I have lots of questions."

Angelique looked at Elizabeth. She was blushing; her shoulders drooped inward. Angelique made a quick decision and poured a cup of Eula Mae's calming tea for her new friend.

They spoke of many things that day and in the weeks to come. They talked about Elizabeth's beloved home, London, city life, castles, and rolling green hills. Elizabeth confided in Angelique about her dire experiences during the war. The loss of her two brothers haunted her. The images stayed with Angelique long after Elizabeth's tears subsided. Jean Marc and Elizabeth had shared hardships that forged a bond between them, one in which Angelique had no part. She truly understood that Jean Marc no longer belonged to her.

Nevertheless, the two women felt as if they had always known each other and delighted in discovering their common interests. They exchanged the few books they owned and embroidery patterns they designed. Angelique taught Elizabeth to cook catfish *court bouillon*—in a tomato sauce—along with several other Cajun dishes Jean Marc loved. Elizabeth gave her the prize-winning cookie recipe and swore her to secrecy.

Jean Marc was elated when he first tasted Elizabeth's attempts at cooking Cajun style. He dipped his finger into the pot on the stove. "Um um, this is really good. *Tante* Odette been here? She helped with this?"

"No. It's Angelique. She came over today and we cooked side by side."

"She's a good woman, Lizzie. I think maybe she could use a friend. She has a hard life with Damon."

"Why, Jean Marc, Angelique's the sweetest thing."

"She's a hard worker," Jean Marc added.

"We find all kinds of things to chat about. I like her. I think you're right about Damon, though. He's a bit of a nasty chap. I can't imagine you two being friends, even as children."

"We were friends growin' up. Oh, we had the usual fights that kids get into, but I don't know, something happened. We were maybe twelve or thirteen when he changed. He was always angry with me. I never understood what I done to him."

"Was it about Angelique? Jean, were you...were you ever in love with her?" Elizabeth waited in the silence for an answer.

"Once, when we were kids, there was a moment when we were sweethearts. It was different then. She was different then. But, it was more than that. I can't explain it."

Jean Marc hesitated. He knelt on the floor in front of Elizabeth's chair, kissed the baby growing inside of her, faced her directly, and rested his forehead against hers. He gazed into Elizabeth's doubting blue eyes. "I'm glad Angelique's got you for a friend. For sure, she's special. But Lizzie, don't you ever forget that when it come right down to it, I chose you. My precious Lizzie." Elizabeth inhaled her husband's scent and kissed him eagerly until their desire pulled them into bed where their need for each other provided comfort.

Elizabeth had months to go and much to do before her baby's arrival. She and Angelique discussed childbirth. Angelique could sense her fear and shared little about the suffering or the possible dangers. Instead, she spoke of the joy of bringing Adelaide and, most recently, Carrie into the world.

Angelique kept repeating, "It will all be forgotten the minute you hear your baby's first cry. And when you hold that little one in your arms, tha's when you know there is a God."

A few weeks later, Angelique and Damon woke up to the sound of Jean Marc pounding with both fists on their front door. Putting on his pants, Damon hopped forward as he scrambled to open the door. "What the hell? All right all right, I'm comin'. Jean Marc, what you want over here?"

"Somethin' ain't right. It's Lizzie. She's in labor, but the baby ain't comin'. She can't take it no more. You gotta fetch Eula Mae for me."

Damon seized Jean Marc by the shoulders. "You go on back home. Don't worry, I'll get Eula Mae." He rushed out, saddled his horse, and disappeared.

Angelique wrapped a shawl around her shoulders and dashed next door. Elizabeth was screaming and thrashing about when Angelique burst into the bedroom. Gus's wife, Odette, was wiping her forehead with a cool wet rag. Odette pursed her lips and shook her head sadly.

"Oh, Angelique, my baby. Do something."

"How long has she been like this?"

"Since midnight. I did everythin' I know. Gus went to fetch the midwife. He ain't come back yet."

Angelique glimpsed the blood soaked linens. She recalled the horrible night when she lost her little boy and was terrified for her dear friend. "Elizabeth. Take a few deep breaths. Thas' it, now, another one." Another contraction started and Elizabeth wrenched in pain.

Jean Marc pleaded, "Y'all got to do somethin' to help my Lizzie."

Angelique took charge. "Jean Marc, go fetch a clean washrag and bring some water. And find some clean sheets." She rolled up a dry wash cloth and placed it in between Elizabeth's teeth. "Here, bite down on this when the next one comes."

When that contraction subsided, Angelique removed the washcloth, dipped it into the cool water, and handed it to Jean Marc. He crawled into bed behind Elizabeth and continually wiped her face and neck. He lifted her for the final push while Odette and Angelique struggled to bring the baby into the world. Eula Mae arrived too late. The midwife never came. The child was stillborn.

While Odette and Eula Mae tended to Elizabeth in soothing whispers, Angelique whisked the baby from the room. She picked up the beautiful white blanket Elizabeth had stitched during their afternoons together and smoothed it open. She cleaned the baby, laid her on the blanket, and swaddled her tight in hopes of breathing life into the tiny thing. Angelique carried the baby to Jean Marc.

Elizabeth whimpered, "Give her to me. I want my baby." Angelique placed the little girl in Elizabeth's arms. Jean Marc leaned over his Elizabeth and the baby and wept. The women left closing the door quietly behind them.

They heard Jean Marc's words: "Oh, sweet Lizzie. I love you. We gonna get through this, together. You'll see."

Elizabeth mourned deeply. She could not come to terms with the loss of her baby. She refused to dress or leave the house. Jean Marc tried to coax her from the bed, only to find her curled up there again. At night, she stood by candlelight beside the baby's cradle until Jean Marc woke up and guided her back to bed. Once, he had tried to remove the cradle. Elizabeth dragged it back inside the bedroom. The rocking of the cradle became a nightly ritual.

"Lizzie, you can't keep goin' like this. You got to focus on gettin' better."

Neighbors made a path to Elizabeth's back door as they brought meals and tried to help lift her out of her depression, but to no avail. She would not eat. It pained everyone to witness her grave sorrow.

Sometimes, Jean Marc ventured into the bedroom during the day and pleaded with Elizabeth to get out of the bed. She would shut her eyelids, turn her back to him, and escape in fitful sleep. Her skin became lackluster, and she grew weaker with each passing day. She began to cough, a dry hacking cough that would not abate. Her body felt hot when touched, consumed with a burning desire to leave this world. Only five weeks after the birth, Jean Marc laid Elizabeth to rest beside their little Janay.

Angelique, Damon, and Adelaide stood across from Jean Marc as he buried his wife. Angelique swayed gently from side to side while Carrie slept peacefully in her arms. The solemn mood of the mourners made Adelaide uncomfortable and she began to cry. Damon whispered to Angelique, "I told you we shouldn't have come." He pulled Adelaide to him and bent to whisper in her ear, "Stop that cryin' or you'll get a whippin'. Adelaide, this ain't nuthin' about you, girl."

Adelaide continued to sob. Her cries resonated out over all of Belair Cove and reminded everyone of the young woman who had touched the hearts of so many. Angelique handed baby Carrie to Damon, and she bent down to console Adelaide. The child buried her head in her mother's chest.

Jean Marc was standing across from them, his suffering and pain registered on his grim face. He kept repeating, "I should have never brought her here."

Uncle Gus gently scolded, "Don't talk like that boy. It ain't gonna do you no good."

Stirring up a cloud of dust, the small crowd left the graveyard and plodded home down Belair Cove Road. As they approached their homes, each family broke away, returning to their own struggles. Damon and Angelique were the last to separate from Jean Marc. They stood and watched as he walked home alone past Elizabeth's azaleas and onto his porch steps. A pall fell over Belair Cove, dark and dreary, the air thick with grief. The somber seasons passed slowly for Jean Marc. Even so, the calendar continued to mark the years from one harvest to the next.

The Hospital Vigil

Mémère squeezed her husband's hand, "Looks like rain's comin'. Good for corn."

"What's that you said, Mama?"

"Oh child, I'm sorry. My addled brain's thinkin' on the past."

Carrie looked across the bed at her mother. "You never talked about how hard life was back then, Mama."

"Aw child, hard times is somethin' none of us can escape. I tried. It's hard times that make us strong."

Carrie tucked the covers tighter around the frail patient in the bed and listened as Angelique told her about the incidences that led to her decision to run away.

Crossing Paths

After Elizabeth's death, Angelique felt an instinctive pull toward Jean Marc. This feeling was stubborn, with a mind of its own. She did her best to pretend it did not matter what side of the road Jean Marc Fontenot walked on, if his crops were faring better this year than last, or if his grieving persisted. She knelt upon the hard wood floor every night and prayed; her fingers ran up and down her rosary beads. Her growing children occupied the rest of her waking moments.

In the meantime, the women of Belair Cove were on the alert. They were busy trying to find Jean Marc a match. "One of our kind. That's what he needs now, somebody like Lena Breaux."

Jean Marc's heart was heavy and he wanted nothing to do with this. "Ain't got nuthin' to do with Lena. I'm just best suited to roam the backlands. I don't want another wife."

Although Angelique and Damon had settled into a comfortable truce of sorts over the past year, he too was watching. They usually worked together by day and went their separate ways at sundown—he to the Fist to Cuffs and she to her mending, sleeping alone. A cross word between them was rare. Nevertheless, Angelique was not surprised when Damon started to stay close to home most evenings.

One Saturday after working in the fields, Damon joined his family on the front porch as they sorted beans. He removed his shirt, dipped his hands into the cool water of the small metal tub near the doorway, and washed away the grime. He turned his shirt inside out, used it to dry off, and glanced at Angelique. She had not said a word since he stepped onto the porch. Her head was bent, her shoulders arched, and her fingers moved swiftly, snapping green beans into a large bowl, snap, snap, snap.

Damon had always thought she was beautiful. Even after all the upheaval of the last few years, her beauty transcended their trials. She reminded him of morning dew on scented wildflowers, fresh and clean. Damon gave the girls a conspiratorial wink and put his finger to his lips. He scrunched up his shoulders, raised his arms high, and swung them wide. He tiptoed toward Angelique. An unsuspecting Angelique found herself suddenly lifted out of her seat and twirled around. The bowl crashed to the floor and beans scattered everywhere.

"Huh, Damon Vidrine, look what you done. Put me down." Angelique caught sight of her girls as they collapsed in a fit of giggles. Her heart lightened and she relaxed. "You girls were in on this trick, well, then, you got lots of beans to gather up. You heard me. Every single one." She pretended impatience.

The girls dropped down on all fours. They scoured the ground tossing snapped green beans back into the empty bowl. Damon continued to press Angelique to him until the sound of horses distracted him.

Lena Breaux's brothers galloped past, yelling and waving their family flag, "Hey Damon, y'all comin' to the dance?" While Damon considered the question, one of the brothers noticed Jean Marc approaching from the opposite direction and extended the invitation to him as well.

Jean Marc hesitated when he saw Damon on the porch with his family, but then he waved. Damon ignored him, grabbed Angelique, and danced her across the porch. Jean Marc turned his back away from the cheery scene.

"Angelique, what say we all go to that dance tonight?"

Adelaide and Carrie held their breath waiting for her answer. Angelique looked from one to the other. "I suppose it would be fine." They squealed in delight.

That evening, while Damon remained outside drinking beer, Angelique tapped her foot, played her fiddle, and reveled in the music that she loved. Angelique and Papa played duets until the music escalated to a fever pitch and the crowd screamed for more. During breaks, she visited with the women and collected tidbits of news from around the Cove.

The weeks went by swiftly. Life with Damon was tolerable. One Sunday, Angelique was surprised to find Damon standing in the doorway dressed for church. "Pack a picnic basket, and after church, I'll take y'all out to the bayou."

Angelique agreed. "That would be lovely."

Damon paddled the pirogue down the muddy bayou. The pirogue dipped as Angelique leaned over pointing to a patch of yellow-green leaves spilling over on the side of the bank.

"Oh, Damon, quick, paddle over there. Eula Mae's been asking me to get a sample of that jasmine."

"Watch out or you gonna send us all over the side. Now, this the last time I'm gonna stop for you. A man's gotta eat. Y'all hungry too, ain't ya girls?"

They ate heartily of the meal that Angelique scraped together at the last minute. Afterwards, she rested in the crook of a fallen limb soaking up the sun. Damon played hide and seek with Adelaide. Their laughter rang out through the piney woods. Carrie busied herself gathering leaves and flowers and brought them to Angelique.

"What's this one called, Mama? What's that one, Mama?" Carrie sneezed.

"That's goldenrod," Angelique answered.

Angelique pulled a few mint leaves from the pile she had gathered and crushed them in her palm for Carrie to smell. Her eyes lit up because she recognized the familiar scent. "I know that one. Tha's mint."

Angelique laughed. "Eula Mae will be very proud of you."

Evening found them roasting peanuts and Damon telling tall tales by candlelight. Once again, Angelique couldn't help feeling that Damon's attentiveness had come too late. Angelique could not bend toward his efforts, not even for her children. She could not bring herself to forgive and trust him. Experience had taught her that this would not last. Angelique remained reticent toward Damon. He stood in the way of what she wanted most: Jean Marc.

Angelique knew she could never act on her heart's desire. She was married and the mother of two children. If only something would happen to Damon, then she too would be free. Angelique dared not confess her sinful wish to her parish priest.

Damon kept a vigilant watch in spite of the fact that Jean Marc had settled into a routine and bothered no one. Damon began to hound Angelique to account for her whereabouts. Angelique resented Damon's constant intrusion. The fragile truce faded, and they began to argue.

It was understandable that Angelique would refuse Jean Marc's offer to ride in his buggy. She and the girls were walking back from

Ville Platte when he slowed down and called out to them, "Hey there, pretty ladies. Want a ride?"

"No thanks, it ain't much further."

"Don't be silly. Get in. Besides what would people think if I left y'all standin' here like this?" Jean Marc teased.

Carrie climbed into the buggy before Angelique could stop her. Adelaide was tired from carrying a heavy bag of flour in her arms, and she did not hesitate either. They rode home with the girls squeezed in between them.

Jean Marc started the conversation. "Last time you gonna get to ride in this fancy buggy. Sold it this mornin' to some folks in Opelousas. They bought it sight unseen. Antoine vouched for me on the phone. They comin' over next Saturday to pick it up."

"Why you sellin' it Mr. Jean Marc?"

"Carrie, a man like me has no need for a fine buggy the likes of this one here. Besides, I still got my old one in the barn, that'll do just fine if I need it. Can't imagine why though."

Angelique inquired, "How are you, really, Jean Marc?"

"I'm gettin' along as best to be expected, I guess. I sure do miss her, though. Angelique I want to thank you for all your kindness towards Elizabeth. It meant a lot to me for her to have a friend."

"I'm glad I got to know her. She was real special."

Jean Marc pretended to clear his throat. "That she was. Well, enough of that. Tell me what's goin' on over at your place. Is Damon gettin' ready to plant?" Their conversation shifted to weather, beans, and planting until they pulled up in front of her house.

Carrie waved and squealed, "Papa, Papa look at us. We rode all the way home in the buggy."

Damon was working on the side of the house sharpening the old plow. He lowered the plow to the ground. It fell with a loud thud. He walked over to the buggy, fists clinched.

"Afternoon, Damon. I found these three lovely ladies back there on the road a ways."

Jean Marc lifted Carrie and handed her to Damon. Damon set her down and reached for Adelaide. He glared at Jean Marc and spoke through clenched teeth.

"To be sure, Angelique's been a hankerin' for a fancy buggy like you got here, Jean Marc." Damon said his name like a bullet hitting a target and smiled a smile that never reached his eyes.

"Seems to me like a waste of good money. Yessiree. I got no need for prideful things. My womenfolk are used to ridin' in the wagon or walkin'. I thank you kindly for givin' 'em a lift this time. Y'all go on inside. Angelique, get down from there." Fully expecting her to follow, Damon fixed his eyes on Angelique and then walked away.

Jean Marc shot back, "What's ailin' you, Damon? To my way of thinkin', I'm glad I bought Lizzie this fancy buggy when I did. It made her happy for a while."

Angelique stumbled and stuttered as she stepped out of the buggy unattended. "Jean Marc, I, I appreciate your kindness. The girls really enjoyed the ride."

Jean Marc eyed a package wrapped in brown paper sitting on the floorboard. "Angelique, you forgot somethin'." He jumped down to hand Angelique the parcel. She reached out to accept the package. On instinct, Jean Marc ran the knuckles of his fingers down the bare skin of her lower arm as she took the parcel from him.

It took only a second for Jean Marc to feel the familiar stirring and convey his feelings to her. He had done it without measuring any possible consequences. The realization hit him hard and he tore his eyes from her lovely face and looked away.

Damon was watching. Damon knew all too well the look of desire in a man's eyes. It was clear to him that Jean Marc still had feelings for Angelique. That evening, he left the house right after supper and headed for the nearest tavern.

Sunday Church

The seasons passed swiftly. Adelaide and Carrie were sprouting faster than prairie grass. Adelaide squirmed as Angelique separated another strand of wet hair and twirled it around a narrow strip of cloth. She twisted the hair into a knot and secured the too-tight curl near her scalp. Eula Mae had taught Angelique well. Little bits of bright scraps of fabric stuck out all over Adelaide's head.

Angelique scolded, "Hold still. Just you wait and see. Tomorrow you will have beautiful bouncy curls when you waltz into church. This is the last one."

Adelaide tugged at her curlers to release the tension on her scalp. "I just look silly."

Carrie giggled as she watched from the old metal tub.

Angelique swatted the back of Adelaide's hand. "Leave 'em alone."

"Carrie, now you scrub behind those ears. I swear, once a week ain't enough to get you girls clean. Lord, your papa needs to quit hauling y'all around like little puppies."

Adelaide teased Carrie, "You can laugh, but guess what? You're next."

As usual, Angelique struggled to make Adelaide mind. Damon kept his daughter close to his side; she had become a notorious tomboy. Adelaide could spit farther and fight tougher than any of the boys could. She had proven herself a good shot when hunting. Carrie, on the other hand, preferred the company of her mama and begged to stay home. She preferred to chase ducks, pick wildflowers, and play with her dolls.

Carrie flung her long hair from side to side. "My hair has lots a bounce, Mama. I don't need them curlers. It's Adelaide's straight hair that ain't ever gonna curl no matter what you do, not mine."

Adelaide stuck out her tongue at her younger sister.

Angelique snapped, "Quit that teasin', the both of you. Y'all are sisters. You gotta look out for each other. It's off to bed with you,

Adelaide. And don't forget to say your prayers. Carrie, dry off and get over here. That wavy hair of yours needs some tamin'."

The rooster flew up to his perch atop the fence post and crowed at the light of dawn. Angelique padded across the floor with hot *café au lait* and buttered biscuits on a tray. The girls' dresses lay on a nearby chair, starched and ironed, ready to wear. She woke them with a nudge.

"Wake up, wake up sleepy heads, I've got a special treat for you this mornin'. Your papa is ready to go, so hurry along."

Adelaide bounced out of bed, ripped out the scraps of fabric wound about her head, and tossed them to the floor. She dressed hastily. "I want to sit by Papa."

Carrie clawed at her curlers, tossed her hair about, and scratched her head. Her hair fell in ringlets. "Mama, why doesn't Papa ever come to church?"

"You just hush and don't let Papa hear you talkin' like that."

Angelique lifted Carrie's arms, placed her dress over her head, and wriggled it down. She wrapped a ribbon around her tiny waist and tied a bow snugly at the back. Angelique inspected Carrie's appearance, and then she hugged her daughter.

"There, a perfect bow. You look mighty pretty."

Carrie took a last bite of her breakfast before they all scrambled out the door. "Hooray! We takin' the wagon and don't have to walk. Ville Platte sure is far, Papa."

Damon lifted the girls into the wagon one by one.

"Carrie's right, Damon, there ain't no sense in us walkin' anymore now that you got the wagon fixed."

Adelaide looked at her Papa. "I don't mind walkin'."

Damon rewarded Adelaide with a conspiratorial wink. "Tha's my girl. Ain't nuthin' wrong with takin' to your feet."

Angelique pulled herself up into the wagon without any help and they headed into town riding in silence, each holding tightly to their own opinions.

Carrie located the cotton gin in the distance. "I see it first. I win the penny."

Ville Platte had grown tremendously over the last ten years. On Main Street, going from east to west, the train depot, cotton gin, and

Blacksmith Shop came first. On the opposite side of the street was the church. Sylvester's Mercantile stood next to the church. The Fist to Cuffs and the Buckhorn Saloons were right in the middle of town across from each other. Scattered in between the two were the bank, the lawyer's office, telegraph office, and several other small places of business.

The wagon bumped over several deep ruts that sent the family bouncing like Roly Poly balls. They grabbed on to the sides of the wagon and held on tight until they arrived at their destination. Damon slowed and came to a halt in front of the Fist to Cuffs Saloon.

"Sooner or later one of them newfangled cars of Henry Ford's gonna try to make its way here. When that happens, y'all gonna see, they do somethin' about this damn road. You women folk pray hard, now hear."

He handed Angelique the reins, stepped down, and gave her a friendly wink. Felix Soileau was leaning against the horse railing waiting for Damon. The two walked into the Fist to Cuffs together.

"How's the blacksmithing business, old friend? Sure wish I had your kind of money. I could do some bettin' then."

Angelique jiggled the reins and guided the mules farther up the street. When they arrived at the church, the girls filed in behind Angelique like yellow ducklings. Adelaide's thin curls were already limp and frizzy in the early morning humidity. Carrie brushed a stray curl away from her face and puffed out like a Bantam rooster, her thick ringlets bounced as she walked. Carrie slowed down when she noticed Jean Marc sitting alone at the end of a pew and waved eagerly as they passed him by.

He lit up when he saw Carrie and whispered, "Don't you look mighty pretty this morning?"

Carrie rewarded him with a broad smile. "Mama set my hair last night."

"*Psst.*" Angelique frowned and signaled for Carrie to follow.

Angelique chose a pew near the altar as far away from Jean Marc as possible. Father Avi climbed the spiral staircase to the top of the pulpit, which stood like a chariot high above the congregation. Father Avi's black robes strained against his bulging waistline as he grabbed hold of the sides of the pulpit and leaned over his congregation. Vengeance and punishment were the themes of most of his homilies. Today, he sermonized about a God filled with wrath, a God with no mercy. Both Adelaide and Carrie quickly tucked themselves securely on either side of Angelique. She understood the kind of fear that rises up with this kind of preaching, she wrapped her arms around her children.

Grand-mère had taught Angelique her catechism. She had been a well-educated French woman and mean as hell. She would strut into the back room of Sacred Heart Chapel, where all the Sunday school students squirmed anxiously. She wore long dresses with three-quarter-length sleeves and carried her Bible under one arm and a buggy whip under the other. That whip met with Damon and Jean Marc's backsides on more than one occasion and struck fear in Angelique.

Angelique could still remember how *Grand-mère* chastised the older girls in the evils of sin. "Every part of you has to be covered. Never show your shoulders. If you tempt a man, you're sinning because you made him sin in wanting."

Angelique loved the traditions of the church, but had long since abandoned some of *Grand-mère's* interpretations of the Bible. She favored a loving God. She looked down at her girls and hugged them closer to her. The Mass ended and the congregation stood up to sing *"Ave Maria."*

Marie Rose whispered to Antoine as they were leaving, "That devil, Damon, ain't with her again this Sunday."

Antoine patted her arm. "It best you mind your own business. Damon ain't seen the inside of church in a long time. I'm thinkin' she better off by herself."

Angelique loaded the girls into the wagon and left quickly to avoid any conversation with Marie Rose. She did not stop until she reached the Fist to Cuffs. Adelaide jumped down, ran to the door, and called out to her Papa. The three of them continued to wait while wagons coming from church rolled on by. The noonday sun beat down on them. Sweat ran down Angelique's cleavage as she sat upright and stared straight ahead. Friends and acquaintances in the passing buggies pretended not to notice her sitting there.

Carrie fell asleep in Angelique's lap. Adelaide pulled a small red ball from the pocket of her dress and bounced it repeatedly against the wooden sidewalk, caught it, and then bounced it again. Giving up on Damon, Adelaide faced the saloon doors and sat cross-legged. Finally, the doors burst open and Damon stumbled out.

"Well, there's my little darlin'." He lifted Adelaide and spun her around before setting her down in the back of the wagon.

"I done won me a whole heap of cash today. Musta been all that prayin'."

Damon winked at Angelique. She breathed a sigh of relief. It was going to be a good Sunday.

"Yessiree, Lady Luck was good to your papa today." he took the reins from Angelique and kissed her roughly. His breath tasted of whiskey, his humiliation of her complete.

Angelique was repulsed. *How much longer can I continue to live like this?*

Running Away

Angelique listened for the distant sound that would signal their salvation. She loosened her white-knuckled grip on the small suitcase, placed it on the ground, and reached for the latch to the gate. In spite of what the church taught about the sacrament of marriage, Angelique was going to leave this life behind; her marriage to Damon was a failure. It had not taken long to save the money for the train tickets. On those evenings when Damon left home to drink and gamble, Angelique had taken in mending. She would fall asleep stitching beside the kerosene lamp. Patience was her friend, and eventually she scraped up enough for the tickets.

Damon's insults, framed as jokes, had become insufferable. Angelique resisted holding on to his words, and she refused to let his insults settle in her bones. However, he had too much influence over Adelaide. She began to imitate him. Adelaide would roll her big eyes to the edge of her dark, thick lashes, place her hands on her hips, and use his tone of voice when speaking. Her words were harsh and demanding. Spanking her with a hickory switch had not helped.

Yesterday's incidence in the bedroom convinced Angelique that it was time for her to leave. Before getting dressed, Angelique had paused to stare at the reflection of her maturing body in the mirror when her husband's sudden appearance startled her. "Damon, what you doin' in here?"

"What you think. Lookin' at my wife. It's my right to and don't you forget dat. You belong to me, Angelique."

Damon tugged on her clothes as she attempted to shy away from him and dress quickly. The tug of war persisted with each garment. He finally relinquished her blouse. Angelique tucked her blouse in as Adelaide walked into the room.

"Oh, by the way, did you get the word? There's gonna be a *boucherie*, Jean Marc's family gonna butcher a hog, on Saturday."

Damon turned to Adelaide and asked, "Want to go to a *boucherie*?" Then, he steadied his gaze on Angelique; his eyes took in the full length of her. "Yep, to my way of thinkin' I'm lookin' at a big fat hog that I could bring to the *boucherie*." He burst out laughing and made grunting sounds like a pig.

Adelaide joined in, "Oink, oink, oink."

Angelique lifted her eyes from Adelaide to her husband. His cruel words sliced through her like a dagger.

"Aw, girl, I'm teasin'. I wouldn't say such a thing if it was the truth. What's wrong with you anyway?'

Again, Adelaide chimed in with her father. "Yeah, what's wrong with you?"

Angelique tapped Adelaide on her bottom. "Adelaide, don't you talk to me that way. It's disrespectful."

"Papa done it first."

Angelique vowed to separate her daughters from Damon's influence. It was time. She struggled to secure the latch of the rickety old gate without making a sound. It crumbled at her touch, one more thing that Damon promised to fix and never got around to doing. She gazed at the rust stains on her palms and dusted them off. Angelique motioned to the girls to pass through.

Adelaide resisted. "Where we goin'? It's spooky out here."

"Shh," Angelique placed her fingers to her lips, "Quiet."

Adelaide stuck her tongue out at her mother. "I don't have to listen to you. I want to go back inside."

"Hush, I told you."

Fog settled in around the three of them as they walked away. Trying to focus on the sharecropper's shack where she had grown up, Angelique scanned the horizon. A black family presently occupied it now. *Papa would forgive her. She would write to him eventually. In a letter, she could write all of the things that she could not say to him face to face. Eula Mae could make him understand.*

She heard the faint sound of the train whistle in the distance. "Hurry girls, or we gonna be too late to catch the train."

"Where we goin'?" Adelaide yelled.

"Washington, Louisiana, to visit your cousins."

Angelique had responded to a help-wanted ad in the paper; the job at a church rectory with room and board would be just fine.

Adelaide persisted, "Is Papa gonna come later?"

Angelique ignored Adelaide and pulled her coat collar tighter around her neck. The sun would not come up for several hours. She saw no one on the road ahead. She had trusted no one with her plans.

Suddenly, Damon grabbed Angelique by the scruff of her neck. "Angelique, where the hell you think you're goin'?"

She tried to jerk free. "Damon, stop it! You're hurtin' me."

Adelaide and Carrie whimpered. Damon yanked the suitcase from Angelique's hand. Tightening his hold on her neck, he forced her to turn back and head home. Adelaide scrambled to keep up with them.

"What's wrong Papa? I didn't want to go. She made me."

Once inside, he threw the suitcase against the wall. Carrie screamed and ran to her mother for protection. Damon pulled her away from Angelique.

"Adelaide, take your sister," Damon ordered. "Y'all go on back to bed right now. Your mama's got it wrong. Y'all ain't goin' nowhere."

Adelaide scrambled to obey. Angelique waited until the children were out of sight. "I can't take it here no more," she screamed. "You ain't no kind of husband to me. I do most of the work around here anyway and you, you drink and gamble. There ain't ever enough to make ends meet. I want somethin' more for my girls."

Damon pointed toward the fields. "Who you think been sweatin' behind that plow all day? I work my butt off in that damn field. Work, work and work some more. This ain't livin'. This ain't nuthin' but hell on earth."

"That's not true. You spend most of your week at the Fist to Cuffs, not here. I'm the one doin' all the sweatin'."

"Bitch, bitch, bitch, that's all you ever do."

Angelique threw herself at Damon. He grabbed both of her wrists in his hands and held her forcibly. Angelique let herself fall to the floor like a ragdoll. Damon released his hold and stomped out of the house.

Angelique unlaced her shoes and removed them slowly. She struggled to rise from this defeat. She slammed the bedroom door shut, kept to her side of the bed, tucked her knees into her chest, and pulled the covers tight around her.

When Damon heard the door to their bedroom slam, his whole body shook with boundless rage. He exploded back into the house and put his fist through the bedroom door, which sent it crashing against the wall.

"This is my house. You ain't got no rights here and you ain't goin' nowhere. Ever. You hear me?" He dragged Angelique from beneath the covers as Adelaide stepped into the room.

"Papa?"

"Get back to bed, you hear me?" Adelaide hustled out of the room in tears. Angelique remained limp and motionless. If she chose not to argue with him, she could claim, at least, that one small victory for herself.

Damon kicked the bedpost and stormed out. He slammed the back door and beat the wall of their bedroom from the outside. He slammed his fist into the nearby tree only to step away bloodied. He cursed under his breath. He picked up the axe wedged in the tree stump and tested the sharpness of the blade. He felt the smooth hard handle and laid it on his shoulder. His anger not yet spent, he walked over to the woodpile, grabbed a log, and set it down on the stump. With one powerful blow, he split the log in two.

In the house, Angelique listened. She had no more tears to shed. Adelaide and Carrie listened. Chop, chop, chop!

Damon chopped until dawn; his muscles ached from the pain of it. His breathing slowed, and his clothes were soaked through. He dropped the ax and sat on the ground amongst the remnants of scattered wood.

Angelique held her breath, the sudden quiet more frightening than the sound of the axe. She waited. Nothing.

Damon lit a cigarette and looked out over the prairie as the sun rose. He rubbed his hand over his bad leg. The dampness always made it hurt. A tear slid down his cheek and he quickly wiped it away. "Damn you, Angelique. I ain't ever gonna let you go."

Angelique woke to Carrie tapping her on the arm. She picked her daughter up and placed her in the empty bed. "Good morning, my little chickadee." Carrie snuggled close to her mother and giggled.

Angelique rose to face the day. She unpacked the suitcase, folded each garment neatly, and placed them back into the bureau drawers. She shoved the suitcase under her side of the bed and stepped into the kitchen. The back door was wide open. Angelique edged toward the door and peeked out into the yard. Shards of splintered wood lay scattered all about.

"*Ca ne fait pas rien,*" she whispered. Never mind the splintered wood, never mind the splintered life, Angelique pushed the door shut.

Broken Fences

Jean Marc had taken a shortcut across the east pasture when he saw Damon's mules lazing in the sun under a nearby tree. Beating a path to his cornfield, the mules had tramped through his garden and left the vegetables in ruins. Jean Marc waved his arms about and cursed the scoundrels. "Git, you, git on back over there." He chased the mules back across the broken fence.

Angelique had Damon's shirt pressed against the scrub board when Jean Marc's curses echoed across the distance to her ears. She tossed the shirt back into the tub of soapy water and peeked out from behind the house. Angelique dashed across the field. She met Jean Marc half way and helped him chase the mules toward the corral. "I'll get the gate," she yelled.

Once the mules were safely fenced in, Angelique turned to him. "I sure am sorry about that. Those old mules got a mind of their own."

Jean Marc could not control his anger. "It ain't your fault, Angelique. This is Damon's doin'. Irresponsible ass, tha's what he is." He regretted his harsh words the minute that they were spoken. "I'm sorry you got to put up with that. I'll take care of the fence. You don't worry yourself none about this. You hear?"

Tramping back to his tool shed, he gathered up a few tools and returned to repair the broken fencing. He tore off his shirt, cut a few notches into the cypress boards, and began fitting them in place. Jean Marc gripped each board and tugged from front to back making sure they were secure.

Angelique hurried into her kitchen. She found Adelaide sitting idle by the hearth. "Where's Carrie? You supposed to be watchin' her."

"I was, until *Grand-mère* took over."

Angelique threw open the shutters above the basin while she worked. From there, she could observe Jean Marc's progress and judge her time. Grabbing a large basket that hung overhead, she carefully selected an assortment of vegetables that she had freshly picked from the garden that morning.

Angelique called out, "Adelaide, get on out to the east pasture and tell *Monsieur* Jean Marc to wait there until I come."

Adelaide put her hands on her hips in protest.

"Adelaide, do as you're told. Go on or I'll take a switch to you."

Angelique filled a small jar with water and tightened the lid. She wedged the jar between the cucumbers. With the basket secured in the crook of one arm, she tried to tame her unruly hair with her free hand. It was a futile effort. She tore off her apron and rushed back.

"That'll do Adelaide. You done good. Get on back and help your *Grand-mère* with Carrie."

"What if I don't want to?" Adelaide whined.

"Go on back like I told you and tend to your sister."

"Adelaide, you ought to listen to your mama."

Jean Marc's words slipped out before he caught himself. He should never have interfered in Angelique's affairs, but that one needed to show her mama some respect. She needed a firm hand.

"I ain't got to listen to you. You ain't my papa."

"Adelaide, that's enough. You get on home and wait for me by the back steps. We gonna have words."

Angelique apologized as Adelaide marched off, "That one's a handful." She handed Jean Marc the jar of water.

Jean Marc drank in quick gulps. Water ran down his chin and glistened on his skin. "Aw, she's got fire for sure. Reminds me of a pretty little thing I once knew." His eyes pierced Angelique and a sudden rosy rush of color settled on her cheeks. He wiped his chin and eyed the basket. "Tha's for me?"

"For your trouble. Picked these fresh this mornin'."

Fresh okra, tomatoes, cucumbers and summer squash filled the basket. Jean Marc looked inside, plucked a plump ripe tomato, and bit into it. "Um um. Delicious. Sweet, too."

"Well if I woulda thought you were that hungry, I woulda washed them vegetables for you."

"Aw, a little dirt ain't never hurt nobody."

Jean Marc tugged on the fence once more. "Looks like she'll hold."

"Like I said, I'm mighty sorry about the mules."

"Ain't nuthin' I can't handle." Jean Marc slipped his shirt over his head, gathered up his tools, and took the basket from her. "Y'all have a good evening." They walked off in opposite directions. Both turned to look back, only once.

Jean Marc had a vexing problem. Angry and frustrated about the events of that afternoon, he wanted to resolve the issue for the last time. He positioned himself near the Fist to Cuffs and the Buckhorn Saloons and waited for Damon to show up. As Damon approached, he was deep in conversation with his drinking companion, Felix Soileau. Jean Marc stepped out in front of them and blocked their path.

Damon tried to shove Jean Marc out of his way. "What the hell? What's ailin' you, Jean Marc?"

"You're what's ailin' me. You owe me four bits for damages done by your mules. I'm gettin' my money one way or the other."

"Jean Marc, what you talkin' about, I don't owe you nuthin'. Felix, let's go. I need a drink." The two men tried to step around him.

Jean Marc blocked their path and inched closer to Damon. "I done told you. For fixin' my fence. That's what. Your mules keep comin' across and you ain't done nuthin' about it. Tha's a problem for me and a bigger problem for you. I get my money before you get your drink."

"You ain't ever gonna get nuthin' tha's mine, you hear me?"

Damon threw the first punch. Jean Marc recovered easily and went after him with all his strength. The two men tumbled into the street, fists flying. Years of pent up anger exploded. They pummeled each other; and neither of the two would give up.

Felix backed away, threw open the saloon doors, and shouted, "Fight! It's a fight!"

Men from both saloons poured out into the street. Jean Marc's cousin tried to step in and break up the fight. Uncle Gus grabbed his arm and held him back. "Son, this one is long overdue. Let it alone."

They tossed money on the top of an oak barrel and laid down bets. By the time the sheriff showed up, Jean Marc had Damon pinned to the ground and was pummeling him. The sheriff motioned to Felix to help him peel Jean Marc off Damon.

"That's enough. You boys break it up or y'all gonna be coolin' y'all heels in jail tonight."

Jean Marc broke free from their grasp, bent over Damon, and reached into his pockets. He counted out the four bits owed to him. Jean Marc threw the rest of the money on the ground at Damon's feet. "Sheriff, I ain't wantin' no trouble, just want what's owed me."

Damon struggled to rise and bent over to gather the coins scattered in the dirt. He wiped his bloody nose and cursed Jean Marc. "You ain't nuthin' but a sorry rotten bastard." Damon hobbled away with Felix and headed into the Fist to Cuffs.

The sheriff turned to the onlookers. "Y'all go on. Ain't nuthin' left to see. Fight's over."

Jean Marc walked across the street to the Buckhorn, dropped the coins on the top of the bar, and drank until the money was gone. Uncle Gus sat beside him without saying a word.

Back at home, Jean Marc lay awake for hours mulling over the problem. Nothing was going to change. He had to come up with a plan.

Antoine Sylvester was at the Buckhorn for a nightcap after closing the mercantile, and reported the whole incident to Marie Rose. "You shoulda heard folks; most believe that whippin' was long past due. They were glad of it too. Why, everyone around here is fed up with the likes of Damon Vidrine."

After chasing Damon's mules out of his field again the next day, Jean Marc straightened his disheveled clothes, dusted himself off, and headed for the Breaux's place. He was not going to let this latest frustration spoil the event. Last week, Jean Marc accepted an invitation to a *cochon de lait*, roast-suckling pig. It was an all-day affair, and he had been looking forward to it.

It would not be like the first time he visited the Breaux's house after Elizabeth died; each occasion became easier. He felt less guilty for finding any pleasure in anyone's company. Still, he was careful not to give Lena Breaux any false hope. He was pleasantly surprised to find Lena flirting with one of Marie Rose's brothers when he arrived.

Jean Marc feasted on the pork and cracklins, drank a few beers, and played cards. On leaving, a tipsy Jean Marc teased old Mrs.

Breaux, "Kind of you folks to have me over. If you weren't spoken for by that old coot sittin' over there, I'd guess somebody would snatch a pretty little thing like you up just like that." Jean Marc snapped his fingers.

Mr. Breaux responded, "You too late to snare a Breaux, Jean Marc. Even my Lena found her another fella."

"Lena don't want no old has-been like me. I think Lena done made her a fine match."

Jean Marc carried home a small platter of sausage from the *cochon de lait*. This would fit right into his plan. There was much to do if he was going to rid himself of those stubborn mules. Jean Marc reached into his pocket for the raw pigskin he had pilfered. He cut the skin into tiny squares. He rolled the squares up tightly and held them securely in place with thread retrieved from Elizabeth's sewing basket.

The next morning, Jean Marc inspected his handiwork. He picked up two chunks of pigskin and shook them around in his big hand like dice. He threw them down on the table. The dried pigskin rattled noisily.

Jean Marc walked to the fireplace and lifted "Essie" from her resting place. He returned to the table and loaded the double-barreled shotgun with the recycled shells. Then he positioned himself in front of the window and checked his view through a knothole in the closed shutters. He crossed his left leg over his right at the ankle and propped the gun up on his knee.

"Now, Damon. Let's see what you got to say about this."

Running his hands over the smooth barrel, Jean Marc studied the shotgun while he waited. He caressed the intricate diamond pattern carved into the wooden handle, and admired the metal plate on the butt of the gun, the embossed hunting dog with a bird in its mouth. He nibbled on the cold sausage from last night.

He recalled the day his stepfather gave him the shotgun. He had set it down quietly on the table. Wrapped in brown sackcloth and tied with a string at the top, the gun was easily identifiable. Jean Marc was hesitant to remove it from the bag. "This is for me? Are you sure? Musta cost a lot of money."

Jean Marc's mother quickly picked it up and handed it to him. "Son, never look a gift horse in the mouth. Take it."

Jean Marc had taken the gun out of the sack and whistled. He looked up at his parents. They seemed somber and strained. The air was thick with tension. His stepfather had walked silently out of the room. When Jean Marc thought back over the years, there had been other occasions like this, moments of undefined discomfort.

Damon had a similar gun, and Jean Marc had marveled at the coincidence when he first moved to Belair Cove. He had fond memories of the first time the two of them spent the night in the woods. They had camped out in the backlands, not returning until daylight. They had what they thought was an impressive kill. Jean Marc recalled the words of his Indian mother when he returned from that first hunt. Attached to his belt were more pelts than they could eat.

"Nature is a fragile thing my son. Take what you need and no more. Make sure you give back to mother earth. Be grateful for bird, rabbit, and deer."

Jean Marc felt ashamed and vowed to honor her words. Today, unusual circumstances called for unusual measures. The years of friendship between him and Damon had been undone. At this point, he could only wish things had been different. Jean Marc eyed the knothole once more. He fingered the trigger.

Damon set his mules out to pasture earlier than usual that morning. Jean Marc watched, sharp-eyed, as Damon knocked out the top board of a section of fencing that made it easier for his mules to cross.

Jean Marc confirmed, "Just as I suspected." He waited until Damon waved his hat at the mules, guided them toward the break in the fence, and turned his back to Jean Marc. Damon went back into his house and shut the door. Jean Marc lifted the shotgun to his shoulder as the mules tramped through his garden.

"Sorry, old fellas."

Jean Marc took careful aim and pulled the trigger. He saw one old mule yelp and kick up his heels at the sting. Jean Marc took aim at the other and pulled the trigger again. Jean Marc repeated the practice for several days. On the third day, the mules took off running into the backlands.

That evening, Damon exploded into the Buckhorn. "What you done to my mules? I ain't seen them in days. I've been lookin' for 'em everywhere. You done somethin' bad to 'em."

Jean Marc looked up from his plate of steamed rice and gravy. He dropped his fork onto the tin plate. "I don't know what you're talkin' about Damon. Go home. Go on home to your family." His voice cut through the room like a sharp blade.

Damon stepped back.

"You leave my family out of this. I'm gonna get you for this Jean Marc. I'll teach you not to mess with me."

Jean Marc pointed his finger at Damon. "And you just better keep your mules off my property."

The One-Room School

The Cove had educated its own since the days when the first settlers cleared the land and planted deep roots. The rich soil offered opportunity and challenge. The backlands and the bayou were a welcome source of nourishment. Beyond the basics, that was all the education anyone had ever needed, at least, until Miss Brown stepped off the train with her satchel and small trunk of books.

Adelaide held no affection for Miss Brown. She had paid Otille, a classmate, to tell Miss Brown that she was sick. And sick she was. School held no interest for her. No one would have been the wiser had Jean Marc not found her playing in the ditch that day.

Adelaide resisted when Jean Marc picked her up onto his saddle. "Adelaide, I ain't leavin' you out here like this. You're supposed to be in school. There's a problem here, and your mama got to know."

Adelaide held the pummel with a firm grip as Jean Marc urged his horse forward. They rounded the bend in a cloud of dust. Carrie was playing on the porch with her ragdoll. She squinted at the bright sun and the approaching horse that was racing toward her. When they got closer, she recognized Mr. Jean Marc, and then she realized it was Adelaide seated in front of him.

"Mama, you'd better come quick."

Angelique stepped out onto the porch drying her hands on her apron. "Jean Marc? What in God's name…?"

Jean Marc dismounted, hanging on to Adelaide, who kicked and screamed at the top of her lungs.

"Look here, I don't mean to meddle none 'cus you might already know. I suppose it's all right if Adelaide ain't been goin' to school? Yesterday, she was out back by the bayou. Today, I found her in the ditch trying to catch crawfish with a net."

Jean Marc handed Angelique the lunch tin she had prepared for Adelaide that morning. Mud covered both Adelaide and the lunch pail. Adelaide hissed, "This ain't none a ya business."

"You hush child. You got some explainin' to do, as soon as you apologize to Mr. Jean Marc. You should be grateful that he done brought you home before Lord knows what happened to you. Jean Marc, you can set her down now. She'll behave or else."

Adelaide squirmed out of Jean Marc's grip and mumbled a curt apology.

"That's better. Spill it out, girl. What's got into you? Why you skippin' school?"

Adelaide rushed the telling of her story. As she spoke, she brushed a tear from her face, but they soon became heart-wrenching sobs as the sad tale unfolded. Her new teacher, Miss Louisa Brown, had announced that the children could not speak French at school anymore. She insisted on English only.

Miss Brown had chosen to make an example out of Adelaide. After recess, Adelaide needed to visit the outhouse. In her haste, she had forgotten the rule and made her request in French. Miss Brown had written the word "dunce" with a black crayon on white paper, and she shaped it into a hat. She made Adelaide sit on a stool at the front of the class with the pointed hat on her head—and wet pants—for the rest of the school day.

"This should teach all of you a good lesson." Miss Brown walked to the chalkboard and wrote in huge capital letters, ENGLISH ONLY.

Adelaide brushed away the last of her tears and placed both hands on her hips. "That's when I decided I don't need no more schoolin'."

Jean Marc curled his fingers into fists. "Whoever heard of such a thing? I ought to go down there and take a stick to that Miss Brown."

Adelaide brightened.

"Jean Marc, I thank you kindly but this is a matter that I'll handle myself," Angelique replied. He left while they went inside. Angelique put on her bonnet and her shoes.

"Adelaide, get washed up. We're goin' to school."

Even though Adelaide was a handful, this rule seemed unreasonable. Adelaide must be leaving out some part of the story. Angelique and Adelaide walked up the steps of the one-room schoolhouse and stood in the open doorway. Miss Brown continued her geography lesson. Angelique whispered to Adelaide to sit in her assigned seat.

Miss Brown smirked. "Well, Adelaide, I can assume you are feeling better and prepared to resume your lessons."

Otille lowered his head as if in deep concentration. He had lied to Miss Brown. Adelaide had paid him a whole penny to tell Miss Brown she was ill.

Miss Brown walked to the door to greet Angelique. "You must be Adelaide's mother."

"Miss Brown, I need a word with you please. Adelaide ain't been sick."

"Wasn't sick," Miss Brown, corrected.

Angelique sucked in air. "Miss Brown, it's very important to me that Adelaide get a good education."

"Then we are in agreement."

"No ma'am, I don't believe we are."

Miss Brown turned to her students. "Children, we are going to have an early recess this morning. Everybody line up and go on outside. I will ring the bell when recess is over."

They were happy to obey. The children lined up like toy soldiers before making their escape into the yard. Vying for positions at various games, they raced to particular quadrants of the playground.

Miss Brown stiffened. "Mrs. Vidrine, I don't understand."

"Adelaide ain't comin' to school because you won't let her talk French."

"I have been sent here with strict orders from the parish school board. Only English is to be spoken in this classroom."

"Yes ma'am, I want her speakin' English good, but I think there might be a better way to get Adelaide on your side."

"Well. You want her to speak English well."

Miss Brown shook her head, turned away from Angelique, and began straightening a student's belongings on a nearby desk. She began arranging the items to her satisfaction, her back to Angelique.

"I do declare this is the root of the problem, ignorance. Adelaide needs to do what she is told."

"Miss Brown, you may speak English well, but certainly no one taught you decent manners. Besides, my Adelaide reads and writes in French. Yes, she speaks Cajun French, but I done taught her some real French. Can you speak more'n one language, Miss Brown?"

"I have no intention of speaking anything except English."

"See here, my Adelaide is a bright girl. If you speak her language well, then maybe she will learn yours. If you will excuse me, I'm takin' Adelaide home. You ain't givin' my child a good education if you teach her to think less of herself."

Miss Brown picked up a book and slammed it down again. "You can't do that."

Angelique stared at Miss Brown. "Oh, yes I can. I'll teach her myself from now on." Angelique brushed Miss Brown's shoulder as she rushed past her. She called out to Adelaide on the playground. Angelique took Adelaide's hand in hers.

"We goin' home, Adelaide."

Miss Brown ran after Angelique. "That won't do, Mrs. Vidrine. Adelaide must attend school."

"Miss Brown, like I said, I'll be her teacher from here on out."

"I can see your mind is set, then. Good day to you, Mrs. Vidrine. I have other willing pupils." Miss Brown stomped off to ring the school bell.

Angelique smiled a friendly smile and replied in French. *"Je te souhaite une bonne journée, espèce de salope."*

Adelaide could not believe what she had heard. Unlike her father, her mother never cursed. She ran to keep pace with Angelique. "I ain't got to go to school no more?" Adelaide cheered.

"Oh you'll get schoolin', all right. I'm your teacher startin' today."

"Oh Lordy, Mama, you're more strict than Miss Brown."

"Got to get us some real good books. We goin' to the store, get Marie Rose to order us some English books. Why, we'll be talkin' just like Mrs. Elizabeth, bless her soul."

Adelaide ran to keep up. "What's my papa gonna say about this?"

"He ain't got nuthin' to say about this, you hear?"

Papa's Passing

Home schooling Adelaide was not easy for Angelique. It was one more thing for her to pack into her already full day. Yet, it was of utmost importance; it was her child's education, but now her Papa was ill. Angelique walked briskly toward Papa's cabin.

"Hurry up, girls. I don't want this soup to get cold."

The silence in the cottage was eerie as Angelique pushed open the door. Her girls followed closely behind.

"I hate coming here," Adelaide moaned. "This place always smells funny since Papa Belair got sick."

Carrie stared at her sister as if she had spoken blasphemy. "What's the matter with you? Papa Belair needs us."

Angelique ignored her oldest daughter's complaints. Their eyes adjusted to the dim light of the disheveled interior. Angelique ordered Adelaide to get some fresh water from the outside pump. She set the pot of soup down and cleared away crumbs on the table. Carrie stacked the dirty dishes in a large gray porcelain basin. Adelaide returned with a full bucket, water sloshing everywhere. Angelique scooped up a fresh cup for Papa and emptied the rest into a pot for boiling. She fueled the dying embers in the fireplace.

"We'll need plenty of hot water to clean up." She placed a soft cloth on the bottom of a wooden tray, and ladled some warm soup into a bowl for Papa. She set the tin of fresh water beside the soup.

Angelique called out Papa's name. She knocked softly on the bedroom door and pushed it open. Its hinges squeaked and frightened Eula Mae, who was sitting on a straight back chair rocking. She had a shawl pulled tight around her shoulders. She looked up at Angelique, shook her head, and continued to run her thumb across her fingers as if she were counting off rosary beads. A solitary beam of light sliced through the plantation shutters and cut across the bed. Papa was frail, skin sagging on a motionless frame. She pulled up a chair next to the bed, tucked the patchwork quilt about him, fluffed his pillow, and lifted his head for a sip of water.

Adelaide attempted to push Carrie into the sparsely furnished bedroom. Afraid for her *Grand-père,* Carrie held onto the doorjamb and resisted. In the sinking quiet, they could hear Papa's labored breathing rise and fall until the distant sound of the train broke the stillness. It became louder and louder as it approached. The sound amplified their fear. The train rushed past, rattled the floorboards, and flattened any sense of false hope. Angelique went to lay her head down beside Papa's head.

He stirred. "What day is it?"

"It's a special day, the first day of the New Year, Papa. And look what I've brought for your dinner, a hearty soup of winter greens." Angelique tried to spoon the warm broth into his mouth.

Papa pushed her hand away and struggled to lift his head off the pillow. In short breaths, he began to recite. *"Bonne année', bonne sante', et le paradis a' la fin de vos jours."*

Angelique smiled and repeated the traditional New Year's toast with him. She scooped another spoon of soup. "That's right Papa, a toast to the New Year. Try another sip."

Papa collapsed back onto the pillow and patted her hand. "No more. I can't. Angelique, we at the end, sweet girl. You gotta let me go."

Angelique dipped a cloth into the water cup and pressed it on his cracked lips. "Tha's enough of that kind of talk. You're gonna be just fine. You'll see, you gonna be just fine."

Papa shut his eyes against her words, patted her hand, and struggled to reveal his deepest regret. He wanted the final unspoken curtain between them to slip away. Angelique shushed him. "None of that matters now. We can talk later. Just rest. I love you always, my dearest Papa."

Framed in the shadow of the doorway, Carrie stood as still as a wooden soldier, unable to enter the room or turn her back. Adelaide finally pulled her away and whispered a long-kept secret; she had seen Papa Belair's casket in the barn. Adelaide had watched him hoist it up to the loft himself, his biceps bulging from the effort. He had made it "just in case, no need to worry your mama none. I trust you to tell her when it's right."

They had spit into their palms and shook on it. She had been surprised that Papa Belair had entrusted her with this secret. Once, Adelaide had wandered to the barn to have a second look at it. She had climbed the ladder to the loft and run her fingers over the smooth wood. It was a beautiful pine box with an airtight seal. Adelaide could not remain silent any longer.

Carrie cupped her hands over her ears. She did not want to hear about caskets. She shuffled to a corner of the room, pressed her back against the wall, slid to the floor, and tucked her knees up to her chest. She imagined that she was back on the front porch making music with both of her grandfathers, Papa Belair with his fiddle and Papa Vidrine with his guitar. With a "one, two, three" they would fill the air with beautiful harmony. The porch would shake from the stomping of their bare feet.

Carrie's grandfathers had been surprised the first time she tapped out the beat of a song with nothing more than a spoon and a tin cup. They thought it best that she have her own instrument. Papa Belair took Carrie with him into town to see the blacksmith. Felix had been busy repairing a wagon wheel when they had arrived.

"Felix, we got us a problem and I think you can help us with it."

Felix made Carrie a *ti-fer*, a triangle shaped instrument and striking rod, small enough to fit her hand. From that day on, they had been a happy threesome. Then Papa Belair started coughing all the time. No, Carrie did not want to hear about pine boxes. Carrie wanted things to be back the way they used to be before Papa Belair got sick. Angelique stayed with Papa until he fell asleep. Hoping for some sign of good news, Carrie studied her mother's face.

"He's asleep and Eula Mae gonna watch over him for a while. Now, I know y'all are sad that my papa's sick. So we gonna ease the time and make ourselves useful. We can clean this place up real good and while we're at it, we can pray for Papa."

Angelique was in the kitchen washing dishes, Adelaide was sweeping the floor, and Carrie was still sitting in the corner praying when he took his last breath.

The Old Place

Papa's old home place had become Angelique's sanctuary. She had left everything intact after his death. It gave her comfort to sneak away from daily routines and find solace surrounded by Papa's simple things. She could hold his cup, pipe, or fiddle and feel closer to him. She would sit in Papa's rocker next to the fireplace, run her fingers over the arms of the high-backed chair, and shut her eyes. Each squeak took her back, filled her with yesterdays, and put a smile on her weary face.

The stillness put thoughts into her head, thoughts once again of being free. It must come from living a meager life, one measured by hard work and lonely nights. Unfortunately, Damon believed Papa's house belonged to him and would not discuss his plans for the place with her. She did not know if he intended to rent it, sell it, or take on a sharecropper. In the interim, Angelique decided to make it her own. She summoned the courage to begin clearing it out.

Angelique spent all morning sorting. She would pick up a chipped bowl or platter and decide to toss it out only to find that it made its way back on the table. She wandered out back to burn some tattered rags. She started a fire in a barrel and tossed the rags into the flames. She watched as the smoke rose and drifted toward the trees.

Angelique noticed a trail that was barely visible through the woods. She had never seen it before. She followed the path and realized that it led straight from Papa's house to Eula Mae's back door. Angelique found comfort in the canopy of the sycamore trees, the mockingbird song, and the scent of dust moistened as a soft rain began to fall.

Angelique hurried to Papa's house. Washed in the memory of the love those two old fools bestowed upon her, Angelique paused and sat quietly for a while. Their love for her had united Papa and Eula Mae in a common goal. Angelique suspected that there was more between them than that. She wanted Eula Mae to live in Papa's house, but Damon would not even consider that possibility. Angelique rose to put bowls on the floor in various places to catch the rain that fell harder with each passing minute. The rhythmic raindrops soothed her.

"I'll need Josef's help to patch this roof. Just needs some new cedar shingles. Tha's all. Papa, what you think about that? After all, you done taught him everythin' there is to know about carpentry."

Angelique abandoned her kitchen tasks and drifted to the bedroom. She shook the bed sheets out and heaped them up into a pile at her feet. It was not until the bed was stripped and bare that Angelique spotted the thin package folded in half and tied with string. It was sticking out of a corner from under the mattress. She read the name written on the package, "For Angelique".

Angelique tore the envelope open and discovered a letter the lawyer had written for Papa along with a legal document. She sat quietly on the bed and read the letter with tears streaming down her face. Papa had acted to make sure that this land was hers exclusive of the Vidrine family. In the letter, he asked Angelique to forgive him for his greatest sin, her marriage to Damon. She set the letter aside and unfolded the document. The deed to the old place lay before her.

A second envelope fell to the floor with Jean Marc's name written on it. Angelique turned the sealed envelope over. She rushed to the window and held it up to the light. All she could make out were the words "sorry" and "good man."

She lowered herself to the bed. "Oh, Papa. What have you done? Is this what you meant by regrets? It is too late to change the past."

She folded Jean Marc's letter in half and tucked it into her apron pocket for safekeeping. She needed time to think about this. If only she dared open and read the full contents of this letter. Angelique busied herself sorting clothes, one pile to burn and one to keep. She took her scissors and cut squares of fabric from Papa's shirts. They would make a nice quilt.

"I'll embroider your name in the corner. Would you like that Papa?" She sobbed softly and paused to gaze out the doorway, "Oh Papa, what am I going to do without you?"

Angelique lifted Papa's worn nightshirt to her cheek. She shut her eyes and breathed deeply. She tossed it into the keep pile and announced to the empty room, "I've got to get out of here." She shut the door quietly and left.

She would return and finish the task another day. "I'll bring Carrie along next time. That one lifts my heart."

Angelique skirted the front of her house. No one was home. She dashed over to Jean Marc's and inched the envelope under the front door. Whatever Papa had written was his gift to Jean Marc, and she would not deny him his last wish. The words could not change the fact that she was bound to Damon. Her life was destined. At least Papa could be at peace. She wondered if Jean Marc would ever have cause to reveal its contents to her. She vowed not to pry.

Carrie loved Papa's old house as much as Angelique did and often followed her there, chattering like a songbird. "Tell me another story, Mama. Tell me more." Carrie liked to hear the stories of Angelique's youth. Her mama was a good storyteller. She tried to imagine her own mama running wild and free through the woods or swimming in the bayou.

However, the constant arguments between her parents about what to do with the old place frightened Carrie. She would hide under the table as heated words churned the air.

Damon kept insisting, "That old place ain't nuthin' but trouble. It's fallin' in on itself. Somebody gonna get hurt."

"Tha's a lie. Ain't nuthin' wrong with it. You just can't stand that it ain't yours."

"You spend more time at that damn rundown shack than in this house. Ain't nuthin' getting done around here. Look at this poor excuse for my supper, bit of *tasso* and cold cornbread."

"It's my place and I'm keepin' it, so get used to it. Josef is gonna fix it all up and rent it from me."

Damon slammed his fist onto the table. "Ha, is that right? You gonna be a landlord? We ain't got time for that. We got seeds to get in the ground, woman."

Carrie would wait until she heard their footsteps fade before crawling out from under the table.

Damon could not change Angelique's mind. One evening, he marched next door to his parents, hoping for support. "It ain't right, her owning land. That's for men folks."

"Son, you ain't thinkin' straight. That land is hers to do with as she pleases. I gave that land to Alduce outright as we agreed. It was a fair deal. He in turn passed it on to her. Besides, the land's still in the family."

Hippolyte set down a bowl of hot gumbo in front of Damon, "You need to give her time. She'll come around to your way of thinkin'."

"Ma, it's been more than a year, for cryin' out loud." Damon's hand hit the bowl and gumbo spilled.

Hippolyte grabbed a dishcloth. "Careful, you could have burned somebody."

Domitile shook his head in frustration, and Damon left in a huff. Hippolyte cleaned up the mess. Domitile stepped out onto the porch. He remembered the day that he had gone to the lawyer's office with Alduce and signed the papers that made him the sole owner of the property. Domitile had handed him the deed to the land, and they shook hands.

Alduce struggled to express his deep appreciation. "Thank you for this. It means a lot."

"Alduce, your Angelique is a good woman."

"That she is. Just like her mama."

While in town, each man met privately with the lawyer. Alduce needed reassurance that the land would go directly to Angelique after his death. Holding his newly signed papers, he stepped out of the lawyer's office and sighed contentedly. He walked over to Domitile and patted him on the back. Afterwards, Domitile went inside. Papa waited for a long time.

When Domitile returned, he handed Papa a sealed envelope. "I need a huge favor from you, my old friend. I need you to keep this safe for me. Can't have it at my place. And if I go before I figure a way to tell the truth and make things right, I know you'll do what has to be done."

Papa looked at the letter. It had Jean Marc Fontenot's name written across the front. "Can't read much, but I can cipher a name. You sure you want to do this? It's like we talked about, Domitile, you was nothing but a boy and you didn't know better."

"Alduce, we old men now, and I'm thinkin' he got a right to know when I'm gone."

"I'm afraid shit gonna hit the fan then."

"I believe things gonna find a way to work out."

The two men became inseparable friends and spent most of their evenings sitting on each other's front porch. Alduce often showed up about suppertime. Domitile would hand him the pouch of tobacco. They would sit there in the cypress rockers with smoke curling over them as they listened to the chorus of cicadas reach a crescendo and then fade into the sunset, only to repeat.

"Sure was a hot one today," Domitile would comment.

"Gonna rain tomorrow," Papa would predict.

"Ya knees gonna bother you then."

"No more than ya aching back."

They would sit until a salmon haze brushed across the heavens and the sun settled in the west. Papa would struggle to lift his withered frame from the rocker.

Domitile would nod. "Tomorrow then."

Papa would meander back to his old place, and then the next evening would be Domitile's turn to make the short journey to Papa's place. The two had formed a strong bond of friendship over the years. Shared secrets and regrets strengthened it. They made promises that they would take with them to their graves. Now, everything was different. His trusted old friend, Alduce, was gone and Domitile was worried. His secrets might unravel right in front of him if he could not find the letter he had left in his safekeeping. Angelique had nearly caught him searching for it the other day. Surely, if she had found it, he would have heard something from Jean Marc by now.

Hippolyte stepped out onto the porch and brought Domitile back to the present. She announced, "All done with the kitchen. Sure wish Eula Mae still wanted to clean. I'm beat. But, she's old and tired like the rest of us, I guess. She only helps a little at Angelique's since Alduce died, nowhere else. Come to bed, old man."

Domitile followed Hippolyte inside. "I can't understand the anger in our boy. Been that way since he turned, what, maybe, thirteen?"

Damon's resentment left him with distaste akin to drinking clabbered milk. He could not reason with any of them about the land and the constant fighting continued. He had to find a solution, a way to keep his wife at home. He concluded that there was only one thing for him to do. Although he hoped it would have gone unnoticed for some time, he was not surprised when Jean Marc pounded on the back wall of their house that night yelling, "Fire! Fire! Angelique, it's your papa's old place. You and Damon need to get out here!"

Angelique sprung out of bed and threw open the shutters. She could see the flames licking the sides of Papa's place. They had to move fast if they were going to save it. She dressed hurriedly, barreled out the door, and raced for a bucket. She stopped to fill it at the horse trough.

Damon caught up with her and stopped her as water splashed around them. "Let it go, Angelique. Stay back, it's too late. That place ain't nuthin' more than kindling."

Angelique kicked and screamed. "Let me go, damn you, let me go!"

"Ain't nuthin' you can do. I done told you that old place was a danger."

Jean Marc was running up and down Belair Cove Road banging on a pot to wake up the neighbors. They rushed toward the old house and formed a bucket brigade between the house and the pond on Jean Marc's property. The intense heat made it difficult for them to get close enough to douse the flames. Jean Marc ordered the men to begin digging a trench around the perimeter of the cottage and the women directed their water on the surrounding trees.

Angelique continued to race to the pond for water, until Jean Marc knelt beside her at the pond and rested his hand over hers. "Angelique, somebody's gonna get hurt if we keep at it."

Eventually, the fire brigade laid down their buckets. Black soot covered their faces, and they coughed from lungs filled with smoke. They could only watch as Papa's place turned to ashes; the last crossbeam fell with a thud that shook the ground. The neighbors trudged home. Tears streaked Angelique's ashen face as they left her standing there.

"Thank you," she said, "thank you for tryin'."

Jean Marc was the last to leave. He touched her shoulder and squeezed gently. "I'm sorry we couldn't save it."

"You did all any man could and I'm grateful for that."

Angelique put her arms around him, shut her eyes, and held on tight. Damon approached them in three long strides. He pulled Angelique away from Jean Marc. Angelique felt his separation in the deep center of her being. Jean Marc forced himself to step aside and leave her there. Now was not the time to confront Damon. He could only watch as Damon dragged her away from the smoking remains of Papa's place.

"Don't you touch me, Damon Vidrine!" Angelique raised her hand to strike him. He caught her arm in mid-air. She threw all of her weight against him and was able to break free. She began beating him with both fists.

"You did this. I know you did it."

Adelaide screamed and rushed in between her parents. "Stop it, Mama. Don't hit my Papa. He ain't done you nuthin'."

Carrie ran to her mother, wrapped her arms around her mama's waist, and sobbed. "Our special place is gone ain't it, Mama?"

Damon stepped back several paces and lifted his hands in resignation. Once again, he had failed to control his wife. He pulled Adelaide to him and reached for Carrie's hand as well. "You talkin' crazy, woman. Come on girls, we goin' home and let your mama be 'til she come to her senses."

Angelique had never felt such blind fury. She knew the truth. Damon alone was responsible for this. Angelique paced; revenge was a fire burning inside of her. She was determined to end it between them. She walked calmly into her house. She floated by Hippolyte, who was washing Carrie's face. She could see Domitile tucking Adelaide into bed. She padded quietly past them and into the bedroom that she shared with Damon. She opened the bureau drawer and searched for the pistol. She lifted the gun and opened the barrel to confirm that it was indeed loaded. Damon was lying down with his back to her. Angelique pointed the pistol at him.

"You thinkin' about shootin' me in the back, Angelique?" He turned slowly to face her. "That old place was a nuisance. I did us all a favor. We can plant on that land next spring."

Angelique took three steps toward the bed, holding Damon in her sights. Without a word, she cocked the gun.

"Oh, shit!" Damon dove for the floor as she fired. He rolled forward and scrambled to reach her. Angelique tried to take aim again, but Damon tackled her to the floor. "*Bon Dieu*, Angelique. You done lost it for sure."

They rolled repeatedly as they fought for the pistol. Finally, Damon wrenched it from her hand. Angelique kicked at him as he stepped aside. Using the bedpost for support, he managed to right himself on his good leg. "I should shoot you for this, woman."

Domitile burst into the room with Hippolyte. "What the hell is going on here?"

"Ask her. The bitch tried to kill me for burning that old place."

"That's enough, Damon, give me that gun." Domitile snatched the pistol from Damon's hands. "Y'all settle down, the both of you. Angelique, you realize what you accusin' Damon of? This ain't the way. Hippolyte, get Angelique out of here."

Angelique repeated her accusation. "Domitile, he did this. He burned down Papa's place. He told me so."

"What the hell? Hippolyte, get her out of here."

Hippolyte began to nudge Angelique out of the room. "You ain't thinkin' straight. Angelique, how you gonna explain this to your girls. God only knows how that old house caught fire."

The two girls were standing by the door. They were confused and frightened. "Girls, y'all can go on back to bed, now. This ain't nuthin' to worry about." The two girls dragged themselves back to bed.

Angelique ran out of the house. "Y'all just can't face the truth. Damon's guilty as sin."

Domitile faced Damon and asked, "Is she tellin' the truth?"

"It had to be done. It's for the best and you know it."

"Jesus, I'm not believin' this. What's wrong with you? You lost your senses. Jean Marc nearly died tryin' to save it and all along you the cause. Why can't you be more like him, son?" The words escaped and struck the intended target a final blow.

Damon threw a strong right hook, and Domitile fell backwards. Blood oozed from his lower lip. Domitile shook his head, wiped his lip, and stared at the blood on his finger. He lifted one hand in mock defeat, and backed away from Damon. Domitile regretted what he had said. *How had it come to this? This was a sorry situation, at least, he did not have to worry about the letter anymore; it must have burned with the house.*

Later, Hippolyte peeked in on her granddaughters. They were asleep. She picked up a light blanket and ventured outside to find Angelique. "Come to bed, child. You'll catch the death of it sittin' out here." She placed the blanket over Angelique's shoulders.

"I'll be all right. I just need to be alone for a little while." Other than adjusting the blanket around her shoulders and patting Hippolyte's hand, Angelique did not move.

Angelique prayed until she felt strength settle into her bones and fill her with determination. She returned home, only to remove her belongings from Damon's room and tiptoe across the house to sleep with her daughters. She slipped under the covers of the girls' bed and settled between them. The miracle of their tiny heartbeats thumped a soothing rhythm that lulled her to sleep.

The next morning, Angelique woke to the sound of Eula Mae singing softly. Angelique followed her sweet voice outside and found her sitting on the porch staring at the burnt remains of Papa's place. Papa's fiddle rested at her side. Eula Mae handed the fiddle to Angelique.

"Eula Mae, where did you find this?"

"Not me child, it was there when I got here. Saw the smoke last night." Eula Mae focused on the charred remains of Papa's place and muttered, "It breaks my heart."

Angelique hugged Eula Mae, and then she examined the fiddle. She was surprised to find little damage, though the strings were missing. She hugged it to her chest and said a silent prayer of thanksgiving for this gift. Angelique wondered if Jean Marc had saved it from the fire and left it there.

From behind his shutters, Jean Marc watched as Angelique picked up the fiddle, gazed in his direction, and walked back into her house. Jean Marc rocked with strong emotions; he felt longing for the young woman he had once loved, and hatred for the man who kept her trapped. Damon had stolen everything from him, even his birthright. The letter dropped at his door left him with no doubt. Its contents were brief, a confession of sorts and a peace offering. Jean Marc had crushed the letter in his palm after reading it. Afterwards, he needed answers and marched over to see Gus. Jean Marc handed Gus the crumpled letter.

"Did you know about this?"

"About what?"

"This, this here letter from Domitile. And there's a deed for a few acres of Vidrine property, signed over to me."

Gus paled. "I don't know what you're talkin' about. You'll have to read it me."

"I get the feeling you might know what it says."

Gus tugged on Jean Marc's arm. "Let's step outside."

Gus grabbed two beers from the well and handed one to Jean Marc.

Jean Marc started reading aloud, "Jean Marc, if you are reading this, then I'm gone but I've got explainin' to do…"

Gus listened intently as Jean Marc continued to read. He was furious. "We had an agreement. This was supposed to stay buried. I know he wrote it, but I don't think he meant for you to have it, not now. This don't make sense to me."

"Why didn't my mama tell me this? I had a right to know." Jean Marc listened while Gus fumbled with the right words that told the story.

"Me, Domitile, and Alduce were scoutin' back then, way up north of Chicot. Tha's when he met your mama. It just happened. They fell in love and he wanted nothing more in life than to be with her. But, it was complicated. He had a wife back here, Hippolyte. We'd be gone for months and months. And it wasn't 'til he come back that he learned Hippolyte had delivered a baby, his son. *Mais*, what could he do? He had to do the right thing and he come home and settle down. Blue Sky, she waited for him all that long summer, but he never went back. He never knew that she had his baby."

"How did she meet my stepfather?"

"The first time Octave saw Blue Sky, she was selling beads and trinkets spread out on a blanket near the outpost north of Ville Platte. He thought her beautiful from the first. She was wearin' beads the color of her name, all her own makin'. You were asleep in a basket at her feet. Octave had a tender heart for kids and he fell in love first with you and then with your mama. He thought she was a fragile bird that needed his protection. They married and lived deep in the woods away from prying eyes, she being a savage and all. Octave, he did not care who your father was. My brother was a good man and he loved you as his own."

"I know that. But, how did Domitile find out?"

"It was rare that Sky brought you into town with my brother. But, one look at you told Domitile all he needed to know. You were maybe four or five when you all walked in that store and Sky come face to face with Domitile. Even he knew, everyone knew. That mean old mule had kicked Octave so hard that many believed that he would never bear children. And you was the right age."

Jean Marc gulped down a swig of beer.

"What happened then?"

"Domitile looked me up and tried to wrangle the truth out of me. I told him that Sky wanted nuthin' to do with him and she begged him to leave them alone. She was happy, you was happy, and Octave was the only father you knew. That was all there was to it."

"He was chicken shit."

"It was for the best. When Sky and Octave died, I went to see Domitile. I told him I wanted to raise you as one of mine. He agreed only because I convinced him it was what Sky wanted. I know he regretted everything that happened and wished he could make it right. Some things can't be undone. Damn it, we agreed. I'm sorry, son."

"You're right about one thing. This don't change a thing. You and Octave were all the family I needed. Funny thing is, I saw Domitile just this morning, and he didn't act like nuthin' was different. I don't think he put that letter on my doorstep. Who else knew about this?"

"As far as I know, me and Domitile, but I always thought Alduce figured it out. I ain't never said nuthin' to him though."

Jean Marc considered the possibilities. Who could have placed the envelope at his door? He paced while Gus waited. "It's Angelique. Domitile musta left it with her papa for safekeeping. And she found it."

"Then, she knows."

"No, the letter was sealed. I'm gonna make up somethin' if she ever asks 'cus I don't want nuthin' from Domitile, not now, not ever. I ain't gonna judge him either. It's like Mama said... 'Don't judge another unless you have walked in his path.' Now I understand why she always kept tellin' me that."

"Tha's for the best, son."

"Gus, I got a confession of sorts. I might be my father's son after all 'cus I know what it's like to love two women at the same time."

Gus nodded his head. "You never got over her. Did you? What you gonna do about that."

"Ain't nuthin' I can do. Might be best if I took off for a while."

"*Mais* me, I think you ought to stay put and let the chips fall where they may."

"Tha's askin' for trouble."

Jean Marc took out a match and struck it on the fence post. He touched the match to the letter and tossed it out into the yard. They watched as it burned. Next, he lit the deed. Uncle Gus jumped up to put the flame out with his foot. "I didn't raise me no fool. No need to burn your bridges."

Jean Marc stopped him. "I meant it when I said I don't want nuthin' from him. The only question left is…Does Damon know the truth?"

After Papa died, Domitile changed. He was often confused and agitated. He could remember things from long ago, but very little about yesterday. He rambled about mapping the land beyond Belair Cove with an Indian scout his father knew. He reminisced about that simple life, the time when he was wild and as free as the deer in the woods. He began to mumble about past regrets, and the sins of a father.

That winter was one of the mildest in years, yet the humid temperatures left the Cove dreary and damp. It was just such a day when Domitile Vidrine followed Papa to his grave. Witnesses were aghast that Domitile had "caught a heart attack" during Father's homily in church one Sunday. Father was preaching about sins of omission. Domitile turned to look at Jean Marc in the pew behind him, and then he was gone.

Damon became the head of the family, but he contributed no more or less than before his father died. He frequented the Fist to Cuffs Saloon looking for a wager of any sort: cards, horses, or cockfights. He began to eat supper out every Thursday night with the gambling crowd down at Pouyee's in Ville Platte and did not return until morning.

On weekends, Damon spent his time at the bush track located on a small clearing of unclaimed land deep into the backlands. The track was nothing more than two lanes hastily set up with posts and split cypress beams at the top and bottom. Damon often acted as master of ceremonies and started the races. He would climb the fence railing, take note of the horses' positions, and raise his pistol.

"I don't see no gentlemen here, so, the rest of you no-good-rotten-scoundrels make your bets. Who's feeling lucky today? What about you, Broussard, or you, Felix? You feelin' lucky? Are y'all ready?"

Trailing their quarter horses behind the wagons, men came from far and near to race their horse against the others. All eyes were on Damon as he whipped the spectators into a fury, fired the starting pistol, and yelled into the crowd, "*Ils sont partis!*"

The men drank, compared horseflesh, and argued about politics. For most, it was more about escaping from the drudgery of daily life and pride in their stock rather than gambling. For Damon, it was all about being in the spotlight.

On those rare occasions when Damon won at gambling, he ventured home with money in his pockets and a smile on his face. "Angelique break out that fiddle and play us a tune. I'm gonna dance with these fine young ladies."

"Me first, me first." Adelaide and Carrie would take turns. They set their bare feet on top of his dusty boots and he would twirl them around the room until they fell in a fit of giggles.

More often, Damon made stops at the home of Mr. Kaplan, who operated a bank out of his house. All of Damon's visits were withdrawals. He kept these visits to himself.

Since Domitile's death, nothing had changed for Angelique or for Hippolyte. They continued to work the fields, care for the animals, and prepare meals. Their days were long and their nights lonely. Angelique was glad to have Hippolyte's company.

At first, Hippolyte carried over only what she needed for a Thursday night stay. Hippolyte moved in, a little at a time, leaving her original home to the spiders and field mice. Adelaide and Carrie were glad of their grandmother's presence as well. Adelaide began to shadow Hippolyte the way she had once followed Damon. Carrie remained at Angelique's side.

One Friday morning, Angelique was searching for her favorite coffee cup, yellowed and stained from the dark brew when Hippolyte stepped into the kitchen. "What you huntin'?"

"My coffee cup."

"I moved a few things around. Was thinkin' the cups ought to be in that cabinet beside the stove. Easier that way. *Mais* me, I think Eula Mae shoulda tossed that old white cup out. It's broken. You gonna cut your lip on it one day."

Finding her cup at last, Angelique ignored Hippolyte. She turned it around to avoid the chip, blew on the hot coffee, and savored the dark flavor of morning. They had this discussion every morning.

Damon was the only drawback. Hippolyte observed her sons comings and goings. From time to time, she tried to set Damon on the right path. "Son, you up to no good? It ain't right. Use your head."

"Stay out of my business, old woman."

"You gotta stay home with your family. Tha's what counts in this world, family."

"I keep tellin' you, old woman, stay out of my business, if you know what's good for you."

Damon's tone was threatening. It crushed Hippolyte to hear her own son speak to her with such disrespect. She shriveled like the few remaining leaves clinging to the trees outside, and spoke no more of it.

Thunder

The Cove tried to hold on to the memory of Papa's old place and its scarred remains. It clung in earnest to the ashes while Angelique marked the long months in mourning. Her children needed her, but she hardly noticed until spring swept across the prairie and began to heal the scorched earth. A variety of prairie grasses sprouted in patches and a few black-eyed susans popped up. The promise of an early spring meant an abundance of summer flowers to come. The azaleas painted the outer edge of the old place in a profusion of pink blossoms. Gradually, Papa's old place was no more. The season continued to bring about change, and Angelique joined in the rituals of rebirth forced upon her; Easter was fast approaching.

Angelique made careful cuts on the fabric of Adelaide's dress, the soft white cotton a luxury. It was lightweight and perfect for this special occasion. She had already embroidered the section that would become the bodice. After stitching several little loops and twirls of her own, Adelaide had added to the design that they had earlier sketched on paper. Adelaide was excited about her first communion, and stood over Angelique to watch as the scissors cut through the fabric.

Hippolyte entered the room carrying a large parcel in her hands. She set it down on the opposite side of the kitchen table with a sigh.

"Mary Beth said we get presents. Is that true? *Grand-mère*, Mama's cuttin' out my new dress."

Carrie chimed in, "And Adelaide been jumpin' 'round like a grasshopper since we got up this mornin'."

"I know dear. And I think I have the perfect thing for the celebration on your special day, Adelaide."

Angelique recognized the quilt covering used to protect the cherished silver punch bowl. Hippolyte began to unwrap the quilt. Adelaide pulled out the bench at the table and sat. She picked up a cup and began admiring the design.

"Can we use it, Mama, can we?"

"*Mais oui*, that would be fine."

Hippolyte smiled. "Oh by the way, once you get it all cleaned up…"

Angelique continued to cut; the sharp scissors followed the curves and lines of the finished dress she envisioned. She whispered under her breath. "Here it comes…"

"Why don't you keep the punch bowl and the cups? It might fit inside that cupboard your papa made, ready to use any old time."

Angelique's scissors were wide open when she stopped what she was doing and gawked at Hippolyte.

Hippolyte faced her. "Well, I think it's right for you to have this, girl. Don't make no fuss. I want you to have it. Tha's all. You done right by my Damon over the years. That way, when I'm gone, I'll know I left you something fine. Damon and his sisters can fight over the rest." She raised her hands, palms out, and hesitated for a moment. "You know my grandpa was a drinkin' man. Seems like Damon come by it natural, but I know he can do better if he sets his mind to it."

Angelique put her scissors down and walked over to Hippolyte. She reached out to hug her. "*Merci*, thank you."

Hippolyte nodded and backed away. "*Puh*! Never you mind. I can see that the dishes need cleanin'. I always find a mess for me to tend to." Hippolyte walked over to the basin and primed the pump, water pouring out into the basin.

Angelique lifted the silver punch bowl and placed it on the sideboard. She carefully arranged the punch cups around it. She placed the ladle gently inside.

Hippolyte bragged, "I knew it would look good sittin' there."

Both women went back to their work. Hippolyte started to hum an old French tune from her childhood, "*Alouette*". Angelique picked up the melody and sang along. Carrie clapped her hands to the beat. Adelaide walked over to her grandmother's side, wrapped her arms around her, and squeezed before dashing through the back door. Outside, the house wrens harmonized.

During a recent storm, Adelaide helped Angelique with the birth of a newborn colt. Adelaide had fallen in love with the colt the instant it stood on its wobbly legs and tipped its nose to hers. She named him Thunder Bolt and claimed him for her own. Ever since then, she spent all of her free time with the colt.

"Carrie, scoot, go after your sister. Tell her we need her back here right now. There's lots more to do if we gonna be ready for Easter Sunday."

Angelique looked to Hippolyte for guidance. "What am I goin' to do about that child? Since that colt was born, it's all she thinks about."

Carrie stopped at the barn door and called out, "Mama says you got to come and help in the kitchen."

Adelaide nuzzled Thunder one more time. "I'm coming."

It was a gorgeous day and Adelaide would have preferred to stay in the barn with its aroma of fresh hay. Pouting, she returned to the kitchen. She sniffed the sweet aroma of pies baking in the oven and changed her attitude. Adelaide swiped her finger inside a mixing bowl and licked her finger clean before Angelique caught her.

"Wash your hands first. Adelaide, you promised to help *Grand-mère* and Carrie today."

"I'm here, ain't I?"

Dying Easter eggs an assortment of colors kept Hippolyte and the girls busy all afternoon. Adelaide had gathered the berries, leaves, and roots whose dyes would best infuse color on the eggshells, some of them covered with Carrie's flowers. Carrie had cut out little flowers from scrap pieces of fabric, arranged them on the eggs, and wrapped each tightly in cheesecloth.

Carrie picked through the plants that Adelaide splayed before them and chose some catalpa leaves to toss into a small saucer of hot water. "I want some green eggs, *Grand-mère*."

Hippolyte tugged on Carrie's pigtails. "Child, you gonna have some strange lookin' eggs if you keep addin' plants to that mixture. And be careful! That water is boilin' hot."

Adelaide snuck a few guinea eggs into the boiling pot for good measure. They were stronger and would be better to *pâques* with. Adelaide looked forward to the contest of butting eggs together to discover which one cracked first under pressure. She chuckled as she imagined duping her boy cousins and collecting their cracked eggs as her prize.

Carrie swiped her finger inside the bowl of blackberry filling. "What about blue eggs? Can we have some blue eggs?"

Hippolyte shook her head. "Eula Mae comin' to help tomorrow, ain't she? She'll be surprised to find all these pretty eggs sittin' here."

Carrie laughed. "She's gonna love the blue ones!"

The eggs were boiled, dyed, and dried. Afterwards, the girls carefully nestled them in a small crate stuffed with fresh hay.

Angelique had been busy baking sweet dough pies, blackberry, fig, and her personal favorite, peach and raisin. Just before noon, she placed the last pie in the keeper. The screen rattled as she secured the latch and sighed, "All done."

Hippolyte offered, "Why don't I get these girls something to eat and you get some fresh air. I'll save a plate for you."

Angelique welcomed the chance to feel the sun on her back.

Hippolyte and the children were sitting down to sample one of Angelique's pies for dessert when they heard the pounding of horse's hooves and Damon's fiery curses. Adelaide ran to the doorway and dropped the plate she was holding. It crashed to the floor.

"It's Thunder Bolt!"

Adelaide raced to the barn. Hippolyte tore off her apron and charged after Adelaide, Carrie followed. Adelaide's colt bolted through the old barn doors barely missing them as it bucked and ran for the pasture. Damon came tearing out of the barn spewing obscenities. Hippolyte turned to Carrie, putting her hands over the child's ears.

Damon yelled, "Adelaide, get back in the house."

"What'd you do to Thunder?" Adelaide screamed.

"Nuthin' yet, but when I catch him, he'll find out who's boss." Damon had a rope tied with a noose draped over his arm and a whip in his hand. "You've spoiled that damn colt and now I can't stable him. Can't let him get away with this. Bad habits are too hard to break."

Damon saddled his horse and took off after Thunder. He found him nuzzling up against his mother. Damon lassoed Thunder and hustled him back to the barn. Both Thunder and his mother were distraught; their cries were haunting. Damon's intention was to walk Thunder into the stall, turn him around, and latch the gate. Thunder Bolt dug in his hind legs, threw his head from side to side, and fought back, neighing repeatedly.

Damon whipped him—*thwap, thwap.* Thunder tugged and yanked on the rope around his neck and struck out at the stall with his forelegs. Damon screamed and cursed as his hands slid across the hemp rope and bled. "I'll kill you before I'll turn you loose."

Hippolyte pulled Adelaide away from the scene. She carried her back to the house as she kicked and screamed. Hippolyte snatched a bunch of rosaries hanging from the nail on the wall inside the back door. She put a rosary in Adelaide's hand and shook her hard.

"All you can do is pray, child."

She thrust a rosary at Carrie as well.

"Kneel down, hurry up."

The louder Damon cursed, the louder Hippolyte prayed. Each time a curse word reached her ears, it was as if Damon had pinched her. Her whole body jerked and she shut her eyes against the devil's work. Adelaide was worried about Thunder and prayed with solemn intensity. On the other hand, Hippolyte's theatrics tickled little Carrie and she had a difficult time containing her giggles. Their prayers rang out across the prairie.

Hippolyte urged the girls, "Louder, louder." They shifted from knee to knee and shouted; Damon spewed words none of them had ever heard before. Hippolyte did not want her granddaughters exposed to any of them either. She rolled her fingers across those rosary beads as fast as she could.

When Angelique heard the mare squealing, she dropped the flowers in her hands and ran for the paddock. The horses were racing back and forth near the fence railing. At first, Angelique could not figure out why the horses were upset. Then, Hippolyte's screams reached her ears and she rushed to the porch. Adelaide stood up when she saw her mother and pointed at the barn. "It's Papa, he's gonna hurt Thunder. Do somethin'."

Angelique sprinted as fast as she could and burst into the barn. "Damon, what on earth are you doin? Stop it. Thunder ain't ever been separated from her mama before."

"I know what I'm doin'. You stay out of this. I'm wantin' to breed that mare again with Felix's quarter horse. Offered me hard cash, he did." Damon pulled tighter on the rope and struck Thunder Bolt.

Angelique winced. "That ain't the way to do it. I'll get her in the stall. Let me. Your hands are bleedin'. Go tend to them."

Angelique and Damon fought to gain control of the rope. He finally released his hold on the rope and threw it at her. "Oh, you think you can do this better than me, do you? Well, let's see what you got then."

Angelique waited until Damon left the barn and she began to whisper softly to the horse. Thunder was resistant and continued to beat the ground with his forelegs. Angelique sang a soothing lullaby. After a while, she was able to get close enough to loosen the rope around his neck.

Damon stuck his head back into the barn and spat. "Ha! Singing, that's just like a woman. That ain't gonna do a whole hell of a lot a good."

"Damon, why don't you move the mare to the north pasture? She'll be out of hearing range. Go!"

"I don't take orders from you," Damon roared, but he left to do her bidding anyway.

Angelique turned her attention back to the colt. "Thunder, that mean old devil's gone. I promise, I won't let him hurt you anymore. You're safe with me." She met Thunder eye to eye, and the frightened colt gradually quieted. Angelique continued to talk to him in a soft voice. "It's gonna be all right Thunder. You just missin' your mama, tha's all. You're a good boy."

Bit by bit, Thunder shook off the tension. His muscles stopped twitching; his nostrils flared. Angelique sat on a bale of hay and held onto the loose rope. Thunder inched toward her. Angelique stood up slowly, reached for a brush, and began to rub him down. Then, with only a "*click-click*" and a slight tug, Thunder followed her into the stall.

Angelique turned him around and closed the gate. She slipped off the rope, fed him some hay, and hugged his neck. "What a good boy. Tomorrow will be a new day and we will get you out of here. I promise."

When Angelique walked out of the barn, Damon was standing there. "Well, I'll be damned. But, I'd already done all the work, wore that horse out before you started with that foolish singing."

"A little kindness goes a long way," Angelique hissed.

Hippolyte was still belting out "Hail Mary's" at the top of her lungs on the back porch. Adelaide saw Angelique and Damon emerge from the barn and dropped her rosary. She ran to Damon and began hitting him. "Why'd you do that to Thunder? Don't you hurt him ever again!"

Damon picked up Adelaide. "Nuthin' wrong with Thunder, girl. You stay away from him for tonight until he settles down. Go on back inside the house." Damon lowered Adelaide to the ground.

"I want to see Thunder," she demanded.

"Adelaide, don't you sass me. You get on back to the house like I told you."

Adelaide stormed off shouting, "It ain't right what you did to Thunder. I hate you."

Damon turned to Angelique and shook his head. "That's your daughter for sure, she got your fire. Tamed you, gonna tame Thunder, and down the road, I guess I'll have to tame that little one, too."

"You got no say with her anymore, Damon. I ain't gonna let you ruin her like you ruin everythin' else you touch."

"Hey, what's the matter with you, woman? I ain't done you nuthin'."

Angelique walked right up to Damon. She was so close to him that he could feel her breath on his face, and he stepped back. "That says it all, Damon, you right. You ain't ever done nuthin'. Hear me well. Stay away from us, stay away from Adelaide."

Money Troubles

The months passed swiftly and fall was upon them. They were busy harvesting the crops. Angelique had an *envie* for pecan pralines. She imagined that they would taste like sweet creamy butter. The crunch under her feet hastened her toward the pecan orchard. The fallen leaves cluttered the trail cleared by generations before her. She had come alone to travel this old worn path. It was one of those rare crisp autumn mornings, uncommon for south Louisiana. She carried Papa's dented milk bucket. The tall grasses whipped softly across her bare legs as she chose a place to begin. She could hear Papa calling to her, a whisper in the wind. It was almost a year since his death and she missed him.

"Not the big ones, the little ones have the juiciest fruit," Papa used to say.

The pinging at the bottom of the metal bucket was music to her ears. She stopped to crush two of the pecans together in her tight fist, the way Papa used to do. Angelique squeezed and listened for the crack that signaled it had begun to split. She squeezed harder and it broke open. She picked the shell clean and enjoyed each tasty morsel. Glancing into the bucket, she realized that she had a long way to go before she would have enough to make a batch of pralines.

Angelique ran her foot over the leaves on the ground, uncovering more pecans. While she picked up pecans, her thoughts turned to fond memories of Papa. She could feel Papa's presence. She breathed in the scent of his old cigar, his essence, the one man who had truly loved her unconditionally. He was always patient with her. It did not matter how tired he was or how often she pestered him.

As a child, she would hide under the table and peek out from behind the worn tablecloth. The instant he held a pinch of tobacco between his thumb and index finger, tobacco pouch resting in his lap atop the worn Bible, she would pop out squealing like a wild banshee. Tobacco flew everywhere.

Papa would lay his calloused palm over his warm heart and pretend to be frightened. "Oh, *Mon Dieu*, you made me scared."

Papa was as gentle as an old Catahoula Hound was, but he would pretend to be upset and chase Angelique around the table. Angelique never ran very fast, and when Papa caught her, he would throw her up into the air and catch her again on her way down. Angelique would succumb to dizziness as he spun her around over his head. It warmed her heart to remember the good times.

"You were a good man, Papa."

They had labored side-by-side most of her life. He had been there for her through both the good and the bad. From his deathbed, he had tried to whisper regrets. Angelique could not bear to listen. She had her own regrets, like the time she turned away when Papa tried to comfort her after the loss of her son.

Papa had been so good with the girls, a good *Pépère*. Angelique wanted to create the same kind of memories with her own children. While they churned butter in the mornings, Angelique told stories. On late summer evenings, they chased fireflies, caught them, and put them in glass jars–magic moments. Today, Angelique hoped they would enjoy making pralines with her as much as she had with her Papa.

A dog barked in the distance and a flock of noisy geese flew overhead. Angelique's grip on the half-full bucket cramped her hand and the small of her back started to hurt. She plopped down on the ground and picked up the pecans at her feet until her bucket was full. "We're going to make a good batch of pralines tonight, Papa. Yessiree, the weather is just right for some pralines. Um um um."

The year after Papa and Domitile died was relatively uneventful. Angelique struggled to scrape a living from the soil and hold on to seed money before Damon spent it. Trying to figure out what to do next, she often stayed up late into the night. Hippolyte woke one morning to find Angelique asleep at the kitchen table, her head resting in her arms. A battered wooden box sat open on the table with a few coins and bills stacked neatly in front it. Hippolyte tilted her head in understanding and padded away on soft feet. She had overheard the conversation between Eula Mae and Angelique yesterday.

"Eula Mae, you are like family to me, but I'm short on cash. I can't keep payin' you to help out around the house. I could pay you in eggs. How would that be?"

"Never you mind, child. I come here and give you some time no matter what. Nobody wants an old lady like me anyway."

"Eula Mae, you are always welcome here and you don't have to lift a finger."

Hippolyte dressed in her Sunday best, although the dress hung loosely around what was left of her once wide girth. She cinched the waist and put on her new bonnet that Angelique had made; the sides of the bonnet covered Hippolyte's face completely.

"Tha's the way I like it," she had told Angelique after pointing out several bonnets at the mercantile months earlier.

In the kitchen, Hippolyte stoked the fire and put a kettle of water on to boil. She turned over one cup, ran her finger against the edge, and searched for possible chips. She reached under the towel draped over the crock and selected three eggs. Hippolyte pecked at each quietly with a fork until they cracked open and dropped each one by one into the hot skillet.

Angelique woke to the smell of fresh ham sizzling in the skillet.

"Morning to you, *ma petite*. I reckon you could use a good breakfast before settin' out for chores. I'll just move all of this out of the way."

Hippolyte pushed aside the money box and placed a plate in front of Angelique. She set two more plates down for sleepy-eyed little girls who would surely shake loose from their beds soon enough. "Angelique, you eat. I'm goin' out. Got somethin' to take care of. I'll be back in a spell."

Angelique was too tired to question her mother-in-law.

Hippolyte did not return until late evening, long after Angelique had tired of Adelaide's questions about where she had gone. At dusk, Hippolyte suddenly appeared around the bend in the road. She stepped into the yard sure-footed. Angelique and the girls stared in relief as she approached the house carrying a tin of baking powder. She stopped to empty its contents on the back steps of the front porch.

"Adelaide and Carrie, y'all go on inside. It's gettin' dark. I need to talk to your mama."

"What about?" Adelaide inquired.

"Never you mind, child. I'll come tuck you girls into bed in just a bit."

Hippolyte kept her eyes on the girls until they disappeared inside. "Angelique, here take this."

Hippolyte handed her the tin to hold, and then she pulled a small roll of bills from her pocket and proceeded to stuff the money into the tin. "This here is between you and me."

"*Mémère*, what have you done?"

"Now, you just hush. I gave it to you and I'm sorry about that 'cus I done sold the punch bowl. We don't need fancy things any more. *Cher*, you and me we can't pull in no more, we gonna set this aside."

Angelique went inside and returned with a glass jar. She placed the tin in the jar and sealed the lid shut. Together they buried it beside the horse trough near the barn, the old barn cat a curious onlooker.

Hippolyte took the shovel from Angelique's hands. "There, and it ain't none of Damon's business what we done here."

Having an emergency fund eased the burden. Angelique was grateful that Marie Rose and Antoine let her put most of their supplies on the credit account at the mercantile. Damon paid it back a little at a time. Today was shopping day and Angelique was anxious to get to the store. The air was already as sticky and thick as cane syrup. They nibbled on cold biscuits as they walked on the road, and the sun burned off the morning mist. Later, the growing heat sped them along.

Adelaide and Carrie were cranky. "Why we got to go all the way to Ville Platte when they got that new store right down the road?"

"I don't think so. Don't y'all want to see Mrs. Marie Rose?"

A small new store had opened up in the Cove, selling the basics. Hippolyte proclaimed it was a den of thieves, a front for moonshine making. She had waved her pointer finger and alleged, "There's more corn and sugar goin' in Alex Breaux's place than I seen flour, salt and the like comin' out. I'm tellin' you something ain't right. They makin' moonshine for sure."

Just in case Hippolyte's observations were correct, Angelique shied away from the new local store. They walked to Sylvester's Mercantile the first Saturday of the month as was her custom. Besides, Marie Rose and Antoine were like family. If circumstances permitted, the two women would sneak off to the back of the store for a brief visit. The girls were content with a piece of hard candy and some time to browse the catalog. Angelique would sip on her cup of steaming *café au lait* and listen to Marie Rose as she filled her in on the town gossip.

Marie Rose overheard all of the telephone conversations that took place in the store. Since its installation, the store had become the perfect gathering place while waiting for a call and for others to listen discreetly. Antoine had bought a few chairs from Widow Comeaux. He put them outside the front of the store with a small table. On sunny days, he hoped to coax the men who stopped by into a game of checkers. Regular games quickly became part of the fabric of the store. On wintry days, they brought the game inside and warmed themselves by the potbellied stove.

"It's good business," he informed Marie Rose. "They stay and after a while, they'll buy a few things."

On the day Angelique and her girls arrived, they looked like wet dishrags. Jean Marc and his Uncle Gus were playing checkers out front. The two men nodded. "Mornin', mighty hot today. Ain't it?"

Angelique grinned. "We drippin' for sure."

Carrie headed straight for the candy jars. Angelique pulled out her supply list from her small cloth purse and went about gathering the things she needed.

Adelaide complained, "Mama, I'm thirsty."

Marie Rose and Antoine exchanged a fleeting look as Angelique approached the counter with her first item, a sack of flour. Antoine angled his head and shifted his eyes to give Marie Rose a sign. She needed to confront Angelique about her bill. Marie Rose stood at the counter, squeezed her hands together, and shook her head slightly. Silently, she pleaded with him. Angelique returned with a tin of baking powder and some coffee and set them down on the counter. Carrie was already sucking on a piece of hard candy.

Marie Rose stepped out from behind the counter and motioned for Angelique to follow. Her voice reached a whispered staccato. "Angelique, I'm awful sorry. I'm goin' to have to ask you to put some money down on your account today, if you can. It's Damon. He ain't been payin' regular no more."

Marie Rose paused to glance at Antoine.

"Antoine says I need to be collectin'. We need the money. Things are gettin' tight around here with lots a folks not payin' up. It ain't jus' y'all. Seems like there ain't no work to be had anywhere. Why, the poor are just gettin' poorer."

Angelique turned ashen, then nodded. "I feel real bad about this. I ain't got nuthin' with me today, Marie Rose. I didn't know I'd be needin' to pay. How far behind are we? Would you consider doin' some tradin'?" Angelique was not ready to dip into the reserves she and Hippolyte had hidden away.

Marie Rose glanced at Antoine who was shaking his head, no. Marie Rose ignored him. "Sure thing hon, let's do that."

"Could you wrap up this stuff for me then and hold it 'til Saturday comin'? I'll be back with some things for tradin'."

Angelique walked home empty-handed.

Monday morning, Angelique was surprised to find Marie Rose at her door with several parcels in hand. She placed the flour, coffee and other staples on Angelique's kitchen table. "Antoine and I had a talk about this, and we decided to extend y'all for a bit longer."

Angelique pursed her lips.

Marie Rose hugged her. "Pay us when you can."

An awkward silence fell between them while Angelique busied herself preparing a pot of fresh coffee. "I'll find a way to pay you back. I promise."

Angelique choked back tears as she filled a small brown sack with grinds and lowered it into the top of the white porcelain pot. She placed the coffee pot in a large black iron skillet and surrounded it with three *demitasse* cups. Pouring hot water into the sack and the skillet, she warmed the cups and brewed the coffee. On a small plate, she set out a few cookies, Elizabeth's recipe.

Suddenly, the door flew open and Hippolyte entered carrying a dented bucket of fresh milk. She placed the half-full bucket on the kitchen counter and wiped her sweaty brow. Angelique poured some fresh milk into each cup.

"I declare this heat ain't fit for old ladies. Marie Rose, I spotted your buggy out front. What brings you all the way out here?" Hippolyte eyed the parcel of goods on the table. "I didn't know y'all took to deliverin'."

Marie Rose stammered, "I was out of baking powder last Saturday when Angelique came to the store. So, I decided to visit my best friend in hopes of enlisting her help. Antoine and I been considerin' new ways to bring in business. I'm here to convince Angelique to do a bit of baking and sewing for us. I think customers would buy some of her cookies and those pretty bonnets, too. I heard several ladies admiring your new one after church yesterday."

Hippolyte preened. "Why, that sounds like a good idea to me. What you think about that, Angelique?"

Marie Rose took a bite of a cookie. "Folks been askin' about them cookies and I suspect you still have Elizabeth's recipe."

Later, a quiet Angelique followed Marie Rose out.

"Like I said, don't you worry about payin' us back. That's all there is to it. This Cove is one big family and we've always been there for each other. Nuthin' is gonna change. I'd be grateful to you for a chance to sell some of your baked goods. Then we even."

"I'd take kindly to doin' that."

Angelique glanced out across the dusty field and the panorama of sky as Marie Rose drove away. Angelique went in search of her straw hat. "No rain today, I reckon."

Pretending to repair the latch, Jean Marc was outside his gate when Marie Rose drove by. Marie Rose stopped her buggy. She simply met Jean Marc's eyes and nodded her head.

"She don't suspect a thing. You done a good deed, Jean Marc."

Jean Marc nodded in turn and went back inside.

"Pop Goes the Weasel"

The first day of picking cotton was done. The sun was setting crimson on the hot August afternoon. Waving as they went by, the hired hands followed Eula Mae off the field.

"We be here same time tomorrow if'n you like, Miss Angelique, for sure."

Angelique waved. "Couldn't have done it without you, great job. See y'all tomorrow then."

Angelique admired the wagon packed to the top, a white cloud of real wealth. Once Angelique had heard about Damon's bet, it had proved easy to convince him to hire extra cotton pickers this year. She had enlisted Josef's help in gathering some good hands.

Damon yelled at Josef, "Move it boy, dump that last load. I'm makin' tracks for the cotton gin."

Angelique stepped into action. "Adelaide get over here, *vite, vite,* quick." Angelique whispered in her ear, lifted her up, and sat her down on the seat beside Damon in the wagon.

Damon's face tightened. He looked back at Angelique. "What you think you're doin', woman? Put that child back down."

"Adelaide, you stay right there." Angelique said, glaring up at Damon. "I heard about the bet between you and Felix Soileau. You gonna beat him to the cotton gin by a whole day, I'm sure of it. Adelaide, you make sure your papa comes back home with money in his pocket. And find out how much he gets for each bale."

"It's Eula Mae, ain't it? I guess she's the one who told ya about the bet. She better stay out of my way."

"No, and don't matter where I heard it anyway." Angelique shook her finger at Damon. "This here is the best grade of cotton we ever got out of this field, clean and creamy. You can settle up with Felix later, after we figure out what's needed around here."

Adelaide looked from one parent to the other. "Papa, I want to go with you. Can't I?"

Damon ignored Adelaide and struck the backs of the mules with his whip repeatedly. They strained against the weight of the full wagon. "Them damn lazy mules ain't got no get up and go."

Adelaide cried out, "Papa, don't be mad at the mules. They pullin' hard as they can."

"Shut up, Adelaide, and get down from this wagon right now. I ain't puttin' up with your naggin', you just like your mama, and I ain't sittin' here all day either."

The wagon lurched forward, almost throwing Adelaide out. She grabbed on to Damon's arm to right herself. He shook free. Adelaide slid as far from her father as possible and held on to the wagon seat. She watched the lonesome prairie pass by swiftly. She remained silent for some time while listening to the steady gait of the mules, the cracking whip, and the creaking wagon. Soon, her curiosity began to unwind like a spool of embroidery thread. She had never been to the cotton gin.

"Papa, how come some call it a cotton gin and others say it's a saw gin. Which is it? We gonna bring Mama back the seeds, right? How they gonna get the seeds out, Papa?" Waiting for words that would signify a truce between them, Adelaide turned her face to her father.

"Stop your yappin', Adelaide. You done caused me enough trouble today. Can't you figure nuthin' out on your own?"

Damon craned his neck to get a better look as they approached town. "Damn, there's wagons waitin'." Damon's sullen mood began to shift. "Humph, I don't recognize anybody from the Cove."

He reached over and gave Adelaide a conspiratorial hug. "Heh heh, that cinches it, I'm the first and win the bet. Felix gonna be mad as hell." He pulled the wagon under the cover beside the noisy gin. He jumped down and ordered Adelaide to "stay put".

Adelaide watched her father as he walked away. She rocked on the edge of the wagon seat and sulked for a while. Finally, Adelaide decided to climb down from the wagon. She climbed on top of a bale of cotton, wiped the dirty office windowpane, and peered inside. The faces were familiar but the conversations faint. Her shoulders slumped; she would have to ask her papa for the answers her mama wanted to hear.

Damon stepped back into the doorway and yelled at the two boys waiting there. "What you standin' around for? Hurry it up. Get this wagon unloaded."

He turned to another customer entering the office. "Looks like I'm the first one here from the Cove. Yessiree, I'm in high cotton this year."

Adelaide jumped off the cotton bale and ducked around the back of the building. She watched several wagons rolling up the street to the cotton gin, but there was no sign of Mr. Felix. She knew her father would want to wait for Felix. Unloading might take a while. She wandered farther down the street until she came upon a few boys playing a game of marbles. She begged them to let her join the game.

Damon paced as the wagon was unloaded and the cotton weighed. He stuffed the cash into his pocket, and then he remembered Adelaide. "Where in the hell is that girl?"

Adelaide was lying on her stomach, her eyes even with the marbles in the circle, ready to throw her next shot. It was a serious game of "keeps." She was about to strike a defeating blow with a borrowed marble when she heard her father shouting.

"Adelaide, Adelaide, you better get over here."

She missed her shot and returned the borrowed marble to one of the boys. "Sorry, I got to go. Papa's callin' me."

She ran up the street. "How much you get Papa?"

No answer.

"What's the grade? Mama says I got to find out."

"Never you mind what your mama says. Go on, get up here."

Adelaide stuck her head inside the cotton gin. "Mr. Lafleur, what's the grade? How much Papa got for our cotton?"

"Ask your papa, girl."

"Adelaide, you better get on up here if you don't want no whippin'."

Damon snapped the reins before she could seat herself. Adelaide grabbed the side railing to keep from falling over. The wagon flew toward home.

Angelique was putting supper on the table when they arrived. "They're here," she called out to Hippolyte as she rushed outside to greet them. "Well, what's the word? How much did we get?"

"What is it with you? Why all the questions?"

"Come on Damon. I want to see the money."

Damon reluctantly stretched out his leg to reach into his pocket. He pulled out a roll of bills and slapped it into Angelique's outstretched hand. She immediately began counting. Joy and relief spread across her face. She made her sign of the cross and then pressed the roll of bills to her chest before tucking them into her dress pocket.

"That's a real good price. What's the grade?"

"Don't make no difference. You got what you wanted, ain't ya?"

Angelique nodded. "I'm gonna save this cash for a rainy day."

Damon shrugged and put one hand in his other pocket. "Huh, every day is a rainy day around here."

"We all worked mighty hard today. We got enough here to make ends meet. Let's make this a real celebration. I've cooked a fine meal tonight, some of your favorites. What you say to that, Damon?"

The aroma of fresh baked bread drifted out onto the porch.

"I chased a plump chicken all over the backyard this evening. Stuffed a piece a smoked sausage up the butt the way you like it. Baked up tender and juicy, skin crispy like duck. Got some smothered okra with tomatoes. And Hippolyte baked a blackberry cobbler."

Adelaide scrambled down from the wagon. "Oh Mama, I'm starvin'."

Angelique waltzed across the porch. "Come on inside."

Hippolyte stood in the doorway waving the apron tied around her waist, "Wait 'til you see what I baked for you."

Adelaide and Carrie pleaded with their father. Damon surrendered and went inside. Hippolyte poured him a cup of hot coffee while Angelique slipped into Carrie's bedroom and hid the money. The evening passed pleasantly. Adelaide recited her addition and Carrie her nursery rhymes, until they succumbed to tired yawns. Hippolyte carted the children off to bed while Angelique cleared the dishes. She heard the door slam. As promised, Damon had gone out to set the fires blazing in the drums to battle the mosquitoes.

After tending the fire, Damon paused to listen to the sounds of life inside the house. He heard Angelique's soft voice as she hummed a tune from the kitchen. The bed in his mother's room squeaked loudly. He slid his hand into his pocket, felt the small roll of bills hidden there, and walked away.

Angelique looked out of the window in time to see Damon mount his horse. The blue crock she was drying broke when it hit the wooden floor as she dashed to her hiding place. She tossed blankets from the cedar chest onto the floor as she searched for the money. She felt the leather pouch, untied the string, and counted. Angelique looked up to the heavens and said a silent prayer. It was all there.

Damon stepped into the Fist to Cuffs and scanned the room for Felix, but he was not there. He shouted above the noisy crowd, "Any of y'all seen that lazy-ass friend of mine, Felix?" Damon suspected that Felix would avoid him for as long as possible. "If you ain't heard, Felix and me, we got some unfinished business. Yessiree."

Damon's throat was parched. He tapped the counter and the bartender poured him a whiskey. He twirled his glass around and admired the dark golden liquid. His thoughts turned to Angelique. He had been stunned at her temerity—sending Adelaide with him to the cotton gin, snatching the money from his hands, and counting it in front of the child. Damon mentally rebuked her. He remembered that when Angelique was younger he had liked her fire; she could get as hot as cayenne pepper when she was a little girl. It was attractive to him then, not anymore.

It took Damon about an hour to spend the cash he had secreted from the day's earnings, and still no Felix. He was squabbling with the bartender, who refused to serve him on credit, when *Madame* Pitre peered into the doorway. She noticed Damon and ventured inside to chat with him. She held up a peculiar looking box.

"Ah Damon, have a look at this. Got it in trade. Come on, turn the handle. Won't cost you nuthin'."

She reminded Damon of an ugly scarecrow and he withdrew. "Get out of my way, you old fool." He brushed past her as *Madame* Pitre began to crank the handle of her old red box. She cranked and cranked until the funny clown popped up from inside.

"Heh, heh, pop goes the weasel," she yelled at Damon as he left. *Madame* Pitre's eyes followed him knowingly. She whispered as she stuffed the clown back inside and snapped the lid shut, "Pop goes the weasel."

An angry Damon headed for the Buckhorn Saloon across the street. Damon scanned the crowded room and found Felix. He shoved his way past several men and squeezed in next to him. Felix was nursing a beer slumped over one end of the bar. Damon drummed his palms on the counter. "Bartender, pour me a drink, my friend here is payin'. I'm mighty thirsty. Felix, you been hidin' from me?"

"Heck, no, my friend, you did good. The first bale, I heard. Congratulations."

"I don't want ya congratulations, I want my winnin's. We had a deal."

Felix stretched out his empty hands before him, his shoulder blades slid down his back. He spouted excuses: poor soil, not enough help, and no cash.

Damon chuckled. "Don't come here tellin' me no sad tales."

He trapped Felix in a pretend headlock and ruffled his thick head of hair until he forced him to pull his last few bills out of his pockets. A forlorn Felix handed them to Damon, who gave a whoop and threw the small bills at the bartender.

"Gimme a whiskey and keep it comin'."

Damon sipped slowly. "Felix, I'm gonna let you slide tonight, old fella, but I'm needin' that money awful bad. So, let's say, first light, you go down to the bank. You got plenty in there. Blacksmithing is what you do best. Leave the farmin' to me."

Felix stared at his hand curled around his beer glass, black soot caked underneath his fingernails. "Thought a change would do me good. Breathe clean fresh air, feel the dirt, and watch things I done put in the ground come up. I'm dog tired of cranking them bellows and hammerin' down steel. My ribs ain't yet healed from when that ornery ol' mare kicked."

Damon finished off his drink.

"Felix, all you need is a little time with that Maybeline who lives on the other side of town. She cheer ya up real quick like. Unless, you fancy winnin' back your money. How about double or nuthin' on the race next Saturday? My horse can beat that skinny filly that Alex Pitre calls a quarter horse."

Felix did not hesitate to shake his head. "Uh, uh, no way. I ain't doin' no more bettin' for a while."

"What's the matter with you, Felix? You don't think my horse can beat Alex Pitre's. In that case, I'll be lookin' you up bright and early in the mornin'. And you better have what you owe me."

Jean Marc was sitting at a table near the back of the saloon when Damon had walked in and gone to meet Felix. Jean Marc paid no attention to him. He was busy entertaining a few friends.

Gus teased, "Jean Marc, don't you be tellin' tales about your old uncle."

Jean Marc stood up and grinned as if on cue. "Why, Uncle Gus here is a brave man, a real hero? Y'all heard about that murderin' thief he got last winter? Uncle Gus done caught himself a chicken thief. Yessiree, he sure did."

Gus chewed on his pipe and clucked, "I guess you be tellin' on me after all."

Jean Marc winked. "Why, Uncle Gus, he heard some noise outside his place. Word was they was a thief abouts. Remember that?" The group all nodded their heads. "So, real quick like, Gus grabbed his shotgun and snuck on out to investigate. Gus was sittin' in the outhouse when he heard that thief. He knew he had to be quick like lightning. So, he took off, lickety split, headin' for the henhouse."

Jean Marc scrunched his shoulders up by his ears, took giant steps, and pretended to be Gus.

"Now, Gus, he ain't quite got the back of his long johns buttoned back up before he took off like that. Fact is, he was shinin' like the silvery moon." Jean Marc threw back his head and howled at his imaginary moon. He had everyone's attention as men poked each other, and their laughter echoed out into the black night.

Damon stepped away from the bar to figure out where all the noise was coming from. There was Jean Marc, his enemy, holding court, surrounded by men who used to be Damon's cronies.

Jean Marc continued, "Gus's dog, Scoundrel, was followin' right behind him. They was sneakin' up, sneakin' up on that thief, real quiet like." He held a fake gun up to his cheek, stepped long, and raised his knees high.

Gus's belly shook as he laughed at Jean Marc's impersonation. Gus leaned his chair back on its two wobbly legs and announced, "If I didn't love that boy like my own son, I think I'd have to whoop his ass for this." Gus turned to the man next to him and whispered, "It's good to see that boy enjoyin' himself. Ain't been the same since his Lizzie died."

Damon hollered at the bartender, demanding another beer.

Jean Marc continued.

"It was pitch black and freezin' cold. Then all of a sudden, Gus heard a commotion coming from the henhouse. Those hens went a squawking. Gus started wavin' that gun of his in every direction. No tellin' where that thief was gonna pop out. Wasn't long before that sorry–no–good–rotten–thief came sneakin' out, carryin' a chicken in each hand."

Jean Marc lifted two beer bottles off the table as if they were the chickens. He squawked and flapped his arms for effect. He was cavorting around the room through the crowd of onlookers.

"Now, don't forget, I told y'all about old Scoundrel. He was a followin' Gus real close like. And when Gus stopped short to face that thief, splat, that old dog ran right smack into Uncle Gus and slathered his bare behind with spittle."

"Gus screamed, 'Yeow!' He tripped, kersplat, and fell. Gun went off. And that thief, he dropped them chickens and went tearin' out like the devil was a chasin' him." Jean Marc slid his open palms across each other.

Damon turned to Felix, "Look at 'em, hanging on his every word. They all a bunch of fools."

Someone shouted, "How we know tha's true, Jean Marc?"

"*Mais*, I was there, me. I hear all that ruckus and got out there in time to see Gus's bare bottom. Uncle Gus was goin' after that thief just a hollerin', 'Enough of somethin' is enough, I'm gonna shoot you dead if you ever come back here'."

Jean Marc finished to an outburst of laughter.

"We ain't ever seen the likes of that thief again. And that's the whole truth! I swear to God."

Damon lurched toward the boisterous crowd.

"You ain't nuthin' but a liar, Jean Marc. Y'all ought not believe a word he says. He was probably the thief. Why, he can't even get his cotton in on time. I'm the first to do that, best grade around."

"I've about had enough of you," said Jean Marc, "Don't be callin' me a liar."

The bartender stepped out from behind the bar. "Damon, I don't want no trouble. You better get out of here."

"You heard the bartender, Damon; get your sorry ass out of here."

Damon pounced on Jean Marc. "You son-of-a-bitch." Damon's drunken punches fell short. Jean Marc had only to dodge a bit to the left or right. Damon stumbled, and everyone laughed. The bartender and Felix grabbed Damon by the armpits and carried him out to the street. Damon struggled to right himself and turned to face the swinging doors once more.

Felix gripped Damon's arm. "Leave it alone. Ain't nuthin' but trouble in there."

Damon followed Felix's advice, mounted his horse, and headed back to Belair Cove. The ride did nothing to sober him. If anything, he had become more determined as his anger boiled. He had enough of Jean Marc Fontenot. Damon bumped into a chair as he fumbled in the dark bedroom while searching for more money and his pistol.

Upon hearing strange noises, Angelique's eyes shot open. Someone was inside the house. She looked around the room to see if she could find anything to use to protect them: nothing. Her breathing came faster and faster. Then she heard Damon's fiery curses. Angelique raced to their bedroom. "Damon, what are you doin'? You'll wake the whole house."

The bedroom was in shambles. Damon took hold of Angelique's hair as she entered and yanked her toward him. "Tell me where you hid it. Where's the money?"

Hippolyte followed Angelique into the room as she secured her robe. She pulled on Damon's arm. "Damon, you let her go. You hear me? Let her go. She ain't goin' to tell you nuthin'. That money's for payin' bills." Damon released his hold on Angelique and raised his hand as if to strike his mother. Hippolyte crumbled to the floor with her hands over her head.

Angelique screamed, "Damon, NO!"

Damon was frustrated and no longer cared about the money. He yanked the pistol from the dresser drawer, searched for a box of bullets, and placed them in his pocket while the two women sat huddled in a corner. Before walking away, he looked at them with disgust. "I ain't got no use for y'all anymore."

Angelique helped Hippolyte up. She walked her back into the kitchen and set her down on a chair. "Let me check on the girls and then I'll make you a cup of warm milk."

Angelique returned. "They're still sleepin'. Thank God."

Hippolyte's face was wet with tears. "I'm really worried this time, Angelique. He got to stop all that drinkin'. It makes him crazy. What's he gonna do with that gun?"

"I wish I knew, Hippolyte." Angelique pressed the cup of warm milk into her mother-in-laws shaking hands.

Damon returned to the Buckhorn Saloon, marched inside, and aimed his pistol straight at Jean Marc's head. "Jean Marc, I'm calling you out. I've had about as much as I can stand of you causin' me trouble and sniffin' around my woman. I done told you before, stay away from us, but, no, you don't listen."

Jean Marc had his right hand in one pocket when Damon called him out. He was feeling around for coins to pay his bill. Uncle Gus stood up as Jean Marc turned around.

Damon glanced at Uncle Gus. "Sit back down, you old fool."

Uncle Gus sat down slowly while the bartender reached behind the bar, pulled out a pistol, and slid it across the uncluttered surface toward Jean Marc.

"Damon, you're one crazy bastard. You don't want to do this." Jean Marc kept his voice calm and steady.

"You don't get it, do you? You're the bastard and you ain't ever gonna get nuthin' tha's mine. Pick up the damn pistol, Jean Marc. 'Cus, I'm meanin' to get this over with."

Jean Marc hesitated. Their eyes met and he realized that Damon knew the truth. They were brothers. It chilled him to the core.

Damon stepped back ready for dueling. He began counting off. "On three. One...."

"Let's at least take it outside, Damon."

"I ain't goin' anywhere. I'm gonna shoot you right where you standin'. Jean Marc, you better pick up that gun."

Suddenly, men were scrambling. Tables were tipped and dragged from the center of the room. Chairs crashed to the floor. The crowd hid behind the tables. A few men dashed behind Damon and escaped through the doorway.

"Come on Damon, don't do this." Jean Marc inched toward the bar.

"…two…"

Damon fired before the count of three. The first bullet whizzed past Jean Marc's head. Jean Marc lunged for the pistol while Damon continued firing. Jean Marc pointed his weapon at Damon, but before he pulled the trigger, a bullet pierced his shoulder. His shot went wild; his usual precise aim was off course. Jean Marc's bullet zinged across the angry space and struck Damon in the neck. Damon fell to his knees and blood gushed from the wound, but he kept firing until he hit the floor. Jean Marc ran to Damon, and Felix ran for the sheriff.

Jean Marc turned Damon over, removed a bandanna from his pocket, and pressed it against his neck, "Hang on Damon, Felix's gone to get Doc." Damon clung to Jean Marc's shirt, a mixture of hate and fear clouded his eyes, until all life drained from his body.

The bartender knelt and felt for a pulse. "He ain't breathin', Jean Marc. You can stop."

Jean Marc pressed on the bandanna even after Damon took his final breath. He leaned over Damon's lifeless body. "You crazy-ass-drunk. *Oh, Bon Dieu, Bon Dieu.* What have I done?"

Uncle Gus came up beside Jean Marc. He put his hand on his nephew's bloody shoulder. "There wasn't nuthin' else you could do, son."

The sheriff stood over the lifeless body and listened to the witnesses; their voices rose and their hands flew as they talked all at once. He chewed on his pencil and scratched some notes for his report. It was self-defense. He and Felix Soileau put Damon in a wagon, covered him up with a burlap sack, and tied his horse to the back. The sheriff drove Damon home. Jean Marc watched as the wagon rolled out of town.

Uncle Gus spoke softly, "Come on, Jean Marc, the Doc, he gonna look at that shoulder." Uncle Gus looked back at the rolling wagon. "*Mais,* I think she gonna be better off, me."

"Gus, how is Angelique ever gonna forgive me. How we gonna get past this?" Jean Marc stayed in town that night. He slept at the boarding house down the street. He could not bring himself to face Angelique and her children.

Part III

Troisième Partie

To Grieve or Not to Grieve

Riding Damon's horse, Angelique left the house before dawn on the morning after his death. She had several loops of rope twined across her shoulder and her fiddle resting on her lap. The sky was a cloudless gray slate with a yellow paper moon hanging low, the horse and the moon her only companions on the journey. The distance to Bayou Debaillon was not far. Angelique left the road and cut through the backlands. She found a tree and tied the horse's reins to it. Angelique located the pirogue, a small flat bottom boat, stashed behind the cluster of river birch trees. She strained to pull the pirogue out of hiding, tied the rope around the tree, and tethered it to the pirogue before she pushed it into the water. She settled in and paddled a few strokes to break from the shore. The current was moving lazily. Angelique shut her eyes against the harsh reality of Damon's demise. She spoke the words aloud for the first time.

"I'm a widow."

It shocked her to hear them. She focused her attention on the colors around her, deep hues of forest green and sky blue. Black was not a color she planned to wear for a whole year.

Angelique drifted out into the middle of the bayou. Once the rope stretched tight, she placed her fiddle on her shoulder and picked up the bow. A slow dirge filled the air with the mournful sounds of deep confusion and loss. She played no particular song. She simply rested the fiddle on her shoulder and let the bow move as it willed; it was music of her own making.

Angelique played until the morning train interrupted her reverie. She heard the familiar whistle in the distance blast the shrill warning at the crossing. The lonesome sound matched her mood; the repetition of the wheels on the track called out to her, "Let go, let go, let go."

She did want to remember Damon, but not the man he had become: not the man who hobbled home late at night smelling of whiskey and who caused her to wonder if he had spent his seed on the belly of some fallen woman. She wanted to remember the man who lifted Adelaide and Carrie onto his back and rode them around, turn by turn, on a blissful day here at the bayou.

Not the man who believed that love meant control, but the man who reached over and tucked a stray hair behind her ear at dawn one summer morning.

Not the man who lost himself in gambling, but the man who surprised her with a package of ribbons and lace for dresses after winning at cards on a Sunday afternoon.

Not the man who was capable of killing Jean Marc, a childhood friend, but the man who held her in his arms as they danced on their wedding day.

Angelique turned her head to face a thicket of trees crowded together along the bank; each tree dipped its willowy branches into bayou waters. There was one gnarled, dead tree wedged in between the patch of evergreens, an old water oak. Once, it had been alive but now vines trailed down the decaying tree trunk and choked it. Angelique shivered, and then she mused, "Damon was like that vine. He smothered the life out of everythin' he touched and took no notice as it withered and died."

A deep sadness ripped through her, and then Angelique opened up to welcome forgiveness. She removed her bonnet, and her chestnut hair spilled out all around her. She rolled the bonnet up, tucked it behind her neck as a pillow, and lay down in the middle of the boat. She lifted her skirt to expose her legs to the light that would surely come. With bent knees, she waited for the sunrise.

Angelique placed her palms across her heart as the sun rose and light filtered through the canopy of leaves above her head. Leaf after leaf tilted to reach the light. A genuine smile spread across Angelique's face as she watched the changing leaves. The gentle sway of the water as it lapped against the pirogue soothed her. She reveled in the sounds of the waking forest and observed a buck with its doe drinking at the edge of the clearing. Two squirrels chased each other around a cypress tree. A male redbird landed on a sturdy branch. *The female ain't far behind,* she thought.

Angelique was serene. The lapping of muddy bayou water, the golden light illuminating the trees, and the sounds of creatures large and small brought Angelique back to wholeness—to freedom's gate. She had only to enter.

Shoe Shopping

Eula Mae was a lot like the chickens she loved. She would give you fresh eggs every morning out of pure loyalty, but cross her and she would peck your bones clean. She appeared at Angelique's door the day after Damon died.

"Gonna stay with you for a while." She set her small satchel of belongings down and opened her arms. Angelique rushed into the comfort of those arms as she had done so often as a child.

Eula Mae slept on the back porch until the winter turned cold. Then, she moved inside to lie down on a pallet near the hearth. She cooked, cleaned, and fussed over Angelique and her daughters as only a mother hen could do. She even tended to Hippolyte.

On a cold Saturday morning, Eula Mae and Adelaide were using shards of bricks as scrub brushes to scour the wooden floor. Angelique decided they should brave the weather to purchase supplies at Sylvester's Mercantile. "We're goin' into town today for supplies and shoes for Adelaide. That's all there is to it." Adelaide sloshed soapy water over her brick one more time, and then she paused to rub her aching back.

"Can we finish cleanin' the floor when we get back?"

Eula Mae chastised Adelaide. "Ain't no shame in bein' poor. Listen here, now, there's plenty shame in bein' dirty. This be a fine house and I say it gonna be a clean one before anybody goin' anywhere."

A mournful Hippolyte ignored the activity around her. She stared across the road at the naked trees bending in the wind. The Cove was as bitter and barren as the ache upon her heart, the trees like the spider veins on the back of her old legs. Both her husband and her precious son, Damon, were gone and her worst suspicions realized; Jean Marc was Domitile's son. She watched as a branch laden with ice cracked and fell.

"Can't we wait 'til it warms up a bit?" Hippolyte walked over to the fireplace and threw another log into the fire. "Coldest winter in years." Sparks and ashes flew onto Eula Mae's clean floor.

"Hippolyte, why don't you say some prayers? Maybe, throw one of your palm branches you got blessed by Father out there, and see if that'll calm this terrible winter storm?"

Eula Mae hurried over to the fireplace, slammed her bucket of soapy water onto the floor, and started scrubbing. The water splashed and soaked Hippolyte's shoes. She backed away from Eula Mae and the warmth of the fireplace.

Angelique pressed her fingers to her aching forehead. "What would y'all have me do? My girls are growin' like weeds. Adelaide's going on eight and Carrie almost five. Adelaide ain't had new shoes in two years. You want me to cut out the leather above the toes? That would look a sight for Sunday church, wouldn't it? Besides, then I couldn't hand them down to Carrie."

Adelaide stood up, faced the two elderly women, and limped around the room in her cramped shoes, her face painfully contorted.

"My big toenails turnin' blue-black. Want to see?"

Angelique pressed the issue. "It ain't money wasted 'cus in time Carrie will grow into the new ones. Marie Rose and Antoine might make me a good deal. Winter is bound to be over soon."

Angelique waved Carrie's coat like a matador; Carrie put her arms into the sleeves of the hand-me-down, and Angelique began to button it up. "Why can't I ever get somethin' new?" Carrie whined as she turned to look at her mother. "Why's it always Adelaide's turn?"

"Because, I'm older than you, and I will always get the new things first! So, there." The two girls stuck their tongues out at each other.

Eula Mae shook her head and shuddered. "Humph, don't look like winter's over to me. I guess I better come along in case these two keep pesterin' each other. Drivin' that wagon gonna be a handful enough for you in this wind, Angelique. Besides, we need more 'n shoes, I got a long list."

All eyes turned to Hippolyte. "Uh, uh, these old bones ain't goin' anywhere. Somebody has to tend that fire. I'll have a nice pot of chicken and sausage gumbo ready for y'all when you get back."

At first, Hippolyte did not mind Eula Mae taking over most of her household duties. It had taken all of Hippolyte's energy to rise and face each dark day. Lately, Hippolyte had begun to resent Eula Mae's presence, and the two old women bickered constantly.

Eula Mae clucked, "I ain't holdin' to puttin' no dried up leaves in that gumbo unless it's *filé*."

Hippolyte bragged, "Well, you ain't makin' it. Are you? I make it like I like it. Tastes better when I make it."

Eula Mae rose, hauled her bucket of dirty water to the back door, and braced the cold to dump it over the side of the porch. She chastised Hippolyte, "That gumbo gonna surely taste a lot like this here bucket of dirty water if she cookin' it." A sudden gust of wind carried her reproach away from its intended ears.

The determined group trudged out of the warm house into the frigid morning. Angelique led the way. Holding each of the girls by the hand, Eula Mae followed. They all leaned into the biting wind and shrunk into their thin coats with each difficult step. Angelique pushed open the barn doors, and they threw themselves into the musty space. Bess, the milk cow, bellowed a greeting. The barnyard cat rose and stretched. Carrie scooped the cat up into her arms, sat on a bale of hay, and began rubbing her soft fur.

Angelique shouted, "Eula Mae, can you hitch up the wagon? I got to check on something."

Angelique and Eula Mae chose not to mention to the girls the tracks they had detected. Angelique tucked the rifle under her arm, grabbed the shovel, and stepped outside. She shut the doors tightly on Eula Mae and the girls.

"I'll be back in a few," she said.

Eula Mae demanded, "You be careful, hear."

Angelique neared the horse trough and rested the shovel against the side. Eyes wide open, she circled three hundred and sixty degrees holding the rifle, raised and ready. No sign of any coyote. She followed the familiar tracks imprinted in the soft earth. This one had been clever. He had already gotten into the henhouse once this winter. She followed the tracks to the edge of the woods and then circled back.

"Another day, then."

Since there was no immediate danger, Angelique returned to the horse trough and propped the rifle up on its side. She clasped the wooden handle, placed one foot on the extended metal edge of the shovel, and pushed it into the hard ground. Her fingers were stiff from the cold and her legs cramped.

"Damn you Damon, this is all your fault."

Angelique hated to dig up their meager savings, but there was no choice. The money from the sale of the cotton had already gone to pay bills. Damon was dead, it was the worst of winters, and her children had no shoes. Angelique hoped that things would fare better after spring planting. She and her mother-in-law had stayed up late into the night discussing the situation. Hippolyte trusted Angelique to do what she thought was best.

Angelique counted out a small number of bills and tucked them into her pocket. She folded the rest, pushed them back into the tin, and buried it once more. With the back of the shovel, she pounded the dirt until it was smooth. A stinging wind chased her all the way back to the barn. Angelique opened the barn door to find Eula Mae and the girls anxiously waiting.

"Oh, *merci Bon Dieu*," Eula Mae exhaled.

Angelique snapped the reins often and pushed the mules to go faster. The old dirt road was full of ruts that made the ride into town even more difficult. It had rained icy buckets the day before. They grabbed on to whatever they could and bounced miserably. Their tight grip left fingers and toes throbbing by the time the cotton gin came into view.

Main Street resembled a ghost town. Angelique slowed to a halt in front of the store. One lone horse stood tied to the hitching post

Adelaide asked, "Where is everybody?"

Eula Mae coughed, shivered, and wrapped her thin coat tighter around her shoulders. "Most got the right idea. Kind of day you best stay close to home."

Shaking off the cold air, the girls ran into the store. Jean Marc and Antoine were sitting beside the potbellied stove, all warm and cozy, with a checkerboard between them. Angelique quickly gathered her girls to her. She had not anticipated this.

A curious Marie Rose stepped out from behind the curtain at the back of the store to greet the new customers. Surprised, she gazed from Jean Marc to Angelique and back again. The wind whistled through the crack in the door, and the firewood hissed, and snapped.

Jean Marc stood up to leave.

Antoine tugged on his arm. "We ain't finished here."

Jean Marc lowered his frame back in the chair. "Probably best I face the music."

Marie Rose jumped into action and stepped forward to greet Angelique. She jabbered enthusiastically while shutting the door firmly behind them.

"Angelique, what on earth are y'all doin' out on a day like this? Such a wonderful surprise. Get on over to the fire. I'll get some coffee for you and hot chocolate for the girls. Warm y'all up right away. How's that sound?" Carrie stepped toward the warmth of the fire with a smile as wide as the Gulf of Mexico.

Angelique whispered, "Marie Rose, I ain't got nuthin' to say to him. It's between him and the Lord."

Adelaide broke free from her mother, threw her weight against Jean Marc, and struck him hard, wailing, "You killed my Papa." Jean Marc stood still while Adelaide pounded out her punishment. Carrie was horrified and burst into tears.

Eula Mae secured the mules to the hitching post and rushed into the store. The bell over the doorway rang out and bounced tension around the room. She scrambled to take hold of Adelaide, knelt down beside her, and shook her by the shoulders. "Child, you stop talkin' like that. It ain't like you think." Eula Mae held Adelaide until she could feel the anger slip from her small body. She pointed toward a stack of shoeboxes. "You go on and see about findin' yo'self some shoes. Go on." Eula Mae pulled a sobbing Carrie to her. "Don't you fret, my precious. Adelaide just got a mighty hurt inside of her."

Jean Marc offered, "This is all my fault. Let me talk to Adelaide."

Eula Mae put up her hand as if it were a stop sign. "Tha's not the way I heard it. It's best we leave her be, Jean Marc."

Angelique remained frozen during the whole outburst. Her eyes never left Jean Marc's face, but she directed her words to Marie Rose. "We gonna get the usual, a pair of plain brown lace ups. Need good leather and a whole size bigger than her foot." She willed herself to walk to the back of the store to see about the shoes. Adelaide was sitting on the floor with her hands folded across her chest. Angelique sat on the floor next to her.

"He killed Papa."

"He didn't mean to, Adelaide. Papa was drunk and actin' all crazy."

"I want my Papa."

"He's gone, Adelaide, and we got to make the best of it." Angelique handed Adelaide a handkerchief. "Now, dry those tears and let's see if we can find you some real nice shoes."

Adelaide looked up at the samples. "I like those." Marie Rose rushed over to measure Adelaide's foot.

Angelique whispered, "By some chance, would these be on sale? It ain't like last time. I got money to pay for everythin' today. Still and all, I prefer the savin's."

Marie Rose smiled and nodded. "I got just the thing."

Eula Mae went about the store gathering the items on their list. Carrie shadowed her so closely that she almost tripped her a few times. Eula Mae approached the counter with her arms full of merchandise. Carrie remained hidden behind Eula Mae's skirt and studied Jean Marc's face. With childlike curiosity, she boldly asked, "Is it true? You killed my Papa?"

Antoine scattered the checkers across the board and Marie Rose spilled the tray of hot coffee that she was carrying. Angelique gasped and darted for Carrie. She snatched her daughter by the arm and pulled threateningly. "Carrie, hush."

Jean Marc stood up. "Angelique, let me talk to her."

He walked over, picked up Carrie, and set her down on the counter before anyone could object. He bent down so that he could look into her tiny face. Carrie began to whimper. Jean Marc reached over, took a few hard candies from an open bin on the counter, and handed them to Carrie. "Go ahead, choose whatever you want."

Carrie shivered. "You ain't gonna hurt me are you?"

He smiled. "You got beautiful eyes, Miss Carrie, just like your mama. No, child, I ain't gonna hurt you."

Carrie reached down and chose a lemon drop, twisted open the wrapper, and popped it into her mouth. "Um, thank you."

"Carrie you're a brave little girl. It's best we get things out in the open." Jean Marc continued, "I see you got a cut on your forehead."

Carrie touched her forehead. "I fell. Mama says it ain't gonna leave a mark."

"Did that hurt?"

Carrie glanced at Angelique for reassurance.

"It wasn't my fault. Adelaide pushed me."

From the back of the store, Adelaide yelled, "I did not. It was an accident."

"Well, that's kind of what happened with me and your papa."

"Papa pushed you?" Carrie furrowed her brow.

"He's lyin'," Adelaide yelled.

Jean Marc ignored Adelaide's outburst. "Well, not exactly. It was an accident."

Carrie thought about this. "Oh, you got a mark to show for it?"

"I got a big scar on my heart, but that don't change nuthin' 'cus your papa's gone." Jean Marc looked at Angelique.

Carrie pointed to Jean Marc's heart. "Can I see it?"

A remorseful Jean Marc answered, "No child, it's not the kind of scar that you can see. It's there all the same. You understand?"

Carrie twisted her lips to one side, the rock hard candy poking out from her cheek; she nodded. "You didn't mean to kill Papa."

"Tha's right. It's just a real bad thing that shouldn't have happened, but it did." Jean Marc reached into his pocket, pulled out a quarter, and handed it to Carrie. "You go and give this to Mr. Antoine to pay for the candy. He'll give you a few nickels in change to keep."

Jean Marc faced Angelique. "Angelique, I'm so sorry. If you need anything, anything at all."

He did not wait for her answer, but turned around and hurried out of the store. He headed straight across the street to the Fist to Cuffs Saloon. Angelique trembled as she stared at his back.

Carrie squealed, "I knew what Adelaide said wasn't true." She turned the palm of her hand to her mother. "*Ga*, Mama, *ga*, look."

Angelique lifted the coin from Carrie's palm and rested it in her own. Circling a memory, she lifted her finger and rubbed the edge of the coin. It haunted her, a reminder of the coin that rested in the white handkerchief with the embroidered initial on the corner. She handed it back to Carrie. "You keep the quarter. I'll pay for the candy."

Adelaide pouted and complained, "That's not fair."

Angelique replied, "Adelaide, you get new shoes and Carrie gets to keep this coin for herself."

They collected all of their parcels, spoke their goodbyes, and braced themselves against the bitter weather once more. Eula Mae dared to glimpse inside the Fist to Cuffs as they drove past. Jean Marc sat at the bar alone and lifeless.

The wagon bumped along rhythmically as they headed home. Angelique concentrated on her driving, her face pinched tight. The wind had died down and that eased the journey. The steady bumpity-bump-bump dulled any need for conversation, until Carrie nearly dropped her quarter.

Eula Mae instructed, "Carrie, give that quarter to your mama 'til you get home. You about to drop it between them floor boards."

Carrie complied. The girls huddled closer together on the floorboard with a horsehair blanket tucked tightly around them. They were soon lulled to silence. Angelique handed Eula Mae her small satchel, and she inserted the quarter.

"Carrie, we're almost home. We gonna tuck this quarter away in a safe place when we get there. You know, I once had a special coin all my own. I kept it as a souvenir. You can do the same thing."

Angelique thought about Jean Marc's nickel throughout the long evening. Adelaide fell asleep wearing her new shoes, a return item from a previous customer. Carrie's eyes grew heavy and Angelique lifted her youngest child from her lap. She tucked Carrie into the bed beside Adelaide. Hippolyte handed her two hot bricks wrapped in a thick cloth. Angelique returned to the bedroom and slipped each beneath the covers near their feet. She tiptoed out of the room.

Angelique set the kerosene lamp on her bureau. She shut the door of her room quietly and knelt on the floor. She pulled open each drawer and looked through her scant belongings. *Where was that handkerchief?* Angelique found the small remnant saved from her childhood. Shutting the bureau drawers, she sat with the handkerchief in her open palm and fingered the embroidered edges of the fabric. She untied the knot in the handkerchief and gazed at the dull nickel inside. *Could it be possible...?*

Angelique smoothed out the wrinkles in the crumpled handkerchief, and then she folded the four corners of the yellowed fabric in upon itself. The dull nickel rested neatly at the center. She clasped the handkerchief in her hand, raised it to her forehead, and prayed. She slipped the delicate handkerchief under her pillow, lay down to rest upon it, and waited for sleep to come.

Time for Forgiveness

Jean Marc had made his home at the Comeaux Boarding House and the Fist to Cuffs Saloon since Damon's death. He could not frequent the Buckhorn Saloon, the bloodstain on the floor still too visible. The Fist to Cuffs was a barbershop and restaurant by day and a saloon by night. It was a place where the inebriated could reside far past the darkest hours. In spite of being sandwiched between the chaos, people left Jean Marc alone. He sought comfort at the bottom of a bottle. He could not bring himself to return to Belair Cove. No one could dissuade him from his guilt. He had been too ashamed to attend Damon's funeral. Jean Marc had concluded that it was better for everyone if he stayed away.

At Eula Mae's insistence, Josef, her grandson, had been caring for Jean Marc's place in his absence. Josef had grown into a strong, handsome young man with a kind and tender heart. He had canned Jean Marc's vegetables and fed his animals. With the help of Jean Marc's relatives and friends, Josef had picked Jean Marc's cotton and placed the earnings in Elizabeth's cookie jar. Josef walked the short distance to Uncle Gus's place and handed the jar over to him.

"For safekeeping," he said.

Eula Mae grew tired of waiting for Jean Marc to return to Belair Cove. One day, she aired out Jean Marc's house, prepared a hot meal, and dressed in her Sunday best. She wrapped a deep plum headdress around her wisps of grey hair and ordered her grandson to bring Jean Marc's old buggy to the front gate.

"I do whatever you want me to 'cus I be a mite curious. What you up to today, Grandma?"

Eula Mae huffed, "I'd best take matters into my own hands. Why it's plain nonsense. Gus should a fetched that boy back home long before now. He be turnin' sour stayin' in town like that."

Josef grinned and was happy to drive her into Ville Platte.

They found Jean Marc sipping whiskey at the Fist to Cuffs. It was not even noon. Eula Mae waited at the door until Clyde Boudreaux walked past. She stretched all four feet eleven inches of her thin body as tall as she could. "Clyde, I need a favor. Would you please ask Jean Marc to come on out? I got to have me a word with him."

Jean Marc moaned when he heard who was waiting for him, and then he went to the door. "Eula Mae, what you doin' here?"

"I need to have a word with you, tha's all. You gonna step outside? I reckon I could still drag you out on your ear. Which way it gonna be?"

Jean Marc rolled his eyes, squared his shoulders, and stepped toward her.

Eula Mae faced him. "Damon be gone. Tha's all there is to it. And to my recollection, he ain't worth all this heartache I see goin' on around me. Damon made choices. They was all bad ones, the way I see it. He has the Lord to reckon with now. Jean Marc, go on home."

Jean Marc opened his mouth to speak, "Eula Mae, you don't understand. I shot my own…"

Eula Mae stopped him with an upright palm to his chest.

"I been livin' here in these parts all my life and I know more than you about folks. Ain't gonna change a thing. What's done is done. Like I told you before. It ain't your fault. Damon a bad seed and tha's all there is to it."

With that said, she pointed to the buggy. "Go on. Get in. Josef will fetch your horse from the livery."

"Yes, ma'am."

Jean Marc allowed Eula Mae to lead him home reminiscent of the prodigal son. He returned to the empty house that he and Elizabeth had once shared. Since Elizabeth's death, there had been no space in it where he felt at ease. It still felt uncomfortable. He began sleeping on the back porch. From that vantage point, he found solace in the stars.

It also gave him his first glimpse of Angelique. She walked in front of an open window carrying a lamp and placed it on a bedside stand. The darkness turned to light and an amber glow filled the room. She was a willowy silhouette that dipped in and out between the shadowy trees and tall bushes. Jean Marc snuffed out his pipe, stepped off the porch, and dared to inch closer. He watched as Angelique prepared her daughters for bed. They knelt for prayers, and then she tucked them in. She leaned over each of them for a brief moment and kissed them repeatedly. Finally, she snuffed out the kerosene lamp and closed the door. The dark house slept. Jean Marc was restless.

Early the next morning, neighbors saw Jean Marc clearing away the brush that separated the two properties. He tackled the project with renewed energy. A cold supper was the best he could do most evenings as he hastened toward the dark cover of night and sat on his porch. He longed for another glimpse of Angelique, and his heart ached. *Was it possible? Could she ever forgive him? How long would he have to wait?*

In deference to the watchful eyes of Belair Cove, Angelique had chosen to follow the customs of grieving widows. The most difficult tradition to adhere to was a world without music. It was hard not to play her fiddle and allow it to mirror the freedom she felt in her soul. She looked at her reflection before turning in each night, the black widow's garb hanging on her bedpost. How had she become this hollow shell of her lost youth? It was not as if her life had gone wrong all at once. A loud alarm had not warned her. Instead, it was similar to misfortunes that slowly dripped from an oak barrel and continued to leak no matter how she tried to stop it. At last, she made a decision.

"Enough of this."

She picked up the black blouse and stuffed it in a drawer. She selected a delicate grey blouse to wear with her black skirt, a signal to all that her mourning was ending. The required six months had not yet passed.

Jean Marc was quick to notice this subtle shift, yet chose to remain a respectful distance. Whatever might happen between them, if anything, had to be her decision. In the meantime, he began to make bold changes around his place. He made an inventory of home improvements that he needed to accomplish. He pulled up Elizabeth's untended azaleas and planted white camellias with dark green glossy leaves. He hoped they would bloom and lift the dead off the next winter. Jean Marc began to wave as curious neighbors passed by.

"Place lookin' better, ain't it?"

With his toolbox in his hand, Uncle Gus stopped by and offered, "Thought maybe you could use a little help around here."

"I reckon that would be fine with me."

Uncle Gus came and enveloped Jean Marc in a manly hug. "It's done then. See, this the reason why you gonna stay right here in this Cove. It's good friends and lots of family, too." Family and friends flocked to his side to lend a hand, a *coup de main*.

"Things are lookin' brighter for sure. Place needed some changes." Jean Marc's home place was alive with the sound of work. Together, they converted the front bedroom that Jean Marc and Elizabeth had shared into a study, complete with bookshelves and a fireplace. He ordered a sturdy desk and placed it in the center of the room with two chairs on either side.

Next, they added a third bedroom to the back of the house, each interior doorway opening from one bedroom to the next. Jean Marc enclosed the back porch and made it into his new bedroom. The combination of rooms lengthened the house on one side. Everyone laughed at the house that now resembled a lopsided letter L.

Jean Marc scratched his head. "Guess I shoulda hired me a draftsman or somethin' akin to it. But, I think I can fix this." Squaring the house off once again, he constructed an additional porch off the new bedroom. This porch faced directly across from Angelique's house. Here he planted hydrangeas, Angelique's favorite. Surely, the flowers would draw her eyes to his place. Jean Marc fell into bed at the end of each day totally exhausted.

Finally, he extended the fence surrounding the house to incorporate a nearby shade tree. There, he attached a rope swing. He even tried it out, his long legs dragging the ground.

Gus commented, "What you need that for?"

"Gus, it's like you said, I gonna let the chips fall where they may."

Gus smiled in approval. "Tha's my boy."

Intuitively, Jean Marc was always aware of Angelique and Hippolyte as they went about their daily chores. He began to tip his hat or nod his head. Neither woman acknowledged his greeting. He was surprised one day by Hippolyte's presence near his outside gate. Warning him that a stranger was approaching, his Catahoula Hound, an offspring of Capsay, barked and barked. Hippolyte stood there holding Carrie's hand.

"Afternoon, Jean Marc. A word with you, please?"

No longer faint of heart, Jean Marc quieted the hound, rose from his gardening, and walked over to them. "Carrie, don't let that old hound dog scare ya. She don't mean nuthin'.'" Jean Marc tipped his hat to Hippolyte. "Mornin' ma'am. I'm glad you dropped by today. I'm not sure what to say. If I could take it back... Except, I didn't mean Damon no harm. It all happened so fast."

Hippolyte interrupted with a wave of her hand as a tear slid down her face. "Jean Marc, the sheriff told me how it happened at the Buckhorn. Other folks say the same. I been thinkin' on it and I'm plenty mad at that boy. It was the war that done it to him. Damon came back different. He had plenty of time to cool off between here and the Buckhorn, no matter what grievance he had against you. I reckon it weren't nobody's fault."

Jean Marc reached out to her. Hippolyte brushed him aside briskly. "Thank you, Hippolyte. If there's anything I can do. Please. Anything."

"Well, come on child, we best be gettin' home. We got lots to do before dark. Our business here is done." Hippolyte lowered her eyes to find Carrie's little hand still resting in her clammy one. The two walked away. Carrie began to swing their arms from side to side. Hippolyte found comfort in the steady swaying and smiled down at her grandchild.

Angelique

Angelique remembered vividly the night when the sheriff stood with hat in hand to explain the events that led to Damon's death. She remembered Hippolyte scrambling into the wagon and rocking Damon's body while she shouted at the sheriff. "If my Domitile was still here, he'd put a posse together and get that Jean Marc. Make him hang for dis." Angelique remembered shielding Adelaide from the sight of her dead father, bloodied and cold.

She recalled the sheriff's words, "Damon was out of his head, acting crazy," and something about a "duel with Jean Marc." Angelique was numb to his words. The sheriff rattled on; his voice resembled the squawk of a crow.

Damon was gone. His time was over. Angelique needed to know if Jean Marc had been hurt. She could not read the sheriff's face because the night was black. "Was anyone else hurt?"

"I ain't ever seen so many bullet holes all over the damn place. Yep, Damon got Jean Marc."

His words hung in the air, until he added, "Went clean through the shoulder. He'll be fine in a couple a weeks. Everyone else scattered this way and that a way. Why, Damon, he just went crazy. Ain't nobody to haul off to jail on this one. It's Damon's doin's. I am sorry for your loss, Mrs. Angelique, Mrs. Hippolyte."

Angelique had been in mourning from the day she married Damon. That had made it easier for her to slip into the black widow's dress. It shamed her to realize that. Angelique carried her regrets as if it were a pail of milk, heavy in her arms. She tossed and turned many a night thinking, *maybe, if I had….maybe if I hadn't….*

She could recall days when she wished Damon dead. On those occasions, she prayed two rosaries a day: one in the morning for forgiveness and one in the evening with the girls and Hippolyte. They gathered and knelt by the bed, the bed she and Damon had shared.

Angelique tried to respect Damon's passing as an example for her girls and out of concern for his mother. However, she could not bring herself to follow Hippolyte to the cemetery to place fresh flowers on his grave. After Hippolyte had gone to visit Jean Marc, she stopped begging Angelique to go with her to Damon's grave. Angelique did not know about her mother-in-law's act of forgiveness, but felt relief all the same.

The harsh winter wind shook off any remnants of paint on Angelique's house as if it, too, were shaking off the past. The old white paint cracked, curled, and peeled away as the March winds descended and released the last of winter's grip. The sky was awash in shades of periwinkle. April showers shattered winter's hold; the spark of rebirth flowed from bend to bend. Spring arrived with the first budding of the pecan trees, the surest sign. The tree limbs curved to the ground and elbowed each other. Angelique Vidrine's house breathed laughter and life.

The Fontenots told the Boudreauxs, who told the Lafleurs, who whispered it to the Duplechins, and so it went until the whole of Belair Cove shared the same dream. Angelique and Jean Marc belonged together. It would soon be their time.

Shortly after Damon's death, Angelique had hired Josef to help her around the place. Angelique had watched as he plowed down the leftover cotton stalks. Josef plowed new ground as well, right up to the fence line near the house. He would have gone all the way to her front door if Angelique had allowed it.

"Miss Angie, next spring, we need every inch of ground if we gonna turn this here farm around. Yessiree, it gonna make money now that...."

Josef choked on his words and the whites of his eyes shown. His near blunder had not bothered Angelique, however. She grieved no more. In fact, Angelique could not remember ever feeling so free.

Josef had been quick to inform Angelique that Jean Marc had returned to Belair Cove. It still surprised her when she heard his voice resonating across the space that separated them one sunny morning. She and Adelaide were brushing down Thunder after a brisk ride.

Jean Marc was yelling at Tess, his goat. "Get out of my way, old girl. You gonna be a tasty supper if you don't. It's too late to help me out."

Tess moseyed over a few yards and continued to pull up roots and munch without concern. Jean Marc thrashed his swing blade across the tall grass. Sunlight glistened off the blade as it swiped across the grass in a fluid motion. His chest was bare except for a stringed pouch hanging from his neck, no doubt one of *Madame* Pitre's potions. Jean Marc's forearms strained and softened in rhythm to the swing blade.

Angelique stared boldly for a moment. Jean Marc paused to massage the stiff muscles around the raised pink scar on his shoulder, a constant reminder of what had happened. Afraid that he might catch her staring at him, she pretended that the wild prairie overhead held her interest. Angelique reluctantly shifted her eyes in the distance.

She focused on the beauty of the Cove, an astounding palette of warm colors. She shaded her eyes against the glaring sunlight. Spring's green, a panorama from dark to light in shades too numerous to name inched slowly across the countryside. The azure blue of the sky was more vibrant than she imagined the ocean to be. Across the heavens, white clouds painted the sky in light delicate sweeps. Angelique inhaled deeply.

"Mama, you ain't listenin'. If I do a good job, can I take Thunder for a ride this afternoon?" Adelaide whined.

"Huh? No child, I got to teach you how to set his saddle first. Sunday might be a good time, Sunday afternoon."

Adelaide hung her lip and slowed her movements.

Angelique let Adelaide walk Thunder out to the fenced-in pasture and turn him loose. They climbed the fence to watch as he trotted off. Thunder lifted his head proudly, shook himself off, and galloped to join the other horses. He played for a while. Adelaide closed the gate, held out some feed, and called to him. Thunder perked up his ears and tail, sniffed the air, and galloped over to feed from Adelaide's hand.

Angelique stroked his mane and hugged him. "Thunder, I get how you feel. It's good to roam free. Ain't it boy."

Angelique worked steadily in the garden all afternoon, Carrie at her side. Every now and again, she would lift her head from her weeding, pretend to massage her aching shoulders, and then discreetly glance across the pasture to find Jean Marc. When she saw him, the palm of her hand leapt to her racing heart, and pounded out an old familiar beat.

Angelique found comfort in the recurring rhythm and allowed her feelings for Jean Marc to wash over her. She would have stood there for some time, but suddenly Adelaide shot across the pasture riding Thunder bareback. Even though she had a tight hold on the horse's mane, Adelaide struggled to stay upright. Thunder was speeding straight for the ancient oaks whose huge limbs stretched out and dipped to the ground. Angelique dropped her hoe and started running.

"Adelaide! Adelaide, hang on!"

Jean Marc was leaning against the trunk of a pecan tree savoring the first sip of a cool beer when he first heard Angelique screaming. Chasing the panic in Angelique's voice, he dropped the beer bottle and sprinted. He saw the horse racing straight toward a tremendous oak tree. If Thunder reached the tree, the lower limbs would crush Adelaide. Jean Marc ran in a wide circle, came up alongside the spooked horse, and held his arms up high.

"Adelaide, Adelaide, hands up. Grab a hold of that branch."

A terrified Adelaide screamed when she saw the tree limb looming ahead of her, but she obeyed Jean Marc. She closed her eyes, lifted her arms high, and when she felt the branch make contact with her body, wrapped her arms around it. Thunder sailed under the limb and raced onward. He traveled the length of the pasture before he slowed down. Adelaide hung there with her legs dangling and the wind knocked out of her.

Jean Marc was out of breath when he reached Adelaide. "Adelaide, I've got you. You can let go of the branch."

"No, I'm afraid. It's too high. I'm gonna fall."

"I'm not goin' to let you fall. Let go."

Adelaide dropped into Jean Marc's arms as Angelique caught up to them. She took Adelaide from him and crumpled to the ground holding her daughter. "Adelaide, you coulda been killed." The reality of what might have happened gripped Adelaide and she burst into tears.

"She hit that tree hard, might have cracked a rib, but we'll know soon enough. Anyways, that'll heal in time." Jean Marc sounded relieved.

"Stop that crying right now. This is all your fault. Jean Marc, thank God you were here."

Jean Marc shrugged his shoulders in response and tried to lighten the situation. "Thank God Adelaide listened to me for once."

"This would never have happened if Adelaide had obeyed me to begin with."

"Aw, a little mischief don't hurt nobody. Looks to me like things just got out of hand."

"Mischief seems to be Adelaide's middle name. I better get her home."

"Good idea. Don't worry about Thunder. I'll fetch him for you."

It pained Jean Marc to stare at Angelique's back as she struggled with Adelaide in her arms and walked away from him. It was something to do with the way she spoke his name. There was so much more he wanted to do to help her, if only she would allow it. His eyes followed her as she walked to her house and climbed the steps to the porch. He watched as Angelique knelt in front of Adelaide and lifted her shirt to examine her for scrapes and bruises. Then, she began scolding; *a tête-à-tête* was definitely in order. Angelique's hair came loose and fell carelessly to her shoulders as she chastised her daughter. Jean Marc's eyes followed the curve of her breasts and hips until he could not bear it any longer.

Jean Marc went home, saddled his horse, and trotted off to round up Thunder. He caught up with the colt in the grazing pasture, managed to rope him, and walk him home. He did not stop to inform Angelique that he had returned Thunder to the paddock. He thought it best to leave her alone.

Jean Marc noticed the beer bottle he had dropped in his haste to rescue Adelaide. He poured out the remaining hot beer. He decided that he would not go the way of Damon. Jean Marc had a reason for living. The past was finished. He had loved his wife. He had tried to breathe life into her after their baby died. The war had taken too much from her. Jean Marc reasoned, *"By golly, I ain't gonna do the same. I want another chance. Me, I choose life."*

Carrie

Jean Marc chose life, but it was a curious little creature named Carrie who brought it forth. She appeared out of nowhere one morning. Carrie grinned, showing off the gap in her mouth where a tooth should have been.

"Jesus, Carrie, you scared me. Where'd you come from?"

"Adelaide bein' mean to me."

"Lookie here, you done got in a fight with your big sister?" Jean Marc teased.

Carrie shook her head and blew air in the space where her tooth should have been. "I done lost my first teef. Mama put it under my pillow last night. See what the mouse brung me." Carrie held out a shiny nickel in her palm for Jean Marc to admire.

"Ooh-wee, what you gonna do with that much money?"

Carrie shrugged. "Think I'll hold on to it for a while. Add it to the quarter you gived me."

"That's my girl," Jean Marc said. "Who's your friend?"

A grey and white spotted Catahoula Hound perked up her ears and stared at Jean Marc with one blue eye and one brown eye. Though still a pup, the dog stood almost as tall as Carrie did.

"This here's *Capon*. She's a coward because she sits under the table tremblin' when it thunders. Mama and me tried to feed her leftovers thinkin' it'd help. It don't. She shivers like clabbered milk in a bowl. Tha's why I named her *Capon*."

Carrie and *Capon* edged a bit closer. "What you doin'?"

Hammer in hand, Jean Marc pointed at the step. "I'm fixin' this step so you don't fall over when y'all come visitin'."

"Can I watch?"

"I reckon so. You might even be of some help."

Carrie and *Capon* soon became regulars at Jean Marc's place. Neighbors laughed as they watched the threesome, Carrie and Jean Marc with *Capon* following close behind.

"Where y'all off to today?" a neighbor would ask.

"Why, me and little Carrie here got big plans for today. Don't we Carrie?"

Carrie showed off a wide-gapped smile. "Big plans."

Carrie often returned home sucking on a hard candy, jabbering about baby goats, and having to take care of wounded birds. One evening Carrie rushed home speckled with white paint. Balancing gingerly, she put her dirty elbows on the table and lifted her bare feet off the floor. Carrie talked so fast that the wind whistled between her missing teeth.

"Mr. Jean Marc said…" or "Me and Mr. Jean Marc caught…"

Hippolyte reprimanded Angelique. "It ain't good for that child to be with him all the time like that." She waved her wooden spoon in the direction of Jean Marc's house. Hippolyte dropped bacon fat into a frying pan, added stale cornbread, and then a pinch of salt. She was making *couche couche* for supper. The aroma of sweet potatoes sprinkled with cinnamon drifted from the oven.

"That child don't stop talkin' ever since she started goin' over there, and she comes home smellin' like a wet, old dog."

Adelaide added, "I saw her over there today while I was gettin' the cedar, Mama. She was supposed to be pullin' weeds in the garden."

Angelique lifted the hot iron from the stove, tapped it, and then pressed it against the cedar leaves. The iron glided easily over her Sunday dress. She looked up briefly. "*Capon* gonna keep an eye on her. Ain't you girl?" *Capon* stood up and wagged her tail.

"You're just jealous. Mr. Jean Marc needs my help. I got to help him paint his house. Mama, I like goin' over there. And I still do all my chores."

Angelique shrugged her shoulders and shook out her next garment for ironing. "Me, I got bigger worries," she responded. "You can help all you like, but Carrie, don't you bother him none."

"No ma'am."

On Sunday, the Vidrine family sat on the fifth pew on the right side of the tiny church in Belair Cove. They filed in together with the exception of Eula Mae, who opted to attend a healing service outdoors in the backlands with gospel singing and Bible preaching. Carrie was pouting because she preferred to go to church with Eula

Mae. She was at the age where she hated the scratchy starch in her dress, the tightness of her shoes, and the silly ribbon in her wavy hair.

"I do declare, that one's turning into a little heathen," Hippolyte impressed upon Angelique. Hippolyte kept a tight hold on Carrie's arm. Somehow, she still managed to wriggle around to face the back of the church. Carrie suddenly smiled happily and started waving wildly with her free hand. The curious turned and followed her gaze.

Jean Marc was walking into church, hat in hand. He had not been there since Damon's death. "Glad to have him back," neighbors whispered and nudged each other in agreement. Uncle Gus motioned for the rest of his family to push over. They made room for Jean Marc in their pew, which was one row behind and across from Angelique. Uncle Gus patted Jean Marc several times on his back; and the *whop, whop, whop* reverberated through the church.

Angelique twisted around and quickly turned back, her face flushed. Father entered the church and the congregation focused their attention on the Mass. Angelique was unable to concentrate. Even though she moved by practiced ritual, twice she knelt or stood after the rest of the worshippers. She recited her prayers and sang the songs from sheer memory; her music book wobbled slightly.

At communion, Hippolyte was slow to rise. She showed the girls how to bow their heads and took her time exiting the pew. Hippolyte motioned for Adelaide and Carrie to step in front of her. Angelique had no recourse but to follow them; she and Jean Marc reached the aisle at the same time. They waited their turn and knelt side by side at the communion rail. Jean Marc kept his head down. Angelique raised her eyes to the crucifix behind the altar and prayed for strength.

After Mass, Father paused to shake Jean Marc's hand as he led the procession out of the church. "We had a good visit yesterday. Glad to have you home, son."

Yesterday, Jean Marc had waited until last to enter the confessional. He had made his sign of the cross and recited the opening prayer before recounting his sin to Father. He had killed his own brother. He had not meant to, but all the same, he had to confess.

Instead of absolution, Father invited him to supper.

"Tha's a bit unusual. Don't you think, Father?"

"Well, I guess you'll just have to think of this as your penance."

"In that case, got no choice in the matter."

They drank a bottle of wine and talked late into the night. Father gave Jean Marc words of reconciliation that reached him and brought him back to the flock. Jean Marc had only to forgive himself.

Carrie climbed over everyone to get out of the pew and reach Jean Marc. She tapped him on the back and placed her hand in his. "Carrie, aren't you a pretty sight this morning?"

Jean Marc sidled up to Angelique. "I see you got all the paint off her face. Sorry about that. Your Carrie is a good helper. She sure is."

Carrie beamed, "See, Mama, I told you I was a good worker."

"You know, I got plenty extra paint. If you want, I could come over and help whitewash your place. Carrie can help me."

Angelique could only nod her head.

Carrie held her mama's hand and the three of them walked out of church together. Angelique and Jean Marc stood on either side of little Carrie. They were the last to leave. Pretending to be engrossed in conversation, several women stood outside the entrance, but their curious eyes were on the threesome. The sun shone brightly through the stained glass in the church as Jean Marc and Angelique exited. The women greeted them with broad smiles and whispered approvals. The men tipped their hats to Angelique and winked at Jean Marc.

All of Belair Cove was hopeful for Jean Marc and Angelique. Marie Rose suggested to Antoine that he schedule a game of checkers with Jean Marc on the first Saturday of each month, the day that Angelique came in to town for supplies. Antoine was happy to oblige.

Jean Marc agreed, "I think tha's a real good idea. Who knows who I might run into some morning?"

The plan worked perfectly. Shortly after that, Angelique arrived at the store alone. Jean Marc sat at the card table in deep concentration. Antoine was beating him at checkers again.

Marie Rose sprang into action. She ordered Angelique to the back of the store for a cup of steaming hot coffee, took the supply list from her hand, and busied herself gathering the items.

Antoine spread his fingers out, crossed them between each other forming a tight fist, turned them inside out, and stretched. "Jean Marc, I got to think on that last play for a minute. Why don't we take a break? Would you be so kind as to get us some coffee?" Antoine raised his eyebrows a few times, and then he pushed his sliding glasses back up on his nose.

Jean Marc slipped behind the curtain at the back of the store and surprised Angelique. He inched closer and closer to her. She pressed her back against the feed sacks. "Mornin', Angelique. I do believe we bumpin' into each other every which way."

"Why, Saturday has always been my shoppin' day."

A curious Antoine crept toward the curtain, but Marie Rose blocked him with a loving hand and an index finger to her lips. The two pretended to be busy, but remained idly by.

Jean Marc said teasingly, "What a coincidence, I play checkers with Antoine here most Saturdays. Where's that pretty little girl of yours, Carrie?"

"Home."

"Well, tha's odd. Ain't it? Both Carrie and Adelaide stayed home. Humph?"

Trying to sound casual, Angelique shrugged. "Not really." She did not want Jean Marc to know that Marie Rose had inadvertently told her about the weekly game of checkers.

Jean Marc poured two cups of coffee from the pot on the stove and winked at her. He stepped through the curtain to the front of the store. Angelique composed herself, tried to hide the Cheshire cat grin that spread across her face, and stepped through the curtain as well.

A week later, the Boudreauxs invited Angelique to dinner. As luck would have it, Jean Marc happened to be there. "This fried chicken is to die for. Who cooked it? Might have to change my mind about staying single and marry a woman who can cook fried chicken this good."

"Angelique brought that," Mrs. Boudreux replied.

"Is that a fact?"

Jean Marc and Angelique found themselves in a subtle dance of discretion and desire. Their eyes followed each other's every step. He would lean his chair back to glance at her while she worked in the kitchen. Angelique watched him as he tossed horseshoes or washed his hands at the water pump. This charade continued week after week.

The Lafleurs hired Angelique to play the fiddle at their son's wedding with other local musicians. Jean Marc was the groom's best man. At the reception, he walked boldly up to Angelique. "What would it take to convince you to put that fiddle down at the end of the evening and save the last dance for me?"

"You'd only have to ask."

"Well, I'm askin' then."

Angelique was surprised at how his nearness left her speechless. Jean Marc noticed how her eyes sparkled and held her gaze as they spiraled around the room until she was giddy. The other guests prided themselves on their matchmaking skills and exchanged bets on how long it would take Jean Marc to propose. The neighbors conspired to throw the two together as often as possible. Conversation between Jean Marc and Angelique became easier— lighter and more playful.

Little Carrie bounced between her house and Jean Marc's with her pigtails flying in the wind. One day, Jean Marc sent her home with a filleted catfish for her family. Angelique returned the favor by sending Carrie back with a blackberry cobbler. Bearing gifts, Carrie tromped from house to house every day. Neither adult spoke directly to each other.

Finally, Carrie balked, "Suppose I spill it? Why don't you go take the stew over there, Mama?"

"Carrie, just do as you're told. You go on. Take this to *Monsieur* Jean Marc and be sure to tell him thank you for the rabbit."

Carrie traipsed back across the pasture, jostling the pot. She delivered her own version of the message when she reached Jean Marc's house and plopped the pot of stew on the kitchen table.

"Mama said to thank you for the rabbit and give you this. I told her she ought to bring it over herself. *Monsieur* Jean Marc, I think my Mama likes you. What you got for me to take back to her, anything?"

Jean Marc

Jean Marc agreed with Carrie. *Sweetpea's on to somethin'. Angelique, she comin' around.*

Yet, Jean Marc needed a bolder sign from Angelique other than Carrie delivering meals. He needed something that truly signaled that Angelique was indeed ready for a new beginning. Nevertheless, it caught him off guard when it arrived.

Angelique stood at the fence and called out, "Jean Marc, a word with you please?" She ran her hands over her waist several times and smoothed out the wrinkles in the front of her skirt as he approached. She was wearing her favorite blue bonnet that matched her blouse.

Jean Marc dropped his trowel to the ground, dusted off his hands, and rushed to greet her. "Mornin' Angelique, I was hopin' you'd come by some time. You lookin' mighty pretty."

"I'm here to talk to you about Carrie. She's spending an awful lot of time under your feet. Like I told you, I don't want her to bother you none."

"Oh no, Carrie's real special. She's a clever girl and a real good helper. She ain't a bother at all."

Jean Marc motioned toward the porch. "You have the time to sit a spell?"

Angelique shook her head. "Not today. I must say though, your place is lookin' real nice."

"Place needed some changes. Have you seen the hydrangeas I planted?" He pointed to the back yard.

A coy grin spread across her face. "They're real nice. Well, if she's no trouble then. I'll...I'll be on my way."

"Like I said, I got plenty extra white paint. You just gotta say the word."

Jean Marc watched her walk away, the sway of her hips like sweet paradise. He pressed his palm to his chest and felt for the small brown sack hanging from a leather string around his neck, a gift from *Madame* Pitre.

"This *gris-gris* is a love potion I made 'specially for you."

Jean Marc straightened his shoulders and went back to work. "*Madame* Pitre, I done had me a sign. Soon *ma belle*, Angelique, soon."

The next time Jean Marc saw Angelique was on the street in Ville Platte. She was leaving Sylvester's Mercantile with her arms full of packages; she looked more beautiful than springtime. He made a mad dash to her side. "Good morning. Here, let me help you with dat."

Angelique smiled broadly. "*Merci*, thank you."

Jean Marc reached for the large bundle and prepared himself to lift something heavy, but it was as light as air.

Angelique explained, "It's a surprise for Carrie. I'll be making her a new dress for Sunday church."

"That one's growin' like a weed, for sure." Jean Marc stumbled in his attempt to make light conversation. He was accustomed to being direct, but did not want to say or do anything that might cause Angelique to bolt. "I'm glad. That sweet girl needs some pretty things."

Angelique was miffed at the idea that he thought she could not take care of her own family, and she responded, "Carrie's needs are my concern." She immediately regretted her words and they stood there uncomfortably. Embarrassed, Angelique broke the silence, "I'm sorry. I don't know what got into me. Well, I best be going now."

Jean Marc followed her to the wagon. He held Angelique's packages in his hands and looked at her with tenderness. He stuttered, "All I meant was that Carrie's real special, for sure. You know, my stomach's tellin' me it's almost noon. Want to join me at the boarding house for a bite before you head back?"

Angelique hesitated.

"You gotta eat." Jean Marc moved closer to her and whispered her name, "Angelique?"

She tried to retreat, but found herself pressed against the rough-hewn boards of the wagon. She could go no further. Her eyes darted to the display window of Sylvester's Mercantile. Marie Rose stared back at her with an encouraging smile and signaled her approval.

Angelique grinned and stared at the man that she had loved for most of her life. "I'd take kindly to that."

While they ate, they talked about many things, being careful to avoid the past. They had awkward starts and stops until it came to Carrie. Jean Marc delighted in telling Angelique stories about their latest misadventures.

"Reminds me of when we were kids. You was always under my feet."

"Why, to my way of recollection, I do believe it was the other way around."

Jean Marc pushed his empty plate aside. "Angelique, being around you like this makes me feel sixteen all over again. I like it!"

"Me too."

"Now, tha's what I want to hear!"

They ate slowly. They lingered over apple pie and hot coffee. Afterwards, Jean Marc walked her back to the wagon, handed her the reins to the mules, and said goodbye. He walked away whistling.

Angelique rode home in bliss, her spirits as light as a puff of snowy cotton. The next morning when she saw Jean Marc leave his house with a fishing pole, it was easy for her to snatch a basket and head for the backlands. She followed the worn path and found him sitting at the edge of the bayou. He was getting ready to cast his line into the water. A twig snapped under her feet and she flinched.

Jean Marc did not seem surprised to find her there. "Angelique, it's too soon for blackberries?"

"I'm here to gather herbs for Eula Mae."

"Want to sit a spell?"

She abandoned her basket and came to sit by his side. "Catchin' anythin'?"

"As usual, you made so much racket that you scared all the fish away."

Pretending to be offended, Angelique pushed him sideways. Jean Marc acted as if he were going to fall into the water. Angelique rolled her eyes playfully. Jean Marc leaned in and kissed her sweetly. "All the same it's nice to have you here."

Angelique was dizzy with wanting. A tear slid down her face and he wiped it away. They kissed several times. Jean Marc could feel his blood pumping through his body and he pulled back to compose himself.

"Angelique, what say you? We destined to be together."

"All I know is that this feels right."

They sat quietly and listened to the familiar sounds of wildlife all around them. Their conversation gradually grew more intimate. They wanted a life together. They dared to dream the same dream.

Angelique hated to pick up her empty basket and make her way home alone. She was concerned about Adelaide's reaction. It was too soon. Unfortunately, Adelaide was sitting on the back porch waiting for her when she returned. The scowl on her face confirmed Angelique's fears.

"Think I don't know where you been? You seeing him, ain't you? *Monsieur* Jean Marc."

Angelique froze. "Adelaide, you don't understand."

"I'm not a baby anymore and I understand everything. How could you? I hate him!"

With those bitter words, Angelique realized Adelaide might never accept Jean Marc after all that had happened. Perhaps there was no future for the two of them after all. It filled her with sadness, but if she had to choose between her daughter and Jean Marc there was no contest. She would choose Adelaide.

Angelique wished her Papa were there. Angelique was convinced that Papa would have approved. After all, he had asked for Jean Marc's forgiveness in the letter he left behind. She was sure of it. She had stolen enough of a peek at the sealed envelope to feel assured of its contents. *Poor Papa! Poor me!*

That evening, Jean Marc showed up at Angelique's door with a grin on his face and a bouquet of flowers in his hands. His intent was to ask Angelique if he could officially court her, but she would not even come to the door. Eula Mae told him to go on home, and she promised that she would have a talk with Angelique. He could not guess what might have changed her mind. Jean Marc wanted to be near her. He wanted to hold her in his arms. He wanted to dance with her. He wanted to share his life with her. He was determined not to give up so easily.

The next morning, Jean Marc was waiting for her outside. "Angelique, I don't understand what's wrong. I want to be with you and I know you care for me. What happened since yesterday?"

"It's too soon, too soon for Adelaide; I got to think of her feelings."

"Damn it girl. We done lived our lives for others far too long. Adelaide's a child. I know we got to be careful, but please don't shut me out. I'll court Adelaide if I got to."

Angelique pleaded, "I'm goin' inside now, Jean Marc. It's best you go on home." Her words were flat. She closed the door softly behind her.

"I'm not finished with this. You hear me Angelique. This ain't over."

❖ ❖ ❖

First, Jean Marc sought out his Uncle Gus. On more than one occasion, his wisdom had been a guiding light. Next, he wanted the advice of Eula Mae. However, Hippolyte called on him to offer her own thoughts about this predicament. And now, he had a plan.

This Saturday seemed no different from any other day, except Jean Marc was in a rush. He hurriedly dispensed with his morning chores. Then he went to the barn, saddled his horse, and headed down Belair Cove Road. He did not stop until he reached the crossroad in front of the church. He dismounted and walked around to the cemetery.

Jean Marc stood before Elizabeth's grave and waited in the silence. He placed a small bouquet of flowers on the grave. He needed her approval. A sudden gust of wind swirled around him and dissipated. He had her blessing.

Jean Marc walked over to Damon Vidrine's grave to speak his sorrow for all that had happened. He pushed his hat back on his head. Peace and forgiveness washed across his face.

Back at home, Jean Marc took out the number three metal tub, filled it with hot water, and scrubbed himself clean with soap. He dressed in his Sunday best: clean khaki pants, starched plaid shirt, hair slicked back curling at the nape of his neck, polished shoes and a buttoned vest. He smiled in the mirror.

"A might dashing, if I do say so myself."

He donned his hat and retrieved the flag with the Fontenot colors, a bold blue and black crest.

Jean Marc mounted his chestnut horse. He secured the Fontenot flag onto the saddle, squared his shoulders, lifted his chin high, and raised his pistol in the air. He fired several rounds as he raced up Belair Cove Road. Then he turned around and headed past his house toward the home of Angelique Vidrine.

Uncle Gus was the first to abandon his chores and chase after Jean Marc. He called out to his neighbors, "That boy's goin' after Angelique. He goin' to get her. Come on."

Family and friends deserted their plows, cattle, or gardens. Hearing the gunshot or shout-outs, they dashed across rows of newly planted fields and followed Jean Marc as if he were the pied piper.

Carrie was swinging under the big oak tree when she heard the crowd approaching. She ran into the house. Hippolyte stepped out to see what was going on. She watched as Jean Marc dismounted at the gate. He stuck the flagpole into the ground, then walked up the porch steps, took off his hat, and slicked his hair back. He nodded at Hippolyte, and then called out loudly.

"Angelique Azalie Belair Vidrine, I need to talk to you."

The door opened a crack and the Vidrine women poured out of the house. Angelique stepped onto the porch with Carrie peeping out from behind her skirt. Adelaide stepped up behind Hippolyte. Eula Mae was not far behind.

"Angelique, time's a passin' and I ain't got no patience for courtin' you like I said I would. It's no secret that you and I was always meant to be. The past is over and done with. It's our turn now. Angelique, I declare my love for you here in front of all these folks."

Jean Marc turned to the expectant crowd standing behind him and waved his hat. They broke out in an exuberant cheer. With renewed enthusiasm, he turned to face Angelique once more.

"If you'll take me, Father Lalonde is ready and waiting at the church. It's all set, Angelique. Come with me. I swear I'll be courtin' you for the rest of our days."

Carrie stepped out from behind Angelique. "Go on Mama, I like Mr. Jean Marc."

Adelaide pointed and yelled, "I ain't goin' nowhere with that man. He killed my papa."

Hippolyte put her hand across Adelaide's mouth to shush her, bent down, and whispered in her ear. Then she said to Angelique, "Go on, child. Jean Marc is right. You deserve another chance at life. Adelaide will be fine with me."

Someone from the back of the crowd yelled, "Adelaide, that ain't true. He was only defendin' himself. I was there and I seen it all, me."

Angelique's love for her oldest daughter tightened in her chest. Yet, she had a deep longing for Jean Marc. Angelique knelt and opened her arms to Adelaide. Her daughter turned away from her and darted back into the house.

"No, No. It ain't right."

Angelique stood and faced the throng, then turned to Jean Marc and said, "I need to talk with Adelaide."

Eula Mae blocked the doorway, rested both of her hands on Angelique's shoulders and she spoke her peace. "Angelique, don't listen to that child. This is y'all chance. I know your papa would approve. We'll take care of Adelaide."

Tears slid down Angelique's face as she made her way around Eula Mae and into the house. She found her daughter sitting on the floor in the bedroom, hitting the wall, and cursing with words she had learned from her father. Angelique wrapped her arms around her and she fought her touch. "Stop that." She held Adelaide as the child wept bitterly. Angelique asked for her daughter's permission.

Friends gathered around Jean Marc while he waited. They whispered words of encouragement and patted him on the back. Jean Marc could not hear a word they were saying; his eyes remained glued to the front door. Little beads of sweat dotted his crinkled forehead and he spun his hat around in his hands. Gus stood beside him.

"Damn, I was a fool. It's too soon."

Suddenly, Angelique stepped through the doorway and waved a small white handkerchief. Eula Mae was fussing around her, tying a ribbon in her hair, and untying her apron from her waist. Angelique hugged Eula Mae and then turned to look at Jean Marc. She placed her hands on her hips and beamed down at him. Jean Marc knew that look. He had won. Angelique stepped to the edge of the porch. Jean Marc stretched out his arms.

"I have loved you my whole life." Jean Marc lifted her into his arms, kissed her firmly on the lips, and then twirled her around for the crowd to see. A cheer went up as he placed his bride-to-be onto the saddle and nudged the horse toward Sacred Heart Chapel. He shouted, "Y'all comin' with us. We got ourselves a weddin' ceremony 'bout to happen."

Angelique reached for Carrie, but Eula Mae intervened. "I'll be bringing Carrie along. Don't you worry none." Angelique looked over her shoulder at the boisterous well-wishers following behind them and agreed.

Josef drove up in Jean Marc's buggy and put his arm out for Eula Mae. She climbed into the wagon and Carrie scrambled up beside her. "Josef, you a fine grandson for sure. Thank you kindly. I been waitin' a mighty long time for this fine day."

Josef extended his hand again for Hippolyte. She shook her head as if to say no. "I don't belong there, boy. I'm gonna stay here and have a nice chat with Adelaide."

"Hippolyte, she'd want you both there."

"Even so, you go on."

Eula Mae commented, "Do as she wants. They gonna be all right. Now, Josef, all I need is to find you a nice girl. Then the Lord can take me." She waved her hands up to the heavens. Josef laughed and clicked the reins.

The ceremony was swift and sweet. Jean Marc kissed his bride and called out, "Y'all all invited to my place for a celebration!" The raucous crowd followed the happy couple. Jean Marc kicked the door open and carried Angelique into his house.

Marie Rose was lighting the last candle on the table when they entered. Fresh flowers graced every part of the room and the table was set for a feast. Marie Rose squeezed Angelique. "I knew you'd come around to his way of thinkin'. I am so happy for you, my dear friend. You deserve a new and better life."

The families of Belair Cove filled every corner of the room. Jean Marc reached for Angelique's fiddle. He placed the fiddle in the cradle of her hands, kissed her cheek, and with a wink asked, "How about shaking up this place with some happy music?" Angelique lifted the fiddle to her shoulder. Several musicians appeared at her side, and they joined in as she struck up a lively Cajun jig.

Resembling a rooster, Jean Marc set his shoulders back, craned his neck, and proceeded to strut across the room. He lifted Carrie in the air and twirled her around. A rowdy applause went up.

Uncle Gus screeched, "*Ayeee!*"

Young men snatched up the all the pretty girls as dancing partners. Children swarmed the food table to savor sweet treats. Outside, the trees hummed with the pulse of fiddles, the leaves trembled, and the Cove swayed to a joyful sound.

It was late when the last of the revelers walked away. They grumbled about having to plow their fields early in the morning. Marie Rose and Antoine packed their wagon with the things that she had brought for the occasion. Eula Mae dried the last dish, folded the towel, and left with Josef.

Jean Marc and Angelique waved until they disappeared. Angelique shut the door. Jean Marc was holding a sleepy-eyed little girl in his arms. Angelique followed as Jean Marc led the way to the bedroom he had prepared for her children. She lifted the covers, and he placed Carrie onto the bed. Jean Marc tucked the covers around her. They watched as she snuggled under the sheets and fell into a deep sleep.

Angelique looked out the window toward where her other daughter slept.

"Adelaide'll come around. We got to be patient with her."

"It won't be easy. That one's like Damon," Angelique's lips quivered as a tear slid down her cheek.

Jean Marc wiped it away. "Give it time."

He paused to let his eyes follow the length of Angelique's lithe body. He reached for the string around his neck, removed the pouch nestled there, and tossed it onto the surface of the dresser. "Won't be needin' *Madame* Pitre's love potion no more."

Angelique glowed. Jean Marc reached out and ran his fingers over the sleeve of Angelique's dress finding his way to her collarbone. He followed the length of it. Angelique paused to stare at her reflection in the dresser mirror across the room.

"Jean Marc, I'm not the young girl you remember."

Jean Marc Fontenot pressed himself against her, the girl of his youth. "Angelique Fontenot, I have loved you since we were children."

"And I you." Angelique spoke no truer words.

Jean Marc reached for her hand, ran his finger across the open palm, and kissed the hollow center of her there. They turned and walked steadily toward their bedroom. Angelique hesitated when she saw the iron bed and turned toward the direction of the side porch. Jean Marc came up behind her, lifted her blouse, and touched the skin of her bare back. He pushed the French doors open and guided them through it to reveal the starry night beyond. There they stood nestled against each other.

"Angelique, you have no idea how beautiful you really are to me."

Angelique leaned the back of her head into her husband's chest, shut her eyes, and cooed as if she were a turtledove.

"Ah, *mon amour*, look. For us, even the full moon shines on our beloved Belair Cove."

The Final Days
The Hospital Vigil

Angelique paused to study the shallow breath fading from Jean Marc's chest, "No, please, not yet. Jean Marc, I am not ready to let you go."

Angelique leaned in closer to her husband of thirty-five years and began to recite there many blessings. Images of the life they had shared flashed before her eyes. She tried to single out the sweetest moments, but the bounty was too great. She rushed the telling of it as Jean Marc struggled to stay with her.

"Jean Marc, my dear husband. I want to thank you for loving me. Why, I was nothing but a small wounded bird when you married me. Your gentle ways mended my broken wings. *Mon amour*, you showed me the vastness of the ocean and the first buds of spring on the pecan trees. You filled our home with so much laughter."

Angelique began to rock in an effort not to sob and she whispered, "I love it when you come from behind and press your palm on my heart. I need that. Your very touch makes me feel safe."

Fear choked her; she swallowed and continued, "I will never forget when you surprised me with my first train ride on our anniversary? The sound of the engine carried us away from Belair Cove. You knew how much I loved that train. You did all of that for me."

Angelique reached for Jean Marc's hand and pressed it to her cheek while feeling for a pulse. "Jean Marc Fontenot, you restored my faith in life. You laid our first-born son, Willis Alduce, in my arms and comforted me when they sent him off to fight in the Second World War. You were the first to heave deep sobs of joy when Willis returned. After working in the fields all day, you did everything you could to help me with the babies. You stayed up late into the night to rock many a sick baby. Together, we raised a beautiful family."

"And Carrie, why you made her feel like she was yours from the very start and you were so right about Adelaide. She came around to lovin' you plenty."

Angelique paused. She placed her open palm on Jean Marc's heart and felt for the slightest beat.

"Lord, I hope you are hearin' all this."

The radio played faintly in the background.

"Jean Marc, you gave me back my fiddle. I loved the way you use to take my fiddle from my hands after I played for a while, set it down, and pull me out onto the floor for a slow dance. Thank you for restorin' the music in my heart. Mostly, for just lettin' me be me."

Jean Marc gasped loudly, and then left Angelique without a farewell. Angelique held her own breath for as long as she could. "Oh, *Bon Dieu,* Jean Marc, Oh God. I love you. Wait for me. I love you. Love you." Angelique wept.

The hospital room had emptied and filled throughout Jean Marc's final day. The nurses navigated around the large family as they attempted to tend to other patients. Jean Marc and Angelique's family had come from all over the South. The nurses had never seen so many people gathered in the hospital before. A radio played in the background, the volume turned down low. Cajun music drifted out each time the heavy door opened or closed. Jean Marc loved that music.

Through morning and night shifts, the family members and nurses exchanged some of the stories that Angelique had told. All the while, Angelique twisted the white handkerchief in her shaky hands. It had a knot near the bottom. When Marc Willis brought it to her, he could feel the round object in the center. He could tell that is was a coin, but dared not ask.

Marc Willis tramped down the hall to share the nightly vigil with his grandmother. As he entered the room, an eerie silence greeted him. Angelique was leaning over Jean Marc. She kissed him ever so softly on the forehead, and then the lips. The final kiss.

She turned to face Marc Willis and spoke softly, "He's gone."

She choked back her tears. Angelique pulled the covers snugly around Jean Marc, touched his arm, and stepped away from the bed. She walked over to stand by her grandson, Marc Willis, and paused to cup her hands over his. "It's all right. Your grandpa and I had a good life."

She tucked the handkerchief into her cleavage and shuffled out of the room. A white mist seemed to slip past, encircle, and follow her out of the hospital room. The door closed slowly and softly. Marc Willis buzzed for the nurse and turned off the radio.

Angelique's Legacy

Many months passed. Marc Willis was on furlough before shipping out to Vietnam. He had joined the National Guard during his first year of college. It had helped to pay his college tuition. Unfortunately, college was going to have to wait. Who knew there would be a war? Marc Willis sped down the winding road toward the old home place of his grandparents.

He parked his car under the trees and stepped out to join the family. The place overflowed with aunts, uncles, and cousins. Each paused to greet him with hugs and kisses. He made his way slowly as he searched for his grandmother. Carrie pointed him in the direction of the big oak.

There she sat and entertained the youngest of the great grandchildren with stories from the old days. She stopped short, choked back a sob, and opened her arms when she saw Marc Willis. He sat at his grandmother's feet and rested his head in her lap for a brief moment.

"Marc Willis, you listen here. I need you to promise me somethin'. You have to promise me that you are goin' to come home safe and that you will finish college. That's the thing to do. Y'all hear dat?"

"Cross my heart, *Mémère*. But first, I am heading for those faraway places you always loved to talk about."

Marc Willis spent the day working with his cousins tearing down the old house board by board in hopes of using some of these materials later on. They stopped at noon to eat a Cajun feast under the shade of the huge oak. Platters and colorful bowls filled with spicy food covered Angelique's blue-checkered tablecloth.

Adelaide explained to Marc Willis as they moved around the table serving themselves, "Turns out your grandpa, in his final years sold off all his land. He never said a word to any of us. Any time we had set our sights on an education for our children, he found a way to provide. He'd slip an envelope in our hand and whisper, 'Got to do what I can. Education's the most important thing.' I remember when folks used to say, 'We ain't like Jean Marc. He can sell a cow any time his family's in need'. At first, he sold the livestock, one cow at a time, and later the land, parcel by parcel."

Carrie came up behind Marc Willis and joined in the conversation. "Probably for the best anyway. Nobody wants to farm anymore. It's too dang hard. Your own father chose to work as a carpenter instead. Your two uncles have stayed with the Lou Anna factory in Opelousas all these years. Your grandma will be better off in town."

Marc Willis fixed his grandmother a plate of food and went to sit next to her. Angelique patted his arm. "Guess what? They think I can't hear what they sayin' about me. Your grandpa and I decided this a long time ago, and I have no regrets. We did what we thought was the right thing. Unfortunately, all that's left is the five acres we sittin' on. The Schiff-Solomon estate owns the rest. I'm only sorry I don't have enough to pay for your education, child. Then you wouldn't be in this fix, going off to fight in some awful place."

"*Mémère*, all I've heard is how grateful they all are. You and *Pépère* did a good thing. That's why everybody is here trying to pay back. They are going to get you a real nice place all your own. Don't you worry about me. I'll be just fine."

Angelique's children purchased a small lot in the middle of an old neighborhood in Ville Platte. They built her a house using the salvaged materials from the home that she and Jean Marc had shared. It was a way of preserving her past.

"I'm gonna love it. I can walk to the grocery store. The hospital is right there, the church, and the cemetery. I will have everything I need," she told Marc Willis. "And my dear old friend, Marie Rose, she lives two doors down."

Angelique became the belle of her new neighborhood. She lived in her simple two-bedroom house for many years. She planted a small garden in the backyard and flowers in the front. She baked Elizabeth's sugar cookies and her personal favorites, lemon cookies, for the great grandchildren.

In the last few years, Angelique's eyesight failed her. She put lemon flavoring in everything she baked. No one ever mentioned to her that her coconut and chocolate cake tasted lemony. It would never do to hurt her feelings.

Angelique died quietly in her sleep late one night. She was ninety-two. There was a lace handkerchief cupped tightly in her hands. It seemed odd to her children that a nickel rested inside of that handkerchief. What did it mean?

They buried her beside Jean Marc in the church cemetery. Their children, grandchildren, and great grandchildren—all forty-five—attended the funeral. Jean Marc and Angelique Fontenot lived, loved, and died in the heart of Belair Cove.

Marc Willis remained at the graveside long after everyone else had gone. He opened up a plastic container of dirt he had dug up from the old home place and sifted it out over Angelique's casket. "Oh, *Mémère,* since I got back from Nam, I been working hard in school. I wanted it to be a surprise, so I waited to tell you. I bought the old home place, all of it. I'm going to breathe life back into it again. I've got some ideas, a family cooperative. *Mémère,* I'll leave this bit of dirt here, to carry you home once again. I want you to know, I'm proud to be a Cajun farmer."

At her craft shop in town, Nanette Comeaux placed the white lace handkerchief on various scraps of velvet with extra care. She lifted the silver coin and moved it about. Marc Willis had walked into her shop a few days ago and asked her to create a shadow box with these two unlikely objects. Marc Willis was quite handsome and unmarried. Nanette wanted this shadow box to be special.

Author's Note

My father's parents were Altere and Ezore Fontenot. My grandmother's first husband was Remie Lafleur, and my grandfather's first wife was Zena. Their story is the basis of this novel, a fictional tale of love and deceit, greed and compassion. It happened long ago in a forgotten place deep in south Louisiana, the place of my Cajun ancestry. Though this fictional tale has its darker side, it is my hope that I have honored my ancestors by sharing some of the old ways—the strong ties—that many currently strive to preserve. For me, it all came together with an old squeaky wooden rocker.

I inherited Grandpapa's rocker. My father lifted it out of his truck and carried the sturdy thing into my house. That is how our Sunday afternoon coffee parties began. My parents talked and I listened. They loved to recount the tales of growing up Cajun in small isolated villages, in a time where French was the primary language and poverty prevailed.

My mother's name is Girlie Duplechin. Her parents were Veillior and Allida Duplechin. She grew up between Bristol and Lawtel, Louisiana. My father's name is Willis Altere Fontenot and he grew up in Belair Cove, near Ville Platte. This story rocks back and forth between their individual reminiscences.

I grew up in the shadow of an indigenous way of life, the French Acadian Culture. We rarely spoke the forbidden language of my grandparents. My mother was determined to shake what she felt to be the shame of poverty and illiteracy, of being Cajun. I needed a sense of place. One Sunday I asked, "Dad, would you take me back to Belair Cove?"

One summer dawn, we headed past the first of many winding curves where he braked to point out the plot of farmland where he had been born. His memories welcomed us bend after bend as he continued to identify parcels of land. As the road twisted and turned, he spoke their names with reverence, his grandfather, father, aunts, and uncles who had owned or farmed this land. He finally came to a stop in front of the church cemetery. We walked its length in solitude as he pointed out the tombstones. It was a time of quiet reflection.

"Why is it called Belair Cove?" I asked as we drove away.

"Because all the Belairs lived near there. Belair Fontenot, Ned Belair, Rosaf Belair. They're all gone now. *Bébé,* you ought to write all dis down."

I am not even sure at what point my parents' truths became my fiction. I only know that the story began to take shape long before my father and I left the main highway to find his home place. Belair Cove is a work of fiction. Some names were inspired by the ancestral pool and assigned to original characters. Thus, specific names and characters are strictly coincidental. Places and incidences are used either fictitiously and or were created from my imagination.

Family Given Names

Henri   Odele   Jean Veillior   Celestine

Domitile

Jehan   Phillipe   Guillaume   Antoinette

Hippolyte

Felicite   Armand Simon   Dominique

Mathurin   ·   Joachim   Bartlelemy   Alexandre

Josephine   Cyprien

Damon

Angelina   Anastasie   Azea   Azelie

Celeste   Genevieve   Delphine   Carmelien

Pierre   Jacque   Altere   Joseph

Jean

Colyn   Rosalie   Batiste   Francois

Marie   Simeon   Clemente   Adelaide

Angelique

Allida   Gabriel   Etienne

Ezore

Truth Matters

Notes from interviews with two Prairie Cajuns, my parents:

Belair Cove, Louisiana

My grandparents were probably married between 1910 and 1915. It was a second marriage for both.

My grandmother was in love with two men. She decided to marry Remie Lafleur, instead of my grandfather, Altere Fontenot. Following a brief ceremony in the church, they ate cake and lemonade served at home. The only ones in attendance were the priest and the parents of the bride and groom.

My grandmother's mother-in-law was mean, a spitfire of an old woman. She hid part of Grandma's wedding cake for herself in a tin can and hung it on a nail over the kitchen. One day, when she left the house, my grandmother decided to sneak into the can and help herself to some cake. She ate her fill then put it back. When my grandmother went to eat the cake herself, she saw that some of it was missing and she simply announced that the cake was no longer worth saving.

Farmers always competed and bet on who would bring in the first bale of cotton. The farmer who arrived with the first bale of cotton at the cotton gin was the winner. The loser had to buy the drinks for the evening. One year, the practice of betting on the first bale of cotton turned deadly. My grandmother's husband, Mr. Lafleur, brought in the first bale of cotton. He drank heavily that night and began arguing with a neighbor.

Mr. Lafleur drove all the way home to get his gun. He called the neighbor out in a duel. The neighbor fatally wounded Mr. Lafleur. His father gathered a posse of twelve men and they went to investigate. The investigation concluded that there was no one to blame. They collected the body and buried him at home.

To my grandmother's dying day, she was angry with her first husband for his actions on the fateful day that ended his life. He had plenty of time to reflect on the dangers and dueled anyway. However, she often repeated, "He was a good man."

In the meantime, my grandfather married a local Cajun girl. My grandfather's wife lost her first baby in childbirth. She stood rocking that empty bassinet for several days, and then she lay in her bed and died. My grandparents eventually married, after their first spouses died.

My grandmother's former mother-in-law raised her oldest daughter, Eunice. The second child, Carrie, lived with my grandparents. My father, Willis, was their first-born, and together they had five more children: Alphan, Jessie, Hilda, Wedna, and Barbara.

My grandparents lived in a shack with a cistern and an outhouse. Houses were twelve-by-twelve flat boxes. They used molding to hide cracks. Dirt and moss or brick was the main material for chimneys. Most of the time, the children slept outside on the porch. They cooked with kerosene on the stove or in the brick oven.

My father, Willis Altere Fontenot, felt life was good back then. Overall, everyone was the same: equally poor, black or white. There were few Native Americans where he lived. However, he was afraid of the Native Americans and stayed away from them. Most of Dad's family lived nearby: Regina, Hanray, Maudrey, Emile, Odette, Gus, and Farreaux.

My father and his siblings would walk to Ville Platte to gather supplies and attend school. The path was a two-lane dirt road. When they blacktopped the road, his mother made fig pies and he would sell them to the workers for ten cents. They cooked the fresh figs in a black kettle over the fireplace until it was sweet and gooey. He walked to school wearing khaki pants or overalls. His teacher's name was Louise Brignac. The school building was one small room, with only one teacher, but the children separated into two groups for instruction depending on age and ability. My father's school lunch usually consisted of peanut butter, figs, boiled eggs, a raw potato or salt meat, and milk. On the way home, he often stopped to play in ditches, trying to catch crawfish and catfish. By the time he arrived home, he was filthy. He only went to school in the winter. The rest of the year, he worked in the fields.

My father's family grew cotton. He had to babysit his little sister, Hilda, while his parents picked cotton. The baby would be in a rocking bassinet at the end of a row. He remembers she was always crying. He would yell across the field at his mother, my grandmother, as he rocked. He would shout "Red pepper," "green pepper," or "yellow pepper," each signifying the degree to which Hilda was crying (red being the more severe). He called out red pepper a lot because she would fuss in the bassinet no matter how much he rocked.

On Sundays, the family went to church. The parish priest was Father Avi. Father's homilies struck fear into my father. As a result, he concluded that he would leave the church going to the women folk.

Capsay was the name of my father's dog. He was a bulldog. He could catch a cow by the throat and hang on. He also had a Catahoula Hound for herding the cattle.

After school and evening chores, my father would play baseball in a field with friends. They competed for pop to drink. Also for fun, they raced horses, held rooster fights, and rode calves if his father was not home. They played a game similar to hockey with a stick and a can. The local boys would make a circle and try to hit the can into the goal. They played marbles.

My father recalled two funny incidents from his childhood. When he was about nine, he tried to get even with his father for punishing him. He soaked a corncob with turpentine and put it on his Papa's dog's behind. The dog squirmed all over the yard and his Papa kept hollering, "What is wrong with my dog?" while my dad giggled under the porch.

My father's uncle, Gus, wore long underwear that opened in the back. One night, Uncle Gus was in the outhouse when he heard a lot of noise in the hen house. He grabbed his shotgun and went out to check the hen house. His dog followed him out. Gus stopped short and the dog ran into his bare skin; it was a cold night. The gun went off and the thief went running.

As a teen, my grandfather allowed my father to borrow the mule and the wagon. On weekends, he would go out to Bayou Debaillon and fish. He would cook his catch and stay the night. My father hunted squirrels and rabbits with his shotgun in the woods.

At sixteen, my father started going to the saloons in Ville Platte. There were two, the Fist to Cuffs and Buckhorn Saloon. Both saloons had a barbershop in it. The men in town played cards (*bourré*, draw poker and stud poker), drank, danced and had a shave. You could even get a good meal at the saloon. There were rooms upstairs for boarding.

A fais do-do was a dance held in the hall of public buildings, or in front of the courthouse and jail. People came from all over to attend the dance. It cost fifteen cents to get in and they stamped your hand. Dad thought the music of the Brothers Balfa was the best.

Sometimes, the locals would have dances in their homes, which lasted as late as eleven o'clock. Saturday was bath day, whether you needed it or not. On Saturday, my father would take a bath in a number three metal tub and "dress up" in a white shirt, socks, and shoes. He rode to the dance on horseback, and brought a half bottle of wine to drink.

My father's grandmother lived in Washington, Louisiana. On weekends, the family would go to visit her overnight, traveling by wagon. Dad loved to watch the steamboats on Bayou Courtableau. His grandparents raised hogs in a boggy area. They would turn the hogs loose in the spring in the backlands, plant good grass in the pasture, and round the hogs up again in the fall. He sold the fat hogs at the market. My father still remembers one particular flood. My father had bought some sow pigs, marked them with a notch on the ear, and turned them loose behind his grandmother's house. The pigs drowned in the flood.

My mother, Girlie Duplechin, lived in Lawtell, Louisiana. My mother's grandmother was a midwife. She delivered the babies, who were born at home. The midwife cut the cord and sewed up the mother. If there was a doctor in the area, he would drop by later. They took castor oil when labor began, to speed the delivery, and then waited for the midwife after taking to their bed. An expectant mother had to help herself during the delivery, so that her baby would not die.

My grandmother gave birth to seven children at home: Thomas, Leonie, Girlie, Vernon, Vernice, Ernest, and Mary.

My mother's father made cypress caskets to sell. She remembers that he kept them in the barn. He pointed out the one he had set aside for himself. That made her very uncomfortable.

For a family member's wake, they wrapped the body in white cloth and laid the deceased in bed. The family stayed up all night with the body and buried the person the next day. Just before burial, they placed the body in a casket, and carried it to the cemetery in a wagon. Sometimes they buried a loved one in a plot in the backyard.

Family members followed the wagon on foot to the cemetery. Everyone in attendance would throw a handful of dirt over the casket in the grave. The family wore black for the first six months afterwards, and then they wore a combination of black and white for the next six months. No one could listen to or play music during the mourning period.

My mother traveled in a stagecoach to Bristol, Louisiana every day to go to school. In the third grade, she spoke French instead of English during class and her teacher punished her for breaking the rule. My mother never returned to a traditional school after that.

My mother also attended dances in the homes of friends and neighbors. The mothers brought their daughters in wagons and stayed to chaperone while the boys arrived on horseback or barefoot and without a chaperon. Everyone would bring cakes. They would move what little furniture there was out of the way and dance in the living room. Uncle Tom played the violin, and her father played the accordion. Everyone encouraged Mom to dance. One time she refused because she had a stomachache, cramping probably, and the next time no one asked. She was disappointed and decided she must be unpopular.

My parents met at a *fais do-do*. My great grandmother was my mother's chaperone. She admired her grandmother, an educated French woman, for teaching her the catechism of the Catholic faith. Lessons were at home several mornings a week. Mom's grandma carried the Bible in one hand and a buggy whip in the other as she lectured to her grandchildren. Every part of a woman had to be covered. One could definitely not reveal the shoulders. If a girl tempted a man, she was sinning, and making him sin for wanting. My mother was committed to the teachings of her grandmother and careful not to "do wrong". My father had to follow all of her grandmother's protocols in order to win her hand in marriage.

My father gave my mother money for their wedding. She bought a dress, a hat, a negligee, and a case of pop. Her parents believed she was marrying a rich man.

My mother remained committed to her Catholic faith. They drove to church every Sunday in a buggy wearing their best dresses. Church clothes were ironed and stiff from heavy starch. Dresses fell below the knees. My mother chuckled and shared that, "back then," she and her sister-in-law would drive by the saloon and drop my dad and uncle off on their way to Sunday Mass. Aunt Hilda's husband was a drinking man, and my dad a gambling man. After church services, they would stop back by and pick them up. They thought nothing of it, at the time.

My parents were farmers who came to own land for the first time when my father went into town and borrowed one thousand dollars from two lawyers who worked out of their house. He planned to pay back the loan over time, once a year, when crops came in.

My father would plow the field behind two mules harnessed to a planter. He would set the wheel on the planter, which would determine how many seeds it would drop. Planting began sometime around Easter, and the cotton was ready to pick in September or October. The cotton gin paid thirty-five cents a pound in those days. A bale was about five hundred pounds. Dad farmed about five or six acres.

Cotton pickers would wear old socks on their hands, cut off at the fingers. Older women took care of the babies while young mothers picked cotton. They would carry a heavy sack on one shoulder and drag it along as they picked. A sack held about twenty-five to thirty pounds. There were few snakes in the fields, but big old stinging caterpillars were a problem. It would burn badly when you got stung. However, you had to keep on picking.

Work continued until the sack was full, weighed and emptied into the wagon. Then they would pack down the load by having the children walk around and around on top of the wagon, mashing the cotton. Later, the cotton would be transferred into a larger sack and put in the barn to dry out.

They also had a vegetable garden, separate from the cash crop.

Life was good then, too. However, as an adult it was much more difficult. Responsibilities of a farm and a family weighed heavily on a Cajun man.

Cajun Glossary of Terms

Alouette [a loo e tuh] a French children's song

Ayeee [ah ye] expression of excitement

bal de maison [bahl duh mazon] a dance at someone's home

Bayou Debaillon [bye you duh bye yon] a waterway that crisscrossed the landscape; and this particular bayou was named after the family surname of people living on its banks, the Debaillons

bébé [bay bay] baby

Bon Dieu [bon dew] good God

Bonne année, bonne santé, et le paradis a` la fin de vos jours. New Year's Day greeting translated: Good year, good health, and paradise at the end of your days.

boucherie [boo shuh ree] Several families would form a cooperative and take turns providing a calf or hog for butchering which they would then share equally.

boudin [boo dah] a sausage made from a blend of pork, rice, onion, parsley and green onion

bouillie [boo yee] dish made from organ meats

bourree` [boo ray] a Cajun card game

café au lait [kaf ay oh lay] coffee with milk and sugar

café noir [kaf ay nwour] black coffee without milk or sugar

capon [kah pon] coward

C'est la vie. [say lah v] That's the way it goes.

Ça ne fait pas rien. [suh nuh fay pa duhyan] It's nothing.

charivari [shiv aw re] a noisy gathering in front of the home of newlyweds on their wedding night

cher [shah] (a as in at) dear

cochon de lait [ko sohn duh lay] roasted suckling pig

cote-a-cote [coat-ah-coat] side by side

courtbouillon [koo be yon] a thick fish stew or soup served over rice

coup de main [koop duh maan] gather together to surprise someone and lend a helping hand

couche couche [koosh koosh] corn meal mush

couillon [koo yon] imbecile

demitasse [dih me toss] half cup

dépêche toi [day pech twaw] you need to hurry

envie [on v] desire

et bien [a byan] oh well

fais do-do [fay doe doe] go to sleep; a dance held in a public place

feu follet [foe foo lay] foolish; trickster

filé [fe lay] a powder made from dried sassafras leaves

ga [gaw] shortened form of *regarder* meaning to look

grand-père [grawn pear] grand-father

grand-mère [grawn mare] grandmother

gris-gris [gree gree] a spell

gumbo [gum boe] a thick dark brown soup prepared with seafood or game, numerous spices, and vegetables served over rice

Ils sont partis! [eel sont partee] They are off!

joie de vivre [zhwa duh veev] a happy-go-lucky attitude

Jolie Jeune Fille [jo lee zhune fee] pretty young girl

maquechou [mock shoo] fresh corn seasoned with tomatoes, onions, and bell peppers

madame [mah dohm] respectful title used when addressing a married lady

ma belle [mah bell] my pretty

ma petite [mah peteet] my little one

mais non [ma naw] but, no

mais oui [ma we] but, yes

merci [mare see] thanks

merci beaucoup [mare see bow koo] thank you very much

mémère [muh mah] my mother; my grandmother, a term of endearment

mon ami [mon ahmee] my friend

mon amour [mon ah more] my love

monsieur [miss your] mister, title of respect for a man

pâques [pock] a boiled egg cracking contest on Easter Sunday; the strongest egg wins and is claimed by the winner

pépère [puh pah] my father; my grandfather; a term of endearment

tante [tawnt] aunt

tasso [tah so] smoked meat used to flavor many dishes

tête dur [teht duerd] hard head, stubborn

tête-à-tête [teht ah teht] private talk to settle differences

ti [T] small, petite, little

Ti Blanc [T blaw] small white

ti-fer [T fair] triangular metal instrument with a striker used to keep the beat in Cajun music

ti pop-a small bird

traiteuse [tray turze] female healer

Je te souhaite une bonne journée, espèce de salope. Translated: I wish you a good day, you stupid bitch!

vite [veet] fast; quickly

Pronunciation Key

"eaux" appears at the end of many Cajun surnames and is pronounced "o". Cajun French phrases often correlate to the specific isolated area from which they originated. Thus, there will be some slight variance in pronunciation and meaning. I based the pronunciations on what I heard as a child. Any similarities in pronunciation and or definitions with other glossaries or dictionaries are strictly coincidental.

Bibliography

I am grateful for the following sources that provided historical background and unique insights that helped to shape this book.

Online Sites

The internet provided a wealth of information, from various sites verifying the existence of colloquial Cajun French words to the medicinal benefits of healing herbs and more:

The Prairie Cajun
http://www.cajunprairie.org/

During the early settlement of the United States, the terrain defined as prairie included a large section of southwest Louisiana. Today, dedicated conservationist work tirelessly to preserve what remains of the ecosystem.

Ville Platte, Louisiana
http://www.vpla.com/site21.php
Information on the history of Ville Platte, Louisiana

Cajun Culture
http://www.lafayette.travel/culture/history/whatiscajun/?gclid=CJ mhlKqO8qoCFQ8j7AodpGO4QA
Answers the question: What is a Cajun?

Books

Brasseaux, Carl A. *Acadiana to Cajun: Transformation of a People, 1803-1877*. University Press of Mississippi: Jackson, 1992.

Calhoun, Mary. *Medicine Show: Conning People and Making Them Like It*. Harper & Row: New York, 1976.

Evans, Patricia. *Controlling People: How to Recognize, Understand, and Deal with People Who Try to Control You.*Adams Media: Avon, Massachusetts, 2002.

Kane, Harnett T. *The Bayous of Louisiana.*William Morrow Company: New York, 1944.

Keyes, Frances Parkinson.*All This is Louisiana.* Harper & Brothers Publishers: New York, 1950.

Post, Lauren C. *Cajun Sketches: From the Prairies of Southwest Louisiana.* U.S.A.: Louisiana University Press, 1962.

Made in the USA
Lexington, KY
29 October 2014